LAST SEEN

LAST SEEN

JOY KLUVER

bookouture

Published by Bookouture in 2021

An imprint of Storyfire Ltd.
Carmelite House
50 Victoria Embankment
London EC4Y 0DZ

www.bookouture.com

ISBN: 978-1-80019-360-4
eBook ISBN: 978-1-80019-359-8

In memory of my father, Eric

PROLOGUE

Such a pretty little thing. Blonde, curly hair and blue eyes. About five years old. She's swinging high on the swing, leaning back, laughter tumbling from her mouth. The baby starts to cry. The mother leaves her daughter and goes over to the pram. The girl scrambles out of the swing and runs over to the slide. She's very near me now. I check again. Her mother is still busy with the baby, her back to the little girl, out of earshot. She thinks she's safe. They're in the park, close to the village. Nothing much happens round here. But the truth is, you're never safe. We've always been taught not to accept sweets from a stranger. And even a lost dog doesn't cut it as a lure these days, but a lost toddler might. Especially if you have a buggy with you. I look once more. The baby is screaming as the mother changes his nappy.

I ask, in a quiet but agitated voice, 'Excuse me, have you seen my little boy? He was running towards the swings but I've lost him.'

She pauses and smiles shyly. Then she shakes her head.

'Are you sure? He was wearing a blue top with a train on it.' You see, if you sow enough doubt into children, they will often change their minds just to please you.

She starts to nod her head slowly and points towards some bushes outside the playground area.

'Could you show me please?'

It really is that easy.

CHAPTER ONE

Friday

Blue and white tape cordoned off Otterfield Park and flapped in the gentle breeze. The air was warm for a sunny, early May afternoon. White blossom snowed gently onto the ground. The park was eerily quiet, apart from a blue tit whistling in the trees like a dog owner. There were no children. No 'helpful' people clamouring to tell the police what they saw. Or even looking out of their windows. No one. Just a few police officers and a lone woman sitting on a bench, with a pram next to her. Where were all the locals? Bernie wondered as she parked her car. All the nosy people that want to help? Something wasn't right. Something wasn't right at all.

She pulled down the car visor and had a quick look in the mirror. Her mascara and eye liner had run from her earlier tears at her grandfather's funeral and smudged on her light brown skin. She took a tissue from her bag and wiped her face. With a sigh, she tied her long, black, frizzy hair into a ponytail. It wasn't the best time to take on an investigation but this was her chance to prove herself. To show that her two years in the accelerated programme to become a DI hadn't been wasted. She also hoped it would take her mind off her grandfather and… other things.

She got out of the car and walked towards Matt Taylor, her DC, tall and lanky, his suit hanging off him. Only twenty-five, Bernie wondered how he would cope. Fast tracked because of his degree in criminology, his two years' pounding pavements in uniform hadn't totally prepared him for the Major Crime Investigations Team. Intellectually very bright but not street savvy. She had DS Kerry Allen for that. She looked round for her DS but couldn't see her anywhere.

'Matt,' Bernie called.

He pushed his brown floppy hair out of his eyes. 'Ma'am. Sorry for disturbing you but I couldn't get hold of the super. He's dealing with another betting shop raid. Trowbridge this time. Happened last night.'

'Another? God, how many is that now?'

'With Swindon and Salisbury it's the third one in Wiltshire. Fifth if we include the ones in Bristol. A man was injured in Trowbridge. He's in a bad way apparently. But what about you? How was the funeral?'

'It was…'

Bernie thought about the heaving church – all the people who had come to say goodbye. And her personal farewell at the funeral home. Her grandfather, Eric Baxter, or Pops as she called him, in his Sunday best. Cold to the touch. There, but at the same time, not there.

She swallowed. 'It was OK. Don't worry. I was on my way back anyway. Bring me up to speed.'

Matt gestured to the young woman sitting down. 'Jessica Cole, mother of Molly Reynolds. Came here after school for a quick play. The baby needed a nappy change. While Mum changed him, Molly disappeared. That's as much as I've got out of her. She's quite distraught.'

Bernie nodded. 'Of course. Are Forensics on their way?'

'Yes. Should be here anytime.'

'Good. We'll need more uniforms down here. We're going to have to start a search before it gets dark. Door-to-door as well.

Especially as no one seems to be around. Bit odd. Can you sort that out while I talk to the mother?'

'Yes, ma'am.'

Bernie sat down on the bench next to the young woman. She was in her mid-twenties. Her fair hair was straggly, her eyes puffy from crying and she held a screwed-up tissue in trembling hands. She was wearing grey jogging bottoms and her pink top had a few stains on it. The aroma of baby sick hung around her. Bernie reached over and gently touched the woman on the arm.

'Jessica. I'm Detective Inspector Bernie Noel. I'm here to help find Molly. I know that you've spoken to my colleague but I have a few questions. Do you think you're up to answering them?'

Bernie saw a slight nod of the head. 'OK. What time did you get here?'

'Just after three p.m. School finishes at three.' Jessica's voice was shaky.

'Was anyone else in the playground?'

'A few other mums and children but they didn't stay long.'

'Do you know their names? It would be good to speak to them, in case they saw anything unusual.'

Jessica nodded and started to cry again.

'We'll get those names later. Can you tell me what happened?'

Jessica wiped her eyes with the tissue. 'I didn't really want to come. Sam was a bit restless but Molly just went on and on at me. So I said we could come for ten minutes. There isn't much to do here so she had to wait for the others to leave before she got a decent turn on anything. I'd been pushing her on the swing but then Sam started to cry. He needed a nappy change. In fact I had to change everything, the poo had gone everywhere.'

'How old is he?' asked Bernie, as she smiled at the sleeping bundle, oblivious to the trauma going on around him.

'Eight weeks. So it took a bit of time to sort it out. And he was yelling his head off the whole time. When I finished, I turned round to tell Molly we had to go but she was gone.' Jessica's voice cracked.

'It's OK, take your time.'

Jessica sniffed. 'I thought she was just playing to begin with; she likes hide and seek. But she wasn't anywhere. I was screaming her name and running round the park with the pram but nothing. So I called the police.'

'Can you remember what time this was?' Bernie knew the time would be noted on the emergency call.

'It was about three forty-five, I think. I can probably check on my phone.'

'That's fine. A long ten minutes, then.'

'As I said, she had to wait for the others to leave before she could have a go on the swings.'

Bernie jotted down the timings in her notepad.

'I'm sure you've already thought of this, Jessica, but have you contacted the mums of any of her friends, just in case she went off with one of them?'

Jessica shook her head.

'Well, we can contact them for you, if you give me their names.'

The young woman shook her head again. 'You don't understand, Molly doesn't have any friends.'

'Oh, are you new to the area?'

'We moved here in January.'

'Ah.'

Jessica's accent didn't quite match the soft local Wiltshire burr. There was a hint of something else but Bernie couldn't quite place it. 'But it's now the beginning of May. Are you sure she hasn't made any friends at school?'

'None. Why else do you think she had to wait? They wouldn't let her have a turn.'

'Have you made any friends, Jessica?'

'No.'

Bernie felt a lurch. She knew the feeling of not belonging. She was neither black nor white, a Baptist in a Catholic school, a mixed-race changeling in her Anglo-Saxon family. Separated not just by colour but by surname too. And now, for the last six months, a former Met officer in rural Wiltshire. It was more like exile than home.

'Is there anyone we can call for you?' Bernie asked. 'You really shouldn't be alone. Do you have a partner?'

Jessica rested her head on her hand. 'Yes, Davy Reynolds. He's my fiancé and Molly and Sam's dad. But he's in the army and on active duty. I can't get hold of him easily.'

'Well, is there anyone else?'

'There's my dad, Derek Cole.'

'Great. If you give me his number, we'll contact him. Also, do you have a recent photo of Molly on your phone? We can Bluetooth it to mine.'

'I have one of her in her school uniform.'

'And that's what she was wearing?'

'Yes.'

'Shoes – colour and size?'

'Black school shoes, size eleven. I had to buy new ones in the Easter holidays.' Jessica fiddled with her phone and showed a photo to Bernie. 'I took it on Wednesday. She looked so pretty that day. She was pleased because she got a sticker from the teacher. I emailed it to Davy. She wanted Daddy to see her sticker.' Jessica put her hand to her mouth and began to sob uncontrollably.

Bernie took the phone from her. Placing her arm around Jessica's shoulders, she stared down at the little girl with fair, curly hair and blue eyes, wearing a white polo shirt under a grey pinafore, with a bottle-green fleece. A big yellow smiley sticker matched an even bigger smile on Molly's face. Bernie felt a lump in her throat.

'We'll find her, Jessica. We'll find her.'

footsteps moving towards her. A woman in her late seventies with grey permed hair opened the door.

'Sticker says no buying at the door.'

Bernie wanted to laugh. *No door-to-door salesman would sell anything in this village.* She showed her warrant card. 'I'm *Detective Inspector* Noel and I'm wondering if you could help with our enquiries.'

The woman gestured towards the card so Bernie passed it over. She looked carefully at it and then up and down at Bernie. She nodded, clearly satisfied Bernie was telling the truth, and handed it back.

'We have a missing five-year-old girl who disappeared from the park this afternoon.' Bernie held up her phone with Molly's photo showing. 'She's called Molly Reynolds. Have you seen her at all this afternoon?'

The woman looked at the photo and tutted. 'Not surprising. Haven't seen her.' She started to close the door but Bernie put her foot in the way.

'Why's it not surprising?' she asked.

The woman shrugged.

'I'd be grateful if you could check any sheds or outbuildings you may have, just in case she's hiding.'

The woman glared at her. Bernie took the hint and removed her foot.

'Thank you for your cooperation. If you do see her, please contact us or call Crimestoppers on 0800 555 111.'

The door swung shut in Bernie's face. She sighed and moved on to the next property. The man there didn't even bother to open the front door but shouted down from an upstairs window – 'Can't help you.'

After several more similar responses Bernie called Matt Taylor.

'Hi, Matt. I'm having a really hard time with door-to-door, like getting blood from a stone. What about you?'

CHAPTER TWO

Bernie looked at the quiet road before her. She heard a song in her head Pops used to sing to her when she was little. He used to sing a lot. Something about little boxes on a hill, made out of ticky-tacky. But Bernie didn't see multicoloured homes like in the song – just sandy-brown pebble-dash on the identical houses. She remembered the tour an officer from the Community Policing Team had given her when she had moved to Wiltshire last December. Otterfield had once been pretty but some Second World War bombs destined for the railway had missed their target and taken out most of the quaint country cottages instead.

'And this is what the government of the day built for them,' the officer had explained. 'Then Margaret Thatcher encouraged the residents to buy them and now they're stuck here, with ugly houses no one else wants to buy. They're a community with a collective chip on their shoulders. Highly suspicious of outsiders.'

Maybe that's why Jessica is having such a hard time, Bernie thought. Armed with Molly's photo on her phone and her warrant card, she walked up the path to the first house in the road. Ringing the doorbell, she glanced around at the neat front garden with its square of lawn and garish orange and purple bedding plants beside the path. There was a small movement at the net curtains but no one came to the door. Bernie rang the bell again. She could hear

'Same. No one's seen her, no one wants to speak, and no one cares. What the hell's going on? She's only five, for God's sake.'

'I know. Have you heard from Kerry?' asked Bernie.

'Yes, she's at the park with uniform. Looks like everyone's turned out and they're doing a thorough search of the area. Forensics are at the playground as well. Sergeant Turner has taken Jessica back to her house to wait for her dad to turn up. He's stuck in traffic. Oh, and I contacted the train companies to warn them. The railway's only a couple of miles away, it's always possible that she wandered onto the tracks.'

Bernie opened her mouth in amazement. Maybe Matt had more initiative than she'd first thought.

'Well done. I'm impressed.'

'Thank you. I'm trying to think out of the box a bit.'

'Good. I've got ten more houses on this road to visit and then I'll have to head back to the park to see Forensics and Kerry. Could you allocate my other two roads to uniforms please? Maybe they'll respond better to someone who actually looks like a police officer. Come to the park when you've finished.'

Bernie hung up and sighed. She didn't really want to knock on any more doors. She didn't understand why no one in the village wanted to help look for a missing five-year-old girl. She braced herself for a cool reception and walked up to the next door.

It was almost seven o'clock by the time Bernie reached the park. Her shoulders were stiff with tension. She had come away from the door-to-door search with nothing, other than the first woman who had not been surprised. *Maybe they'll have discovered something at the park.*

She found DS Kerry Allen at the entrance to the playground. Petite with cropped blonde hair, her right-hand woman had proved invaluable in the six months they'd been together. They'd bonded over being the new girls in town – Bernie from London and Kerry from Manchester.

'Our leader returns,' Kerry said. 'How was London?'

Bernie shook her head. The emotion of her grandfather's funeral and now a missing girl weighed heavily on her. Before she could say anything there was a crackle from Kerry's radio.

'Didn't catch that. Say again,' Kerry said.

'Got a green fleece. Near the back gate,' replied a male voice.

'Where is it?' asked Bernie.

Kerry showed her a map of the park she had divided up into smaller areas. She pointed to the top left-hand corner. 'Here. There's a gate in that area but it's not used because the pathway beyond it leads to the railway line. It should be bolted shut with a padlock and chain.'

'But it's not?'

Kerry shook her head, her face grim. 'Chain's been cut.'

'Right,' said Bernie. 'We need a photographer and a CSI. I'm going there now.'

'I'll send them on.'

Bernie ran across the park as best she could, cursing the heels on her shoes. *Back to flats tomorrow.* She saw a uniformed officer waving at her.

'Over here, ma'am,' he called.

Bernie slowed down. 'Where is it?'

'Under this bush here.' The officer lifted some branches and shone his torch.

Bernie crouched down. The bottle-green fleece was camouflaged by the undergrowth but Bernie could see something yellow.

'Can you direct the light a little more to the right please?'

The torch moved and the yellow gleamed in the light. It was a sticker with a smiley face.

*

The Coles' house was the last in the village. A sign saying, 'Now leaving Otterfield, thank you for driving safely', was only a few metres away. They really are on the edge, thought Bernie. She knocked at the wooden door. It looked new and the little sandy pebble-dashed house appeared to have new windows as well. *Making improvements.* The door was opened by Sergeant Alan Turner, a rotund man who would normally be found manning the custody suite at Wiltshire Police headquarters, back in Devizes.

'Thank God you're here, ma'am. Jessica's really struggling,' said Alan.

'She's about to struggle more then.' Bernie held up a brown paper evidence bag. 'Molly's fleece.' She stepped into the hallway, Kerry behind her.

'Oh God. She's in the lounge, rocking the baby back and forth. She can't seem to stop. Can't get anything out of her. Still waiting for her father to come home.'

'What about Davy Reynolds?' asked Bernie.

'I've put a call into the MoD. They're sorting out contact. He's on manoeuvres so we can't get hold of him directly.'

'DNA samples?'

'Trying to work on that but can't seem to get through to Jessica that we need to take these things.'

'OK,' said Bernie, 'let me try. I sort of made a connection with her earlier. I won't show her this just yet. Can you hang onto it for now, please, Kerry? Just wait by the door. Keep it behind your back.'

Bernie followed Alan into the lounge. The room was painted mostly white but with a turquoise paisley-patterned wallpaper on one wall. The beige carpet felt soft under her feet and Bernie wondered if she should have taken off her shoes or, better still, put blue plastic covers over them. She couldn't help but feel that maybe there was crucial evidence in the house.

Jessica Cole was sitting on a brown leather sofa, rocking back and forth with the baby in her arms. Bernie knelt down in front of her.

'Jessica? It's DI Noel. Remember we met at the park earlier.'

The young woman raised her head. Her eyes looked vacant as she stared at Bernie but then she gave a slight nod of recognition.

'Have you found her?' she asked, her voice barely a whisper.

Bernie shook her head. 'Not yet but I've got lots of police officers out looking. And we've been going through the village knocking on everyone's doors and asking them to look out for her.'

'Huh! Good luck with that one. No one round here cares.' Anger flared into Jessica's voice.

Bernie sighed. She didn't have the heart to tell Jessica she was right on that score. 'Jessica, there are some things we need to do here to help us find Molly.'

The young woman focused on Bernie's face, all the while still rocking.

'What? Just say and I'll do it.'

Bernie looked across briefly to Kerry. 'Please be aware that what I'm about to ask for is standard practice for all missing persons. We need to have DNA samples – her hairbrush or comb and her toothbrush. We'll also need more photos if you have some. We'll scan them and make sure you get them back. And...' Bernie hesitated. This was the part she hated the most. 'We'll also need the sheet on Molly's bed.'

Jessica looked at her, perplexed. 'I don't understand. Why do you need her sheet?'

'As I said, it's standard practice.'

'Bullshit.'

Bernie suddenly realised Jessica had stopped rocking and her attention was fully on her.

'Why do you need the sheet?'

Bernie took a deep breath. 'Because we need to make sure Molly was safe at home. You said yourself – you didn't hear Molly cry out at all. Maybe it's because she was taken by someone she knew. Someone who knew her a little too well.'

Bernie watched as realisation dawned on Jessica's face. 'No. No, you're wrong. No one was abusing Molly. You want to check for semen, don't you? Well you can't. I washed her sheet this morning, in fact all of her bedding. She wets herself at night still. And I told her off for it this morning.' Jessica raised a hand to her face as she started to cry. 'I told her off for her stinky wet sheet. I told her off.'

Bernie moved from the floor to the sofa next to Jessica and put her arm around her shoulders. 'You didn't know what was going to happen today. I'm sorry to say these things to you but a lot of detective work is ruling people out as much as ruling suspects in. I would like Forensics to check her mattress since you've washed the sheets. And there's something else.' Bernie nodded at Kerry and she came over with the brown paper bag. 'We found this at the park earlier.' Kerry broke the seal on the bag and opened it for Jessica to see.

'It has Molly's name on it and the sticker you were telling me about,' said Bernie. 'I just need you to confirm whether or not she was wearing it when you last saw her.'

Jessica took a sharp intake of breath and nodded. 'Yes. She was wearing it. Oh God, where did you find it?'

'In the park. Are you sure she didn't take it off?'

'Positive.'

Moving back into professional mode, Bernie removed her arm from Jessica's shoulders. 'OK. This is what's going to happen now. It's time to move this up a level and get the press involved. Social media too. I'm going to make a statement tonight. If we haven't found her by the morning then I'd like to do a full press conference with you and your father. We're working on getting hold of Davy.'

'But how will you find her tonight? It's getting dark.'

'I've spoken to Detective Chief Superintendent Wilson and we're sending up a police helicopter with an infrared camera. At some point we'll have to stop as we'll need some sleep, and the residents of the village will need some too. But a helicopter hovering overhead for a while won't be such a bad thing. It will remind them a child is missing and we need their help.' *Despite what they might think.* 'I don't know why people here are being so unkind to you, Jessica, but I was on the receiving end of similar treatment today. The press are going to invade this village and it will probably shame them all into helping.

'This is DS Kerry Allen and she's going to stay with you for the rest of this evening,' Bernie continued, 'and she'll help explain things to your father when he gets here. She'll oversee the CSI who will come soon. I know you aren't keen about that, but tomorrow at the press conference I want to be able to portray Molly as a happy little girl at home. I'll appoint a family liaison officer to you tomorrow, someone who can be with you most of the time. I'll ring you later, after I've made the statement, so you know what's been said before it goes on air on the news tonight.'

Bernie paused for breath and saw a slightly stunned expression on Jessica's face. 'I know things are moving quite fast now and this isn't how you thought your day would be.' She glanced down at the sleeping baby in Jessica's arms. 'I can also get someone in to help you with Sam.'

A look of horror appeared on Jessica's face. 'No. I'm not having social services take him away.'

'Oh God, no. I wasn't thinking of that. Technically, it probably should be them but I was thinking of referring you to Home-Start. They're a charity that helps families with children under the age of five. All their volunteers are DBS checked. I know one of them and she's fairly local. Leave it with me.'

Bernie stood up. 'I'll call you later. Please be assured we're doing everything we can to find Molly. Hopefully your father will be back soon and then you'll have some family support.'

Bernie nodded at Kerry and they both left the room and walked to the front door where Alan was waiting.

'Thanks so much for coming in on your day off, Alan. Kerry's going to stay so you can go now.'

'No problem, ma'am. Anytime. Not like I've got much going on at home. See you tomorrow.' He opened the door and left.

Bernie turned to Kerry. 'If needed, could you sleep here tonight on the sofa please? Just in case Derek Cole gets back really late.'

'Yes, of course. So who is it you're thinking of to help with the baby?'

'I think I'd better check with her first before I say. I'll call you later. Let me know when the CSI has been.'

'OK,' said Kerry. 'We got interrupted earlier. How was the funeral?'

'It was… all right.' Bernie's thoughts lingered on the condolence card wrapped in a plastic bag in the boot of her car. Hand-delivered that morning. Unsigned. Its message ominous. She instinctively moved her hand to her side, aware of the scar that still itched occasionally. 'I'd better get on. Speak soon.'

She walked back to her car with Molly's fleece in the evidence bag and glanced at her watch. It was just after eight p.m. She scrolled down the contacts on her phone and then dialled.

'Hello, vicar, it's DI Noel… Yes, nice to speak to you too… Actually, I need some help, not just from you but from Anna too. I think she's a volunteer with Home-Start, isn't she?'

She wasn't out for long. Surprisingly, she hasn't cried. Instead, she's like a cat – not exactly hissing at me but definitely scratching. The scratches on my arms are long and shallow but they're short and jagged on my hands where she's dug her fingernails in. She's drawn blood in a couple of places. Somehow I have to subdue her but I don't want to use force; not unless I have to. I don't want her to be scared of me. I want her to be... compliant.

CHAPTER THREE

Bernie had watched the late-night news report on the TV at the police station, cringing to herself. *Do I really sound like that?* She'd been pleased though; the case had made national news, not just local. She was still in two minds as to where to hold the press conference in the morning. The police station was the obvious choice but something was telling her to go local – the hall of Molly's primary school sprang to mind. It would be Saturday morning so no children would be at school. She wanted to keep this case fresh in the minds of the Otterfield villagers. All the house-to-house reports were now in and no one had seen Molly. Nor had they particularly cared. A few of the mums who had been at the park had been found. One or two had noticed her there and one had remembered she'd been wearing her fleece. The police officer had noted down the woman had found this odd, as it had been such a warm day. This caught Bernie's attention. She highlighted the name and the address. Someone to go back to, she thought. All the mothers had left through the main entrance. No one had used the back gate, close to the train track.

She glanced at her watch. Ten fifty p.m.

Her phone buzzed. 'Kerry, what have you got for me?'

'The CSI has checked the mattress, both sides. Definitely urine present. You could tell by the smell. No obvious signs of semen but it's been sent to the lab for further checks. Derek Cole finally turned up just after ten o'clock. There was a major accident on the M4 and nothing was moving. Jessica seems a little brighter now her father is here.'

'What's he like?'

'Pleasant enough. Mid-fifties. Engineer by trade. Works in Bristol. He's doing the "good dad" routine and being strong for Jessica. I've told them we'll do formal statements at the station tomorrow after the press conference.'

'Actually, I was thinking of asking the head teacher of Molly's school if we could use the hall, keep it local.'

'You mean rubbing the villagers' noses in it.'

'Something like that.'

'Hmm...'

Bernie could sense the hesitation in Kerry's voice.

'...I'm not sure. It could backfire on you. Plus it's May bank holiday weekend. You might not get hold of the head anyway. Oh, can you hear that?'

Bernie listened carefully. She could hear a whirring sound. 'Is it the helicopter?'

'Yep,' said Kerry. 'Been round a few times now. I'm sure they'll report in to you soon. Check with the super about the press conference.'

'Yes, I will. You're probably right. I forgot about the bank holiday. Oh, can you get some of Molly's clothing, please, preferably unwashed? We've got the sniffer dogs in tomorrow. Going to concentrate the search along the railway line. Uniform did what they could today but we're going to need extra help in the morning. Bring it in with you tomorrow.'

'Will do. Is anyone else still there with you? What time are you going home? You need to get some rest.'

Bernie looked around the empty office. The silence weighed heavy.

'It's just me. I sent Matt home. I'll wait for the helicopter crew to get back to me and then I'll grab a few hours' sleep. You try and do the same. I want you in for a meeting at eight.'

'OK, see you in the morning.'

Bernie's finger hovered over the text message icon on her phone. She wondered if her mum had seen the news. She hoped her mother had put two and two together and figured out her daughter had left straight after the funeral because of the missing girl. Of course, if Denise Baxter thought about it clearly, then she'd know that the times didn't add up. Bernie had just turned off the M4 on her way back when the call had come through. The image of the card with a lily on the front and 'Sorry for your loss' embossed in gold danced around in her mind. A lily. The flower most commonly associated with funerals and death. It was now in her desk drawer. She resolved to speak to the super in the morning and send it in for processing. If the death threats were starting again, she had to protect her family. Plus, she'd just realised: national coverage was good for Molly but not for her. She'd given away her location.

Saturday

Bernie slept fitfully. She found herself running through endless dark tunnels, shouting out Molly's name. The tunnels then turned into a maze, chasing a shadow that was always a step ahead, and finally a house of mirrors, where she saw Molly at every turn. In frustration, she started to smash the mirrors, Molly splintering before her. She woke trying to catch her breath. Sunlight was filtering through her curtains. Bernie put her hands to her head. She knew the dreams weren't real but the reality of Molly's disappearance loomed large before her. Music started to play on her clock radio. Six a.m. She knew four hours' sleep wasn't really enough but adrenalin would get her through. And caffeine, lots of caffeine.

The incident room was starting to fill up. Bernie checked the interactive whiteboard again. Everything they knew so far was typed up on her laptop and had been entered into the HOLMES database that would help process any information coming in. The door to her right opened and the smell of doughnuts wafted in. Matt Taylor was carrying six large, white bakery boxes.

'Courtesy of the baker's down the road. They saw the news last night and made these for us this morning, with a pledge they will provide us with breakfast every day, until Molly is found. Danishes tomorrow.'

'Ooh, the baker's that makes doughnuts as big as your face?' asked a uniformed officer.

Matt laughed. 'Yeah, that's the one.'

Bernie smiled. She still couldn't work out what was wrong with the residents in Otterfield but at least the people of Devizes seemed to care. She took some of the boxes and passed them round the room, grabbing a huge chocolate iced doughnut for herself. 'Well, as partial as I am to a free pastry, I hope there won't be too many mornings like this.'

As she sank her teeth in, her stomach rumbled. She realised the last thing she had eaten had been before the funeral. She washed down the doughnut with some coffee, her third cup of the morning. She knew she'd be buzzing soon. She saw Kerry Allen come in, a large brown evidence bag in her hand. Everyone was now here.

'Right, ladies and gentlemen, if I could have your attention please.' Bernie pointed to the board behind her. 'Thank you very much for being here this morning, especially those of you who've come in to do an extra shift. Let's go through what we know already.'

She clicked on her computer and an image of Molly in her uniform appeared on the screen.

'This is Molly Reynolds, five years old, who went missing yesterday from the playground area in the park at Otterfield, at approximately fifteen forty-five hours. She was wearing her school uniform, including this green fleece, which was found about nineteen hundred hours, under a bush in this area of the park.'

Bernie clicked again and a map came up. She zoomed in.

'This is close to a gate that's normally locked by a padlock and chain because of its proximity to the railway line. However, the chain has been cut. Uniforms started to search this area last night but had to stop because of fading light. This morning, we're sending in the dog handlers. We have an item of Molly's clothing and we're hoping the dogs will pick up her scent.'

Bernie looked at the people before her, about fifty in all. Some she knew well. Others had been drafted in from neighbouring forces. Many had given up their days off.

'As you can see from the map, the park is on the edge of the village. There are no houses beyond it for a significant distance, just the railway, woods and farmland. The helicopter went up last night but didn't find any hotspots.'

'Except for the couple who were shagging in a car,' laughed a young male PC. A few others sniggered. Bernie glared at him. 'Sorry, ma'am.'

Bernie looked back at the board. 'House-to-house enquiries didn't produce much except for one woman,' she referred to her notes. 'She mentioned she thought it odd Molly had her fleece on when it was so warm. Matt, I think you have her details. I'd like you to go and see her. And Lucy…' Bernie looked around the room for the young CSI who had taken the photos of the fleece and bagged it. 'Jessica has confirmed the fleece belongs to Molly.

So can you check with the lab and see if they can get any trace off of it? I'm guessing that prints will be a no.'

Lucy screwed up her nose and shook her head. 'Unlikely but I'm sure they'll do their best. But they can check for DNA trace.'

Bernie continued, 'There will be a press conference at twelve hundred hours, here at the station, with Jessica Cole and her father, Derek. We're still trying to get hold of Molly's father. In the meantime, we have a lot of searching to do. Remember, the press and the public are watching. Hopefully, we'll start to get some calls coming in from the public soon.'

Kerry began to distribute sheets of paper. 'If you look at the handouts coming round to you now,' said Bernie, 'you'll see you're divided into teams. Most of you are out with the search but a few of you will be needed to distribute missing persons' leaflets and posters. I want to see a poster in every shop in Devizes.

'Matt, I'd like you to update social media before you go out please. We have officers from other divisions on standby to join us. I'll be leading the search initially, along with DS Allen. I need everyone to report back in by eleven forty-five hours so we can prepare for the press conference. Let's hope and pray we find her before then, alive and well.'

Otterfield was almost empty as Bernie drove through the village. The few people on the streets averted their eyes as she went past. She expected more of them. Maybe overnight, their hearts had softened and they would want to help find Molly. There was no one hanging around the park, though, as she pulled up. Bernie looked at the houses opposite. Even though she couldn't see anyone around, she couldn't shift the feeling she was being watched.

She heard the dogs before she saw them. The police van was parked by the main entrance to the recreation ground. Two white, male, uniformed police officers stood next to it. Bernie held her hand out to each of them.

'DI Bernie Noel. Thanks for coming.'

'Not a problem,' said the taller of the two men. 'I'm Sergeant Keith Lincoln and this is PC Dan O'Connor. And these two beauties are…' He walked round to the back of the van. One of the doors was already open and Bernie could see two springer spaniels behind the wire mesh. 'Bonnie and Clyde. They're brother and sister, bred especially to be sniffer dogs. Parents were police dogs as well.'

Bernie looked at the brown and white dogs. 'They're beautiful. I was expecting German shepherds.'

'We generally find when a person has gone missing, especially someone vulnerable, it's a lot less scary for them if a spaniel finds them, rather than a German shepherd,' said PC O'Connor.

'You do realise we may not be looking for someone alive, although I hope to God she is.'

Lincoln gave a grim nod. 'Clyde is our search and rescue dog and we use Bonnie for cadavers. We figured it was best to bring both.'

Bernie glanced at her watch: nine a.m. 'Right, well, we'd better get started. We have an item of clothing for Clyde to sniff. How do you want to do this?'

'Clyde is Dan's dog so he'll take him to the last known place Molly was at. I'm assuming it was the playground.'

Bernie nodded. 'Yes, I can show you.' As they crossed the park, she asked Dan, 'How long have you been doing this?'

'I transferred to Dogs two years ago. I've had Clyde for almost a year now. Is that officer over there waving at us?'

Bernie looked across the park. Kerry was with a group of about twenty uniformed officers by the playground.

'Hi, Bernie. We've done another search around here but haven't found anything else,' said Kerry.

'Did you go into the playground?' asked Dan.

'Yes.'

'How many of you?'

'Myself and about three other officers. Why? Is that a problem?'

Dan sighed. 'It could be. That's four other recent scents you've just put in there. Clyde may have a hard time. It's going to be difficult as it is.'

Kerry's face dropped. 'I'm so sorry, I didn't think.' She looked across at Bernie. 'Ma'am, I was only doing what I thought best.'

Bernie mentally kicked herself. She should have known that and told Kerry not to search the playground again. 'Well, it's done now. Let's all keep back and let Dan and Clyde do their jobs. Do you have Molly's clothes?'

Kerry reached for a brown bag that another officer was holding. 'They were from the washing basket. It only had Molly's clothes in it.' She handed it over to Dan, looking rather shamefaced.

'Thanks.' He held it open for the dog to smell. 'OK, Clyde, go find.' Dan took him off his lead.

They all stepped back as Clyde ran around sniffing the grass. He stopped at little patches but didn't appear to be following a specific trail. He then ran into the playground. Bernie watched as Clyde followed a trail around the swings and slide, and then back to the little gate at the entrance to the playground. He sat down.

Dan scratched his head. 'Clyde – find.' The dog didn't move.

'What's going on?' asked Bernie.

Dan looked at her, slightly confused. 'I'm not sure. It looks as though he can't find a scent trail beyond the gate.'

'But what about when she came in with her mum? Surely there would be a scent from the main entrance.'

Dan shook his head. 'I don't understand it. He was picking up a sporadic trail which might have been their way in but her scent only appears to be strongest in the playground. Where did you find the fleece?'

Bernie pointed behind her in the distance to a set of bushes near to the back of the park. 'Over there. It's close to a back gate. It's been unlocked and we assume Molly was taken that way.'

'OK. Let's take him over there. Clyde, come.'

The dog brushed past her legs, his fur beautifully soft. 'He's gorgeous. He reminds me of a cadaver dog we used earlier this year, called Tilly. Very sad case. An old man with Alzheimer's had gone missing. She found him.'

Dan nodded. 'I remember. That was awful. Tilly's another sister of Clyde's. There was a litter of five, two boys and three girls. All fantastic dogs.'

As they got nearer the bush, Dan held open the brown bag for Clyde to smell again. 'Clyde, find.' The dog sniffed the ground again, seemingly aimlessly.

'Still no scent?' asked Bernie.

Dan shook his head. He went and stood right next to the bush. 'Clyde, here.' The dog obediently followed his master and trotted over towards him. As he reached the bush, he put his nose to the ground and went straight under it and sat down.

'Well, he's found where the fleece went, at least,' said Bernie. 'Is it worth taking him out of the park, over there, through the back gate?'

Dan scratched his head again. 'I really don't understand this. I think we need to get Keith here. He's got twenty years of experience. I'm just a rookie with the dogs. I'll radio for him to come.'

Bernie left Dan talking to his sergeant and walked back to Kerry.

'Ma'am, I'm really sorry about searching the playground again…'

Bernie held up her hand. 'Don't worry about that for now. We've got bigger issues. Molly's scent is strongest in the playground and under the bush where her fleece was found but weak elsewhere. Why is that? She didn't fly in.'

Kerry looked thoughtful for a moment and then smiled. 'Buggy board.'

'Pardon?'

'A buggy board explains why her scent isn't very strong outside the playground. We'll need to check with Jessica but I bet you anything she has a buggy board attached to her pram so Molly doesn't have to walk everywhere.'

Bernie nodded. 'Good idea. But what about when she was taken? There didn't appear to be any scent at all in that direction until we got to the bush.'

'The abductor carried her?'

'No, that wouldn't have completely wiped out the scent,' said a male voice from behind.

They both turned to see Keith Lincoln standing there with Bonnie. 'Unless held very tightly, the body, if moving, would still give off scent. She would have to be completely immobile.'

'Go on,' said Bernie.

'The best way to do that would be to knock her out, probably with chloroform or something similar, and then put her in a buggy.'

'A five-year-old in a buggy?' asked Bernie.

'Actually, I checked her health record in her red book last night and she's small for her age,' said Kerry. 'She wouldn't necessarily look out of place in a pushchair.'

'And yesterday was warm. Put a big sun shade over it to conceal the child inside. Of course, a plastic rain cover would do a better job of keeping the scent in,' said Keith.

Bernie put her hands to her face for a few seconds. She took a deep breath. 'So there's nothing we can do?'

'It might be possible to pick up a secondary scent for the abductor but so many officers have tramped through here it's not going to be easy.'

'Let's see if that will work.'

'I'll go and talk to Dan,' said Keith. 'Of course, there is another scenario.'

'What?' asked Bernie.

'That Molly left the same way she arrived. In which case, you need to interview the mother.'

Bernie pondered Keith's words. Was that why the residents of Otterfield were being unhelpful? Did they think Jessica was responsible for her own daughter's disappearance?

CHAPTER FOUR

Bernie pulled into her usual parking space at headquarters. She glanced at her watch – eleven twenty-three a.m. – just over thirty minutes away from the press conference. Massaging her aching temple, she braced herself for the next onslaught: Detective Chief Superintendent Wilson.

As she strode through the station, she was greeted with the same response from everyone – 'Anything?' – and her reply was the same – 'No.' She knew she had to talk to Wilson before anyone else. She knocked on his door.

'Enter. Ah, Bernie. This is Jane Clackett from the press office. Your paths might not have crossed before. Jane advises us on the media for our most serious cases.'

Bernie turned to her right and saw a woman in her thirties with chalk-white skin, raven-black hair cut in a sharp bob, matching black eye liner and bright red lips. Her black trouser suit and white shirt added to the monochrome look. Bernie wasn't sure if she was a media expert or a vampire. There was little enough natural light in the building to make the latter a real possibility. Bernie hadn't personally met Jane but knew of her reputation. Loved by the top brass for her ruthless efficiency but not so much further down the scale as she trampled over investigations to get what she needed. She nodded in greeting.

'The big question is, do we have enough to issue a Child Rescue Alert, Bernie?' asked Wilson.

'I think so.'

'You think so?' asked Jane Clackett. 'Either you do or you don't.'

Bernie clenched her fists and then slowly released her fingers, deliberately keeping her eyes on her senior officer. 'Well, she's been missing since yesterday afternoon. We've got nothing from house-to-house or the helicopter search. We've got the dogs in today. The only thing we've found is her fleece stuffed under a bush and it's unlikely she took it off herself. And the thing that clinched it for me this morning is that the dogs can only find her scent in the playground and under the bush. She didn't fly out of there. Someone has taken her.'

'No scent? That's very odd,' said Jane.

Bernie resisted the urge to turn her head. 'I'm going to ask Jessica if she has a buggy board. It would explain how Molly got to the playground without leaving much scent.'

'But how did she leave the playground then… Unless… Oh God. Maybe it's the mother after all? Some people will do anything to get sympathy these days. And money. You know, sell the story to the papers,' said Jane.

Bernie couldn't hold her displeasure in any longer. 'If you don't mind, Ms Clackett, I'm addressing Detective Chief Superintendent Wilson, as he's the one who'll have to make the decision. Please don't interrupt me again.'

Bernie looked back at Wilson, his bald head glowing slightly in the warm May heat. He was only a few years away from retirement. His bulging, frog-like eyes sent her a warning that she'd overstepped the mark. Bernie ignored him and continued.

'We can't be sure how Molly left the park. It may have been on a buggy board or even in a buggy. Perhaps Jessica is responsible. They're fairly new to Otterfield and haven't settled. Maybe it is a

ruse to gain attention and sympathy from their neighbours, but,'
Bernie shook her head, 'I don't think so. Jessica's devastation seems
genuine to me. It's so… raw. You'll see what I mean when she
gets here for the press conference. I believe Molly Reynolds has
been abducted. I know we have nothing to go on at present in
regards to a possible suspect but when I left the park, the search
dog had picked up a secondary scent that led out the back gate.
So, in answer to your question, yes, I think we have enough to
issue the CRA.'

Wilson rubbed his chin. 'Even if the mother has taken her and
hidden her, she could still be in danger of harm. Jane, are we going
to be live on *BBC News 24* and *Sky News* at the press conference?'

Jane gave a smug smile. 'Yes, and the other networks and papers
will be there. When you issue the alert you'll get a newsflash on
BBC West and South West, and it will be read out every fifteen
minutes on Spire and Heart for four hours. *Salisbury Journal* and
Swindon Advertiser will put it on their websites, as well as have it
in their next edition. Of course, the press will want to know why
you didn't issue it sooner. She's been gone almost twenty hours.'

Bernie's face burned with anger.

'As you well know, Jane,' said Wilson, 'we don't issue these alerts
lightly. The vast majority of children are found quite quickly. I
think DI Noel has done everything she could to find out what's
happened. If the residents of Otterfield aren't helping us, then
we do need to turn to the public at large for their help. Issue the
CRA, and I want Crimestoppers in on this too. There may well
be someone who saw something, but would prefer not to speak
to us directly. We'll do it just before midday and then hopefully
that way, people will turn over to watch the press conference.'

The telephone on Wilson's desk began to ring.

He picked it up. 'Hello… right, I'll let her know.' He put the
phone down and looked up at Bernie. 'Jessica Cole is here with
her father. You and Jane need to prep them before they go in

front of the press. Afterwards, I want you to ask them some hard questions, find out if they're responsible in any way. Have you been in contact with social services?'

'Only to find out if they're on the register and they're not. I've brought in someone from Home-Start, though, to support the family.'

'Well, I suppose that's better than nothing but you'll have to bring social services in if you have any doubts about the Coles. Keep them in the loop anyway.'

Bernie remembered Jessica's terrified face at the thought of social services becoming involved. She nodded her head. 'Yes, sir.'

Wilson looked at the clock. 'You two have fifteen minutes to spend with the family so they're prepared.' He flicked his hand at Bernie and she knew it was time to leave. She held the door open and allowed Jane Clackett to go out first.

'Oh, Bernie?' said Wilson.

She turned back to him. 'Yes, sir?'

'Play nice,' and he raised his eyebrows at her.

Bernie sighed and closed the door. Immediately, Jane was in her face.

'You may not think what I do is worthwhile but let's get this straight, right now. I know how to handle the media. Don't you ever put me down in front of the super again.'

Bernie felt spit on her face. She wiped it away with her hand and pushed past Jane. The vampire is alive and well, she thought.

Bernie took Jessica's hand and squeezed it. 'We'll do this together. The only thing I need you to say is how much you love Molly and want her back. Detective Chief Superintendent Wilson and I will deal with the rest. And your dad will be right there with you as well, won't you, Mr Cole?'

Bernie looked across at Derek Cole. She hadn't been too sure what to expect of him. He was smartly dressed with short grey hair and a neatly trimmed beard. He was quite tall, well built, but with a harshness to his face. She had already checked him out, Jessica too, just to make sure. Neither had criminal records.

'I assume I have to be.'

'Of course you do,' said Jane. 'And you're already dressed for it.' She pulled Bernie away and whispered, 'Unlike his daughter. Sort her out, Bernie. She's got dry snot on her face and judging by the smell, baby puke on her top.'

Bernie managed a smile. 'Ah, but that's not my job. You know what the media wants. Take her to the ladies' and tidy her up yourself. But...' Bernie placed a hand on Jane's arm, 'be kind.'

Jane glared at her but gently led Jessica away.

Bernie smiled at Derek Cole. 'Where's Sam?' she asked.

'That lady from Home-Start has got him downstairs. I think you sent her. Irish woman. She did tell me her name but nothing is staying in my head at the moment.'

'That's understandable. She's Anna Bentley and from Northern Ireland. She's married to the vicar at Marchant. Now, Mr Cole, after the press conference, there are a few questions I have to ask you and Jessica and we also have to take your fingerprints and DNA.'

'What do you want those for?' Cole's voice rose in anger. 'We haven't done anything wrong.' A vein pulsed in his forehead.

'It's OK, Mr Cole.' Bernie reached out her hand to reassure him. 'This is normal procedure. We need yours and Jessica's to rule out your prints and DNA on any evidence we find.'

'Oh, I'm sorry. We're just so stressed. I don't think Jess slept at all last night. If it weren't for the baby, I'd suggest having her sedated. She's feeding him herself.'

Bernie nodded. 'I understand. We can talk to your GP though. There might be something else we can do to help her sleep.'

'She needs Davy. I can only do so much.'

'We're working on that too with the MoD.'

'Working on what with the MoD?' asked Jane.

Bernie turned to see Jane and Jessica behind her. Jessica looked far more presentable with her face washed and hair tied back. Jane had even lent Jessica her jacket to wear to cover up the vomit stains.

'That was quick.'

'Well, I don't like to muck around.' Jane turned her head to the side and muttered, 'Quick splash of water and hair tied back. No time to comb it properly. My jacket – job done. Now, what about the MoD?'

'Davy Reynolds, Molly's father, is in the army. He's on manoeuvres at the moment. We're trying to get him home.'

'Oh, I see. Where's he served, Jessica? Iraq? Afghanistan?'

'Afghanistan,' said Jessica quietly. 'Two terms. He was lucky to come back alive.'

Jane nodded and Bernie knew she was plotting her media strategy. 'Any commendations?'

'Yes. He got a medal for saving some fellow soldiers after a sniper attack. Carried the injured to safety whilst dodging bullets,' said Jessica, proudly.

Jane looked at Bernie. 'Well then. We have to ask the people of Wiltshire, a proud army county, to help us find the daughter of a hero. Don't you agree, DI Noel?'

Bernie took a deep breath. The search was difficult enough without Jane playing power games with her. 'Of course.' She glanced at her watch. 'It's time. There'll be a glass of water for you and some tissues. Don't be afraid to show how upset you are but keep your language clean when you speak. No swear words please. This is going out live.'

Jessica paled. 'Live?'

'There'll be a few seconds' delay and it's only on a few channels. As I said earlier, you just have to say you want Molly back. We'll do the rest. OK? Let's go.'

*

The room was packed and stiflingly hot. Bernie felt Jessica tense as she led her and Derek Cole out. Wilson followed them. Bernie's heartbeat increased and she suddenly regretted all the coffee she'd drunk – she needed a cool head. She saw Jane at the side of the room, talking to a couple of journalists. Bernie wondered if she was feeding them questions.

'Ladies and gentlemen…' started Wilson.

And members of the press, thought Bernie.

'…we're here to update you on Molly Reynolds, aged five years old, who went missing yesterday from the park in Otter-field around three forty-five p.m. We believe she may have been abducted. We need help from members of the public to find her. Behind me is a photo of Molly as she was dressed that day, in her uniform. We would like to hear from anyone who thinks they've seen Molly, or if they saw anyone suspicious in the local area. Think carefully. There may be someone you saw a few days ago, hanging around. You can contact us directly at the station or ring Crimestoppers. Detective Inspector Noel is leading the investigation.' Wilson nodded at her. She knew it was her turn.

'We've been searching the local area but we really do need help from the public if we're to find Molly quickly. In particular we want to speak to anyone who was at the park at the time. You may have seen something you hadn't realised was important. Now, this is Molly's mum, Jessica, and she has something to say to you.'

Bernie placed her hand on Jessica's arm. She whispered, 'Remember what I said, you want Molly home.'

Jessica raised her head. Light bulbs started to flash and cameras clicked. 'I just want Molly home. If you have her, please let her come back to me. I love her so much.' Tears started to stream down Jessica's face and Bernie passed her a tissue.

'Are there any questions?' asked Wilson. Hands shot up. 'Yes.' He pointed to an older man in a tweed jacket on the front row.

'Clive Bishop, *Salisbury Journal*. You've just released a Child Rescue Alert. Why's it so late?'

Wilson nodded. 'As you'll know, we don't issue these alerts readily. There's criteria that has to be fulfilled. As Jessica didn't see her daughter leave the park, we couldn't be sure she'd been taken. She could have been playing hide and seek or run off with another child. However, as time has gone on, we now believe Molly didn't leave the park by herself. Next question.' He pointed to one of the journalists Bernie had seen Jane talk to.

'Trudy Smith, *Swindon Advertiser*. This is a slightly delicate question. Is Molly's father on the scene? Could he have taken her?'

'DI Noel knows more about the family.'

Bernie paused. She saw Jane looking at her, mouthing, 'Army hero.'

'Molly's father is Davy Reynolds. He's in the army and currently on deployment. He's very much on the scene as he and Ms Cole are engaged.' Bernie hesitated. She really didn't want to play into Jane Clackett's hands but knew she had no choice. 'He's a very brave soldier, a hero, in fact. We're hoping to get him home very soon.'

Jane pulled a face at her. She clearly wanted more but Bernie thought that was enough. If the journalists wanted the full details then they could investigate – it was their job, after all.

More questions were asked but Wilson handled them. Bernie became aware of Jessica shaking next to her. It was time to stop. Before Wilson could choose another journalist, Bernie spoke up, 'I think we need to leave it there for the moment. We will of course update you all at regular intervals.' She leaned across to Jessica. 'Come. You've had enough for now.'

CHAPTER FIVE

Jessica took Sam in her arms. A brief smile appeared on the young woman's lips as the baby nestled into her.

'She's a good mother, in case you're wondering,' Anna Bentley said to Bernie. 'I know I've only been with her a few hours but she's still managed to care for Sam despite everything else. I've had to persuade her to let me help.'

'The super wants me to call in social services.'

'I guess you have to but I don't think Sam's in any danger. And I'm willing to stay as long as it takes.'

'What about Paul?'

'Oh, Paul'll be fine. In fact he'll be glad I'm out doing something. Since I left work I've been moping about the place. Doing Home-Start is the best thing for me. I'm sure social services will be OK with me being there.'

'What, with you being a former social worker and all that?'

Anna sighed. 'At least this way I get to care for families without any hidden agenda.'

'Well, about that…' said Bernie.

'No. I won't spy for you. If I think there's any reason to believe Sam's in danger or if there's anything you need to know about Molly, then I'll tell you. But I won't go looking for it; I won't snoop.'

Anna's long red curls were tied back in a bushy ponytail. A smattering of freckles sprinkled her nose and cheeks. Only the wrinkles around her sparkling green eyes belied her age of mid-forties.

Bernie nodded. 'OK. I'll trust you to tell me things when you need to. But I will ask after Jessica's well-being. I have a duty of care to her. The family liaison officer will be along soon for me to introduce to the family. I'd like you to be there for that. But now, I have to take Jessica and Derek's fingerprints and DNA. We need them for elimination purposes. Derek was a bit weird about it at first.'

'People don't like the idea of the police having their prints. I can understand that.'

Bernie glanced at Jessica and realised she was feeding Sam. For a brief moment they were a picture of serenity in amongst the bustle of the police station but Bernie knew the turmoil going on inside the young mother. 'We'll do Derek first,' she said.

'OK, Mr Cole, as I said to you earlier, we'd like to take your fingerprints for the purpose of elimination. I need your consent for this as you're not a suspect. I'd also like to take your DNA for the same reason. I'll be asking your daughter to do this as well.'

'And what happens to this information afterwards?'

'We only keep records if you're a suspect. You've already accounted for where you were yesterday and a whole office of people have corroborated it. You're currently not under suspicion. As I've already said, this is just for elimination.'

'Currently not under suspicion?'

The vein in Derek Cole's forehead was pulsing again.

'I'm sorry, Mr Cole, that was the wrong phrase to use. More often than not, a missing child is abducted by a family member.

I have to remain open to all possibilities. Do I have your consent to take your fingerprints and DNA samples?'

The harshness in Derek Cole's face crumbled slightly. 'Yes. I'll do anything to get our Molly back. Anything.'

'Thank you. I'll need you to sign a consent form. Then I'm going to hand you over to another officer who will take you to the fingerprint machine and take your DNA sample.'

'Fingerprint machine?'

'Oh yes, all high tech these days. No more ink. The machine will scan your whole hand.' Bernie looked across the room for Alan Turner. She caught his eye and he nodded.

'Hello, sir, I'm Sergeant Turner. If you'd like to come with me and we'll sort this all out.' Turner winked at Bernie as he led Derek Cole away. She mouthed 'thank you' back to him.

Bernie's phone buzzed in her trouser pocket. She glanced at the screen before answering.

'Matt, got anything for me?'

'The lab called. Just urine on Molly's mattress and it's hers. And there've been a few calls in from the public. Nothing concrete though.'

'That's good about the mattress. What about the woman you went to see?'

'She wasn't in. Had taken her daughters to ballet. She'll be in later so I told her husband I'd call back at three p.m. But to be honest, I don't think she's going to be much help.'

Bernie leaned back against the wall to let some officers pass.

'OK,' she said. 'I still have a few things to sort out with the family here but I plan to join the search after that. Have you heard from Kerry?'

'Yes, about half an hour ago. They're following the secondary scent down the path by the railway line but haven't found anything yet.'

Bernie glanced at her watch. Just after one p.m. 'Right. Well, you keep fielding the calls but get some lunch before you head back to Otterfield. We'll speak later.'

At the thought of lunch, Bernie's stomach rumbled. She needed to eat something. She'd be no good to the investigation if she didn't keep her strength up.

Bernie sank her teeth into the bacon butty and allowed herself to savour the combination of salty meat and tangy ketchup. She caught sight of the lady serving behind the bakery counter smiling at her. It was a relief to see the friendliness of Devizes after the cold shoulder from the residents of Otterfield the day before.

'You keep coming to see me and I'll make sure you and all the team are well fed. Did you like your breakfast earlier?'

Bernie nodded, her mouth full of food. 'Yes, great, thanks. It's very kind of you.'

'No trouble at all. We feel so helpless, so anything we can do. We saw the news last night and the press conference today. Are the family still with you at the station? Do you think they'd like some sandwiches? On the house.'

Bernie smiled. 'That's very kind of you but I can pay.'

'It's no trouble. I'll get you a selection to take back, and some other bits too.'

Bernie's phone buzzed again. Paul Bentley's name appeared on the screen. She hesitated. She didn't really have time for a social call but she did need to hear a friendly voice from outside the investigation.

'Paul,' she mumbled.

'Hi, Bernie. Sorry, have I interrupted lunch?'

'Only a bacon butty. No time for more than that. Did you want to speak to Anna? I'm not actually at work at the moment.'

'No, it's you I want to talk to, about the missing girl.'

'OK.' Bernie put her butty down and licked ketchup off her fingers.

'Anna told me about the press conference. So I decided to get together a search party. We all met at the pub so we could see the news first. I was engrossed, you were very good by the way…'

'Thank you.'

'…but I was aware of the pub door opening and closing. I thought more people were joining us but when I turned round at the end, practically everyone was gone.'

'What do you mean "gone"?' asked Bernie.

'Well, they'd left, without a word to me.'

'What about the landlord? Did he say anything?'

'Well, he said something a bit weird. Said they can't be expected to look for an Otterfield child. Does that sound strange to you?'

'Yes, very odd. Thanks for letting me know. Catch you later.'

Bernie put her phone down, her mind thrown into confusion. *First the people of Otterfield, now the villagers of Marchant not wanting to help. What the hell is going on?*

Bernie was lost in thought at her desk when someone tapped her on the shoulder.

'DI Noel? I've done the fingerprints for both Derek and Jessica Cole. They're settled in the visitors' room with the lunch you brought. Mrs Bentley is with them. Is there anything else you need me to do?'

Bernie turned and looked up at Sergeant Alan Turner. He was a large man with a kind face, much better suited to being in a station rather than chasing down criminals on the streets.

'Question for you – a child goes missing, how does the public react?' Bernie asked.

Turner pulled up a chair and sat down.

'Well, in my experience the public are very helpful.'

'And who would you expect to help the most?'

'Family, friends, people in the local community.'

'Exactly. So why aren't the people of Otterfield wanting to help? No one wanted to know when I knocked on their doors.'

'We're getting telephone calls in,' said Turner.

Bernie could hear the phones ringing from the incident room. They were the main reason she preferred to work in MCIT away from the bustle. Easier to concentrate. Matt and Kerry were the same.

'Yes, but not from anyone in Otterfield,' she said. 'I've just heard from Paul Bentley, Anna's husband. He'd organised a search team from Marchant but most of the volunteers left as he watched the press conference in the pub. Why would anyone not want to search for a missing girl? Marchant's only a few miles away from Otterfield.'

Turner scratched his head. 'No idea, ma'am. I'm from Bournemouth originally. Been here since ninety-nine but I still can't fathom some of the locals.'

Bernie pushed her chair back and stood up. 'I need to get a formal statement from Jessica about yesterday's events. She was too traumatised last night. Will you scribe for me please? I think I may need to ask some hard questions after that. There's something else going on here.'

'I'm sorry this is taking so long. I just need to get a formal statement from Jessica about yesterday and ask a few more questions. Then we can let you go home,' said Bernie.

She surveyed the small family group in front of her. Baby Sam was out for the count on his mother. With some food inside her, Jessica looked a little better and Derek seemed to have relaxed a bit. Anna Bentley sat next to Jessica, her hand on the young woman's arm. Bernie sighed a little.

'I'm sure you won't thank me for this but I'm wondering if Anna should take Sam out while we talk. I know you'll probably get upset, Jessica, and I wouldn't want Sam to pick up on that.'

Anna's eyebrows rose and a sceptical look appeared in her eyes. 'That's very sensitive of you, DI Noel, but I think we ought to leave that up to Jessica. What would you like to do, love?'

The young woman hesitated. 'I'm not sure. I don't want to disturb him but maybe you're right. I know he's only little but babies can pick up on things. If you could take him please, Anna.'

The red-haired woman nodded. 'OK, but I'll just be outside if you need me.' Anna took the sleeping bundle from Jessica. 'Come with me, wee man.' She left the room, giving Bernie a look she recognised as 'go easy on her or else'.

'Right. You've already met Sergeant Turner and he's going to take down your statement about yesterday afternoon. If you could start from meeting Molly at school right up to the time when you realised she was missing.'

Bernie listened carefully to Jessica as she said what had happened. The young woman told the same story Bernie had heard in pieces the day before. She hasn't deviated at all, thought Bernie, everything is the same. Can't decide if that's suspicious or not. She watched Sergeant Turner as he wrote down each word. An idea popped into Bernie's head.

'Sorry to interrupt you but one question – how did Molly get to the park from school?'

'We walked. It's not far.'

'So Molly walked?'

'Yes… oh wait, she started to moan about being tired so she got on the buggy board. She's too big for it really. One of Dad's colleagues gave it to us and Molly loves it. Anyway, I was cross with her because I thought, if you're tired, why are we going to the park? And then as soon as we got into the playground she jumped off and ran to the slide. The little tyke.' Jessica put her head in her hands and started to cry. 'I just can't believe I spent so much time being cross with her yesterday – the bed-wetting and then having to go to the park. Oh, how I wish we'd just gone home.'

Bernie reached across and gave Jessica a tissue. 'I know. You're doing really well. You're almost done now. You've got up to the part where Sam started to cry.'

Jessica continued. Bernie looked at Derek Cole and saw tears welling up in his eyes. Maybe this is the first time he's heard all this, thought Bernie. Maybe I misjudged him.

'I changed his nappy and it took a while because it had leaked everywhere. I called for Molly when I'd finished but she didn't answer. I turned round and saw she'd gone. I thought she was playing hide and seek with me, it's her favourite game, but when I couldn't find her, I got scared. And that's when I called the police and said Molly had gone missing. I still don't understand how anyone got away with her so quickly.'

'That's my job to find out,' said Bernie. 'Thank you for going through it all again. If you could read the statement and let us know if we need to make any changes before you sign it.'

Turner handed the piece of paper to Jessica to read. She looked through and nodded. 'Where do I sign?' she asked.

'Just there,' said Bernie. 'Thank you.' She smiled at the Coles. 'You're doing really well. I'm going to sort out a family liaison officer for you who'll be the link person between us.'

A look of alarm appeared on Derek Cole's face. 'Aren't they for when a death has occurred?'

'What?' asked Jessica. Her eyes widened.

'Sorry, I didn't mean to upset you. Yes, they are usually there for when a death has occurred. But I think in this instance you need the support. I have every hope we're going to find Molly alive. I need to ask you some more questions first though. Is that OK?'

Jessica looked to her father and he gave a nod.

'OK. It was quite warm yesterday but you said Molly was wearing a fleece. Why? Wasn't she hot?'

Jessica sighed. 'She's a funny little thing. She loves her fleece, says it feels nice against her skin. I think it's like a security blanket for her at school. She's supposed to take it off in class but I think her teacher has given up asking.'

'I see. You said yesterday Molly doesn't have any friends at school. Why do you think that is?'

Jessica shook her head. 'Kids can be so cruel. It's a small village school, they've all known each other since birth. And Molly's a bit different.'

'What do you mean?'

'I'm not sure exactly. She's sensitive. She likes things to be done a certain way.'

'Like wearing her fleece even when it's hot,' said Bernie.

'Yes. Her teacher thinks we ought to take her to the doctor. Get a referral to CAMHS to have her assessed.'

'So Molly may have some special needs then?'

Jessica hesitated. 'Maybe. No one likes to think there's anything wrong with their kids, do they?'

Bernie nodded. 'Of course not.' She paused. 'My next question is a bit more delicate. You've explained why the locals in Otterfield are being unhelpful and I understand that.' Bernie leaned forward and rested her arms on the desk. 'But why do you think the people of Marchant, the next village down the road, don't want to help find Molly either?'

CHAPTER SIX

'Do you believe them?' asked Alan Turner.

Bernie watched the family get into the police car to be driven home. Jessica's eyes had seemed haunted as Bernie had said goodbye.

'Jessica, yes, I think I do. She hasn't changed her story but she was able to add details when asked. Derek – I'm not so sure. Her reaction seemed genuine but his seemed a little delayed.'

'What do you mean?'

'Well, she couldn't believe that people in a village she's never been to could be so cruel. But Derek?' Bernie shook her head. 'I'm not sure I can explain it. I have a feeling that he's been to Marchant. He hesitated just a second too long saying that he had only ever driven through the village, had never stopped.'

They walked back in and headed for the lift.

'But they only moved to Otterfield in January. Where were they before?' asked Alan.

'Jessica told Kerry last night she'd been living on an army base but hated it. Don't know where Derek was. That's a good point, Alan. Perhaps you could get previous addresses for me. Actually, haven't you done family liaison training in the past? Our normal FLO is dealing with the family of the man injured in the betting raid. He's in a bad way, apparently.'

'Yes, but it was a while ago. I was going to pursue it but then Tracey got ill. Made more sense at the time to go back to uniform and stick to a definite shift pattern. But since I've lost her...'

Bernie put her hand on Alan's shoulder.

'Well, fancy getting out from custody for a bit then? You were good with Jessica last night and now Derek's met you too. What do you think?'

Turner looked thoughtful for a moment and then nodded. 'Yes. I've been stuck at headquarters for too long. It'll be good to stretch my legs a little in the real world. As long as there's no running; I can't do running any more.'

The lift doors swished open.

Bernie smiled at the rotund man in front of her. 'I don't think there'll be any running. I'll square it with the super. I need to see him now before I go to join the search. If you could sort out those addresses in the meantime? You can use a computer in MCIT to do the search. Oh, and get those fingerprints and DNA samples sent off to Forensics please. They'll need them for elimination from the crime scene.'

'Already on it, ma'am.'

Bernie knocked on the super's door.

'Come in. Ah, Bernie. I was just about to send for you.'

'I've only just finished with the family. Jessica's given a statement and we've done fingerprints and DNA. Alan Turner's been helping me with all that. He got on well with the family. Seemed to make a real connection with Derek and was very gentle with Jessica. I know he hasn't done family liaison work for a while but I think he'd be a perfect match for them. We do need someone working closely with them.'

Wilson sighed and wiped sweat from his forehead with a handkerchief. 'Bernie, sit down. I've had the chief constable on the phone.'

'Oh. What did he want?' Bernie had a sinking feeling in her stomach. 'You're not taking me off the case, are you?'

'No, no, not at all. He's very happy with the work you've done so far but he's a little concerned with your lack of experience. This is your first major case since becoming DI.'

'I closed plenty of cases on my own in the Met when I was still a DS.'

'Yes, I know. But nothing as big as this. Anyway, the chief constable has suggested you have someone with expertise. There is a very experienced FLO who has just joined us from Scotland. He's been instrumental in solving several crimes where the families have been suspects.'

'But Jessica and her father aren't suspects.'

Wilson drew in a deep breath and exhaled slowly. 'In your heart of hearts, are you totally sure about that?' he asked.

Bernie paused. She felt sick. 'I don't think they did it. But…'

Wilson raised his eyebrows.

'I think Derek knows why the locals won't help,' she said.

'Well then. I think DS Anderson will be very useful in ascertaining that information. He will be here shortly. Although, of course, you're still very much in charge.'

Bernie nodded. Her heart sank a little. She found it hard to believe Wilson. She had worked so hard to build her team and now a stranger was about to come in and turn it upside down. 'Yes, sir. I have to go and join the search though. I've spent far too much time here today.'

'I think it's better if you wait for DS Anderson. Then you can take him with you. Bring him up to speed.'

Bernie stood up. 'Sir…' She wondered if now would be a good time to mention the card sealed in an evidence bag. She was supposed to log all threats.

'That's all for now. Just keep me informed.'

Obviously not a good time. Bernie closed the door behind her and leaned back briefly against it, her eyes raised to the ceiling.

God, I don't need this. She was aware of Jane Clackett walking past, a smirk on her face.

'Everything OK, Bernie?' she called.

'Yes, fine.' Bernie smiled sweetly at her. You already know, don't you? she thought. You, back-stabbing bitch, probably came up with the idea.

'Alan, I need to talk to you.'

'Yes, but before you do, ma'am, you have a visitor.' He inclined his head towards Bernie's desk. 'DS Anderson, the new FLO.' He pulled a slight face.

Bernie leaned in and whispered, 'I'm so sorry, Alan. The super's pulled rank on me. Apparently, the chief constable has sent him. I don't have a choice but I'll still need your help.'

Alan nodded but his shoulders slumped with disappointment.

She walked across to the man who was facing away from her, sitting at her desk. He appeared to be looking through her notes. She took a deep breath.

'DS Anderson,' she said as brightly as she could. 'I'm DI Noel.' She held out her hand as he turned round. He smiled and leapt to his feet.

'It's a pleasure to meet you. Please call me Dougal or Dougie.'

Bernie caught herself as she felt her smile deepen. Although he had a Scottish accent, his looks were Italian – olive skin, slicked back dark hair, molten chocolate eyes and just the right amount of stubble. He was a few inches taller and Bernie thought he was maybe a little older than her but not much. You're gorgeous, she thought, and you probably know it. Maybe you charm the truth out of people.

'I'm Bernie but you can call me ma'am, *DS Anderson*.'

*

Bernie was unnerved by DS Anderson. She hated not being able to choose her own team. Wilson's words 'very experienced' told her all she needed to know – she wasn't fully trusted yet in her new position as DI. As she drove, she told Anderson everything about the case from when she first received the phone call to the interview she had just had with the family. She knew she was prattling on but she couldn't seem to stop herself. She kept her eyes on the road but in the end she had to flick them across for a quick look at him. He was staring out of the side window, seemingly unaware of everything she had just said. Bernie's temper rose.

'Have you being listening to me?' she asked.

Anderson slowly drew his gaze away from the window. 'Yes. Molly went missing yesterday about fifteen forty-five hours from the playground in Otterfield. Her fleece was found under a bush, a fleece that she likes to wear all the time, suggesting the abductor took it off. Mother is Jessica Cole. Father is Davy Reynolds, currently serving in the armed forces. Grandfather is Derek Cole and the baby brother is called Sam. They don't have any friends in Otterfield and no one seems to want to help. The people of Marchant don't want to help either which is a surprise to you. But you think Derek might know why. How am I doing so far?'

Bernie bit her bottom lip in embarrassment. 'I'm sorry, I thought you were ignoring me.'

'Not at all. I apologise for giving that impression. I was doing a rare thing for a man and multi-tasking – learning the routes as well as listening to you. I don't want to be totally reliant on a satnav.'

Bernie nodded. 'That's wise. It took me quite a while to work out the roads around here, especially all the little ones connecting the villages.'

'Well, I actually have a photographic memory so once I've seen something, I know it.'

Something clicked in Bernie's brain. 'Wait a minute, you didn't get all that information from listening to me. You read my notes at the office.' She laughed inside. Anderson was obviously 'very experienced' in reading reports.

Anderson smirked. 'Not all of them. You hadn't written anything down about Marchant or Molly wearing her fleece all the time. Sorry, ma'am.'

Bernie glanced at him. 'I don't know whether to laugh or throw you out of the car.'

'Well, don't throw me out just yet. I need to know how to get to Otterfield.'

'We're not going straight there. Kerry texted to say they've found something so we're heading to the search party first.'

CHAPTER SEVEN

Bernie turned right into a side track that ran down to the railway line. A few officers were milling around. The two sniffer dogs were lying down, enjoying a well-earned rest. She parked her car a few metres before an area that had been cordoned off by tape. Kerry waved to her as she and Anderson got out.

'What have you got for me?' Bernie asked. Kerry's eyes lit up as they drifted over Anderson. 'Kerry?'

'Yes, sorry.' She pulled Bernie over to one side and whispered, 'Oh my God. Who is he? He's mint.'

Bernie rolled her eyes. 'DS Dougal Anderson. The chief constable has appointed him as FLO to Jessica.'

Kerry giggled. 'Dougal? He should have blond floppy hair then, and a friend called Zebedee. Seriously, though, he is sex on legs.'

Bernie gave her a puzzled look.

Kerry laughed. 'Just because I'm gay, it doesn't mean I'm not appreciative of the male form.'

They both joined Anderson at the cordon.

'DS Anderson, this is DS Kerry Allen, my right-hand woman. Kerry, this is DS Dougal Anderson. He's going to be FLO.'

The two officers shook hands and Bernie could see the faintest of smiles on Kerry's lips.

'Call me Dougie.'

The smile widened.

'So what's going on here?' Bernie asked.

Kerry turned back to Bernie, her eyes resting on DS Anderson for another second. 'Well, as you can see, we're the other side of the railway line. Clyde followed the secondary scent, hopefully the abductor's, for nearly two miles along the footpath from the park. We did the usual search and CSIs have taken photos. Didn't find any more clothing. There were a few marks in the ground that looked like tracks from a buggy which would tie in with our earlier theory. We then reached an unsupervised pedestrian crossing where you can walk across the railway safely.' Kerry turned and pointed behind her. 'Over in that direction.'

'And the scent continued across there?' asked Anderson.

Kerry smiled and nodded her head. 'The scent continued for a little bit longer but then stopped here in this clearing, suggesting the person had left the scene. There are tyre tracks, which have been photographed.'

'So we might be able to get a make and model for the car?' Bernie asked.

Kerry shook her head. 'Unlikely. The CSIs thought they looked quite generic. They're searching around this area now for any other clues. They've taken soil samples.'

Bernie could just make out two CSIs in white suits behind a large hedge. 'Was the car behind there?'

'We think so. It's a good spot to hide it.'

'Is there CCTV on the crossing?' asked Anderson.

'No. It's an old pedestrian crossing, hardly used, apparently. Network Rail is due to put gates up soon to block it.'

'Shame. We might have had a nice clear picture then.' Anderson looked towards the railway line for a moment and then nodded his head. 'But the abductor already knew that. You're looking for someone local. Ma'am, what motives do you have for this abduction?'

Bernie shook her head. 'There's no clear motive yet as to why it was Molly but it was obviously planned.'

'But was Molly the actual target?' Kerry asked. 'Could it have been any child from the park? There's still an element of an opportunist here.'

'I'm not so sure and I won't know for definite until I meet with the family,' said Anderson.

'What are you basing this on?' asked Kerry. 'A hunch?'

'No, experience. But before I see the family I'd like to see the park and playground for myself first. We need to go now, ma'am.'

Bernie looked up into his eyes. *Who do you think you are, giving me orders? I need to be able to look you straight in the eye. Back to my heels tomorrow.* She caught Kerry mouthing, 'What the…'

'No,' said Bernie. 'This is an important step forward and that takes priority over your requests, DS Anderson. Both of you come with me.'

Bernie strode off to her car, the other two following in her wake. She was struggling to keep her anger with Anderson under control but she had to, for Molly's sake. She couldn't allow personal feelings to cloud her judgement. She pulled out a map from the back of her car and opened it on the bonnet, scanned it and then pointed to something.

'Look, we're here. This little road links the main roads to Devizes and Salisbury. It's quiet now because it's a Saturday but it's a bit busier during the week at rush hour times. Maybe someone saw a car pulling out from here. We need to get this info to Jane Clackett so she can add it to the alert for the media.' Bernie glanced at her watch. It was close to four p.m. 'How long do you think it would take to walk from the park to here, Kerry?'

'Hard to tell because we did it so slowly but maybe thirty to forty-five minutes. It's just over two miles altogether. Why?'

'Because it might be worth getting Traffic to set up a road block to see if any drivers used this road yesterday around this time.' Bernie was aware of Anderson sighing behind her. 'Do you have something to say, DS Anderson?'

'Yes. Most of the drivers yesterday would have been commuters. They're hardly likely to be driving round here today. You're not really going to be able to get hold of them until Tuesday with the bank holiday on Monday. This is a waste of time. I need to go to the park first and then meet with the family. That's who we need to be concentrating on.'

Bernie made direct eye contact with Anderson. 'May I remind you that I'm in charge of this investigation?'

Anderson frowned. 'And may I remind you I was put on this investigation by the chief constable of Wiltshire?'

Bernie narrowed her eyes and was about to speak again when a police van appeared.

'Ah,' said Kerry. 'The lift back to headquarters for some of the officers and the dogs.' She gave a tight smile. 'They have to go via the park to drop the dogs and their handlers off. Why don't you go with them, DS Anderson? Then I could get DC Matt Taylor to meet you there – he's already in Otterfield and he could take you to the family. DI Noel could join you later. Does that sound like a plan?'

Bernie's heart beat faster, adrenalin pumping through her. Was Anderson going to back down?

He slowly nodded his head. 'That could be an option.'

'Great,' said Kerry. 'I'll text Matt and get it all set up. Just go over to the officer over there and tell him you need a lift to Otterfield.'

Bernie watched him walk away, all too aware he did not like conceding. 'You're bloody wasted here, Kerry. You should be chief negotiator for the UN.'

Kerry gave a wry laugh. 'Arrogant prick. Sod him. If you want road blocks, then do it. And fast.'

A shout of 'Ma'am' went up behind them. Bernie turned quickly. 'Yes?'

'CSIs have something,' shouted an officer.

Bernie and Kerry ran back to the cordoned off area.

'What have you got?' Bernie asked.

A suited CSI looked up. 'There are brambles round here,' he said. 'We've found some cream thread that might be from a blanket but, better than that, they've scratched the car. We'll need to get it under a microscope but there is a trace of paint.'

'Colour?'

The CSI pursed his lips. 'We'll need to do tests to confirm exact shade but looks blue to me.'

'Is there enough to tie it into a make and model?'

'What do you want, a miracle? I really don't think there's enough paint here. Interesting thing about the tyre imprint though.'

'What?'

'It's a new tyre. All the tread marks are there. So, if the abductor is forensically savvy, then he would know to change the tyres to a more generic make before the abduction.'

'OK, well, that might be something to go on.'

'Yes, but if they're really savvy, then the tyres will be changed back.'

Bernie smiled. 'It's a start. Kerry, get Traffic onto the road blocks and say we're looking possibly for a blue car, and that info needs to go to Jane as well. Then we need to track down all the tyre fitters between Devizes and Salisbury. Even if the tyres are changed back, they must have been bought fairly locally to keep the tread that well. I hate to say this but DS Anderson was right. Our abductor had this carefully planned and, more than that, he's local.'

CHAPTER EIGHT

Bernie sat at her desk, her head in her hands. The sun was setting and only a few pink and orange rays penetrated through the slats of the blinds in MCIT. She had sent everyone home at eight p.m., telling them to get a good night's sleep and to be back for seven thirty sharp in the morning. She thought through the previous few hours. The road blocks had happened swiftly but not many people had driven in the area on Friday, and those who had didn't remember a blue car pulling out of the side track. The tyre fitters had already finished for the day and some weren't reopening until Tuesday because of the May bank holiday. Forensics had promised to fast-track the paint traces but without a make and model, Bernie knew there was still little to go on. The public had phoned in but there were no credible leads.

She left MCIT in search of the super. Not surprisingly, he was still in his office. In the last six months she'd learnt how dedicated he was. He'd taken on her mentorship personally and she reported directly to him. She knocked at his door.

'Come in... Ah, Bernie. Sit down. I've just read your notes for today. Progress is slow.' He shook his head. 'Sorry, that isn't a dig at you. We're not just accountable to the family these days but also the media.'

Bernie shuffled uncomfortably in her seat. Of course, it wasn't just her senior officers watching her closely. 'I was wondering about sending the helicopter up again tonight?'

Wilson pursed his lips. 'This is a tough decision. The new evidence suggests she was taken in a car. I hate to say it, Bernie, but if she's outside now, then she's probably dead and her body temperature will be dropping fast so any infrared search will be pointless. So I'm afraid it's a no.'

'But sir—'

'It's already been agreed with the chief constable. Along with something else. We're telling the media that I'm leading the investigation.'

'But you announced that I was. Are you kicking me off already?'

'No, of course not. But… you don't come over very well. Some of the journalists Jane spoke to suggested you don't exactly inspire confidence. I'm sure it's just lack of experience in these matters. Much better to leave the press to me. '

She walked out, aware her hands were clenching into fists. *Bloody Jane.* She didn't want to go home just yet. She wanted to check on the family first.

Bernie realised she didn't have Anderson's mobile number yet. She didn't want to go back and ask the super for it so called the home telephone for the Coles and got through to the answerphone.

'Hi, it's DI Noel. If you're there can you pick up please?'

There was clicking on the line as someone answered.

'Hi, it's Jessica. Any news?'

'Not really. There are a few lines of enquiry that we're looking into though. Is everything all right with DS Anderson?'

'Oh yes.' Bernie could hear an unexpected brightness enter Jessica's voice. 'Thank you so much for sending him. He's been brilliant, so reassuring. In fact he's cooking us some dinner. He says we have to keep our strength up for Molly's sake. He says I have to stay positive, that we'll find her.'

'I'm glad he's being so helpful. Could I have a quick word with him please?'

Bernie could hear Sam crying in the background while she waited for Anderson.

'Yes, ma'am?'

'Just wondering how things are. I hear you're being very reassuring?'

Anderson cleared his throat. 'It's all part of the job, ma'am. Most important to look after the family at this time.'

'Jessica's in the room with you, isn't she?'

Anderson hesitated. 'Yes.'

'Perhaps she could check on dinner.'

Bernie heard a muffle over the telephone and Anderson saying something to Jessica.

'Right, she's gone. You mentioned earlier about Derek maybe knowing why the locals aren't helping. I've asked him a few questions and got nothing concrete in response. In fact, I haven't found anything untoward happening here at the moment but if there is I'll find it out.'

Bernie sighed. 'Personally, I'm not convinced they're involved. I'm conscious you don't have a car. Do you want someone to pick you up later?'

'I'm staying here tonight, on the sofa.'

'Is that wise?'

'It's how I work and besides, I gather Kerry stayed here last night.'

'That was different. Derek Cole was home late and Jessica was in no fit condition to be left. That's one of the reasons I got Anna in to help.'

'You mean the Irish woman? Oh, I sent her home, told her she wasn't needed.'

Bernie thumped her desk. 'What? You had no right to do that.'

'She was obstructing me. Every time I asked Jessica a question, she would get in the way. I can't do my job with a goody-two-shoes hovering over my shoulder.'

'Anna is a volunteer with Home-Start, a former social worker and a vicar's wife—'

'Exactly,' Anderson interrupted, 'a goody-two-shoes.'

'Well, we'll discuss this further in the morning. I want you here for a briefing at seven thirty. I'll send someone to get you at seven.'

'Could you make it six forty-five please? That way I can pop back to my hotel room for a quick shower and change of clothes.'

Bernie was surprised. *He really is newly arrived if he's staying in a hotel.* 'Yes. Is there anything else you need?' she said through gritted teeth, cross at his demands.

'No, I'm fine. Oh, wait a minute, Jessica is asking something… she wants to know if the helicopter is going up again tonight to look for Molly?'

Bernie paused. 'Sorry. After… much discussion with the super, the helicopter won't be going up tonight.' She sighed.

'OK. I know that wasn't your decision.' Bernie heard a softness in his voice. 'I'm sure you argued as best you could, ma'am. I'll see you in the morning.'

'Yes, see you then.'

Bernie put the phone down. God, that man's infuriating, she thought. So arrogant and then so tender. Anderson was really starting to get under her skin. And it was only his first day on the team.

She opened her desk drawer to fetch her handbag. Underneath was the opened card, its message in black capital letters visible through the clear plastic of the evidence bag. She pulled it out.

She'd been in the kitchen, drying up the breakfast dishes. Granny refused to have a dishwasher. She took the saying, 'The Devil makes work for idle hands' a little too seriously. The letter box clicked and there was a gentle thud on the carpet. Bernie looked from the kitchen door and saw a white envelope on the doormat.

Another card. They'd been flooding in, ever since the news of Pops's death. He'd been a popular man, well-loved in the community. Bernie picked it up and went to put it on the hall table when she saw it had BERNADETTE written on it. No one had called her Bernadette in years, not since the nuns at school.

She smiled. Maybe it was her favourite nun, the one she was named after. The nun who had stood by Bernie's mother, Denise, when she gave birth at just fifteen. *How kind of her to think of us.*

She ripped open the envelope and pulled out a card. There was a picture of a peace lily on the front. 'With Sympathy' was embossed in gold. Very Sister Bernadette. She opened the card.

DEAR BERNADETTE,

SO SORRY TO HEAR ABOUT YOUR GRANDFATHER. I KNOW HOW MUCH HE LOVED AND PROTECTED YOU. NOW HE'S GONE, THERE'S NOTHING TO STOP US FROM MEETING. HOPE TO CATCH YOU SOON.

Bernie frowned. The card wasn't from Sister Bernadette. It was unsigned. And hand-delivered. She reread it. Her heart beat faster. She remembered the obituary her grandmother had placed in the local paper. Wonderful words about Pops but also the details for his funeral. Making Bernie's whereabouts known.

'Shit.' With trembling hands, Bernie took the card and envelope into the kitchen and found a plastic bag to put them in. It would have to do until she could get hold of a proper evidence bag. She'd left London and the Met because of past death threats. And now they knew she was back. She'd hoped she'd been out of sight, out of mind, but clearly not. Someone had been keeping tabs on her family. *He* might be in prison but his family and friends weren't.

Bernie carried the bag into the lounge and looked at the large photo of Pops that had been placed on the table. It helped her to make a decision. She'd stay for the funeral but then leave straight away. She wouldn't put her mother and grandmother in danger.

Her mind clicked to the present. She really needed to hand the card in for processing. She'd talk to the super tomorrow.

Finally, she's asleep. She's peaceful now. At least I think so. She keeps twitching, murmuring 'Mummy'. It took a while for her to calm down, to placate her, to persuade her she's safe with me. I need her to trust me. I reach out and touch one of her golden corkscrew curls. It's soft to touch and I wonder, if I have to cut them all off, will her hair grow back curly or will it be changed for ever? The scissors are ready, cold in my hand. I close my eyes. Steady myself. I don't need to cut them all yet. Just one is needed for now. Tied up in a red ribbon. A message that won't be misunderstood.

CHAPTER NINE

Sunday

The radio came on at six a.m. Bernie was about to turn it off when she heard a newsreader on BBC Wiltshire mention Molly's name.

'Police are still searching for missing five-year-old, Molly Reynolds. She was last seen on Friday afternoon at a park in Otterfield. Detective Chief Superintendent Wilson, who's leading the investigation, has asked for the public's help. They would particularly like to hear from anyone who saw a blue car on the Otterfield Road on Friday between three p.m. and five p.m.

'In other news...'

Bernie turned the radio off. *Leading the investigation, my arse. It'll be my head that'll roll if we cock it up.* She lay back on her pillow. She knew she had to get up. She was thankful she had slept well. Exhaustion had overtaken her and any dreams she may have had were forgotten. She picked up her phone to look for messages. There was a text from Anna Bentley about a special church service to pray for Molly and the family. She was about to reply when her phone began to ring. She didn't recognise the number.

'Yes?'

'Ma'am, it's me.'

The voice was faint but sounded like Anderson. 'How did you get my number? I can only just hear you.'

'From Jessica's phone last night. Reception's rubbish. Anyway, I thought you might like to know Davy Reynolds is back and not best pleased to find a strange man sleeping on his sofa. I think I might need an ambulance. For a Sassenach, he does a very good Glaswegian kiss.'

The early morning sun was shining on Otterfield as Bernie drove through the village. The little box houses had their curtains pulled shut, protecting those inside from the outside world. She had spotted a couple of people out walking dogs and shuddered at the thought of getting a phone call from one of them: 'I was out walking the dog and she found something.' No member of the public should ever find that, she thought, but they so often do.

She pulled up outside the Cole house. A paramedic car was already there but no sign of a police car. She knocked on the front door and Jessica answered. She pulled her dressing gown tighter around her.

'Oh, DI Noel. Davy's so sorry. He didn't mean to do it.' Jessica blinked back tears.

'It's OK. We'll sort that all out in a minute. Where's DS Anderson?'

'He's in the lounge with the paramedic.'

'And Davy?'

'He's in the kitchen. He knows he'll have to talk to you.'

Bernie walked into the lit lounge, the curtains still pulled. She nodded a greeting at the female paramedic.

'Where's the police guard from outside?' she asked Anderson.

'Oh, hi, ma'am,' Anderson replied, and then, in a higher voice, mimicking Bernie, '"I can see you've been injured there in the line of duty, Detective Sergeant, are you OK?" Well, yes, ma'am, I'm fine, thank you very much for asking.'

Bernie stared impassively at Anderson. 'Where's the police guard? Because if he'd been out there, he would've spoken to Davy Reynolds first and you wouldn't have been hurt.'

'I sent him home last night. Didn't seem much point us both being here.'

Bernie shook her head in anger. 'How many times have I got to tell you that I'm in charge? You sent Anna home without my permission and now you've told a fellow officer he can leave his post. He was meant to shield the family from any opportunistic journalists. And don't give me that shit you've been put here by the chief constable. You can go just as easily as you came.'

Bernie took a deep breath and turned to the paramedic. 'What's the damage?'

The paramedic smiled. 'He'll live. Just a small cut above his eyebrow which I've glued. Probably get a lovely bruise too. He needs to be careful in case he has concussion. No running around today.'

Anderson had blood on his white shirt.

'How did this happen?'

'I don't think Davy liked being greeted at his own front door by a strange man. And my warrant card was in my jacket pocket.'

Bernie looked up to the ceiling and tried to contain her frustration. 'You're bloody lucky to still be alive, or have you forgotten he's a soldier?'

'Erm, sorry to interrupt,' said the paramedic. 'He's going to need someone with him for the next twenty-four hours, just to make sure he hasn't got concussion.'

'Great, just what I don't need,' said Bernie. 'Well, you're not staying in this house, that's for sure. I'll get Alan Turner to take over your duties here and you'll have to come into MCIT and sit in the office. I can't afford to have an officer babysit you at your place.' Bernie glanced at her watch. 'It's almost six forty-five anyway. Matt should be here any minute to pick you up.' Bernie looked at the paramedic. 'Thanks for patching him up.'

She smiled at Bernie. 'No problem. It wasn't exactly a hardship.'

No, thought Bernie, I bet it wasn't. A cut and a blossoming bruise just seemed to enhance Anderson's Italian good looks.

Davy Reynolds looked exhausted. There was blood on his forehead and he smelt heavily of sweat. He was a big man and Bernie knew he would tower over her when he stood up. She decided to keep him sitting down.

'Good morning, Davy. I'm Detective Inspector Bernie Noel and I'm…' She paused for a moment and then thought, Sod the super. 'I'm leading the search for Molly. Would you like to tell me what happened this morning?'

The young man rubbed his tanned face with his hands. It was only then she realised he'd been crying.

'Erm, I overreacted.'

'I think we all know that. Tell me everything.'

Davy sniffed. Jessica came and stood next to him and put her arms around his shoulders. She kissed him lightly on the cheek. 'Just tell her, love,' she said quietly.

Davy sighed. 'I've been travelling for the last twenty-four hours to get home. I can't tell you where from. I've been awake for most of that time, just thinking about Molly. You know, she's my little girl and… the thought that someone has her…' He wiped his face again. 'I got back to base about five this morning and was dropped off here just before six. Didn't have my key so I knocked at the door. I expected Jess or Derek to answer but… there was this strange man. I thought I had the wrong house to begin with I was so tired, so I asked for Jess. He said she was still sleeping and then asked who I was. He didn't have any ID or anything and I think, well… I didn't think, that was the problem, I just reacted.

There was this man in my doorway and how did he know Jess was asleep…'

Bernie nodded. 'I understand you were confused. It wasn't the right thing to do though. Technically, we should press charges but I don't think it's in anyone's interest to do so.'

A cry came from Sam upstairs. A brief smile appeared on Davy's lips.

'Have you seen your son?' asked Bernie.

'Only for a few days after he was born.'

'Then I'll get out of your way so you can spend some time with him and Jessica. You must get some sleep, though, as well. Jessica, did you get a text from Anna about going to church this morning?'

The young woman nodded. 'I had thought about going but now Davy's home, I'm not so sure.'

'Why would we want to go to church?' asked Davy. 'And where? There isn't a church in Otterfield.'

'There's a church in Marchant,' Bernie answered. 'The vicar's wife, Anna, was here yesterday helping out with Sam. The plan is to pray for you all, especially Molly. I'll be there as well. The media will cover it so Molly stays headline news. We really need the public's help with finding her.'

Bernie watched Davy's face. She could tell he wasn't entirely happy. He slowly nodded. 'What time?' he asked.

'It's going to be at eleven a.m. You don't have to be there, Davy. You must get some sleep. I'm sure Derek could come with Jessica and Sam.'

'No,' answered Jessica. 'Dad's an atheist, he won't come. Look, I'd better go and see to Sam. He'll want feeding. Could you give us a call later please?'

'Yes, of course. If you don't feel up to it then that's fine. We'll talk more after the service and I'll fill you in on what's happening. DS Anderson needs some rest today so I'll send Sergeant Alan Turner over to you later.' Bernie turned back to Molly's father.

'Davy, tomorrow, can you come to headquarters so we can get a DNA sample from you and take your fingerprints? It's OK, it's only for elimination purposes. Jessica and Derek have already done it.'

Davy nodded. 'Of course. Anything for my Molly.'

Bernie turned to go and Davy stood up. She was right, he did tower over her. She looked up at him. He was built like a barrel and for a moment she pitied the abductor. *If he ever finds you, you are so dead.* He held out his hand.

'Thank you, Inspector, for looking for Molly and for not pressing charges.'

Bernie smiled as Davy squeezed her hand. 'Go and spend some time with your son. We'll see ourselves out.'

She walked back to the lounge and found Anderson sitting back on the sofa, his hands behind his head, looking like he owned the place.

'So, ma'am, we're going to church then this morning, are we?'

CHAPTER TEN

One solitary bell rang out as Bernie and Anderson crunched along the gravel path leading up to the church. She was still irritated he'd come but in the end she had decided it was safer to keep him with her than leave him in charge back at the office.

'Sounds a bit mournful, doesn't it?' said Anderson.

Bernie remembered her local history lesson from when she first arrived. 'The other bells were melted down during World War Two. They've never replaced them.'

'What happens at weddings then? I mean, its fine for a funeral but not exactly jolly for a wedding.'

'Tape.'

'Tape?'

'Yes, they play a tape. Well, it might be a CD now or a music file. A lot cheaper than buying new bells.'

Bernie had a brief memory of her grandfather flash before her. They were in their little kitchen in Clapham having breakfast. The local church was ringing its bells. 'Those blasted bells,' Pops had said.

'I like them, they're pretty,' she'd replied.

'Pretty annoying. I don't need a stupid bell to tell me when to worship God like all those Anglicans. I give thanks to the Lord all the time.'

Bernie smiled at the recollection.

Anna Bentley was on the door, welcoming the congregation and handing out service sheets. She smiled at Bernie as she approached. 'I wondered if you might be coming this morning,' she said. 'I didn't hear back from you.'

'No, sorry about that. Something came up. Davy Reynolds is home.'

'Oh, that's good,' said Anna. She stared at Anderson's face. 'You appear to have been in the wars, Detective Sergeant Anderson.'

'Just a bit of a misunderstanding,' he replied. He looked away.

'How busy is it in there?' asked Bernie.

'It's almost full. Paul cancelled the early morning service, said he would do a brief service now. I think the word "brief" has pulled most people in. I take it Jessica isn't coming if Davy has just come home.'

'No. He needs sleep and some family time.'

Anna nodded. 'Probably best. Some of the media are here. I told them to sit at the back on the left. Paul has said they can take notes but no recordings of any kind.'

'Good. We'll sit near the back too. That way we can keep an eye on them. I'll see you at the end.'

Bernie walked in and Anderson followed. The air inside was cool despite the sun streaming through some of the stained glass windows, the colours glowing like confetti on the grey stone floor. The church was almost full, just as Anna had said, so Bernie and Anderson had to sit in the last pew on the right. A few people had turned their heads as they'd come in and had nodded at her.

'How many of these people do you know?' asked Anderson.

'Some. I've been to church a few times so I know the vicar and his wife a bit. And there's a good pub in the village. Matt's dragged me there for a quiz night and they do a great roast on Sundays. Not for us today though.'

'Shame, I could do with a good roast dinner.'

'Shush, be quiet. I think they're about to start.'

*

Bernie felt herself going through the motions – stand, sing, sit, kneel, pray, listen to readings – but she was finding it hard to concentrate. She was all too aware of Anderson sitting closely next to her, his knee brushing against her leg. But she was also thinking about the briefing from that morning, where she had had to admit there was still little to go on. Forensics were hoping to get back to her in the afternoon and she desperately needed a make and model for the car. There were still plenty of jobs to be done though – searching woodland, handing out leaflets and posters, knocking on people's doors to ask them to check any outbuildings, asking farmers to look out for Molly as they walked their fields, taking calls from the public who had apparently seen Molly in at least ten different locations and, of course, looking after the family. Alan Turner had been pleased to take over that role for the day.

'I have a couple of gentle questions to ask them,' he had said. 'Been having a few problems tracking down previous addresses.'

Bernie had nodded. She knew Jessica liked Anderson but she had a feeling Davy and Derek would warm better to Alan.

She was suddenly aware of her name being mentioned by Paul Bentley, the vicar. She looked up and saw his kind face smiling at her. He looked resplendent in his white cassock and vestments.

'I would just like to thank Detective Inspector Noel for taking a short time out of her very busy schedule to join us this morning. I'm sure you were all, like me, very shocked to hear of the disappearance of Molly Reynolds on Friday. I did invite the family to come this morning but they didn't feel able to do so, which is very understandable.'

Bernie thought she saw an imperceptible shudder move across the congregation. She glanced across to her left at the journalists. They were busy writing notes and hadn't appeared to notice.

'The more observant among you will have realised I didn't stick to the lectionary for one of our readings this morning. Instead, we had the parable of the Lost Sheep from Luke fifteen. Having taken one liberty already, I'm going to take another. We all know Jesus tells this parable to explain how much God rejoices over people returning to him and Jesus is the Good Shepherd who will not stop searching for those who are lost.

'As a servant of Jesus, I also have a duty to search for those who are lost and help them in any way I can. In fact, if we all love and follow Jesus, then we share that duty. So, yesterday, I tried to gather some of you to do just that. To search for Molly. But just like the guests in the parable of the Great Banquet in Luke fourteen, who gave plenty of excuses for not attending, it appeared many of you had better things to do with your time. I don't know what those things were but I do know there is a beautiful five-year-old girl who has gone missing and we have a duty to aid the police in whatever way we can.'

Paul Bentley's voice was rising and righteous anger burned on his face. Bernie could see the effect it was having on the congregation. People were shifting uncomfortably in the pews, the journalists were now furiously writing.

'It's a lovely sunny day today and maybe you have plans to have a picnic, play with your children, mow your lawns or just read a book. But I am asking you all, right now, to consider changing those plans, and join with me to help look for Molly. Who's with me?'

'I am,' said a voice from behind Bernie. Without even turning, she knew it was Anna.

The rest of the congregation stayed still, as though everyone was collectively holding their breath. Even the journalists had put down their pens. Paul Bentley's steady gaze continued to move across them all.

It was almost a minute before there was movement near the front of the church and a woman in her mid-fifties with shoulder-length mousey hair stood up. 'I will,' she said, looking at the vicar. Then she turned to face everyone else. 'I will,' she repeated.

Heads jerked up. Bernie recognised the woman, she'd seen her in the pub. She wanted to applaud her, bravely standing alone.

People were turning in their seats, their eyes silently saying something to each other that Bernie didn't understand. Then, finally, a man stood up – Ron Willis, a local farmer.

'I will too.'

His wife joined him.

Then others rose up from their seats and the motion rippled across the church until only a few elderly people were left sitting.

Paul Bentley nodded his head, his hand clasped to his chest. 'Thank you, thank you. Detective Inspector, we are at your disposal. Please use us in whatever way you can. And as we're nearly all standing, let us pray for the family…'

Bernie's cheeks were wet. She hadn't felt the tears but she did feel something significant had just happened. She wiped her face.

Anderson leaned in close to her and spoke quietly. 'Who's the woman at the front?'

'Lesley Cooper. I don't really know her though.'

'Why did she make all the difference?'

'I don't know but I think we need to find out.'

Bernie and Anderson waited by her car for the congregation to leave.

'The last thing we need is for the press to realise we want to talk to one individual in particular,' she said. She had noticed a few photographers attempting to take photos and some had aimed their cameras at her.

'So how do we talk to Lesley Cooper then?'

'It's OK, I know where she lives.'

Bernie felt her phone buzz. She answered it. 'DI Noel.'

'Ma'am,' said Matt Taylor. 'Molly's teacher has rung in and she'd like to come and see you today.'

'When?'

'Sort of now. She's already on her way.'

'What?' Bernie spotted Lesley Cooper leaving the church talking with Anna Bentley. Anna's arm was round Lesley's shoulders, comforting her.

'I'm really sorry. She'd been away camping and had only just heard the news. She sounded very distraught and wanted to speak to you straight away. There wasn't much I could do.'

'OK, Matt. Don't worry about it. We'll come back now. I forgot to ask you earlier about the woman you spoke to in Otterfield yesterday. Did you get anything interesting?'

'No, she still wasn't in when I went back. That's why I didn't mention it this morning. I was hoping to try again today.'

'Hmm, I suspect that one's a lost cause. She's avoiding you. Let's hope Molly's teacher is more forthcoming.'

Bernie put her phone away and turned to Anderson.

'What was that about?' he asked.

'We need to go back to headquarters. Molly's teacher is coming in.'

'But what about Lesley Cooper? Do you want me to go and have a crack at her?'

Bernie looked at the cut and bruise above Anderson's eye. He wouldn't make the best first impression.

'No, I think it's better I do it. I know her a little but I think you're more likely to scare her off looking like that. Plus sometimes people respond better to higher ranking officers; it makes them think they're important.'

Bernie thought she saw Anderson grimace at her last comment as they got in the car. What was his problem?

*

Bernie smiled at the young woman in front of her. She was in her late twenties but still fresh-faced with freckles across her nose and cheeks. Her blonde hair was pulled back in a loose ponytail. She gave Bernie a nervous smile back.

'I'm Detective Inspector Noel, but please call me Bernie, Miss…?'

'Oh, Miss Williams, sorry, Megan Williams. Sorry, I'm a bit nervous. I've never spoken to the police before.'

'That's all right,' said Anderson. 'In fact it's a good thing you haven't had to speak to any officer before.' He leaned forward towards her. 'It means you've behaved yourself.'

Megan Williams blushed. Bernie hadn't really wanted Anderson in on the interview but after knocking him back for Lesley Cooper, she felt she ought to let him in on some of the action. Besides, she thought, his charms might be useful on a young woman.

'So, Megan, you've been teaching Molly since she arrived in January. What do you make of her?' she asked.

The young teacher turned her gaze back to Bernie. 'Oh, Molly is a sweetheart, but…'

'But?' asked Bernie.

'I don't know if her mum mentioned it to you but I think Molly may have some issues. She's on her own most of the time—'

Anderson interrupted, 'Through choice or bullying?'

'A little bit of both, I'm afraid to say. I've tried to get her to integrate more with the class but she's in a world of her own most of the time. The others don't say unkind things, they don't say anything at all to her. They completely ignore her.'

'What about Jessica Cole? Do the other mothers ignore her too?' asked Bernie.

'Yes. This is my third year at the school and the parents are only talking to me more this year. It is very cliquey. At least I don't live in the village, I can escape it at the end of the day.'

'What kind of issues do you think Molly has?'

'Well, I think she may be on the autistic spectrum. As I said, she's often in a world of her own, talking to herself. She shies away from the others. I've managed to get her to talk to me but she doesn't give any eye contact. She has lots of sensory things going on. I've given up trying to get her to take her fleece off and she likes to smell my hair. She struggles to sit still, she's always fidgeting. But she can read like an eight-year-old, as long as she's lying on her stomach on the floor, kicking her legs. I've suggested to her mother she gets her assessed. In fact, I've written a letter for her to give to her GP, outlining my concerns.'

Anderson leaned forward again. 'Megan, do you think Molly could have wandered off by herself?'

Megan thought for a moment and then shook her head. 'No, she loves her mummy too much. Jessica is like an anchor for her.'

'But, as you said, she's often in her own world.'

'No. Molly wouldn't have gone off by herself and she wouldn't have gone with a stranger willingly. We talked about Stranger Danger the other week at school and she shouted the loudest when we practised calling for help.'

'What if it wasn't a stranger?' asked Anderson. 'What if it was someone she knew?'

'You're not suggesting her mother is lying?' Megan looked aghast.

'No, no, not at all. It could be anyone she's seen in the village or at school. We've not been able to account for all the staff's whereabouts. It seems most of you have been or are away. Including your head teacher. And your caretaker.'

Bernie looked sideways at Anderson. *What the hell are you playing at?*

'Am I correct in thinking the head teacher and the caretaker are the only two male members of staff?' asked Anderson.

Megan stared at him and nodded slowly.

'I do apologise, Megan. We haven't offered you a drink. What would you like, tea or coffee?' Bernie interrupted.

Megan turned her gaze to Bernie and nodded. 'Tea please.'

'I'm sure Detective Sergeant Anderson won't mind getting you one. Milk? Sugar?'

'Milk, no sugar, please.' Megan's voice was quiet.

Anderson stood up quickly, scraping his chair back across the floor, and let the door close noisily behind him on his way out.

'Actually,' said Bernie. 'I might have a cuppa too. Give me a minute.' She smiled at Megan as she left the room.

'Anderson,' she called down the corridor. He turned and glared at her as she walked towards him.

She leaned in close as she caught up with him and spoke in a hushed voice. 'What the hell were you doing in there? You completely hijacked my interview.'

'Well, it seems to me, ma'am, if you're so sure the family isn't involved, then we have to start looking round at other suspects. I think the head teacher and caretaker are fair game to look at.'

Bernie nodded. 'I agree we look at them but we don't give them a heads up by telling another teacher that info first. She'll almost certainly contact the head and let him know. Honestly, Anderson, you're like a bloody bull in a china shop. Get the tea, and I'll have one too please. Milk and one sugar.'

Bernie watched as Anderson strode down the corridor, his head held high. The chief constable might have sent him to help but was Anderson also part of a test? Checking to see if she could really handle the responsibility of a serious case as a new DI? A spy in the camp?

CHAPTER ELEVEN

Bernie passed the tea over to Megan. 'There you go. Milk, no sugar.'

Megan nodded in thanks.

'Sorry about my colleague. He's spent some time with the family so he knows the hell they're going through. We all get a bit worked up when children are involved. Anyway, probably better just for the two of us to have a chat.'

Megan sipped her tea. 'I understand. I'm distraught too. But the other officer was right. Mr Jenkins and Eddie Parker – he's the caretaker – they are the only male members of staff.' She drank some more, her head down. Avoiding eye contact.

'Megan, is there something you'd like to tell me?'

Her eyes darted up and back down again. 'It's probably nothing.'

Bernie picked up her pen. 'If it's nothing then it'll be fine.'

'It can't come from me. Officially, that is.'

Bernie tilted her head to one side and smiled. 'Only you and me in the room.'

Megan put her tea down. She squeezed her hands together. 'Molly's been playing by Eddie's shed. He keeps his tools there. It's all padlocked and out of bounds for the children. But she keeps going there and I don't know why. Eddie finds her and brings her back each time.'

'Maybe she prefers to be away from the others,' Bernie suggested, although her thoughts were going somewhere else. She jotted down 'Eddie Parker' and 'shed' on her pad.

'Perhaps.' Megan picked up the tea again but didn't drink it, just cradled it in her hands.

Bernie waited. There was something else, she knew it.

'Eddie… well, I'm not sure if he was on site all the time on Friday afternoon. He was meant to come and fix a dripping tap in my classroom as soon as the children left. But he didn't turn up. It was almost four thirty by the time he arrived. Said he didn't have time to do it and it would have to wait. I wasn't happy because I'd stayed to make sure he did it and I was going away for the weekend.'

'A dripping tap?'

'Yeah, I know it's not that important but it's been doing it for weeks now and, well, it's annoying me. Stupid thing is I could probably fix it but I'm not allowed to. My dad's a plumber and I spent most of my summer holidays with him on jobs. Eddie's not that great a caretaker. I don't know why Mr Jenkins took him on. Anyway, he seemed out of sorts when he came in. He's normally easy-going but he was really stressed. As I said, it's probably nothing. Isn't it?'

After a few more questions, Bernie waved goodbye to Megan Williams. She felt for the young woman; it was horrible to have doubts about your work colleagues. Bernie knew that all too well from her time in the Met. Her hand drifted to the scar on her abdomen. She pushed the thought away. She didn't have time for that now. She had planned on going back to see Lesley but Eddie Parker was more pressing. If he wasn't at school on Friday afternoon at the relevant time, where the hell was he?

She sighed. Looked like an afternoon of paperwork and reading through witness statements from the park. Had anyone there seen Eddie?

*

Bernie's phone buzzed in her trouser pocket. She put down the statement she was reading and glanced at the screen before answering. 'Kerry, what's happening?'

'Bloody hell, Bernie! What did the vicar say this morning? We've had nearly two hundred volunteers turn up this afternoon. Some of them are Davy's mates from the base but most of them were from Marchant. We've covered loads of ground today. I know the trail went cold after we crossed the railway line yesterday but I thought we ought to continue the search along both sides of the track, just in case.'

'And?'

'Nothing. Except for a dead fox that the cadaver dog went a bit loopy over. But that's an area of ground we can cross off. I even got some of the press involved. I told them to stop being a waste of space and if they really wanted to help they should join in with the search.'

'Oh God, you didn't, Kerry.'

'I was politer than that. But they got stuck in. I did hear a couple of them try to start up conversations with the locals, try and find out why they were so late in joining the search. They didn't get very far.'

'Good. I want to be the one to uncover that little secret and I think I know who to ask.'

'Who?'

'Lesley Cooper. She lives in Marchant. She was the first person to stand up at the service this morning and offer help. After that, practically everyone else stood up. In fact' – Bernie glanced at her watch: four thirty p.m. – 'I might try and see her this evening. How much longer are you searching for?'

'Probably another two hours and then we'll have to call it a day. Want people to get home before it gets too dark.'

'OK, that sounds wise. Text me when you finish.'

Bernie put her phone away. She picked up the statement again as Anderson came into MCIT.

'Ma'am. I was right to check out the staff. The head teacher seems clean but the caretaker has previous for drugs and burglary.' Anderson handed her a printout.

She quickly read through it. 'Hmm, fifteen years ago.'

'He must have lied to get that job, ma'am.'

Bernie paused and thought about what Megan had said. Knowing what they knew about timings, could Eddie Parker have been involved somehow? None of the witness statements she'd read so far mentioned him.

'Come on, ma'am. Let me have a little chat with him.'

It was worth talking to the caretaker but she worried about how Anderson would conduct himself. 'OK, you and Matt go and see him. But it's for a friendly chat. For now, anyway.'

She hoped to God she'd made the right call in sending Anderson. But he wouldn't do anything stupid with Matt there – would he?

CHAPTER TWELVE

Bernie knocked on the door of interview room four and entered.

'Ah, Detective Inspector Noel, how kind of you to join us,' said Anderson. 'I was just explaining to Mr Parker about the situation. He had no idea Molly was missing.'

Bernie looked at the man before her – late thirties, thinning hair with a gaunt face. An earring twinkled in his right ear. But more importantly she was wondering why the 'friendly chat' was happening at the station and not at Eddie's house as she had requested. Matt had been on edge when he'd told her where to find Anderson and Parker. There was clearly something he was unhappy about. Were Bernie's doubts in sending Anderson justified?

'You haven't seen the news or read the papers?' she asked.

'No, we've been away at a wedding up north. Only just got back.'

'I suggested to Mr Parker we should have our conversation here rather than at home because he's got kids and I didn't want to upset them,' said Anderson.

Bernie stared at him and raised one eyebrow a little. *That explains it – you want him to feel intimidated.* She looked at the caretaker, beads of sweat forming on his brow. *And you're succeeding.*

'Mr Parker, what's your first name?' she asked. She already knew, of course, but she needed to bear in mind Megan's desire to stay anonymous.

'Eddie.'

'Well, Eddie. Please don't worry. My colleague and I just want to ask you a few questions.'

Anderson picked up his pen, ready to take notes. He had a list of questions in front of him.

'Eddie, how long have you been caretaker at the school?' he asked.

'About seven years now.'

'And are you originally from the area?'

'No, but my wife is. We met at school. She used to work in the school office.'

'And you have two small children?'

'Yes.' Eddie beamed. 'They're great kids. I could show you a photo?' He reached into his pocket.

Bernie smiled. Pops had had one of her in his wallet. Had her own father ever had a picture of her? She doubted it. 'No, that won't be necessary, thanks. You'd feel awful if anything happened to them, wouldn't you?'

'God, yes. Doesn't bear thinking about. I can't believe little Molly has gone missing.'

'So you know who she is then?'

'Yes. I know all the kids. Only fifteen to twenty kids per year.'

'Have you ever talked to her?'

'A little, but no response from her. She's a funny one.'

'In what way?'

'Doesn't talk to anyone and they don't talk to her. Plays on her own. Caught her playing behind my shed. Had to take her back round to the playground. My shed is out of bounds, you know, because of all the tools.'

Ties in with what Megan said but she suggested it happened more than once. Bernie leaned back in her chair.

Anderson spoke as he wrote his notes. 'So none of the children talk to her. It's interesting you say that because no one in the village has offered to help look for her.'

'Haven't they?' Eddie Parker looked astonished. 'That really surprises me.'

'Oh,' said Bernie. 'So you didn't have any problems settling in to the village then?'

'No, but...'

'But?' asked Anderson.

'I started going out with Paula fairly quickly so I guess I was accepted. People don't really move to Otterfield. It's not the prettiest of places. I think Molly's family is the first family to move in since I've been there.'

'And your wife hasn't mentioned anything to you about them? Why no one is talking to them? Because it's not just Molly who's not been accepted, it's her mother too.' Anderson's voice rose a little.

Bernie could hear the tension in his voice. He had obviously started to form a bond with Jessica. That wasn't good news; she needed him to stay objective.

Eddie Parker stared blankly and shook his head. 'No, she's not said anything.'

'Let's talk about Friday,' said Bernie, before Anderson could interject. 'Let's start from when school finished. What time was that?'

'Three o'clock. As it was a bank holiday weekend, lots of the staff were keen to get out early so we agreed I would close up at four thirty.'

'So what did you do between those two times?'

'I was on site making sure the cleaners got in and did their jobs. I checked everyone had left before I locked up. Then we were straight in the car and headed off for the wedding.'

'And where was the wedding? You said up north.'

'Bolton. We stayed overnight with my family because the wedding was at eleven on Saturday morning. Then we drove back today.'

Bernie was aware of Anderson drumming his fingers on his notepad. She decided to ignore him.

'So, Eddie, what time did the cleaners arrive?'

'Just after three p.m.'

'And you locked up four thirty p.m.? Did you see anyone during that time?'

Eddie's eyes darted around. 'What do you mean?'

'Well, as you said, it's a small village with no new families other than the Coles. Did you seen anyone else you don't know hanging around?'

Eddie visibly relaxed. 'Oh right, that's what you mean. No, not really. We get deliveries at the school and sometimes the drivers are different. It's been a different guy bringing the school dinners the last couple of weeks. People drive through the village occasionally, or cycle, quite often tourists, thinking it might be picturesque. They get a bit of a shock. But I can't think of anyone actually hanging about.'

Bernie leaned forward. 'What did you think I meant?' She sensed Anderson tense next to her.

Eddie gave a faint laugh. 'I thought you were asking for an alibi.'

'Well, yes, I suppose I am. Molly went missing around three forty-five p.m. Can anyone vouch for you at that time?'

Eddie paled.

'Were you on site for the whole time between three p.m. and four thirty p.m.?'

He shook his head. 'No.'

'So where were you?'

Eddie glanced down. 'Am I a suspect?'

'No. But you are a person of interest.'

Eddie looked up, his eyes wide. 'What does that mean?'

'It means we would like to know where you were between three and four thirty p.m. when you should have been at school.'

Eddie rubbed his face with his hands. 'Oh God. Paula's going to kill me. I can't afford to lose this job. She's working two jobs as it is.'

'You don't have to tell your wife, just us.' Bernie wondered if Eddie was having an affair.

Eddie wiped more sweat from his brow. 'I went to Devizes on my bike to put a bet on for the weekend races. I only just got back in time because I was chatting with the woman there. Her name's Elaine and it's the bookies in The Brittox. Pretty certain they have CCTV.'

'Why would your wife be angry about a bet?' It didn't make sense to Bernie and then realisation dawned. 'God, Eddie, how much do you owe?'

Eddie looked away. 'About ten grand. I put an accumulator bet on at the races at Newmarket for Saturday and Sunday. Had a good tip. First two came in but lost everything on the last.'

'How much would you have won?'

'Enough to clear the debt.'

Anderson was like a coiled spring next to Bernie. He was desperate to speak.

'Detective Sergeant Anderson, do you have any more questions for Mr Parker?' Bernie asked.

'Yeah, a few. You said you locked up at four thirty. When did the teachers leave?'

Eddie looked at Anderson, confused by the change of questioning. 'Er, I'm not sure. They were all gone by the time I got back. Except Mr Jenkins. Oh, and Megan Williams. I should've fixed a tap in her room. She wasn't very happy with me.'

'Mr Jenkins, he's the head teacher?' Anderson wrote a few more notes.

'Yes, Tim Jenkins. He left with me. We did the final walk through together to make sure everything was locked.'

'So you get on well with him then?'

Eddie looked puzzled. 'Yes, Mr Jenkins is great. I don't see what this has to do with—'

'Is that why he overlooked your criminal record when you got the job as caretaker? Or did you not disclose it?'

Eddie put his hand to his head. 'I wondered when we were going to get to that.'

'Well, it looks as though it's now, Mr Parker.'

Bernie was tempted to elbow Anderson in the ribs.

Eddie Parker rubbed his hands over his face. 'I had a few problems in my twenties, got into drugs. Became an addict. My parents decided to practise tough love and threw me out. I had to find a way to fund my habit so I started stealing. I got caught, went to prison. When I came out, I went on a rehab course. The leader knew Tim Jenkins and put me in touch with him. He knew everything but he took a chance on me anyway. I thank God every day for him. But those are my only crimes. I would never hurt a child. I wouldn't hurt anyone. Not intentionally. But I guess my gambling is hurting my family. Just changed one addiction for another, haven't I?'

Bernie nodded. 'Thank you very much for your honesty, Eddie. You must be tired after your long journey today. I don't think we have any more questions for you now. We'll be checking your alibi with Elaine. And you're right about your gambling. I strongly suggest you get some help.'

Eddie Parker looked confused. 'I can go?'

'For now, yes.' Bernie stood. 'But we might need to talk to you again at some point.'

Eddie gave a nervous laugh. 'So don't leave town, then?'

Bernie gave a brief smile. 'Something like that. But I was also thinking that maybe you could speak to your wife about the Coles. Find out why they're so disliked in the village. See if she'd be willing to talk to us.'

Eddie sucked in his cheeks. 'I can't promise you anything.'

Bernie raised her eyebrows.

Eddie flushed. 'But I can give it a go.'

'Thank you Eddie,' Bernie said as she opened the door. Matt Taylor was walking past.

'Matt, could you take Mr Parker home please? And then you can head home yourself.'

'Are you sure, ma'am? There's still plenty of things to do. It's only just after seven.'

'No, it's fine. Come back fresh in the morning.'

'OK. By the way, someone called Gary rang for you. From London.'

Bernie's forehead creased. She didn't know anyone called Gary.

'Mr Parker, if you would like to come with me?' said Matt.

Bernie held her hand out to Eddie as he walked past her. He took it.

'Thank you, Eddie. You've been very helpful. And if Paula does think of anything then please let me know.' A thought crossed Bernie's mind. 'Out of interest, where were you on Thursday evening?'

'At home with the missus. We had things to get ready for the trip. Why?'

Bernie shook her head. 'Don't worry about it. Just another line of enquiry.' She caught Matt's eye and he gave a slight nod. He'd grasped her meaning. Was Eddie so desperate for money he'd raid a bookies? She watched the two men walk off down the corridor before turning her attention back to her sergeant, still sitting at the desk.

'What the bloody hell was that, ma'am?'

'Excuse me?'

He looked up at her. 'I'm not going to apologise. You're supposed to share information before an interview. I assume you got some of that stuff from Megan Williams about him not being on site. I looked a bloody idiot.'

More like I stole your thunder.

'You were only supposed to have a friendly chat with him at his home, not bring him in,' Bernie said. 'I wanted to see if he would offer up where he was willingly. Then we could have formed a coherent interview strategy. But you thought you knew better.'

'He came willingly. Didn't want to upset his kids.'

'God, Anderson. What am I going to do with you? If Davy Reynolds will have you back in his house, then I think you need to go back to family liaison tomorrow.'

Anderson got up and stood right in front of Bernie. 'Are you fed up with me already, ma'am?' He leaned into her as she had done to him earlier that day. 'Because, you know, someone has to lead this investigation and you seem too inexperienced to do it.'

Bernie narrowed her eyes. She saw anger in his. They were getting nowhere. 'Go home, Detective Sergeant. I will see you in the morning.'

Bernie sat at her desk and read through the final witness statements they had from the park. All the mums corroborated one another and none of them mentioned Eddie Parker as being there.

Despite Megan's misgivings, there was no evidence at present to suggest Eddie was involved and if his alibi checked out then she could definitely cross him off her list. Bernie sighed. She still had to type up her notes for the day and they weren't looking promising. DCS Wilson would be at the team meeting in the morning, along with Jane Clackett. She needed something.

Maybe Lesley Cooper could help with that. She glanced at her watch. It was almost eight o'clock so a bit late for a visit. Perhaps a phone call would be better. She looked up Lesley's details and found a landline number for her. She rang but it went straight to answerphone.

'Hi, Lesley. It's DI Bernie Noel here. I was at the church service this morning and I'd like to have a chat with you about Molly Reynolds. Could you call me back please?' Bernie rattled off her mobile number and ended the call. She put her phone down as she heard someone approach.

'Hi, Kerry. I didn't expect you to come back here from the search. I thought you'd go straight home.'

Kerry looked shattered.

'Nah, Debs is away this weekend visiting her parents. I'm home alone so thought I'd pop by first. I knew you'd still be here. Besides, I have some good news for you.'

Bernie smiled. 'I need some of that. Go on.'

'Well, I've already told you we carried on the search on both sides of the railway tracks and didn't find anything. But just as we were leaving, a member of the public spotted something in a bush. It was near to yesterday's site where we believe the car was.' Kerry beamed.

'Go on then. I can tell you're desperate to tell me. What did you find?'

'We think it's an old gate post. It looks as though it'd been knocked down and then hurled into a bush.'

'So why wasn't it found yesterday?'

Kerry sighed. 'It was just beyond where we put the cordon up. We were all so focused on the tyre tracks and other forensic evidence that that particular area didn't get searched. It's quite close to the road and we concentrated nearer to the railway.'

Bernie nodded her head. 'OK. How is it helpful?'

'Because it looks as though it was knocked down by a car which just happened to leave a beautifully large scrape of paint which matches the colour found on the brambles – a nice shade of dark blue. Forensics are more hopeful now of getting a manufacturer. They're going to work through the night.'

'Yes!' Bernie punched the air. 'Finally, we might be getting somewhere.'

'So, not a good day here then?'

'No, not really. Molly's teacher raised a concern about the caretaker, Eddie Parker, but I wasn't ready to bring him in just yet. I wanted Anderson and Matt to have a friendly chat first. Anderson ignored that.' She rolled her eyes.

'Hmm, Matt texted me earlier.'

'Saying what?'

'Sounded like DS Anderson was never planning on a "friendly chat". Told Matt they were bringing him in.'

'Oh God, Kerry. I don't know what to do with him.' She buried her head in her hands.

Kerry placed a hand on her shoulder. 'I know we're all stressed with this case but is there something else? You haven't talked about the funeral.'

Bernie looked up. 'You're right. There is something else.' She pulled open her bottom desk drawer and took out the evidence bag. 'I got this the morning of Pops's funeral. I left straight after the service. Didn't even go to the crematorium. Told Mum I had urgent police business. I was a bit of a shit, really, but…'

'But this is serious,' said Kerry. She turned the bag over. 'Just your name on the envelope, so, hand-delivered.' She flipped it back. 'And the card unsigned. Have you told the super?'

'No, not yet.'

'And your family?'

'God, no. Only Pops knew about the death threats after the trial. Mum and Granny just thought I was starting over by moving here. They didn't know it was for my own safety. Theirs too. The threats stopped when I came here but of course my name's been on the national news now. And other than the super and the chief constable, you're the only other one that knows.'

Kerry handed the bag back. 'Then you have to give this to the super and tell your family. They need to know you left early because you love them and wanted to protect them. And that you're not a shit. Call your mum. Now.' Kerry hugged her. 'See you in the morning.'

Bernie knew Kerry was right. She and Pops had agreed not to tell the rest of the family about the death threats after the Ambrose murder trial. Her evidence had been crucial in securing a conviction. But as the card had suggested, Pops was no longer there to protect them.

She picked up her phone to call her mother, and immediately put it down again. Maybe she should finish her report first. Her fingers brushed the keys but she was too restless to concentrate now. She turned her attention instead to a pile of telephone messages. She scanned them until she found the message that Matt had mentioned. Gary, plus a mobile number and the phrase 'personal call'. She contemplated doing a search on the number. But she didn't need the distraction. She had to focus. She put the note in one of her desk drawers.

Bernie picked up her phone again and scrolled until she found the number. It rang four times and then clicked over to voicemail. *Damn. This isn't something I can just leave as a message.* She hung up. Kerry wouldn't be happy but it would be better to find out exactly what she was dealing with first – wouldn't it?

It's getting hard to keep her occupied, to stop her from asking for her family. I got some craft things out and we made a pop-up book together. She loves all the hidden pictures. I wonder if the police have found the clues I left hidden for them. A trail of breadcrumbs leading them to the real perpetrator. After all, I'm not the person with the biggest guilty secret round here.

CHAPTER THIRTEEN

Bank Holiday Monday

There was a hush in the room as DCS Wilson walked in. Bernie was relieved most of the officers had already polished off their breakfast iced buns from the bakery. Only a few were still munching, and were now doing so discreetly.

'Please, don't let me interrupt you, Detective Inspector Noel. Carry on.'

Jane Clackett was hovering over Wilson's shoulder, her mouth close to his neck. God, that woman looks more like a vampire every day, she thought, as she pressed a button and PowerPoint clicked onto the whiteboard.

'So, yesterday was interesting.' Bernie glanced over at Anderson, his forehead now a nice shade of yellow and purple. 'We managed to get some more help with the search from the public – some of Davy Reynolds' soldier friends and the villagers from Marchant. Kerry, can you fill us in please?'

Kerry stood up and began to explain where they had searched the day before. Bernie looked at Wilson. His eyes were mostly on Kerry but he kept stealing a glance towards Bernie and then Anderson. She wasn't sure what the look meant but it unsettled her. *Has Anderson put in a complaint about me?*

'So, although we didn't find anything else, we're hopeful about the gatepost. Ma'am?'

Bernie started, suddenly aware Kerry had finished. 'Yes, thanks, Kerry.' She paused. 'OK, the upshot is we still have little to go on. There are some leads like the possible blue car but we're waiting on Forensics for more details. So we're a bit stuck at the moment. Today is bank holiday Monday and, of course, the weather is looking a bit doubtful. Up until about midday it's due to be dry so we need a really big push this morning with the public. I'd like to get a mobile incident room down to the Market Place. Although we've had plenty of calls, not many people have actually come into the station. I know there are posters everywhere but I think a more obvious police presence is needed.

'I also think we ought to scale back the search a little. If we're right about the car, then she could be miles away by now. The fact the gatepost was knocked down shows us that either the car drove in or reversed quickly, or it was done at night.'

Swallowing slowly, she thought carefully about what she was going to say next. She glanced across at Wilson whose gaze was still flicking between her and Anderson.

'Plus DS Anderson has suggested we may be looking for someone with local knowledge,' she said. 'The path along the railway, the crossing over the tracks and the hiding place for the car – it all adds up to someone from the area. We've checked our usual suspects and they're all accounted for. Someone, somewhere, knows something.' Bernie paused. The thought that someone local was responsible weighed heavy in the room. Strangers were easier to deal with. For everyone concerned. 'So we need to get out there and find that information. Kerry has the team allocations so she'll let you know what you're doing. Sir,' Bernie turned to Wilson, 'is there anything you wish to add?'

Bernie watched Wilson take a deep breath. His jacket buttons were straining over his paunch. 'By three forty-five this afternoon, Molly will have been missing for seventy-two hours. I don't need to tell you how that looks to the family and the media. We must find her. And soon. Off you go.'

The officers started to get up and the noise level increased. Bernie was aware Wilson was moving closer towards her. There was no escaping him.

'Bernie.'

'Sir.'

'My office, please, and bring DS Anderson with you. I think you both have some explaining to do.'

Bernie looked over her shoulder and beckoned Anderson. He grimaced at her so she mouthed 'Wilson' to him. She watched him reluctantly stand and walk towards her.

'What does he want?' he asked.

'An explanation.'

'What for?'

'No idea. Better go and find out.'

As they approached the door, Bernie saw Jane was still there, clearly waiting for her.

'Well done on a fantastic speech, Bernie. "Someone, some-where, knows something." Have you got any more little gems like that from TV cop shows?'

Bernie breathed deeply, allowing Jane's sarcasm to roll off her. *You're not getting on my wick today.* She was conscious of Jane looking over her shoulder, her eyes lighting up.

'Oh, Detective Sergeant Anderson, I don't think we've been formally introduced. I'm Jane Clackett, in charge of the press office.'

Jane's hand and arm slithered like a snake past Bernie to grasp Anderson's right hand. She pulled him towards her. 'I do believe your presence is required in the super's office. Let me take you there.'

Bernie followed as Jane led Anderson down the corridor, a proprietary hand on his arm. She felt a flash of emotion. Annoyed, she realised it was jealousy.

*

Bernie and Anderson stood by Wilson's desk while he wrote. She knew he was deliberately keeping them waiting. Like being back at school, when Sister Philomena had kept her waiting for ten minutes before suspending her for smoking in the toilets. She risked a glance at Anderson. He was getting impatient too. She had to do something.

'Er, sir? What is it you want us for? We really need to get back to the investigation,' she said.

Wilson wrote a few more words then put his pen down. He slowly looked up at them. 'It's not nice having your time wasted, is it?'

'No, sir,' replied Bernie.

'But you wasted people's time yesterday. I had a phone call from Tim Jenkins this morning. He's the head teacher of Molly's school, in case you'd forgotten.'

'I hadn't forgotten, sir.' Bernie's hands went clammy. She knew what was coming.

'His caretaker, I think his name is…'

'Eddie Parker,' answered Bernie.

'Yes, that's the fellow. He was a bit unhappy when he got back from here yesterday. The thing I don't understand is why he was brought in at all.'

Bernie opened her mouth to answer but Anderson got in before her.

'That was my doing, sir. As he has children, I thought it would be better to ask him some questions here rather than at his home.'

Wilson stared hard at Anderson. 'I see. Presumably there wasn't a room in his house you could have gone into and shut the door. Or even gone out to the garden. I believe your sole intention in bringing him to the station was to intimidate him. And you succeeded.'

'Sir,' Bernie interrupted, 'we had information that made him a possible person of interest. I was in the interview room as well—'

'Yes, I know. Were you ready to bring him in, Bernie?'

She shook her head. 'Well, no, not yet.'

'To be fair,' said Anderson, 'DI Noel sent us to have a friendly chat, not bring him in. That was my decision. I'm sorry, sir. It was wrong of me. It won't happen again.'

'No, it won't. And is Eddie Parker still a person of interest? He wasn't mentioned in the briefing.'

'I'm not ruling him out completely, sir, but it looks unlikely,' Bernie said. 'He said he was in Devizes putting a bet on. I'll send someone down to check their CCTV and talk to the staff. From what Eddie told us it sounds like he has a gambling addiction. He owes a lot of money and he's worried about losing his job.'

'Hmm. In that case I don't suppose you asked where he was Thursday evening?'

'I did, sir. Said he was at home with his wife. Do you want me to look into it?'

'No, I'll do that. Right. Well, next time I want to hear about possible suspects from you, not members of the public. Understood? And I'm not entirely sure what to do with you, Detective *Sergeant* Anderson. Don't forget why you're here in the first place. Bernie, where were you thinking of sending DS Anderson today?'

'Despite what happened yesterday morning at Jessica's house, I was thinking of sending him back to family liaison duties, if they'll have him.'

Wilson nodded. 'Yes, we haven't even started on that little incident. At least he hit you rather than the other way round.' Wilson rubbed along his eyebrows with his fingers, as though he had a headache. 'As much as I'm giving you grief, it's nothing compared to what I'm getting from the chief constable's office. Not just this case but the betting shop raids as well. We have to make progress, and fast. Do you understand me?'

Bernie nodded. 'I know, sir. We desperately want to find her.'

'The only good news I have is we have the green light to spend as much money as is needed to find her. Tell Forensics to pull out all the stops. Get the paint details on the car as quickly as possible and then get the info to Jane. We all have to pull together on this one, Bernie. We've no time for personality clashes.'

Bernie looked down briefly. As much as she thought Wilson was pompous, she knew he wasn't a fool. Nothing got past him. She nodded.

'Right. I want a report back from you at fourteen hundred hours to let me know how things are going. I will see you then.'

Bernie wondered if now would be a good time to mention the condolence card but Wilson waved his hand in the air to dismiss them.

She opened the door to find Jane hovering outside. She was tempted to make a comment but knew she was still in earshot of Wilson. Jane gave Anderson a dazzling, white-toothed smile.

'Careful there, Jane,' said Anderson, 'you're going to blind someone with those teeth.'

Bernie concealed a snigger as the smile abruptly left Jane's face. She glanced at Anderson who raised an eyebrow at her. Maybe it's better to have you on my side after all, she thought.

'Are you going to rule out Eddie Parker then?' Anderson asked.

They were at Bernie's desk. Bernie tapped a pen against her lips. 'If Elaine and CCTV at the bookies can place him there then yes.'

'So what was the super on about with Thursday then?'

'Betting shop raid in Trowbridge. There have been five in total over the last couple of months. Eddie owes quite a bit of money. The super was probably wondering if he was involved somehow. I was thinking the same thing.'

'Hmm. Maybe. Am I really going back to the family?'

She nodded. 'Yes. Jessica sent me a text message asking for you. I think she got on all right with Alan but you seem to have made an impression.'

'What about Davy Reynolds?'

'Well, we know you made an impression with him,' she looked pointedly at the large bruise on his face, 'but he accepts he was in the wrong. He just wants what's best for Jessica.'

Anderson smiled. 'I think it was my charm and cooking skills that won her over. Erm, thanks for trying to stick up for me in there.'

'I'm your commanding officer. I have to be prepared to stand up for my team. One thing, though – what did the super mean about why you're here?'

Anderson glanced down. 'Just a little reminder this is a fresh start for me. I'll head off now then.' He looked directly at her, deadpan, and Bernie sensed he wasn't going to elaborate any further.

'OK. Check in with Alan Turner before you go. I think he's back in. And can you send him up to me afterwards please.'

Bernie watched Anderson walk away, his shoulders slumped a little. So different from the day before.

'Kerry?' Bernie beckoned her over.

Kerry pulled a chair up next to Bernie. 'Yes?'

'At some point, when you get a chance, could you tap into that police grapevine of yours and find out more about our Scottish friend please?'

Kerry looked amused. 'Really?'

'No, not like that. The super said something in his office, reminding Anderson why he's here. And he said "Sergeant" in a strange way too. Just see what you can find.'

'And it's not odd that you keep calling him Anderson rather than Dougie? You don't do that to anyone else.'

Bernie pursed her lips. Kerry was right. She called her team by their first names. 'I… I just need some distance from him.'

Kerry shook her head. 'Then maybe you should send him back to Scotland.'

Bernie poured boiling water into her mug and stirred the coffee, her third of the morning.

'Ma'am, you wanted to see me?'

She looked up to see Sergeant Alan Turner smiling at her.

'I always want to see you, Alan,' she laughed. 'How did it go yesterday with the family?'

'Well, it was fairly quiet. Davy wanted to go out on the search but I managed to persuade him to stay with Jessica and the baby. Said they needed him more at the moment. But I think he'll want to help today.'

Bernie nodded. 'That's to be expected. I'll tell Kerry. Anything else?'

'Yes. I spent most of my time with Derek. He's taking it very badly. He was in a bit of a state when I arrived. He's trying to be strong for Jessica but he's struggling. He clearly adores his grand-daughter. They were living in Spain before they came here. He had a bar which he ran with his Spanish wife. When they divorced, he came back to the UK and Jessica followed when she was old enough. She doesn't seem to get on with her mother.'

'No wonder I couldn't place her accent. But she doesn't sound Spanish.'

'No, not when she's speaking English. She went to an international school plus they lived in an expat area that's popular with British tourists. But when she's speaking Spanish, then you can tell she's from there. She called her mother last night. Derek told her she had to. I don't think it went too well. I think the mother wants to come over and Jessica doesn't want her to.'

Bernie sighed. 'They really are a very strange family. There's something off about them. I can't quite place my finger on it.' Whatever it was she was missing, she hoped it wasn't the cause of Molly's disappearance.

CHAPTER FOURTEEN

Bernie stared at the blank screen in front of her. She needed to write a report for Wilson but she had nothing new to tell him. Quite a few people had come into the mobile incident room but no one had any concrete information for them, and Kerry hadn't turned up any new evidence from the ongoing search. Bernie wanted to ring the Forensics lab but she knew they were working flat out and would call as soon as they had anything. Matt had visited the bookies in town and confirmed Eddie's alibi.

'He's well known in there,' Matt had said. 'As a loser. Even Elaine thinks he has a problem.'

Bernie hoped Eddie would get some help now. She rubbed her eyes and looked at the screen again, sighing deeply. 'How do I do this?' she said quietly to herself. 'What is it I'm missing here? There has to be something.'

She glanced at her watch. One forty p.m. She started to type.

Wilson scanned the piece of paper in front of him.

'Nothing new then?'

'No, sir.'

'So we're at the mercy of Forensics.'

'Not quite. Some of the garages are open today. I've sent uniform out to see if any of them changed tyres for a dark blue car recently. We might get something on that. And the rest will be open tomorrow.'

'Bernie, it's been almost seventy-two hours.'

She nodded. 'I know. You don't have to tell me. I know what the statistics say.'

'If Molly was the intended victim rather than a chance one,' said Wilson, 'what's the motive? Just a pretty face? Or something else?'

There was a knock on the door.

'Come in.'

Matt Taylor stuck his head around the door. 'Sorry to interrupt, sir, ma'am, but Forensics are on the phone. They know the car.'

Bernie looked at Matt in astonishment. 'What? Already? That's unheard of.'

Wilson shooed Bernie away with his arm. She ran down the corridor to MCIT and grabbed the phone on her desk.

'DI Noel.'

'Hello, Therese here from the lab. I have something for you. You're looking for a dark blue Ford Focus.'

Bernie raised her eyes heavenward in a silent prayer. 'Thank you so much. I know the team worked through the night on this one. And you have the green light from us to do whatever is necessary to get what we need.'

'Well, if there's any chance of finding her alive, then we'll do whatever it takes. We were fortunate with the car though. We dealt with a sample from another blue Ford Focus last month. It won't be the same car because that was a write-off but it's likely to be the same year as they only used that particular paint for that year. I checked with the manufacturer. The first car was sixty-one so second half of two thousand and eleven. Your car may be eleven or sixty-one. There's something else.'

'Hang on a sec,' said Bernie.

She cradled the phone against her face as she grabbed a pen and notepad and quickly scribbled down what Therese had said.

'Go on.'

'The fleece. We've been able to get a few DNA samples but they match with the family.'

'So our abductor was probably wearing gloves.'

'It's something to consider. Or, and I hate to say this, the family are involved somehow.'

Bernie paused. Therese wasn't the first to suggest this and probably wouldn't be the last. But she hadn't spent time with Jessica in the way Bernie had. She hadn't seen the pain. 'Having spent some time with Molly's family I don't think that's the case. Thank you very much. I owe you all a drink.'

Bernie put the phone down. 'Yes! We have a make and model. Dark blue Ford Focus.'

'That's excellent news,' said Matt. 'Do you want me to tell Jane Clackett?'

Bernie hesitated. 'No, I'll do it.'

Matt raised his eyebrows at her.

'It's OK. I'll behave myself. You put it out to everyone else.'

Bernie walked down the corridor, feeling elated. Even Jane couldn't put her in a bad mood now. She opened Jane's door and then walked in. Her office was minimalist to its core. Everything was in its right place – even her pens were lined up in size order. Jane was on the phone.

'Yes, OK… I'm sorry but I have to go as someone has just walked into my office without knocking. Yes, I'll call back.'

Jane put the phone down and glowered at Bernie. 'You should knock and wait.'

Bernie held back a smirk. 'I'm sorry to interrupt your call but we have a development. We're looking for a dark blue Ford Focus. I need that information to go out now but don't mention the tyres.'

'What about the tyres?' Jane's hand hovered over her pens as she chose which one to use.

'The tracks found suggest the tyres are fairly new. I don't want the abductor to know we have that information. They may change the tyres back.'

'OK, I'll get onto it straight away.'

'Thank you.'

Bernie turned to leave the office.

'Oh, Bernie?'

'Yes?'

'I was just wondering about Dougie. Is it best that he's with the family? Wouldn't it be better to have him here at headquarters with us?' There was a gleam in Jane's eyes.

Bernie felt a glimmer of a smile appear on her lips – *subtle, Jane, subtle.*

'No, I think he's better with the Coles. Family liaison is his speciality, after all. Besides, I think he works better away from the *distractions* of the station.'

The phones in the incident room were ringing off the hook. The information about the car had gone out an hour before.

'How's it going?' she asked Matt.

'Well, there are a lot of dark blue Ford Focus cars in the UK.'

'Ha. Tell me something I don't know.'

She saw movement from across the room. An officer was waving at her.

'Think we've got something, ma'am,' she called.

Bernie wove in and out of the desks until she reached the officer.

'Got a lady on the phone who had a family who were booked to stay at her farm this weekend. They had a dark blue Ford Focus. They arrived Friday around teatime but left Friday night as they said their daughter was ill. She didn't see her properly but she thinks she matched the description of Molly.'

Bernie smiled. 'Get her details and tell her someone will be over to see her in the next hour. Great work.'

Bernie looked at Matt who was talking to another PC. He beckoned her over.

'Craig's found a garage that changed the tyres for a dark blue Ford Focus. The driver was female.'

'Description?'

'Yes, ma'am.' The officer opened his pocket book. 'White, late twenties, early thirties, about five foot five to five foot seven. She was wearing jeans, white T-shirt and a black baseball cap.'

'Any writing on the cap or T-shirt?'

'No, both were plain.'

'Did he get a good look at her? Any CCTV? Registration?'

Craig glanced at his notes. 'No, ma'am. No CCTV and he didn't get a good look. She kept the cap down and didn't hang around for long. Doesn't remember the reg. Paid cash.'

'Damn. No card to trace. Don't suppose he still has the notes?'

'No. He paid his takings in for the day. This was on Thursday. To be honest, ma'am, this garage owner is just on the right side of legal, if you know what I mean.'

Bernie nodded. 'I see. Well it's something to go on. That description might be helpful for us. Matt, a woman's rung in saying a family was supposed to be staying at her farm but they left Friday night. They had a dark blue Ford Focus and a little girl that matches Molly's description. I think we ought to go and have a chat with her.'

Bernie let Matt drive to the farm. She normally preferred to drive herself but she needed time to think. She hadn't considered the possibility of two abductors. She knew she had to follow the evidence but she was also looking for that light-bulb moment, when everything would suddenly become clear. She rubbed her temples, willing her thoughts to flow. A child with a couple wouldn't stand out that much and this family left late at night before the Child Rescue Alert had been activated. Could this be it? She knew she mustn't jump ahead of herself but with the trail growing colder by the hour, she needed a breakthrough, fast.

They were near the farm when Bernie noticed something blue and white flapping at the side of the road.

'Slow down a minute, Matt.'

'Sure. What is it?'

'It's the police tape. That's where we think the car was.'

Matt pulled over and they crossed the road. The tape had come undone and the wind was picking it up and lashing it down like a whip.

'The weather's changing. That rain will be here soon,' said Matt as he retied the tape.

Bernie was looking down the overgrown track to where the car had been hidden. 'You definitely wouldn't have been able to see the car from the road. It was a good hiding place. How far are we from the farm?'

'Not far at all. Probably only another five minutes' drive.'

'That close? Oh, that's clever. This has been very well planned.' She looked across at Matt and noticed a bemused look on his face.

'What?'

'Ma'am, you're always telling us to follow the evidence and here you are, theorising. This couple may be completely innocent.'

She nodded reluctantly. Matt was right, but couldn't he let her hope for a minute, at least? 'I know, I know. But if it is them, then this was clever. Come on, let's go. What's the name of the farm again?'

'Pear Tree Farm.'

'Sounds very quaint.'

Matt laughed. 'Well, it is more geared to holidays rather than farming these days. I had a quick look at their website. They've converted some of the outbuildings to be holiday lets and they don't have much land. They've been there nearly twenty years though.'

They drove down the road for only a matter of minutes when they saw a sign saying 'Pear Tree Farm, next left'.

'Look, it's just coming up, it's a bit hidden,' said Bernie.

Matt slowed down but not quickly enough. The tyres screeched as they turned left and they almost collided with a cyclist coming down the narrow lane.

'God that was close,' he said.

Bernie glanced back. The cyclist, a woman by the looks of things, had just carried on. 'She seems OK. Are you all right?' Bernie asked. 'You're trembling. My heart's going like the clappers.'

Matt swallowed slowly. 'That's never happened to me before. I'm such a careful driver normally. I'm amazed she didn't yell abuse at me. I deserved it.'

'Do you want me to drive?'

'No, I'll do it. I'll go slowly, it's not far.'

The farm soon appeared on the right-hand side of the lane. There was a large farmhouse which Bernie assumed belonged to the owners and then two smaller cottages that had presumably once been outhouses or stables. There was a large courtyard for parking and beyond the farmhouse was a field. She could hear chickens and caught sight of a small gaggle of geese strutting around. She hoped they would stay in the field. She could still remember being chased by geese in a park when she was little. It was the last time she'd asked Pops if she could feed the ducks.

A woman in her mid-fifties stood at the front door of the farmhouse. She was dressed in jeans and a faded black T-shirt, had short brown hair and a screwdriver in her hand. She smiled at them as they climbed out of the car.

'You must be the police. I'm Naomi Phillips.' She had a strong Bristol accent. She held her hand out to Matt first.

He shook her hand. 'Detective Constable Matt Taylor.'

Bernie then took her hand. 'Detective Inspector Bernie Noel.' A look of surprise passed across Naomi's face. Yes, thought Bernie, you're surprised the woman's in charge, aren't you?

'Gosh, I didn't know the top person was coming out to see me. I heard your name on the radio. Come in, come in. I bet you've not had much chance to eat, have you? I've got a few bits out already. Mind the toolbox, I was just fixing the lock on my front door. Husband buggered off last year and took all the power tools with him.'

'Anything I can help you with?' Matt asked.

'No, you're all right, my love. I've got my dad's old tools and he taught me how to fix things.'

Bernie and Matt followed her through a darkened hallway to a large traditional farmhouse kitchen. A huge pine table took centre stage. Spread across it were bread, ham, cheeses, preserves, scones, cream and cake. Bernie saw Matt's mouth fall open.

'This is incredibly generous of you. Are you sure?' asked Bernie. She felt guilty for misjudging the woman.

'Yes, of course. Tuck in. I bet you haven't had anything for lunch. What would you like to drink – tea or coffee?'

'I've had far too much coffee today so tea please. Matt?' Bernie gave him a quick nudge.

'Um, yes, tea as well please.'

Naomi laughed. 'You're looking a bit surprised there, officer. It's no trouble. I do this for all my guests. Ellie's already had hers. You might have seen her on your way here.'

Matt glanced across at Bernie and grimaced. 'Was she on a bike?'

'Yes. So you did see her. Lovely girl. She's an artist. In any case, it's my other guests that I need to tell you about.' Naomi poured boiling water into a large teapot and placed it on the table. 'Just give that a couple of minutes to brew. Please dig into the food.'

Bernie didn't want to appear greedy but she was famished. She cut a few slices of bread for them both and took some ham and cheese to make a sandwich. She sank her teeth into the soft white bread and tasted the saltiness of the smoked ham.

'Bread was freshly made this morning by me and I bought the ham and cheese at the market earlier. It was on my way back I heard the news on the radio. It was the blue car that caught my attention. I had thought it a bit odd at the time but not enough to worry about it.'

Bernie managed to choke back a laugh. Naomi Phillips was going to be one of those witnesses who didn't need lots of questions – she would tell them everything. Matt got out his notepad.

'Just tell us what happened, from the beginning,' said Matt.

'Well, this couple booked a few weeks ago. They turned up about five o'clock on Friday in a dark blue Ford Focus. It was just the man who came to the door.' Naomi picked up the teapot and gave it a little swirl. 'The woman was sitting in the back of the car with the girl. He said she wasn't feeling very well. Thought she was just a bit car sick but they didn't want me to show them round the cottage in case it was a bug, which I was relieved about. I'm a bit paranoid about sickness bugs. So I didn't see the little girl close up but I did see the man carry her into the house. She definitely had fair hair but it was hard to see how long it was. She looked a bit floppy.'

Naomi poured the tea and handed the mugs to Bernie and Matt. Bernie wondered if Naomi always talked this much.

'Help yourself to milk and sugar. So, I left them to it but then at about eleven that Friday night, the man knocked on my door. He said his daughter had taken a turn for the worse and they would have to go home. He apologised for leaving and said they had cleaned up as best they could. I saw the woman bundling the child into the car and then they went off. She'd been sick in the cottage, in the bed. They hadn't cleaned up very well at all.' Naomi wrinkled her nose in disgust. 'I spent most of Saturday sorting it out. So I didn't really know much about the missing girl until yesterday but it was only when I heard on the radio today about the car that it all clicked.'

Matt made copious notes.

'OK. I'm presuming you have their details from their booking,' said Bernie.

Naomi squirmed a little in her seat. 'Not exactly. He rang up and spoke to my cleaner. He said his name was Mick O'Connell and he asked if he could pay cash because they were in the process of changing banks. Which sounded dodgy to me. Stupidly my cleaner said yes. She had no right to. Especially as she's been away this weekend so I had to do all the work. I was very cross with her. I would never have agreed to it myself. And I only have a mobile number for them. Sorry.'

'And did they pay cash?'

'Yes. I paid it in on Saturday morning. I was worried they might ask for it back but they left the cottage in such a state.'

'So you've given the cottage a really good clean?' asked Bernie. 'Washed the bedding?'

'Yes. That doesn't help you, does it?'

'Not to worry. We'll get a forensics team in anyway. Let's focus on the man and woman and see if you can give us a good description. Think back to when you first met the man at the door. You can close your eyes if it'll help.'

Naomi nodded and shut her eyes. 'He's white, early to mid-thirties, quite tall. I had to look up at him so maybe six foot. Dark hair and dark stubble. Brown eyes. Wore a blue T-shirt and jeans. He looked… stressed. A little bit agitated. He was certainly keen to get in the house and not have me there.'

'OK, that's good. What about the woman?'

'I didn't really see her. She was in the car. I think she had fair hair but that's all I can say. Same with the girl.'

'And now I want you to think about the car. Did you see the registration?'

'Not all of it but it did have XBX at the end because it reminded me of Xbox. And the number was sixty-one. Don't know the rest though.'

Bernie thought carefully about what to ask next. She knew she mustn't ask a leading question.

'Is there anything else about the car you remember?'

Naomi paused. 'It was quite dirty and had obviously been in the wars – a few bumps and scratches.'

Bernie exchanged a look with Matt.

'Whereabouts?'

'The scratches were down the side and a dent at the back.'

Bernie could feel the adrenalin start to pump round her body.

'Naomi, you've been very helpful. I know it's a bit rude to ask but could I take a slice of your delicious chocolate cake with me please? I think we need to get back to work.'

CHAPTER FIFTEEN

Bernie rubbed her hands with glee.

'I've got a good feeling about this, Matt.'

Matt gave her a cautious smile. 'They could still be innocent though.'

'I know. But we're finally moving in the right direction.'

They sat in the car outside the farmhouse. She had already called in the information.

'Or it could be a false name and a pay-as-you go phone. They may have changed the number plates. And why book a B&B for the weekend at all? Why didn't they just drive away?' Matt continued.

'God, Matt, we may have something here and you're the harbinger of doom and gloom. Come on, let's get back to the station, and watch out for cyclists on the way back. We don't want any more accidents.'

Matt blushed. 'I do feel bad about that. I wonder if she saw the family or the car. I might have to come back and ask her at some point.'

Bernie laughed. 'Yes, that would be a good idea. You can give her an apology. In the meantime, back to MCIT.'

Bernie walked into the bustling incident room, buoyed up by the new information.

'OK, everyone, listen up. We have some new information which I called in. Have we got anywhere with it yet?'

'Yes, ma'am,' called a female voice from the back. The room was still noisy.

'Hey! I said listen up. PC Fraser has something to share with us all.' The noise faded away. 'Please go on.'

'OK. The DVLA has a ridiculous number of Michael O'Connells on their database but only one with a dark blue Ford Focus with a registration ending in sixty-one XBX. He lives in Oxford and the mobile number is registered to him too.'

'PC Fraser, I owe you a drink. Matt, get on to Thames Valley and find out the nearest police station. See if they can get an unmarked car to check out the address for us.' Bernie caught sight of Jane, her face even paler than usual against her black suit. 'But,' she said loudly to everyone, 'we have a media blackout on this and the car registration for the time being. We don't want to alert them. The last thing I need is the number plate and tyres being changed. If this proves to be fruitless then we may have to go to the media.'

Bernie saw Jane give her an imperceptible nod. Bernie's skin prickled. *She's already given it out, hasn't she?* She quickly made her way towards Jane.

'Who have you told?'

Jane picked at her nails and refused to make eye contact with Bernie. 'Everyone,' she said quietly.

'When?'

'When you phoned in. I was walking past and heard about it.'

'That was nearly half an hour ago. Can you ask them all to sit tight?'

Jane shook her head. 'It's too late. BBC are already running it on News 24.'

Bernie took a deep breath and fought the temptation to shake the stupidity out of Jane Clackett. She stood closer to Jane and lowered her voice so only she could hear her. 'I understand the media is your thing and you know far more about it than I do. But detection is *my* thing and you do not release information without my say-so. We do not publicly alert potential suspects unless we really have to. We do not put a little girl's life at risk. Do you understand?'

'Yes,' she hissed back.

'Good. Now go back to your little hidey-hole and don't issue anything else without my approval. Stay out of *my* incident room.'

Bernie watched Jane slither away and turned back to find Matt. He was talking on the phone. She quickly made her way to him and mouthed, 'Who are you talking to?'

'Excuse me just a minute, sir, I think my inspector wants a word.' Matt handed her the phone. 'It's a DI at St Aldate's, they're the nearest.'

'Thanks.' She grabbed the phone. 'This is DI Bernie Noel.'

'Hi. DI Terry West. Your DC was just filling me in.'

'Yes. I'm afraid we're going to have to move quicker than we thought. The press officer has fucked up and issued the partial registration to the media. The BBC are already going with it.'

'No problem. I have the name and address. I'll send in an unmarked car first and get my guys to do a recce. If no one's there, do you want us to go in?'

Bernie caught Matt's eye. 'Check with the neighbours first. It's entirely possible this is an innocent family, and I don't have a warrant yet. We're still doing searches here on them. Perhaps you could do the same; local knowledge and all that.'

'Yes, of course. I'll take the lead on this and get back to you ASAP. What's your mobile number?'

Bernie gave it to him and then put the phone down. She ran her fingers through her hair. It felt dry. It needed treating. *Damn, I left the new bottle in London.*

'You hate being away from the action, don't you?' said Matt.

Her mind snapped back. 'No. Well, yes. I want to be the one to find Molly. Not because I want the glory but because I promised Jessica I would.'

'Should we tell them about this latest development?'

Bernie sighed. 'Best not to. Don't want to get her hopes up. But I really should see them today. I'll wait until we know what's happening.'

Bernie thought she was going to go crazy with the waiting. It was almost an hour since she had spoken to Terry West.

'What's taking him so long?' She paced the incident room.

'He had to read the stuff we sent over, get a team together, do a briefing and then get over to the house. Without a warrant they can't just barge in there,' Matt said, far too reasonably in Bernie's opinion.

'Yes, you're right. We don't have enough for a warrant. The guy has no prior and we only have one witness who thinks the girl might have been Molly. Still bloody frustrating though.'

She glanced at the clock on the wall. It was nearly five thirty p.m.

'Can I get you a coffee, ma'am?'

She shook her head.

'Well, eat your chocolate cake then. I ate mine earlier. Naomi Phillips certainly knows how to bake.'

Bernie smiled. 'Yeah, I wouldn't mind being one of her guests. I'd be the size of a house by the end of it though.'

She sat down at her desk and began to eat the cake. The dark chocolate sponge melted in her mouth. 'Oh, this is good. She ought to be doing afternoon teas as well as the cottages. She'd make a mint. Plenty of tourists come out this way to see the White Horse, or they're en route to Salisbury for the cathedral. Surely a motorist saw the car on Friday on that stretch of road.'

Bernie's phone began to ring.

'Bernie Noel.'

'Hi, it's Terry West. Do you want the good news or the bad news?'

Bernie shut her eyes. A sense of dread came over her. 'Bad news.'

'No one's here. No sign of the car.'

'OK, good news.'

'Mick O'Connell has some lovely, chatty and a bit nosy neighbours. Apparently he's only just bought the house. Sale went through two or three weeks ago. He's living at the address alone because he has a new job in Oxford but the house needs work. He's told the neighbours that his wife and daughter are in Birmingham staying with her parents until the end of the school year and then they're moving in the summer. Also mentioned to them he was going away for the bank holiday with his family. Said he'd been planning it as a surprise for his wife's birthday.'

Bernie opened her eyes. She felt despondent. 'What's your gut instinct on this one, Terry?'

'Well, I think it's worth following it up. It's possible they went to the in-laws in Birmingham but you'll have to find them. I know your press officer screwed up but the release might go in your favour. They may see it and come forward. That's assuming they're innocent. If, on the other hand, Mick O'Connell is your man, then you've got one hell of a job trying to find him.'

Bernie knocked at Jessica's front door, not wanting to ring the bell in case the baby was asleep. She hadn't seen Davy and Jessica for over twenty hours and was wondering how they were bearing up. She was still in two minds as to whether to tell them about the latest sighting. Out of all of them, it seemed the most credible, but she didn't want to give them false hope.

Davy opened the door. He had dark shadows under his eyes. He clearly hadn't slept.

'Hi, Davy. Can I come in?'

The huge man in front of her nodded his head and shuffled away from the door. Bernie gently laid a hand on his arm.

'Are you all right?'

Davy sniffed and shook his head. 'Can't seem to do anything right. I tried to help with Sam last night but I couldn't settle him because he doesn't know me. And when he wasn't crying, Jessica was. And Molly is just in my head all the time. Feels as though my heart's been ripped out.'

Bernie sighed. 'I wish I had better news for you. We're doing everything we can to find her.'

'I know you are. I joined the search team. Your DS Allen is very good, very thorough.'

'I know, that's why I put her on that job. Look, I have a small bit of information for you. Is everyone downstairs?'

'Yes. Jessica is feeding Sam and then she'll put him to bed. Looking after him is the only thing that's stopping us from completely falling apart. Come through.'

Bernie followed Davy into the lounge. If she didn't know better, the family appeared to be having a quiet night in front of the television, with nothing to worry about. Jessica was stretched out on the sofa, Sam nestling into her, and Derek Cole was in an armchair, a newspaper open on his lap. DS Anderson came in from the kitchen, his shirtsleeves rolled up.

'Ah, ma'am. I thought I heard your dulcet tones. I was just doing the washing up.'

Bernie looked for a hint of sarcasm in his face but didn't find any. Jessica looked up at her, expectantly.

'I'm afraid we still haven't found her but I wanted to bring you up to date. Davy, why don't you sit down next to Jessica? I'll—'

Anderson placed a dining chair behind her. 'Ma'am?'

'Oh, thank you, DS Anderson. Right. You know we thought there may have been a dark blue car involved.'

Davy, Jessica and Derek all nodded.

'We think it may have been a Ford Focus.'

'Yes,' said Davy. 'We saw it on the news earlier. There was even a partial number plate. Would've been nice if you'd told us yourself.' There was a tremor in his voice.

'I'm sorry about that. The registration shouldn't have been released to the media. You should never have found out that way. I'm not trying to keep you in the dark. I just don't want to give you false hope every time possible leads turn up.'

'The news mentioned a couple were in the car,' said Jessica. She raised her head away from Sam and looked at Bernie. Her eyes were almost lifeless, the colour draining out of them. 'Did they take my Molly?'

'We don't know for certain. A witness has told us there was a girl in their car who looked like Molly but she was only seen at a distance. They could be completely innocent. We're trying to find them now. We know who we're looking for.'

'Who?' asked Derek, sitting forward in his chair.

'I can't give you names because they could be innocent. But what I can say is this person doesn't have any prior convictions. The details have gone out to all the police forces and the ports and airports. We will find them.'

'But it could be too late,' said Derek, his voice rising. 'She went missing on Friday and now it's Monday evening.' He shook his head. 'I blame myself. We should never have come here.'

Jessica started to cry. Bernie reached in her pocket for a clean tissue and pushed it into her hands.

'Mr Cole, you can't blame yourself. This is no one's fault. You're not responsible either, Jessica. The perpetrator is. He or she is the one who took Molly.'

'You know, I would die for that girl.'

Bernie looked at Molly's grandfather, tears rolling down his ashen cheeks. He seemed to have aged ten years in a couple of days.

'I would. I would die for her.'

'I know you would, Mr Cole.' Bernie felt a lump in her throat. 'I think we all would.' She stood up. 'I'm sorry I've upset you. As soon as we know anything more, I'll be in contact. I won't let you find out things from the press again. We will find Molly.' Bernie reached over and took Jessica's hand. 'We will find her. I know it's difficult but try and get some sleep. All of you.'

Jessica gave her a quick glance and a small nod.

'I'll show you out,' said Davy.

'No, it's OK. You stay where you are. I'm sure Detective Sergeant Anderson can do that.'

'Of course, ma'am. I'll walk you to your car.'

Bernie and Anderson stepped out into the cool air. The sky was heading towards sunset with dusky pinks and orange mixing together. After the earlier rain the May bank holiday was ending on a high. The road was quiet except for a few birds singing and the fragrance of roses lingered in the air. No curtains twitched from the neighbours as they walked towards Bernie's car. She felt slightly awkward with Anderson. The antagonism between them had gone. Their shared telling-off from Wilson had brought them together somehow. She wasn't sure how to behave. When they reached her car, she spoke quietly.

'I'm worried about Derek. He seems to be falling apart.'

Anderson nodded. 'Yes, he was in that mood when I got here today. I wasn't going to sleep here tonight, I know you've lined up a patrol car to be outside. But…'

'Ask them. If they want you to stay then do.'

'I'll come in for the morning briefing though.'

'That would be good.' She paused, wondering whether to be cheeky or not. She decided to risk it. 'I think Jane Clackett will be pleased to see you.'

'What? Dracula's daughter?' He laughed. 'Naw, she's too easy. I prefer my women to be a bit more... challenging.'

Bernie looked at him and he held her gaze for a few more seconds than was comfortable. She reached for the car door handle and found his hand already there.

'Let me get the door for you, ma'am.'

She pulled her hand away slowly, her fingers brushing his palm. He opened the door and she climbed in. As she was almost ready to drive away, he knocked on the window. She pressed the button and it wound down. He leaned in a little.

'Drive carefully, ma'am. I'll see you in the morning.'

Bernie tried not to look at Anderson directly. She couldn't work out how he'd gone from foe to supposed friend in one day. She let her eyes flicker quickly towards him. He gave a knowing smile and then walked away, back to the little sandy-coloured box house at the end of the road. Watching him in her rear-view mirror, she saw a flash of light as he opened the door. It wasn't until she was almost home she realised the light had been from outside the house, not in. Bloody journalists. She'd ask Jane to have a word with them.

I print out the photo and then stick it to the wall, adding to the patchwork of other pictures and news reports. I run my finger over it. I can only learn so much from the media. Sometimes I have to turn detective myself. I hate leaving her but I only go when she sleeps. And it's worth it. I'm learning lots about the detective inspector and her team. The young guy with floppy hair looks like he's seventeen. Then there's the short blonde woman who has a hard face. But the officer the inspector was with this evening. He's quite something. I saw the way she looked at him. It didn't look appropriate to me. Honestly. Is this the way to behave when you're supposed to be looking for a missing child?

I heard what the detective inspector said. The grandfather is falling apart. Good. I won't be satisfied until I've brought the whole family to their knees. They don't deserve her. I hear a murmur. She's stirring. I smile and close the door on my own incident room.

'Coming, little one.'

CHAPTER SIXTEEN

Tuesday

Bernie's phone vibrated on her bedside cabinet. She forced her eyes open, grabbed the phone and squinted at the screen. There wasn't a name but the number seemed familiar.

She shook her head before answering to get rid of her sleepiness. 'Hello?'

'DI Noel?'

'Yes.'

'It's Terry West from St Aldate's.'

Bernie pushed herself up to sitting. 'Hi, Terry, sorry. Do you have some news for me?'

'I think I do. You may have to say a big thank you to your press officer.'

'Oh God, do I have to?' Bernie sank back on her pillow.

Terry West laughed. 'Yes, I'm afraid so. We think we have the car. A nurse rang in to us. She's just finished her shift and heard the report on the radio. The car's at the John Radcliffe hospital.'

Bernie swung her legs to the floor, the carpet soft beneath her feet, ready to get up. 'Our witness did report the girl was ill. She had vomited everywhere.'

'According to the nurse, she's critical. She's actually been the one looking after her. The little girl has meningitis.'

'Oh shit. So not Molly then?'

West sighed. 'I think it's highly unlikely. They gave GP details. And the nurse doesn't think it's Molly either. This girl has brown eyes rather than blue.'

Bernie rubbed her forehead. She could feel it starting to throb. 'How does the nurse know it's their car?'

'She got something out of the car for them yesterday. I really don't think it's Molly but I will go to the hospital if you want me to.'

Bernie thought for a moment. 'I don't wish to add to their distress but it is important to completely eliminate them from the inquiry. It's also possible they may have seen something on Friday. If you could go then that would be good but I'll trust your judgement on how much you ask them.'

'OK. I'll go about nine o'clock. Don't want to be too early.'

Bernie glanced at her clock radio. The red digits flashed 7.11.

'Oh shit. I've overslept. OK, I'll hear from you later. Thanks. Bye.'

Bernie rushed into headquarters, aware she wasn't quite her normal self. She hated oversleeping but she remembered now that she had switched the alarm off so she could keep dreaming. Her cheeks flushed a little as she recollected the images of her and Anderson together. She hoped she could look him in the eye at the briefing. But there was something else she was dreading more. She was going to have to thank Jane Clackett for releasing the car information to the press.

There were about twenty people assembled when she walked into the incident room, including DCS Wilson. As the search area shrank, so did the team.

'Good morning everyone.' Bernie looked around and gave a brief smile. 'Right, I had some news this morning that's probably going to eliminate Mick O'Connell from the inquiry. DI Terry

West from St Aldate's rang me earlier to say that the car's at the John Radcliffe hospital in Oxford. The little girl is very ill with meningitis. So it's probably not Molly. Terry is going to pop in and see them in a while but obviously he'll be sensitive towards their needs.' Bernie paused and swallowed before carrying on. 'The nurse who rang in about the car had heard about it on the radio so I have to thank… Jane, for releasing the information to the media. In this instance, it paid off.'

Bernie couldn't bring herself to look fully at Jane but out of the corner of her eye, she could see her looking smug.

Matt Taylor stuck his hand up.

'Yes, Matt?' said Bernie.

'Where does this leave us with the car? Are we looking for a different Ford Focus now or did Mick O'Connell drive down that track for some reason?'

'That's a good point. Note that down. We'll get Terry to ask them.'

'So, Bernie,' Wilson's voice boomed across the room, 'are you saying that we're no further forward this morning in finding Molly? The press are baying for our blood. She went missing on Friday, it's now Tuesday.'

Bernie steeled herself to look at DCS Wilson. His large face was red and his eyes were bulging. Her heart beat faster. She was used to him berating her privately in his office but not publicly, in front of her whole team. Everyone was looking at her. She tried to speak but words failed her. From over her shoulder, she heard a male Scottish voice.

'Sir, I think it's fair to say there's been little to go on since the beginning. The leads we've been chasing may be false but at least we've discovered them. I think our perpetrator has local knowledge and is likely to be forensically savvy. I mean, who isn't these days? He or she may be one step ahead of us but I think we're closing in. And besides, Jessica Cole trusts DI Noel. It would be a mistake to make changes now, sir.'

Wilson looked at Anderson and nodded slowly. 'You may be right, Detective Sergeant Anderson. You have a good team, Bernie. You need to make better use of them.'

Bernie could feel relief flood through her body. 'Yes, sir.'

'Right, carry on with your briefing. Report back to me at fourteen hundred hours.'

Everyone stood up as Wilson and Jane left the room.

'Shall I tell everyone where we're up to with the search, ma'am?'

Bernie nodded, the power of speech still evading her.

'OK. We've covered on foot a five-mile radius of farmland and wooded areas. Apart from the fleece at the park, we haven't recovered anything else of Molly's. We've been searching along the banks of the River Avon and the canal and the army are checking the top part of Salisbury Plain for us. I didn't want to say in front of the chief super but I honestly don't know where else to search. If there was a car then she could be anywhere.'

Bernie smiled weakly at Kerry. 'I think we're all feeling a little despondent at the moment. Matt, any phone calls overnight?'

'No, nothing.'

'Right. It looks as though we're going to have to start again. We need to go back through all the information we've received from the public so far. It's entirely possible we're still looking for a Ford Focus. Who had the info about a woman getting her tyres changed?'

Bernie saw a young uniformed male officer raise his hand.

'Go back to the garage and look for any CCTV in the area and get tapes. See if the owner remembers anything else. Kerry, keep going with the canal and the rivers and check all the tributaries. I'm assuming you've already spoken to the Environment Agency.'

Kerry nodded. 'Yes, they've asked all their volunteers to keep an eye out.'

'DS Anderson, go back to the family and let them know that the O'Connells are in the clear. From what Terry West told me, I don't think the little girl with them was Molly and I don't want them to find out through the press. I can't trust Jane to keep her mouth shut any more. Not after releasing the car details actually paid off.'

'OK, ma'am.'

Bernie knew Anderson was looking intently at her but she kept her gaze focused on the room.

'Ma'am?' asked Matt. 'What do you want me to do?'

'We're going to wait for Terry West to get back to us but before then, pop down to the front desk and see if the bakery has delivered anything this morning. I'm starving.'

Bernie was wading through paperwork when her phone rang.

'DI Noel.'

'Hi, it's Terry West. I've just had a very interesting chat with Mick O'Connell.'

Bernie put the paperwork down and signalled to Matt to come over.

'I'm going to put you on speakerphone so that Matt, my DC, can hear you as well.'

'Tell him to grab pen and paper. You're going to want to write this down.'

'Really?' Bernie looked at Matt in surprise. She had only expected to eliminate Mick O'Connell, not gain any relevant information.

'OK. First off, the little girl is definitely not Molly. Her name is Emma and… it is as bad as the nurse said.'

Bernie shook her head. 'Oh no. Poor girl and poor parents.'

'I know what you mean. I really hated intruding on them at this time but when I explained a girl had gone missing, they were more than willing to help. They had no idea about Molly. So we've eliminated them. I got your message about the car and I asked them if they had gone down the track.'

'And?'

'It was them.'

'Damn.' Bernie rubbed her forehead. 'Looks as though you were right, Matt. I was hoping it wasn't the case.'

'Well, I'm afraid it was them,' said West. 'They were coming from Salisbury, they'd been to visit the cathedral. They missed the turning for the farm and had to go back. So O'Connell pulled into the track, drove down it to try and turn round. His daughter thought she was going to be sick so they got out of the car. She wasn't sick at that point though.'

'No,' said Bernie. 'But she was very sick at the cottage.'

'Yes, well at that moment they just thought it was travel sickness. Mick turned the car around and his car got scratched by some brambles. He then drove back to the road, was about to pull out when a car came whizzing round the corner and he had to reverse quickly.'

Bernie looked at Matt and sighed. 'Let me guess – he hit a gatepost?'

'Yes. He was pretty angry and threw the gatepost into the bushes.'

'Did you ask about his tyres?'

'The car had its MOT last week and all four tyres had to be replaced so he went for cheap unbranded ones.'

Bernie shook her head. 'Oh my God. The super is going to do his nut when he hears that we've just been on the biggest wild goose chase ever.'

'It's not all doom and gloom,' said West.

'Isn't it? It's looking pretty bad from this end.'

'That's because I've given you the bad news. I've got good news as well.'

'It had better be good after all that.'

'When Emma got out of the car to be sick, her mum stayed with her. Mick had a little wander around and found something pushed underneath a bush. Something that looked as though it was in reasonable nick; something his wife, as a new childminder, needed; something that clearly nobody wanted. So he took it and put it in his car.'

Bernie smiled at Matt as she began to realise what it was. Matt still looked perplexed. 'Go on, Terry. I think I know but Matt's a bit unsure.'

'Well, I have, wrapped up ready for your forensics team, one buggy with rain cover. My DS has taken Mick O'Connell down to the station to get his fingerprints for elimination and I've got my CSIs here taking samples from the boot of the car for the same reason. Now, do you want me to send it to you or do you want to collect? I'm happy either way. I appreciate you might not be able to spare an officer at the moment.'

Bernie was so happy she thought she was going to cry. 'If you're able to send someone then that would be fantastic. I'll let my CSIs know it's coming. Terry, thank you so much. Oh God, I know we still don't have her but this could make all the difference. If you can get Mick O'Connell to describe exactly where it was then I'll get someone back to the scene. We were so focused on the tyre tracks it's possible we may have missed something.'

'Ma'am,' said Matt. 'There was a thread found on some of the brambles. Is it possible to check if Emma had a blanket?'

'Did you hear that, Terry?'

'Yes. I'm at the car now. I'm just looking in the back. Yes, I can see a cream knitted blanket. Does that match?'

Matt rifled through some papers and then pulled out one. 'Yes, it was cream but it might be useful to take a sample so we can check and rule it out.'

'Yes, of course. Right, I'll get all the evidence gathered including the elimination samples to send down with someone and I'll email you the fingerprints. The wife didn't touch it at all so it will only be Mick O'Connell's.'

'Terry, you are a star and I owe you,' said Bernie. She beamed at Matt.

'Well, come and see us at Oxford some time and you can take me to the Randolph for dinner,' said West.

Bernie laughed. 'Oh, I see. Expensive tastes, Detective Inspector West. You might have to make do with a curry.'

Terry laughed. 'Oh, all right then. Keep me informed. If there's anything more we can do, just let me know. You will find her, Bernie.'

'Thanks. Speak to you soon.'

Bernie finished the call and put up her hand to high five Matt.

'Yes, yes, yes! Finally. We may have something with the abductor's prints or DNA on.'

'Ma'am, this is good news, no doubt about it, but…'

'But what? This is excellent news.'

Matt shook his head. 'I don't know, maybe I'm wrong about this.'

'Wrong about what?' Bernie's excitement slumped.

'This is the second piece of evidence that's been hidden under a bush. Remember, Molly's fleece was under a bush in the park, and now the buggy. Either we have a perpetrator who's not very smart or he or she is playing games with us. Don't be surprised if we only find evidence of Molly and no one else.'

CHAPTER SEVENTEEN

Bernie stood in front of Wilson's desk while he finished a phone call. Unlike Jane's, Wilson's was covered in paperwork – folders tottering in large piles.

'Yes, Chief Constable, I fully understand. Detective Inspector Noel is here with me now. There's been a development. I'll ring you back. Goodbye, sir.'

Wilson put the phone down and sighed. 'This had better be good, Bernie.'

Bernie nodded. She was still smarting from Wilson's angry outburst from the morning briefing. She filled him in on her conversation with Terry West and how the O'Connells were in the clear. Wilson raised his eyes to the ceiling. Before he could interrupt, she told him about the buggy.

Wilson rubbed his chin. 'Hmm. It sounds as though it could be something. People don't normally shove buggies under a bush, unless it's broken.'

'O'Connell said it looked in very good nick.'

'Well, as you may have guessed from that phone call, I'm up against it with the chief constable on this case and the betting shop raids. The injured man suffered a major heart attack overnight and is now on life support. It's not looking good. I'm sorry I yelled at you in front of everyone this morning. From now on, I'll only yell at you in my office.'

Bernie smiled. She was so focused on Molly she'd forgotten about the betting shop raids that Wilson was also overseeing. 'Yes, sir. Any news on the raids?'

Wilson sighed. 'No, not really. It's a very professional outfit. Actually, sit down a minute. I'd appreciate your thoughts on this.'

Bernie perched on the edge of the seat. 'Go on.'

'There have been five raids so far. Two in Bristol and three in Wiltshire. Different companies, different times of the day. No pattern at all. Our colleagues in Bristol think the shop owners or managers know more than they're letting on.'

Bernie frowned. 'Some kind of insurance claim?'

'It's a possibility but now this man, David Chaucer, has been hurt... he was just a punter trying to be a hero. The stakes have really gone up now.'

Bernie gave a little smile. The super hadn't noticed his unintended pun. 'It might look random but it also seems very organised to me. Hmm. Interesting. I'll have a think.'

'Well, I should let you go. I'll stall the chief constable for as long as I can but you need to start getting results and soon.'

'Thank you, sir, and I will do my very best.'

Bernie turned to leave.

'Oh, one other thing before you go. The schools are back today. It might be prudent to go and visit Mr Jenkins, the head teacher, at some point. But don't take DS Anderson with you.'

Bernie smiled. 'I won't. He's back on family liaison, permanently.' She glanced at her watch. It was nearly eleven o'clock. 'I might leave it until this afternoon, just before home time.'

'Why?' asked Wilson.

'Because I want to arrive when the other parents are there and see the gauntlet that Jessica Cole has to go through every day. And it won't hurt to remind them a child is missing.'

*

Lucy, the CSI, was already waiting for them when Bernie and Matt arrived.

'Sorry to drag you out again, Lucy,' said Bernie.

'No problem at all.' The young forensic officer smiled at her and nodded towards Matt. 'DC Taylor filled me in on the phone. I gather all the effort over the car paint has been fruitless.'

Bernie nodded, her face grim. 'It's definitely looking that way. Thames Valley have confirmed the girl isn't Molly and the parents are fully cooperating. But, this information about finding a buggy might just help.'

Matt Taylor appeared next to Bernie, clutching two forensic suits. 'We probably ought to suit up.'

'Yes, please do,' said Lucy.

'I've just thought, Matt,' Bernie said. 'After this we ought to quickly pop down to Pear Tree Farm and let Naomi Phillips know about the O'Connells. I think I'll drive this time though. Don't want any more accidents.'

Matt gave Bernie a wry smile as he picked up the police cordon for her to go under.

'After you, *ma'am.*'

Bernie gave him a little grin as they walked down the track.

'I didn't come here on Saturday,' said Matt. 'I know about the tyre tracks but what about footprints?'

'Too many to isolate properly,' replied Lucy. 'The whole search team piled in, dogs and all. I also think the car possibly rubbed some out when turning round. I certainly hadn't spotted any child's prints but then we did mostly focus on the tyre tracks.'

'Also,' added Bernie. 'The dogs had lost the scent so we put two and two together and…'

Matt nodded. 'You came up with the getaway car. On the surface, it certainly seemed plausible.'

'But we were wrong,' said Bernie.

'Wrong about this particular car. There might have been another.'

They came to a stop next to the patch of brambles where the paint trace had been found. The tyre tracks were no longer visible, washed away by the rain.

'So,' said Lucy, 'this is where the Ford Focus was. Where's the bush the witness mentioned?'

Bernie pulled out her phone and looked up the email sent by Terry West. 'OK, Mick O'Connell said he walked past the brambles, towards the railway.' She looked up and scanned the waste ground in front of them. There were lots of bushes to choose from.

'Oh God, which one?' asked Matt.

'Hang on. I'm just reading a description… it's a sharp one – he got scratched.'

All three of them looked around trying to pinpoint the exact bush.

'Are you sure he doesn't mean brambles?'

'Don't think so, Matt. He must know what brambles are.'

Lucy moved forward, stepping over weeds. 'No, it's not brambles. Look over there, it's a hawthorn bush. Personally, I think they're worse than brambles. Great big thorns. Come on.'

Lucy led the way, carrying her forensic case. They slowed down as they neared the hawthorn, looking at the ground for any clues.

'I'm guessing the biggest problem here is we unwittingly contaminated the crime scene,' said Bernie. Another stuff-up. She remembered Anderson's words – *too inexperienced to lead*.

Lucy nodded. ''Fraid so. Some of the grass is flattened, suggesting that people have walked here but no distinct prints.' She crouched down next to the bush and shone a torch under it. 'There is space underneath here to put something.'

'Big enough for a buggy?' asked Bernie.

Lucy looked back at her. 'Yes, I'd say so.' She looked under the bush again. 'But I don't think it was here for very long though. The ground doesn't look too disturbed. Oh, wait a minute, what's that? Matt, could you hold the torch for me please?'

Lucy opened her case and pulled out some tweezers and a small evidence bag which she passed to Bernie. 'Right, hold it steady, Matt. I'm going in.'

Lucy lay flat on her stomach and commando-crawled a small way into the hawthorn. Bernie watched as she reached out her right arm, tweezers in hand.

'Are you all right? Not getting too scratched?'

'No, I'm fine. Oh the glamour of this job. I'm sure this is some animal's toilet underneath here – stinks a bit. Nearly there… got it.'

She shuffled back. 'Got that bag ready, Detective Inspector?'

'Yes,' answered Bernie, as she bent down. Lucy sat up, pulling her right arm carefully out of the bush, the tweezers holding on to a long, blonde, curly hair. Bernie smiled.

'Look,' said Lucy, 'it even has a root. We can get DNA.'

'And maybe match it to Molly?'

Lucy smiled. 'Maybe.'

By the time Bernie and Matt finished at the scene it was lunchtime.

'You do realise Naomi Phillips is going to think we only pop by when we're hungry?' said Matt, with a laugh.

'I think her food is definitely preferable to the burger van.'

They stripped off the forensic suits, bagged them up and put them in the boot of the car. Lucy was continuing to search the area. A uniformed officer was on the way to stay with her.

'Do you think Lucy will find anything else?' asked Matt.

Bernie shrugged. 'Maybe, maybe not. We'll just have to wait and see.'

'I've been thinking more about this bush business,' said Matt. Bernie started to interrupt but Matt lifted his hand. 'Just hear me out.'

Bernie nodded. 'OK, go on. Give me all your criminology, psychological insight.'

'Having a degree is not a bad thing.'

'I know, I know. I'm just jealous because I didn't have that opportunity. I've spent nearly fourteen years in the police force learning the hard way. Seriously, tell me what you think.'

'OK, but let's get in the car first. I don't like the way those clouds are building up.'

Bernie glanced up to the sky and saw grey clouds moving rapidly in. 'Hmm, I think you may be right. Oh dear, poor Lucy.'

They got into their seats as thick blobs of rain started to come down, hitting the windscreen with hard splats.

'Right,' said Matt, 'as I said to you earlier, there are two choices here. Either the perpetrator is a bit thick and is just shoving evidence under bushes, or, it's being done for a reason. I suppose the hair could have been left there accidentally. It could be for a bit of fun, to wind us up. Or a message is being sent. I'm not sure what the message is and whether it's for us or the Coles. Does Molly like playing hide and seek, for instance? I don't think we should dismiss the significance out of hand.'

Bernie rubbed her forehead. Her muscles were starting to tense, suggesting another headache was on its way. 'Actually, Jessica said she thought Molly was hiding to begin with. All right. We'll keep an open mind on it. Let's see what Forensics have to say about it tomorrow after the buggy's been processed. And then there's the DNA match on the hair that we need to wait for.' She laughed a little. 'Do you know what this feels like?'

Matt shook his head.

'It's like horses at the start of the race when they have to get into the gates. We're waiting for everything to slot into place and then we'll be off – galloping down the course after the abductor.'

Matt laughed. 'Reminds me more of the dogs. The hare has got a head start on us but we'll catch up.'

Bernie's eyes widened. 'Bloody hell, that's it.'

'What is?'

'The betting shop raids.'

Matt stared at her. 'OK, I'm really confused now.'

'Sorry, I was talking to the super earlier. He said the attacks were random. What if they fit with the sporting diary? Not the really big events – nothing too obvious. Maybe the raids happen afterwards?'

'Or maybe just prior,' said Matt. 'Before money is paid out. It could even be tied in with fixing.'

'Hmm. Change of plan. Back to headquarters so I can talk to the super before heading to Molly's school. You can ring Naomi and leave her a message.'

Matt looked forlorn.

Bernie laughed. 'Oh all right, we'll go to the baker's on the way back.'

A gaggle of mothers was waiting for the school gates at Otterfield Primary to open. Bernie wasn't sure she wanted to deal with them just yet. She spotted a small corner shop opposite the school. Unlike almost all the shops in Devizes, this one didn't have a 'Missing' poster in the window. *Why's that?*

A bell tinkled as she pushed the door open. Although the shop was small, it was piled high with shelves full of tins, cereal boxes and cleaning products. A fridge at the back hummed. Bernie browsed. She thought it might be easier to talk to the owner if she bought something. She headed to the chocolate near the till, passing the newspapers on her way. Molly's face filled the front cover of the local papers. Bernie spotted Clive Bishop's name on one so grabbed a copy.

Bernie hadn't spotted anyone behind the counter when she came in but an old man stood up as she approached. He had more tufts of hair growing out of his nose and ears than on top of his head and his breathing was laboured. Bernie smiled but he scowled back. She placed the paper on the desk and picked up a bar of dark chocolate.

'That all you want?' the old man rasped. His voice was slow and stretched out all the vowels.

'Yes, thanks.'

'Two pounds.'

Bernie handed over the money. She pulled out her warrant card. 'Good afternoon, sir. I'm Detective Inspector Noel. I'm investigating Molly Reynolds' disappearance. I think we may have forgotten to give you a Missing poster to display.'

The man gave an empty stare. 'No. Got one.'

Bernie's eyes flicked to the empty window. 'But you don't have it up.'

'No need.'

'Why?'

'We knows she's missing.'

'But…' Bernie was baffled. What was it with these people? 'The police details are on there in case anyone remembers anything or sees something.'

'We knows how to contact police. Ring nine nine nine.'

Frustration bubbled up but Bernie pushed it down. 'It would help us if you could display the poster please.'

'That an order?'

'It's a very strong recommendation.'

Bernie snatched up the newspaper and chocolate and headed out of the shop, the bell tinkling as she left. She stowed the items in the car and slammed the door. It was time to brave the mothers at the school gate. God help anyone who got in her way.

Their chatter slowed as Bernie approached them. She could feel hostility crackling in the air and wondered if they would start pecking at her like the geese. Then they parted, leaving a small gap for her to squeeze through to reach the keypad at the gate. She pressed the buzzer and heard a muffled answer. She hesitated before she spoke but then decided she would draw attention to herself. In a loud, clear voice she said, 'It's Detective Inspector Noel, here to see Mr Jenkins.'

Bernie heard one mother murmur, 'Police,' and the sound rippled round her. The gate clicked open and Bernie pushed it.

'You haven't found her then?' said one mother.

'Yeah, what about our kids? Are they safe?' said another.

Bernie turned to them. 'We haven't found Molly yet. We'd certainly appreciate some more help from the local community. It's been decidedly lacking.' She flashed her most insincere smile at the group. Two can play the intimidation game, she thought. No wonder Jessica found this impossible, she couldn't intimidate a fly.

Bernie followed the signs for the school office and soon found herself by a door with a second buzzer. The door swung open after she introduced herself for a second time. It was the smell that hit her first. A mixture of polish, school dinners and vomit. She looked through the office window and saw a pasty-looking boy sitting on a camp bed. Bernie gave him a brief smile before turning her attention to the receptionist.

She flashed her warrant card. 'DI Bernie Noel. I rang earlier.'

'Yes, of course. If you could please sign in I'll let Mr Jenkins know you're here. Here's a visitor's badge for you as well.'

Bernie wrote her name in the visitors' book and then settled down to wait, her eyes wandering over the wall displays near her. She saw one called 'Things that make us happy', and stood up and moved closer. There were various drawings with seemingly random letters and then an interpretation by a teacher in pencil. She caught her breath when she saw a picture labelled 'Molly'.

'My baby brother makes me happy,' Bernie read. Tears pricked her eyes. She took a deep breath. Losing Pops was playing havoc with her emotions. She had to remain focused, for Molly's sake. She thought about the hateful mothers outside. Even the receptionist hadn't mentioned Molly. How can they not care? she thought. How can they just not care?

CHAPTER EIGHTEEN

'Ah, Detective Inspector. Would you like a drink – tea or coffee?'

Bernie smiled at Tim Jenkins. Despite only being in his forties, he looked like a typical old-school headmaster: suit and tie and brown hair, neatly parted.

'No, thank you. I won't take up too much of your time. I really just wanted to check on you all, especially the children and Megan Williams. I was just looking at Molly's picture here.' Bernie gestured to the display.

'Yes, we took a conscious decision to not take it down. We're all devastated by Molly's disappearance. The children were very upset in assembly today.'

'Were they?' Bernie struggled to keep the surprise out of her voice.

'Yes, of course. What makes you think they wouldn't be?'

Bernie paused. She knew she'd been wrong to let her emotion show. 'It's just, I got the impression from Jessica Cole that Molly didn't have any friends.'

Bernie watched the colour rise in Jenkins' face. 'Well, Molly was, sorry, is, a bit of a loner. She hasn't really connected with anyone in particular. But the children are still naturally concerned about her.'

For themselves more like, thought Bernie.

'We talked about Stranger Danger and the children know what to do if someone approaches them.'

'That's a good idea,' said Bernie, 'but it's not always a stranger who abducts or abuses a child. Often it's someone they know.'

'Do you think Molly knew her abductor?'

Bernie shook her head. 'I've no idea.' She wasn't going to let him know any more than that.

'I only say because,' he lowered his voice, 'there are rumours going round the parents that Jessica's responsible.'

'Then I hope as head teacher you're squashing those rumours.'

'Yes, of course.' He looked abashed. 'I'm guessing you'd like to see Megan. School has almost finished. I'll walk you down there.'

As Bernie followed the head teacher, the lanyard with the visitors' badge attached swung round her neck. A thought popped into her head. 'Have you had any visitors to the school in the last two terms?'

'We have visitors every week. Why? Do you think one of them is responsible?'

Bernie paused. 'I'm not sure but check to see if you had anyone new come in. Maybe someone who offered their services rather than you inviting them.'

Jenkins nodded his head. 'I'll get the office staff to look into it and we'll send you a list.'

There was a rush of sound as Jenkins opened a door. Some children were disappearing off to the hall, trailing book bags and packed lunch boxes behind them.

'After-school club,' he explained.

'But it wasn't running on Friday? Eddie Parker said he locked up at four thirty with you.'

'No. Eddie's wife Paula runs the club and they were going away to a wedding so she cancelled. The infant classrooms are off the hall.'

Jenkins opened one half of the double doors leading into the hall. 'After you.'

Bernie walked through into a cacophony of screaming children. A harassed-looking woman with short dark hair was standing in the middle of it all. Mr Jenkins clapped his hands loudly in a rhythm. The children stopped what they were doing and clapped back the pattern.

'Children, what are you doing? This is not how you behave at after-school club. Are you all right, Mrs Parker?'

The caretaker's wife blushed bright red. 'I'm sorry, Mr Jenkins,' she said in a shaky voice. 'One of my staff members has called in sick so I'm on my own for the next twenty minutes until Eddie can get here to help.'

'Well, we can't have that. I'll stay. Detective Inspector, the reception class is at the end there on the left, if you're OK to go there on your own.'

Bernie smiled at Paula Parker. 'Yes, of course.'

Bernie could feel Paula glaring at her as she walked towards Megan Williams' classroom. She was secretly cursing the head for letting on who she was. She didn't like Eddie Parker's chances now for persuading his wife to talk to her.

Bernie knocked on the door and then entered the class. She was greeted by bright classroom displays and a row of almost empty pegs. Megan Williams looked up from her desk and then burst into tears.

'Oh, Megan, what's wrong?' asked Bernie.

Megan Williams grabbed a tissue and blew her nose noisily. 'You've got bad news, haven't you?'

Bernie sighed. 'No, I don't have any news. Molly's still missing. I was just here to speak to Mr Jenkins and to check in on you.' She reached out and placed her hand on the teacher's. 'I'm guessing you're not doing so well.'

Megan sniffed and shook her head. 'No, not great. I keep seeing her little face. She's such a beautiful girl and then I start to think about who might have her and what they're doing…' She broke down again.

Bernie put her arm around Megan's shoulder. 'I know. It doesn't bear thinking about, does it? I'll let you into a secret – I'm struggling too, we all are. Somehow, we just need to focus on finding Molly. We will only deal with the worst *if* it happens.'

Megan wiped her eyes with another tissue. 'I assume you checked out what I said. About… you know.'

'Yes. I'm pretty certain it's fine. So don't worry about that and he'll never know from us what you said.'

'Good. I hated doubting him. I keep thinking about Molly's mum. Maybe go and see her but if I can't control my own emotions, then I won't be much comfort.'

'You could write to her. I'm hoping to see her later so I could take a note for you, that's if you want me to.'

Megan gave a half smile and nodded. 'Yes, that would be good, thank you. I haven't got a nice card though.'

'I don't think that matters. I saw a drawing that Molly did on display in the foyer. Maybe you have something else of Molly's I could take for her. Your note could be about that and saying you're thinking of her.'

'Molly did a lovely picture of a lamb at the beginning of term. We'd been on a school trip to a local farm and seen the new lambs. It's on the wall over here.'

Bernie followed Megan over to a large display full of paintings of different farm animals. She saw Molly's lamb covered in white cotton wool, supposedly running around in a green field.

'Which farm did you go to?' Bernie asked.

'Greenacre. It's the largest around here. Been going for several generations now.'

Bernie nodded. 'I know it. It's Ron Willis's farm. The whole family has helped with the search – checking their fields and outbuildings.'

'Molly loved it there but it was the lambs she fell in love with. They let her feed one with a bottle. It was all she would talk about after that.' Megan put her hand to her chest. 'Oh God, in some ways I don't want to take it down. It would be like admitting that... that she's not coming back.' She wiped her eyes on the sleeve of her top. 'Would it be selfish of me to keep it for a while longer? I mean, if the worst does happen then I will give it to her mum but...'

Bernie reached and touched Megan on the shoulder. 'It's not selfish. It's lovely to see how much you care for Molly. You don't have to give any of her work if you don't want to. Just a note would be fine but there's no pressure to do it now, honestly.'

Megan nodded. 'I think I'd rather get a nice card and I'll hand deliver it tomorrow after school. And I'll find something else of Molly's. She did a lovely chalk picture of the White Horse which we had on display. She's a good little artist. It's around here somewhere.'

'No problem. How were the children today?'

'Yeah, they were quite upset after assembly when Mr Jenkins told them. Some of the older ones already knew but four- and five-year-olds don't often watch the news and the parents were shielding them from it. We've talked about Stranger Danger again today.'

'Do you think...' Bernie paused. She knew she had to say it the right way. 'Do you think the children were more worried about their own safety rather than Molly being missing?'

Megan swallowed slowly. 'It's hard to tell. I know what you're getting at, the fact that Molly doesn't have any friends. Probably a bit of both. They're scared someone might be out there who would take them but there did seem to be genuine concern for Molly. A couple of the girls were upset they hadn't been nicer to her.'

The classroom door banged open and a small girl ran in.

'Sorry, Miss.'

Megan smiled. 'What is it, Sarah?'

The girl stared at Bernie. 'Packed lunch box.'

'You left it behind?'

Sarah nodded, her eyes still on Bernie.

'Go and get it then.'

Sarah didn't move. 'You the policeman looking for Molly?'

Bernie smiled. 'Yes, I'm the police officer looking for Molly. My name's Bernie. How old are you, Sarah?'

The girl shifted from one foot to the other but raised her hand to show five digits.

'Five. A big girl then. Is there something you want to tell me?'

She shook her head and then nodded it.

Megan beckoned her over. 'It's OK, Sarah. You can tell Bernie.'

Sarah fiddled with the bottom of her school polo top, rolling it up and down. She dipped her head so her mud-brown hair swung into her eyes. 'I was in the park.'

'The day Molly went missing?' asked Bernie. 'Did you see something?'

Small nod. 'There was someone in the park.'

Bernie leaned slightly closer to Sarah. 'Who?'

'A grown-up with a buggy.'

'Do you know this person? Was it a man or a woman?'

Sarah shrugged her shoulders. 'Didn't see. They were behind the trees. And had a hoodie on. My granny hates them. Says you can't see faces.'

'Your granny is right. But you definitely saw a buggy?'

Sarah nodded her head vigorously. 'Yes, but there was no baby.'

'One last question, do you know what time it was?'

'After school.'

Bernie smiled. She couldn't expect a five-year-old to know the time. But she was surprised the abductor had taken such a risk.

There was a knock at the classroom door and the receptionist poked her head round.

'Oh good, you're still here. There's a phone call for you, Detective Inspector, from the police station. It's a Detective Constable Taylor.'

Bernie smiled at Megan Williams. 'I need to go but I'll keep in touch.' She held her hand out to the teacher. 'Keep strong. You have my number if you need to contact me. Oh, and could you mention to Mr Jenkins and to Sarah's parents that she's spoken to me?'

She turned to the little girl. 'Thank you, Sarah. You've been really helpful.'

Sarah beamed. 'I promise to play with Molly when she comes back.'

Bernie bit her lip and followed the receptionist across the hall. She raised her hand to the head teacher. He nodded in response as he sat with a group of children playing a board game.

Bernie picked up the phone in the office. 'Matt?'

'Yes. Sorry to call you at the school but it's impossible to get through to you on your mobile when you're in Otterfield.'

Bernie pulled out her mobile and saw it said emergency calls only on the screen. 'Of course, I'd forgotten it was a black hole here for mobile signal. God knows how the residents cope if their landlines go down.'

'There's a telephone box in the village. I put a Missing Persons' poster in it with the Crimestoppers' number.'

'Good thinking, Batman. Anyway, what are you ringing for?'

'Thought you might like to know the evidence has arrived from Oxford. Lucy wondered if you wanted to see it before she takes it all to the lab. They're going to work on it all tonight.'

'Oh, I see. I was going to pop in on Jessica as I'm here but I could come back later. And I still haven't seen Lesley Cooper. But I want to see this buggy and we definitely need to get some photos of it. I've just spoken to a girl who saw an adult with a buggy in the park that afternoon.'

'Really? How old is the girl?'

'Five. I know, not a reliable witness, and she couldn't tell if it was a man or a woman. But it's a confirmation of sorts. OK, I'll come back now and see Jessica this evening.'

As Bernie approached her car, she had the strange sensation that someone was watching her again. She flicked her head around. Maybe it was the school receptionist. Or a parent. Or the old man in the shop. Or... someone from London? Whoever it was, Bernie showed no apprehension. She couldn't afford to reveal she was unnerved.

CHAPTER NINETEEN

Bernie looked at the vast array of evidence bags in front of her and the folded up buggy wrapped in plastic. The rain cover was attached and the seat was purple. It looked to be in reasonable condition.

'Wow. Someone has been thorough.'

'It'll help Therese at the lab,' said Lucy. 'Most of them are elimination samples plus I've got my own samples in the van. But, I don't want to get your hopes up. We didn't find any additional trace on Molly's fleece, so chances are we might not find the abductor's prints if gloves were worn. In fact, if it was wiped down, there might not be any prints at all, other than Mick O'Connell's.'

'Oh great. Anything else the lab can do?'

'They'll swab for DNA. Hopefully they'll find Molly's and perhaps another. But like the prints, we could be looking at multiples. They're moving this to the top of their list. They hope to have results tomorrow, late afternoon.'

Bernie nodded grimly. 'Shame we're not trialling the two-hour machines.'

Lucy sighed. 'I know. Eventually it will be the norm but cost will always be an issue.'

'Talking of which…' – Bernie waved her hand towards all the evidence bags on the table before her – 'do you think they'll need to test all of it?'

'Yes, pretty much. I'm going to ask them to pull that buggy apart and go through the lot.'

'Well, I'm not going to put a price on Molly's life. Test whatever you need. The chief constable has given us the green light to go ahead. Although he might change his mind when he sees the bill.'

Lucy smiled. 'We'll do our best to keep costs down. Before they take the buggy apart I'll ask them to take lots of photos you can use. Maybe someone will recognise it.' She started to gather up the evidence bags before her.

'I'll send someone along to help you,' said Bernie. 'I'm assuming we've logged it all.'

'Yes, Matt did. He's very efficient.'

'I'll see if he's free to help you.'

Bernie left the evidence room and headed for the lift back up to MCIT.

Matt was on his own, speaking on the phone.

'Yes, well, thanks for ringing me back. Just thought you'd like to know the O'Connells are in the clear.'

Matt looked up at Bernie and mouthed 'Naomi Phillips'. She nodded in response and pulled up her chair to sit next to him.

'No, it's so important to report these things, you know, better to be safe than sorry… I don't think they're angry, they were happy to help… Yes, the little girl is very ill… I will pass on your regards. Thank you very much, Mrs Phillips… Oh, something else. Could you ask your other guest to contact me please? Maybe she saw something suspicious that day. She can contact me here. Yes, thank you. Goodbye.'

Matt turned to Bernie as he put the phone down. 'Naomi Phillips. I left her an answerphone message earlier.'

'Thanks for sorting that out. And if her guest rings you, make sure you apologise for nearly running her over.'

Matt flushed. 'Of course.'

Bernie laughed. 'Matt, I'm teasing you. Go and help Lucy with all the evidence that came from Oxford. It needs to go to the lab. Oh, and it might be worth getting someone to talk again to the parents at the park. If this little girl at school saw something, maybe one of the parents did as well and might be more willing to tell us now.'

She walked over to her desk and saw a note. 'Matt, did you put this here?'

He looked over at the yellow Post-it note. 'Yes, telephone call from Gary again. He really needs to speak to you.'

'But it's not to do with the investigation?'

'No. He said it was a private matter.'

A thought wandered into her mind but then she dismissed it. If he had anything to do with the London gang he wouldn't ring up and leave a name and number. Hand-delivered and unnamed cards were more menacing. 'Well, he'll still have to wait. Kerry will be reporting in soon and I ought to ring Anderson over at the Coles' house. I need to try and get hold of Lesley Cooper too. You go and help Lucy. We'll chat later.'

Bernie finished writing up her notes in the logbook. She looked at her list of things to do which seemed to grow longer every day. At the top was Lesley Cooper's name. It was odd she hadn't phoned back. Bernie tried calling again but it still went to answerphone. She wrote next to Lesley's name – 'visit tomorrow'. She sighed and put her head in her hands, her thumbs rubbing her temples.

'Are you all right, Bernie?'

Bernie lifted her head and saw Kerry had come into MCIT.

'Long day. What about you?'

Kerry shook her head. 'Nothing. We covered the canal in Devizes but not a dicky bird.'

Bernie tapped her fingers on the desk. 'I went to Molly's school this afternoon. Apparently the class went on a school trip a few weeks ago to Greenacre Farm. Has that been searched?'

'Yes,' said Kerry as she rammed a biscuit into her mouth. 'Sorry, I'm starving. Gaggin' for a brew as well. Didn't get lunch. Erm, I didn't do it but uniform did with the owners. It's really big but it was clear. Why do you ask?'

Bernie sighed. 'When we first spoke to Molly's teacher she said they'd talked about keeping safe from strangers and Molly had shouted the loudest when they had a practice. I still can't decide if Molly was targeted and knew the person, or if it was just completely random – that it could have been any child. Anyway, I've asked the school for a list of visitors, especially anyone new to them or had offered to come in. And I wanted to rule out anyone from the farm. Apparently she loved it when her class went on a trip.'

'I can check all the workers on the farm again tomorrow if you want but I'm pretty sure they all had alibis. They were all needed to deal with the new lambs – cutting off tails and castrating, if I remember rightly.'

'I can see why you didn't go now,' Bernie said.

'Yeah, it's not easy being a veggie when you're surrounded by farms.' Kerry laughed. 'Anyway, unless you need me for anything else I'm going home now. I've typed up my report for today. It's quite short.'

'Yeah, that's fine. See you tomorrow morning.'

'Oh, have you spoken to the super about your anonymous card?'

'No, not yet. I have to focus on Molly for now.' Bernie hoped Kerry wouldn't mention her mother. She still hadn't spoken to her.

Kerry raised her eyebrows. 'Don't forget about it though. Get it tested just for your own peace of mind. You're not staying here for much longer now, are you?'

Bernie glanced at her watch. It was just after six thirty. 'I spoke to Anderson earlier. I'm going to pop in on the family. The head teacher at Molly's school said there are rumours flying around that Jessica's responsible for Molly's disappearance. Poor woman. Then I'll head back home for my microwave meal for one.'

Kerry reached and touched Bernie's shoulder. 'When this is all over, Debs and I will have you round for dinner. Matt too, and maybe even the Scottish/Italian stud.'

Bernie gave Kerry a hard stare. 'Leave. Now. While you still can.'

Kerry laughed as she left the office.

Bernie collected up her things and pulled on her coat. She was almost at the door when she caught sight of a newspaper on a desk. It was the same paper that she'd bought from the little shop and was now in the boot of her car. Molly's picture stared up at her. But it was the headline for the story below Molly's that captured Bernie's attention.

'Name Change for Worst Pub in Wiltshire'. Bernie laughed. She knew the pub and was aware this wasn't its first reincarnation. Bloody hell, she thought, it doesn't matter how many times they change the name, unless they change the man in charge, it will never improve.

The words lingered in her brain along with Tim Jenkins mentioning the villagers' suspicions. Something clicked. Names can change, she thought, but it's still the same man. She gasped. *Names can change… but not fingerprints.*

Bernie pounced on the phone as soon as it rang. She'd been waiting for over an hour.

'DI Noel.'

'Hi, it's Therese. I've had the report on the fingerprints.'

'Hi. Thanks so much for staying on to do this. Can't believe I didn't think about running the prints through the database before.'

'Well, if their names didn't bring up any records you didn't really have any reason to. I've just sent you an email.'

Bernie glanced at her computer and saw the message ping into her inbox.

'Brilliant, thank you so much. I hope it's not been in vain.'

'It hasn't,' said Therese. 'There's a hit. I'll leave you to decide if it's relevant or not. I'm heading home now. If you need anything else I'm back in tomorrow.'

'OK. Thanks again for staying late. Bye.'

Bernie opened the email and read quickly. Was her hunch correct? If so, the implications would be huge. Not just for the case but for her career as well. She'd made too many mistakes as it was. She stopped dead.

'Shit, shit, shit, shit, shit!'

She grabbed her mobile and dialled the landline for Jessica Cole. It was engaged. She knew she had to get hold of Anderson. She tried his mobile and it went straight to voicemail.

'Oh God! Why hasn't that village got decent reception?'

She rang Matt.

'Ma'am?' She could hear the sound of voices and music in the background.

'Matt, I need you to meet me at the Coles' house now.'

'Er, I'm in the pub. I'm on my second beer and the quiz is about to start. I thought I was off duty.'

Bernie gave a loud sigh. 'Great. I'll have to try Kerry then.'

'Is DS Anderson still there?'

'I'm not sure. I can't get through on his mobile and Jessica's phone is engaged.' Bernie could feel her heart beating faster. She didn't have time to muck about. 'Look, don't worry. I'll ask uniform.' She hung up before Matt could say anything else.

Bernie knew it was probably pointless but she tried Anderson one more time. This time it connected.

'Oh, hallelujah, it's actually ringing. Thank you, God.'

She heard Anderson answer.

'Yes, ma'am?'

'Can you hear me?'

'You're very faint.'

'I'll speak up. Do you have the whole family with you?'

'Sorry, ma'am. You're breaking up. Do I have what?'

Bernie clapped her hand to her head.

'Is all the family with you?'

'No, I really can't hear you.'

Bernie was on the verge of screaming, she was so frustrated. 'I'm coming over now. Don't let anyone leave.'

'You want me to leave?'

Bernie screamed down the phone, 'No! Stay there. I'm coming now.'

'You're coming?'

'Yes. I'll be there soon.'

Bernie almost chucked her phone across her desk. 'Oh God!' She grabbed a notepad and wrote down Jessica's home phone number and a message for Anderson. She tore off the note and ran down the stairs to the front desk, throwing the piece of paper at the officer there.

'Keep ringing that number until you get through and then get DS Anderson on the phone and tell him what's written there.'

'Yes, ma'am.'

'And I need uniform back-up. Two officers with the van at the Coles' house in Otterfield. The duty sergeant will have the address. Silent alert until the outskirts of the village and then blue lights off. Have you got all that?'

Bernie stared at the slightly bewildered officer.

'Would it be easier for you to talk to the duty sergeant yourself?'

'No, I don't have time!'

Bernie flew out the front door and ran round to her car. She raced out of the car park with her blue lights flashing. She always preferred silent alerts. It allowed her to think as the adrenalin started to pump round her body. She mulled over what she had read in the email attachment. The police record spoke for itself and she was kicking herself for not running the prints earlier.

Twilight was setting in as she hit the country lanes. She slowed a little as she swung round the twisty roads, thinking through how she was going to approach the situation. She could already imagine the headlines in the papers – the super would be furious and Jane would be unbearably smug as she dealt with the fallout. And Bernie knew her job would be on the line.

She saw the sign announcing she was about to enter Otterfield, switched off the blue light and slowed down to normal speed as she drove through the village. She went past the school and the telephone box Matt had mentioned. It was quiet. There were no kids out on the street. TVs flickered in lounges and some curtains were already drawn. Bernie took some deep breaths, trying to slow her racing heart as she neared Jessica's house. She hoped Anderson had heard her say he was to stay with them. Back-up was on its way but she really didn't want to do this alone.

Parking behind Anderson's car, Bernie blew out a huge sigh of relief. He was still there. She took a big breath and slowly exhaled. Going in all guns blazing wouldn't be right. There was baby Sam to think about. She would be calm and collected. Murmuring the words to herself, she walked up the path and rang the doorbell. Davy Reynolds answered the door.

'Evening, Inspector.'

Bernie could hear Jessica's angry voice coming from the lounge.

'What's going on?' she asked, realising that Jessica was speaking Spanish.

'She's on the phone to her mother in Spain. They always argue. That's why she came over here in the first place, to get away from her mum.'

Bernie hovered in the lounge doorway.

'I've been trying to ring. I guess this is why I couldn't get through. Where's DS Anderson?'

'He's in the kitchen making some tea. He was waiting for you to come round before he left.'

Bernie headed through the lounge to the kitchen, Davy following close behind.

'Thank you, Davy. Is Sam OK with all the noise Jessica is making?'

'That's a good point. I'd better check on him.'

Bernie waited for Davy to leave before beckoning Anderson over. He was a picture of domesticity with a tea towel over his shoulder.

'Sorry about earlier, I really couldn't hear what you were saying. I only had one bar of reception and that's good for round here.'

'Don't worry about that now.' She lowered her voice and leaned in to him. 'When this first happened I ran the names of all the family and they were clear.'

Anderson nodded. 'Yes, I know. There are no records for any of them.'

'But it's just dawned on me that I only checked the names, not the fingerprints.'

Anderson stepped back a little and stared into Bernie's eyes. She wanted to pull away from his gaze but found she couldn't. 'There's a hit. It's not good,' she said.

'Who?'

'Where's Derek?'

Anderson looked alarmed. 'His own granddaughter? But how? He has an alibi.'

'Where is he? He's not in the lounge.'

'No, he's in the garage at the end of the garden. He's got a classic car in there he's been working on. But it doesn't make sense. We both saw him the other day. He said he'd die for Molly. How could he have taken her?'

Bernie swallowed slowly. 'All I know is we need to talk to him, and fast. He's got form. Back-up should be here any minute but it would be good to speak to him now while the others are distracted. Between the two of us we should be able to handle him, if necessary.'

'Yes. We'll need a light now it's almost dark. It's quite a long garden.'

With Anderson using his phone as a torch they crept past a climbing frame, trampoline and sandpit, moving through the dark garden as silently as they could. Bernie could see the light on in the garage through small glass windows near the top of the large door. There was something odd about it but she couldn't quite work it out.

'I can't tell if those glass windows are frosted or not but they seem to be moving. Am I imagining it?' she asked.

Anderson shook his head. 'I'm not sure. But I can hear something.'

Bernie's heart jumped. 'And I can smell something. Petrol. Shit.'

They both started running at the same time and pulled open the garage door. Exhaust fumes spiralled into the air and they held their sleeves over their mouths and noses. Anderson ran in. Bernie heard glass smash and then the car engine was turned off. He appeared, coughing, a moment later, dragging Derek Cole out into the garden.

By the light of the garage, Derek's lifeless body looked unnaturally well. Anderson put his hand on Derek's neck and then under his nose. 'Shit. No pulse and not breathing.' He immediately started chest compressions.

Bernie called for an ambulance. 'They'll be ten minutes.' She coughed, the fumes irritating her throat.

'Not. Quick. Enough.' Anderson said, matching each word with a pounding on Derek's chest.

Bernie was about to ask Anderson if he wanted her to take over when a scream filled her ears and she turned to see Jessica staring at her father.

CHAPTER TWENTY

Bernie held a sobbing Jessica in her arms as Anderson did chest compressions on Derek. The paramedics were still five minutes away but she knew he had gone.

'Ma'am,' Anderson panted between compressions, 'you need to take Jessica back into the house and get Davy to come out here and help me. I can't do this for much longer.'

'Davy is dealing with Sam. I can take over until uniform get here. Where the hell are they?'

With that, Bernie heard running footsteps and she could just make out two figures coming round the side of the house.

'About bloody time. Where the hell have you been?'

The two male police officers ran up to them.

'Sorry, ma'am, there was—'

'Explain later. One of you take over from DS Anderson and the other help me get Jessica back into the house.'

One of the officers took Jessica's arm and together they tried to lift her but she was a dead weight, her legs completely collapsed. Bernie stood up.

'Stay with her. I'll get her partner. He'll be able to pick her up, he's built like a tank.'

She sprinted back across the garden towards the lights of the house. She could hear Sam crying before she reached the back door.

'Davy!' Bernie called out. 'We need you. We need to get Jessica back in the house and we can't lift her.'

She stopped dead when she saw Davy's ashen face. In contrast, Sam's tiny face was getting redder by the second as he bawled.

'He won't stop… I can't get him to stop. I don't even know what's going on any more. I saw it all from the kitchen window.'

Bernie reached out and gently took Sam from Davy. She wasn't really used to babies. He felt awkward in her arms.

'I know. I'm still trying to work it out myself. But we must get Jessica back into the house. I'll deal with Sam and listen out for the paramedics. You're the only one who can lift her. Go.'

She watched the huge man, shaking like a leaf, walk out into the dark garden, then turned her attention to Sam.

'Right, young man, what's this all about?' She popped him over her shoulder and rubbed his back. She'd watched mothers in coffee shops do this and it normally achieved something. She heard a large belch and then smelt something sickly sweet.

'Oi. I'm pretty sure that puking on an officer is a punishable offence.'

The baby turned his head into her neck and gave a little sigh. 'You have no idea of the hell your family's going through, do you? Probably better you're blissfully unaware.'

She caught sight of blue flashing lights. 'Well, the cavalry's here, but I have a horrible feeling it's too late.'

She walked to the front door and opened it as two paramedics came up the path.

'He's out the back in the garden. I don't know how much you were told but it's a possible suicide attempt using car fumes. We've been doing chest compressions but I'm not sure it's working. DS Anderson and another officer are with him. His name's Derek. He's mid to late fifties.'

As she was speaking, she led them quickly through to the back door.

'His daughter is out there too but we're trying to get her back in the house. It's probably best to tell you now this is the abduction family.'

She turned and looked properly at the two medics. The man was older and she recognised him from other scenes. The woman was young, so young that Bernie thought she was probably newly qualified. She didn't have to say any more. She could tell by the looks on their faces what they were thinking.

They jogged off into the garden. Bernie walked back into the lounge with her precious bundle. She was fairly certain he was asleep now and she carefully placed him in a bouncer chair. He stirred a little so she gently rocked the chair until he settled again. But her mind was a-whirr with all her mistakes. What would the super say? And the chief constable?

Bernie heard sobbing. Davy walked into the room carrying Jessica, followed by the other police officer. He gently placed her on the sofa and then knelt down by her, stroking her hair. Bernie pulled the officer to one side and kept her voice low.

'Is he alive?'

'He's not responding to CPR, ma'am. Paramedics are trying the defibrillator now. Doesn't look good.'

'I don't know what radio reception is like here but I know mobile is appalling. We need CSIs down here now and someone needs to contact the super and tell him what's happened. If you can't get through on the radio then we'll have to use the landline but I'd rather not, if possible.' She nodded towards Davy and Jessica. 'Go outside and do it in the car.'

'Yes, ma'am.'

Bernie fetched a dining room chair and sat by Davy. He turned his head briefly to glance at her.

'I don't understand… I don't understand.'

Bernie looked at Jessica. She had barely been holding it together since Molly's disappearance as it was. Jessica's skin was sallow, her eyes dead.

'You have no idea why he might have done this?' Bernie asked.
They both shook their heads.

'OK. I'm not sure if this is the right time to tell you something or not. You're both in deep shock.'

'Will there ever be a right time?' asked Davy.

'No, probably not.'

'Then just say it. Jess may not take it in but I will.'

Bernie rubbed her face with her hands, pushing back her own tears that threatened to burst out.

'I was planning on coming to see you tonight anyway but then I found out some information. I ran your fingerprints – all of you.'

'But we're not suspects. You said that yourself.'

'Yes, I know. You and Jessica are clear. Derek, however, has a criminal record.'

'No,' said Jessica.

Bernie turned to her and took her hand. 'I'm afraid he does.'

Jessica pulled away. 'No, no. My father's a good man.'

'I'm sorry. This is going to be very hard to hear.' Bernie swallowed. 'Derek was guilty of a few petty crimes, but in 1990 he was the main suspect in a case that has never been solved. A young girl was abducted from this area. A girl called Sophie Newell. She was never found.'

Jessica's face turned white. Bernie ran to the kitchen and got back just in time with the washing up bowl as Jessica gagged and then spewed.

'God, thanks for getting that,' said Davy.

'Well, I'm pretty certain your son has already puked down my back. Didn't really want any more.'

Jessica rested back down on the sofa, her forehead damp with sweat.

'I think it might be better if I get a doctor over. She might need something to help her sleep.'

'No,' muttered Jessica. 'I need to be able to feed Sam. I don't want a doctor. I want Anna.'

Bernie heard the rustle of police uniform before she saw the officer.

'All done, ma'am.'

Bernie nodded. 'Good. I need you to do something else now. Drive over to Marchant and go to the vicarage. It's the large house next to the church, you can't miss it. Bring Anna Bentley here. Just say that Jessica has asked for her. Don't say anything else.'

She looked back at Davy. He had sunk down on his knees so that his head touched the sofa as he clung on to Jessica's hand.

'And bring the vicar as well. I think we're going to need him too.'

Detective Chief Superintendent Wilson was standing by the garage when Bernie joined him. He turned to face her.

'Bloody awful business.'

'Yes, sir, I know. I'm sorry. I should have run the prints. Now I understand why he was so cagey about having them done.'

'He had a cast-iron alibi. There was more reason to suspect the mother than the grandfather. I'm not blaming you.'

Bernie put her hand to her chest in relief. 'Thank you but it doesn't stop me blaming myself. We still have more questions than answers.'

Wilson nodded. 'I agree, which is why – and I don't say this lightly – we need to get a DCI in to take over the investigation.'

'But sir…'

Wilson raised his hand. 'No buts, Bernie. The chief constable has been on at me for the last couple of days to get a more senior officer in charge. And this isn't the only fatality we've had tonight. The man injured in the Trowbridge betting shop raid died earlier this evening. So we're looking at murder or manslaughter for that one now.'

'But this is a probable suicide,' said Bernie. 'I don't think it's murder.'

'Even so, you have to admit you've been struggling a bit with this case. DCI Worth is just wrapping up a job at Swindon—'

'DCI Worth*less*, more like!' Bernie looked at Wilson in disbelief. 'You are not giving my case to him. He's dreadful. I'm not working with him.'

Wilson sighed. 'You won't have to. He'll bring his own DI. You'll be off the case.'

Bernie shook her head. She tried to speak but no words came out.

'I'm sorry, Bernie. It's not my choice either.'

Bernie coughed and managed to find her voice. 'How long have I got?'

'I'd say forty-eight hours or until the end of play on Friday.'

'To find her?'

'Ideally, or at least significant progress.'

Bernie rubbed her hands. 'Right, in that case I'll go back to the station and start—'

'No, the only place you're going is home, to sleep. And shower. You stink of baby sick.'

Bernie grimaced. She was grateful Anna Bentley had sponged down her jacket shortly after arriving but Sam's vomit was still in her hair.

'Anyway,' continued Wilson, 'it's close to midnight and the CSIs have done all they can tonight. They'll be back in the morning. What's happening with the family?'

'The Bentleys are taking them back to the vicarage to stay there for a few days. We're going to have to rip this house apart for answers and they can't be here. Besides, I want them out of this hateful village.'

'I agree. They'll be well looked after and that will give DS Anderson a break. He can come and help you.'

Bernie's natural instinct was to rail against that idea but she stopped herself. She remembered how Anderson had collapsed onto a chair at the dining room table, exhausted after trying to save Derek. He had glanced up when she'd called his name, his eyes red. He wanted to find Molly as much as she did. And with only forty-eight hours now to crack the case, she was going to need all the help she could get.

'Yes, sir. I think that would be a good idea.'

'Well then, let's all get home. We've got an early start in the morning.'

They walked back up the garden together.

'Is it worth me talking to the family?' asked Wilson.

'No, not at the moment. They're in no fit state to take anything in. I'll see them tomorrow. They just need looking after and I can't think of anyone better than Paul and Anna Bentley.'

'I agree. I'll go round the side then. Eight o'clock briefing?'

'Yes. I'll see you then.'

Bernie walked back into the house. Packed bags sat in the lounge, ready to be loaded into a car. Anna Bentley was putting Sam into a car seat, her long curly red hair pulled back into a loose ponytail.

'Now then, wee man, we're all ready to go.'

Bernie loved Anna's Irish accent – there was a soothing, lyrical tone to her voice.

'Thank you so much for doing this, Anna.'

Anna glanced up. 'No problem. I would have been here every day if I'd been allowed.' She gave Bernie a knowing look. 'But to be fair, it seems as though DS Anderson's been good for the family. He's helping to pack the car. Actually, he won't admit it but I think he's in a bit of a state. You'll need to keep an eye on him.'

Bernie nodded. 'I think we're all in a bit of a state. I'll be over in the morning to talk to Jessica. I wish I could leave it longer, give her some time to recover, but there are lots of questions to be answered and…' Bernie paused before continuing, 'I've only been given until Friday, maybe Saturday if I'm lucky, to sort this. After that, another, more senior, officer will take over the case.'

Bernie felt Anna's eyes study her. 'And you don't want that, do you?' she said.

'No, and it's not just about my reputation. I promised Jessica I'd find Molly.'

Anna smiled. 'Then you will. I have faith in you. Now, would you be able to pick up those last two bags for me, please, and I'll take the wee man.'

They walked out into the chill of the night air. The boot of Paul Bentley's car was rammed full with bags and baby things. Jessica was already sitting in the back of the car, her head slumped against the car window. She appeared to be totally unaware of anything. *How much more can this poor woman take?*

'Right,' said Paul Bentley. 'That's everything for now. If we need anything else…?'

'Then just say,' Bernie said, 'and I'll get someone to bring it over, assuming it's not relevant to the investigation.'

Watching the car driving off into the night, Bernie turned to DS Anderson who was sitting on the front garden wall.

'Have you got keys to lock up with?'

He nodded and raised a hand. 'I've got Davy's keys.' He sighed. 'I'm bloody knackered. What the fuck happened here tonight?'

'You did really well.'

'Yeah, but it wasn't enough.'

Bernie reached out her hand to Anderson. He took it and she pulled him off the wall. He was close enough for her to feel his breath on her cheek. She didn't dare look at him. She was having enough problems with her emotions without adding attraction into the mix.

'Let's lock up and hand over to uniform for the night. Then I'll explain everything as I drive you home.'

*

The quiet country roads were deserted as they headed back to Devizes.

'So, let me get this right,' said Anderson. 'Derek Cole is actually Derek Hayes and he has form.'

'Yes,' said Bernie. 'Mostly trivial things but then in 1990 he was a suspect for a child abduction – a five-year-old girl called Sophie Newell. I didn't read too much of it but it remains unsolved. And guess what address was given for him?'

'Their current house?'

'Yep. We've assumed all along Derek Cole bought the house for Jessica and Davy and they were outsiders coming into the village. I think he inherited the property from his parents and the villagers know exactly who he is.'

'And they've been blanking them.' Anderson turned slightly in his seat towards Bernie. She was aware of his gaze upon her. 'But what I don't understand, is why not grass him up?'

Bernie shrugged. 'I don't know. I don't even want to consider this but what if the whole village is in on this abduction? What if it's retribution? Derek was at work when Molly went missing so we know he didn't do it.'

'Or maybe,' said Anderson, 'Derek had a partner back in 1990 and that's who's got Molly.'

'Well, whatever it is, I'm sure there's a link with Sophie Newell. We'll have to look at it in the morning,' said Bernie.

'In the morning? Why not now?'

Bernie slowed down as they drove into Devizes. 'Because I promised the super that I'd go home and get some sleep. You need sleep too.'

'Bollocks to that. Sorry, ma'am, but we need to find Molly.'

Bernie fell silent. She knew Anderson was right but she was shattered. On the other hand, her remaining time on the case was ticking away. She pulled up outside headquarters.

'Stay here,' she said. 'I'm going to email the file to my home address. I know I shouldn't but things are getting pretty desperate now. There's something I haven't told you. We only have forty-eight hours to solve this. After that, a DCI will be brought in and I'll be off the case.' She couldn't quite bring herself to look at Anderson. She wasn't sure if she would see sympathy or smug satisfaction in his eyes.

There was a roughness to his voice when he spoke. 'We're not going to let that happen. Send the email and we'll work on it at yours.'

'Well, that's very forward of you, inviting yourself back to mine,' she teased.

'Just being practical, ma'am. I'm at a hotel for the moment until I find something permanent. Not ideal for discussing a confidential case – I'm fairly sure the walls are made of papier-mâché. I'm assuming you have your own place.'

She nodded. 'I'll send the email.'

CHAPTER TWENTY-ONE

Bernie flicked the light switch. The energy-saving bulb produced a warm glow.

'You can dump your coat here.' She hung up her own jacket on one of the hooks screwed into the wall, Sam's puke mark still visible on the back despite Anna sponging it down. 'And the bathroom's there should you need it. Tea? Coffee?' She could do with a shower but it didn't seem wise with Anderson there.

'Tea please, ma'am.'

Bernie left Anderson to it. What would he think of her tiny flat with its mismatched furniture that was clearly not her choice? She switched on the kettle in the kitchenette. The estate agent had billed it as a bijou kitchen but two cupboards on the wall – one for food and one for crockery – along with a small fridge, sink and a two-ringed Baby Belling cooker, didn't really equate to a kitchen. She'd brought her own kettle, toaster and microwave and that was all she needed.

Anderson was settled on the pink floral sofa as she handed him a mug of tea.

'Have you just moved in?' He nodded at some boxes piled up in a corner.

Bernie thought about the items in the boxes with their attached memories – GCSE and A-level certificates, a few books, drawings and designs from her teenage dream of being a fashion designer, and photo albums. But most precious of all, a framed picture of her and Pops after her passing-out parade at Hendon. They had stayed in the boxes because if she took them out then she'd be admitting she definitely wasn't moving back to London. She couldn't tell Anderson that though.

'No. Six months ago. There's not enough space to put everything out and this place was meant to be temporary. Turns out, saving for a deposit is harder than you think.' She put her mug down.

'So what is there to do around here then? Apart from solving crime. I'm trying to decide whether to find a place nearby to live or go a little further afield.'

Bernie was bemused. They needed to work, no time for small talk. She humoured Anderson though. It had been a difficult night. Maybe a short conversation about normal things would be good for them both. 'To do? Not a lot. Unless you like walking. If you want the cinema or ice skating you have to drive over to Swindon. Plenty of nice restaurants and pubs around though.'

'Oh yes. Matt was trying to persuade me to go to a pub quiz.'

'He loves his quizzes. Bit odd for someone so young but each to their own.'

'And Kerry told me she does martial arts. Runs self-defence classes. So what do you do after work?'

Bernie sighed. Was this Anderson's way of asking her out? She shrugged her shoulders. 'I work. I come home. I eat. I watch Netflix. Then I go to bed.'

'You know what they say – "All work and no play makes—"'

'Me a very good officer.' Bernie opened her laptop. 'We need to work. Come on. It's very late and I broke the rules sending this file home.'

'All right, you're the boss.'

Bernie tried to focus on the words on the screen but her conversation with Anderson took her back to her past. To a time when she did go out and enjoy herself. Her scar burned as though it had been seared there for the first time. Her failure branded into her skin. An image of a netball match on a hard court next to a council housing estate floated into her mind. Teenage girls laughing, cheating, trying to turn it into a basketball game. Bernie blowing her referee's whistle every five seconds. The glowing face of a girl who scored her very first goal. Laughter that turned to screams later that night. A girl's face morphing into a death mask. She pressed her nails into her palms and brought herself back to the present.

Bernie was conscious of Anderson next to her – from the way he blew across his mug to cool the tea, to the creases in his trousers. There was something contained about him. She thought he was probably holding in his thoughts on the earlier events of the evening.

'So it looks as though Derek Hayes used to be quite a naughty boy.' Anderson pointed to the laptop screen. 'Shoplifting, joy-riding, possession of drugs.'

'Doesn't explain the abduction though.'

'No.' Anderson yawned. 'Sorry, ma'am. It's been a long day. I'm sure the tea will kick in soon. It's going to be hard with us both looking at one screen. Would it make more sense to email me the file too?'

'Hmm. Probably. But you have to delete it later. Hang on.' Bernie opened her email and forwarded the case notes to Anderson. 'You take the initial police report and I'll focus on witness statements.'

Anderson leaned back into the sofa, phone in hand. 'Sure.'

Bernie turned back to the screen. There were plenty of witness statements to read through.

Her eyes were drooping when a name jumped out at her. 'Oh my God.' She read through the witness statement once and then again. 'Anderson. Have a look at this. Now I know why Lesley

Cooper stood up in church. She's Sophie Newell's aunt. But more than that – she was Derek's alibi. Oh God! No wonder she hasn't returned my call. I should have seen her on Sunday.' Bernie rested her head in her hand. 'Oh God, what have I done? If I'd seen her Derek might still be alive. Anderson?'

She looked at Anderson. He was sound asleep, his lips slightly parted. She thought about waking him but what was the point? They couldn't do anything right now. It was the middle of the night. And she didn't want to admit to more mistakes on her part. She grabbed a throw from another mismatched chair and gently placed it over him. She stared at the screen for a couple more minutes then closed down her laptop. She would face the mess in the morning. Maybe it would be a better idea to have DCI Worth take over.

Bernie stood. Tiredness hit her like a giant wave. She stumbled into her bedroom and crashed onto the bed, fully clothed. She was asleep in seconds.

I wake in a sweat, the dream still playing like a movie in front of my eyes. I'm running along a cliff in a storm. I'm screaming 'Stop!' but thunder swallows my unheard words. Lightning crackles and for a split second I see them on the edge. I run forward but the wind and rain whip at me and propel me back. Another flash makes the night as bright as day and they are gone.

I sit on the end of her bed, watching her sleep. Her little chest moving up and down. Up and down. I thought the dreams would stop now I have what I wanted but no. I feel sick to my stomach. So many things are swirling in my head. So many thoughts. So many images. So many voices. I clap my hands over my ears and shut my eyes tight. But they don't stop. They keep coming. My heart is thumping so hard I fear it will burst. I throw open a window and gasp the cool night air. It doesn't help. I watch her breathe again. Up. Down. Up. Down. Slowly, my breathing begins to match hers until we're in sync. We're meant to be together. No one else can understand her like me. No one else can have her.

CHAPTER TWENTY-TWO

Wednesday

'Wakey, wakey. It's six thirty.'

Bernie stirred, momentarily confused as to why a Scottish man was in her flat. Then she remembered – Anderson. She turned over, hastily wiping away a trail of dribble.

'I've got a coffee for you, ma'am. I don't know if you'd realised but your tea is decaf. No wonder we couldn't stay awake.'

Bernie pushed herself up and took the mug. 'Thanks.' She didn't want to think about how she looked.

'Did you find out anything else last night?'

Bernie nodded. It was awkward having Anderson in her room. She was grateful she was still in her clothes, and that her dirty laundry was in the washing basket for a change. 'There are a few things. We'll talk about them at the briefing later. I'm sure you want to go home and get showered and changed.' She wasn't ready to confess her stuff-up just yet.

'So, you're not offering me breakfast then, ma'am?' He raised his eyebrows, a wry smile on his face.

Bernie thought of her virtually empty food cupboard. 'Cheeky. No. You'll have to wait and see what the bakery sends.'

She took a mouthful of coffee as he left the room.

He turned back. 'By the way, ma'am, you might want to do something with your hair.'

Bernie pushed herself off the bed as she heard the front door shut, and headed to the bathroom. She looked in the mirror. Her hair, in desperate need of some treatment, was sticking out all over the place. And there was still the sickly-sweet vomit smell to deal with.

'Oh shit.'

'Right, listen up, people. Grab a yum-yum from the bakery box if you haven't had one already. You're going to need all the sugar you can get today. And then sit down and shut up!'

Bernie surveyed the room. The team had shrunk again from the beginning of the week. The super stood at the back. She knew this was her last chance to win him over. Slowly, the noise in the room simmered down.

'I think it's pretty fair to say that things have taken a shocking turn. I'm sure you've all heard Derek Cole died last night. Looks like suicide but we'll leave that for the pathologist and coroner to decide. However, we've also discovered he'd changed his name at some point. He'd previously been known as Derek Hayes and he had form.' Bernie clicked on her laptop and Derek's record appeared on the white screen. 'Minor things to begin with but in 1990, a five-year-old girl called Sophie Newell went missing in Marchant. Hayes was the main suspect but there wasn't enough evidence to charge him. He disappeared after he was released. Now, this could be a complete coincidence and not related to Molly's abduction, but I don't think so.'

Bernie looked at her team and their stunned faces. They needed to move past their shock and get back into action.

'It's now Wednesday, five days since Molly went missing. This is a new lead and we have to throw everything we have at it. Kerry, I'm scaling back the search to just uniform. I want you here with Matt going through the original Sophie Newell case.

Use that criminology degree of yours, Matt. What was missed over twenty-five years ago?'

Bernie steeled herself and looked at Anderson. He was sitting with a pen in his hand, ready to take notes. 'DS Anderson, you know the house better than anyone here. I want you to lead a thorough search at the Coles'. Before, we were looking for Molly herself and didn't find anything. We now need to look at Derek's life in detail. Focus initially on the garage and his bedroom and then spread out to the other rooms.'

'Yes, ma'am.'

'You can have some uniform to help you.'

She glanced at the super and he gave her a nod of approval. She needed to make sure everyone knew what they were doing.

'Forensic results are due in this afternoon on the buggy and strand of hair that was found by the railway line. I'm going to see Jessica and Davy later this morning to find out how much Jessica knows about her father's past. Given her reaction last night, I have a feeling she knows nothing. I'm also going to see a family member of Sophie Newell's. There's still one in the area.'

Bernie knew she was glossing over her mistake. She glanced at her watch. 'Right, it's coming up to eight fifteen. I want "check-ins" every four hours, please, earlier if you find anything. Any questions?'

Matt raised his hand. 'Ma'am, there were a couple of calls to Crimestoppers overnight that are worth listening to.'

'OK, if you can set that up, Matt. Kerry – go and find the original case papers. Anderson, choose three officers for the search. The CSIs will meet you there to finish processing the garage. The rest of you, please go downstairs to Sergeant Turner and he will allot you areas to search. Off you go. Remember, check in at twelve fifteen hours, or before if you find anything.'

Chairs scraped the floor as officers began to move and chatter filled the air. Wilson made his way over to Bernie.

'You look tired. Did you get any sleep?' he asked.

'A little. I was looking at the case at home. You only told me not to go into the office.'

'I told you to sleep, not work. So you decided to not mention the deadline for solving this?'

'They're under enough pressure as it is. No point adding to it. I'll bear the brunt of that.'

'Well, we're keeping Derek Cole's death under wraps for the moment. The press will go berserk when they find out everything and they will, eventually. Someone will talk.'

Bernie shook her head. 'Not from Otterfield, they won't. They won't talk to anyone. That's the whole damn problem. At least now we're beginning to find out why.'

Wilson nodded. 'If I can stall DCI Worth coming in then I will. But you have to get me something, Bernie, and fast.'

'OK, it's all set up to listen to. I'll just press play.'

Bernie and Matt sat in an interview room, away from the bustle of the rest of the station. Matt had the tape from Crimestoppers.

'Oh, hello, my name is Ellie Du Plessis and I was asked to ring a Matt Taylor at the station but I've lost the number. I'm staying at Pear Tree Farm...'

Bernie reached over and pressed the pause button. 'Is that a South African accent?'

Matt nodded. 'Sounds like it and I think Du Plessis is an Afrikaans name.'

'Hmm, so the cyclist is from SA then. Let's hear the rest.' She pressed play.

'...and Naomi who owns it said the police wanted to know if I saw anything suspicious last Friday with that little girl who's gone missing. Oh shame, man, sorry, I didn't notice anything. I really hope you find her.'

Matt pressed pause. 'So it looks as though she can't help us at all.'

Bernie tapped her fingers on the table. 'Well, we can cross her off the list for potential witnesses, not that we really have any. Next one.'

There was a crackling noise to begin with and then a muffled female voice spoke.

'Er, I don't want to give my name and I don't want to talk to anyone at the station. I saw a man last week in Otterfield, a man I didn't recognise. He was hanging around the school gates during the day and looked a bit suspicious. He walked off as I approached him. He was white, in his late thirties, early forties with light brown hair. He was quite tall and he was wearing jeans and a black jacket. That's all I can tell you. Please don't ask me to come forward. I hope you find her.'

Bernie bit her thumbnail. She glanced across to Matt.

'What are you thinking, ma'am?'

'I'm wondering if that's Paula Parker. I asked Eddie to talk to her about the Coles. Do we have a telephone number or was it blocked?'

Matt smiled. 'It was the pay phone in Otterfield. For both of them, in fact.'

'Both? That's surprising. Mind you, it's the second one I'm more interested in.'

'Yes, me too. There's something not quite right about it. I think it's a woman but it's quite muffled. She's obviously trying to disguise her voice. I'd like to send it for analysis.'

'What? How much is that going to cost? And we don't have time anyway.'

'But ma'am, I know some guys from uni who have set up their own lab to do this kind of work. They're specialising in audio and visual stuff – you know, audio tapes, cleaning up CCTV images. They've even got a forensic artist. They're based in south

Birmingham so they can get a courier down to us. They'll make it top priority.'

Bernie rolled her eyes at Matt. 'You've already spoken to them, without checking with me first. Matt, we really don't have time to waste on this.'

'They have the most up-to-date equipment. It won't be as long as you think.'

Bernie rested her head in her hand. Lack of sleep was creeping up on her and she didn't have the energy to argue with him. 'Matt, you don't understand, I only have until Friday to solve this. After that, DCI Worth is taking over the investigation.'

Matt sat back in his chair. 'Shit. He's awful.'

'He's the only DCI in the whole of the county who can take it on.'

Matt sighed. 'Ma'am, you know me, I always follow the evidence rather than my gut. But there's something about that message – I just can't put my finger on it but I know people who can. If it takes too long and proves to be fruitless then it will be DCI Worth who'll have to foot the bill. I think I can get it cheaper anyway.'

Bernie raised her head slightly to look at Matt. He always reminded her of a puppy with his floppy brown hair, eager to please. She suddenly felt very tired, the fight falling out of her.

'Go on, then. Ring them and organise the courier. I'm going to make myself a very strong cup of coffee and eat any yum-yums that are left. I need energy, desperately.'

'And then are you going to see this family member of Sophie Newell's? Who is it?'

Bernie pushed herself up from the desk. 'Someone who I should have spoken to on Sunday when I had the opportunity. If I had, maybe Derek would still be alive and able to answer our questions. Sophie Newell's aunt – Lesley Cooper.'

CHAPTER TWENTY-THREE

Bernie sensed a warmth come over her as she drove into Marchant. The atmosphere was so different from Otterfield. She loved this village and its inhabitants. They greeted each other with smiles and quite a few had already waved to her. She drew up outside Lesley Cooper's terraced cottage. Bernie let her eyes drift to the cottage next door with its For Sale sign outside. She couldn't believe no one had bought it after five months on the market. It was her little dream home, the only house she'd seen that made her want to stay in Wiltshire. But it was beyond her price range. If anyone ever suggested to her that the police earn too much money, she would show them her payslip. Her mother had mentioned there might be a small inheritance from her grandfather but Bernie wasn't sure it would be enough for a deposit. She felt bad she hadn't contacted her family again. And the condolence card was still sitting in a drawer in her desk. She still hadn't spoken to the super about it.

She got out of the car. The sun was beginning to make an appearance from behind the clouds. The trees by the pub were in full blossom, alternating pinks and whites. She looked towards Lesley's cottage and thought she saw movement at the curtains. She took a deep breath and walked down the path of the small, manicured garden. The door opened before she got there.

'Hello, Bernie. I thought it was you.'

Bernie looked closely at Lesley. She didn't know her well but sometimes saw her in the pub. Her mousy hair was lank and her skin dull. She wasn't wearing any make-up which was unusual for Lesley. She was normally so well turned out.

'Hello, Lesley. I've been meaning to come and see you since Sunday. I called a couple of times.'

Lesley nodded, a sad look on her face. 'I know. Sorry. Come in. Do you want a cuppa?'

'Maybe just a glass of water, thanks.'

Lesley showed Bernie into the lounge. 'Take a seat.'

Bernie looked round the room. It had pink stripy wallpaper. There were very few personal items – no photos, just ornaments. There was a vague hint of vanilla, probably from a plug-in air freshener somewhere, which tickled her nose. She sank into the dark green sofa. She wasn't sure if it was meant to be that soft or if some of the springs were gone. It didn't look particularly new so she decided on the latter. The carpet had a swirly pattern with various shades of oranges and browns. Lesley was in her fifties but the decor still felt too old for her somehow.

'Here you are and I've brought some biscuits too. I bet you're hardly eating at the moment.'

Lesley sat down in a hard-looking armchair.

Bernie reached for a chocolate digestive. 'Well, I am eating but all the wrong things. One of the bakeries in Devizes is giving us breakfast each day at the moment. Still, I'm managing to burn it off.' She took a bite and waited to see if Lesley would broach the subject first. It was a tactic she often employed. It paid off.

'I'm sorry I didn't call back. You've come about Sophie, haven't you?' Lesley said.

Bernie nodded. She had some water to wash down the biscuit crumbs. 'Why don't you tell me about it? I've only read the bare minimum so far.'

Lesley gripped the arms of her armchair. 'You know, I have this… air about me. Everyone thinks of me as happy, an optimist, glass half-full – despite everything that's happened.' She paused.

Bernie looked at Lesley's face. It was true; even as a relative newcomer she'd gained that impression. Lesley let go of the chair and started wringing her hands.

'It's only when I'm at home on my own that I can really be me. Let the old misery guts out.' She gave a half-hearted laugh.

'You don't have any photos up.'

'No. Not on display. It's too painful, see. But I have photos in albums upstairs that I go through from time to time. I haven't forgotten. Not once.'

Bernie tried to sit forward to reach out to Lesley but the sofa was determined to swallow her. 'Can you tell me how it all started?'

'Well, I was the rebellious second child. Karen was nine years older. Married with two children – Steven and Sophie. Steven was ten and Sophie five at the time. I was very immature for my age, really. Still doing stupid things even though I was twenty-six. Didn't make the best choices when it came to men. Quite liked the bad boys. Which is why I was attracted so much to Derek Hayes. He made me think we'd conquer the world. Bloody stupid. And he loved the kids. Always playing football with Steven and giving Sophie piggybacks. Of course, Karen didn't approve. I put it down to jealousy at the time. Derek was a very good-looking man back then. Certainly charmed me into his bed.'

Bernie finished her biscuit before speaking. 'What happened with Sophie?'

Lesley stared ahead, looking at the blank TV screen, as though she could see her memories playing on it.

'He really loved Sophie. She even called him Uncle Derek. I guess I thought we'd get married. You know, I could have taken it if it had been another woman or even another man.' She laughed, painfully. 'But a child! He only wanted me to get to *her*. It was her he wanted.' Tears started to fall down Lesley's face.

'Lesley, what happened?'

She turned her head to Bernie. 'He took her. That's what happened.' She sobbed.

Bernie waited for her to continue.

'It was a beautiful, sunny summer's day,' said Lesley. 'The kind of day you should be out enjoying the weather, not in bed with your lover. But we were here, in this house, in my room. My parents were away so we were making the most of it.' She sucked in her lip. 'And it was good. He was good. It was the happiest I've ever been in my life.'

Lesley paused. Bernie had no intention of interrupting, knowing that dredging up the past was an incredibly painful experience for anyone.

'I hadn't planned for us to get up. I wanted to stay in bed all day. But Derek had brought his dog with him and he was whining, so he took him for a walk. I fell asleep.' Lesley shook her head. 'I have no idea what time he went or when he came back. But it must have been a few hours because I slept for a long time. We'd been up half the night, drinking and having sex. God, we were like rabbits.' Lesley blushed as she glanced quickly at Bernie. 'Sorry, that's probably too much information.'

Bernie felt a wry smile form on her lips as she thought about her own past lovers. 'Don't worry, carry on.'

'I was woken by the phone. It was Karen. She was frantic. Said she couldn't find Sophie anywhere. She'd been playing in the field nearest their house but was gone. So I went over there to try and help find her. Karen had already called the police and they were on their way. We searched for hours but she was just gone. Nowhere to be found.' Lesley flung her hands up and then covered her face as tears began to fall again.

Bernie released herself from the sofa's grip and passed a tissue box that was next to her over to Lesley. 'Just take your time. There's no rush.'

Lesley pulled her hands away abruptly and took a tissue. 'And now there's another child missing – his granddaughter. How could he do that to his own flesh and blood?'

Bernie reached across and patted Lesley's arm. 'We'll get to Molly in a minute. Just tell me about Sophie.'

Lesley blew her nose noisily and wiped her tears with her hand. She nodded. 'When I finally got back here, Derek was already in. Before I could even say anything about Sophie, he started going on about losing the dog in the woods, how he'd tripped over something, and he was all dirty and scratched. He'd found the dog eventually, somewhere.' Lesley glanced up at the ceiling. 'And I remember thinking as he told me, *Sod the bloody dog – we've lost Sophie*. And when I got a chance to speak, that's exactly what I said. We've lost Sophie. And he was shocked. Genuinely shocked. I had no reason to doubt him. He went back with me to Karen and Bill's to help look after Steven. It was starting to get late by then so they called off the search. The next day, everyone came to help. There were so many people.'

'Even from Otterfield?' Bernie asked.

'Oh God, yes. We used to take Sophie over to Derek's mum and dad all the time. Everyone in Otterfield knew Sophie. Wait here a minute. I'll get you a photo.'

As Lesley went upstairs, Bernie pulled out her phone. There were no text messages or emails. There was another hour and a half before check-in at twelve fifteen.

'Here we go,' said Lesley, as she came back into the room. 'This was the last school photo – well, it was the only school photo of them both together. Sophie was in reception and Steven in year five.'

Lesley passed the photo to Bernie, who looked at the smiling pair – Steven with a protective arm around his sister's shoulder. Sophie had twinkly blue eyes, a fringe and two blonde plaits with red ribbons matching her red and white checked school dress. Bernie thought there was a mischievous look about her. She looked at Steven. There was a more sombre look in his blue eyes and his light brown hair was short and swept to the side. His smile was awkward, his lips tight. Each of them had a slightly turned-up nose like Lesley. The photo made her want to smile and cry at the same time.

'Did they get on?' asked Bernie.

'Oh yes. Well, I say that. They did fight, like all siblings do, you know.'

'Actually, I don't know, I'm an only child. Tell me more about them.'

Lesley sank back down into the armchair. 'Steven would tease her from time to time but really he was wrapped round her little finger. She called him Stevie. "Stevie, do this, Stevie, do that" and he did.' Lesley nodded her head, grimly. 'It was Steven who found her teddy bear. He insisted on going on the search with his father.'

'When and where?' asked Bernie.

'The day after. It was under a bush. He caught sight of it somehow.'

Bernie flicked her head up quickly and reached into her jacket pocket for her notepad and pen. 'Under a bush? Actually placed there or just dropped? Do you know where exactly?'

Lesley shook her head. 'In the woods somewhere. I wasn't there, I was with another search party so I don't know. I suppose she might have dropped it. But she did like hide and seek. They found dog hairs on the teddy which matched with Derek's dog. But because we were often with Sophie they couldn't prove that the hairs were recent. And a witness thought she had seen Derek with a child answering the description for Sophie but she couldn't pick him out of a line-up.'

'And you gave him an alibi,' said Bernie.

Lesley paused before whispering, 'Yes.' She looked down at the floor. 'I'm very ashamed of myself. At the time I really didn't think he had done it and I didn't know what time he'd left the house.'

'Lesley, I have no interest in charging you for perverting the course of justice. I simply want to find Molly. When did you realise Derek was responsible?'

'After he was released without charge. He simply left. He wrote a letter to me explaining he couldn't stay with all the gossip, that it wasn't fair on his parents to have a slur on their good name.' She paused. 'He didn't ask me to go with him. He didn't even say that he loved me. He just left and I knew then, in my heart, he'd taken her.'

'But you didn't know for certain? It was a feeling rather than fact.'

Lesley nodded. She rested her head on her hand and stared at the carpet.

'What happened to the rest of your family? You're the only one left here.'

Lesley twisted her head to look at Bernie. 'Karen and Bill managed to hold on until Steven was eighteen, then they drove to Beachy Head and jumped off the cliff together.'

Bernie willed her face to not show shock but her heart beat it out instead. She swallowed before speaking again. 'And Steven?'

'He sold up and went and joined the Royal Navy. I've not heard from him since. My parents died ten years ago, a few months apart. None of us ever recovered from Sophie.'

Bernie looked up from her notes. 'I'm beginning to understand why no one wanted to help with the search. Your communities must have been destroyed by this.' She hesitated. 'Did you receive any backlash for giving Derek an alibi?'

Lesley looked down but nodded. 'Yes, to begin with. Especially Karen. She never forgave me.' She glanced up. 'That was the hardest thing of all. Knowing I wasn't forgiven by her. I was in pieces after her and Bill's deaths. People round here were kinder after that.'

'I'm sorry to have to ask this but where were you last Friday afternoon?'

Lesley sighed a little. 'Don't be sorry, you're only doing your job. I was working at the charity shop in town. I'm there every Friday and there was another assistant plus customers. They can vouch I was there from ten until five thirty. To be honest, I didn't even know Derek was back. I don't go to Otterfield any more. And I don't talk to anyone from there either. It was only when I saw the press conference on TV last Saturday that I realised. I had absolutely no idea before that. The name was different but I knew him, even with that beard. I was in the pub with the rest of the village, waiting to join the search. As soon as I recognised him, I left. I must have been seen and the others quickly followed. I'm sorry. It wasn't my intention to derail the search party.'

Bernie nodded. 'I know. It was very brave of you to stand up in church.'

Lesley shook her head. 'If I'd been brave, I wouldn't have given him an alibi all those years ago, or I would have returned your phone calls. I know your priority is to find Molly but will you ask him what he did with Sophie? You won't let him get away with it again, will you? I'll retract my alibi. I had thought about storming over to his house but I didn't want to upset his daughter. I know how desperate it is to have a missing child. But I need to know where Sophie is. I need to bury her with her parents. I need to have justice, I need to have closure.'

Bernie looked into Lesley's pleading eyes. 'I'm very sorry, Lesley, but I won't be able to do that. Derek won't be answering any questions. He killed himself last night.'

CHAPTER TWENTY-FOUR

Bernie closed Lesley's door quietly behind her. She hated leaving her in such a state but she had no choice. She had to go and see Jessica and Davy at the vicarage. At least Sue from the pub had come over to stay with Lesley. Bernie would need a statement from her at some point but it could wait.

She started to walk down the path when she heard a noise behind her. She turned to see a smartly dressed young man coming out of the empty property next door. She pulled out her warrant card and walked back towards him.

'Excuse me, can I ask what you're doing?' Bernie asked.

The young man looked up and jumped when he saw Bernie's ID. He held up some keys and a pile of post.

'I'm the estate agent looking after the property. I just came to get the post and make sure everything's OK. I've got someone interested in viewing it.'

Bernie's heart sank a little. She knew someone would buy her dream cottage one day.

'Would you like to see it?' He reached into a pocket and pulled out a card. He handed it to Bernie. 'Take it, just in case you want to see it or any other property.'

'Oh, um, I can't really afford to move at the moment. I don't have a big enough deposit.' She took the card and read the name 'Alex Murray'.

'Well, we have a mortgage broker who can help with things like that. It might not be as bad as you think. We could take a look now, if you like. Come on, you know you want to. Your face dropped when I said someone else wanted to see it.'

Bernie looked at Alex Murray. He reminded her of Matt. Not as tall but just as eager to please. He seemed nicer than most estate agents she'd met in the past.

'You've just taken this property on, haven't you?'

Alex smiled. 'Oh God. Is it that obvious? I only started working here last month and I was given this one to shift.' He wrinkled his nose up. 'Are you sure I can't tempt you to have a quick peek?'

Bernie laughed. 'I've already seen inside, thank you.'

'Oh, you've already had a viewing with another agent.'

'Erm, not exactly. It wasn't on the market when I was in there.'

'Oh… oh.' Alex looked slightly perplexed. 'Did you know the late owner?'

'A little bit. I met her in an official capacity. She was the victim of a particularly nasty mugging at the end of last year. She passed away not long after. She had cancer.'

Alex put his hand to his head. 'Of course. I thought you looked familiar. You're the officer looking for the missing girl. You were on TV last weekend.'

Bernie nodded. 'Yes, and if you don't mind, I do need to get on, especially now I know you're not a burglar.' She held his card out back to him.

'No, keep it. You never know when you might need to come and see me. And if there's anything we can do to help with finding the little girl, then please just say. I know we have a poster up in the window.'

'Thanks.' Bernie put the card in her jacket pocket and walked down the path. Alex seemed nice enough but now wasn't the time to be thinking about buying her dream cottage.

The morning was warming up as she walked round the corner to the church and the vicarage. The scent of early sweet peas wafted in the air. She wanted to smile at the beauty of the spring day but it felt like a betrayal of Lesley, Jessica and Davy to be happy. Her phone buzzed in her pocket. She pulled it out to see a text from Anderson.

Found a suicide note. Just says, 'I'm doing this for Molly.' Bagged it. Will bring it later.

Bernie sighed sadly. She remembered the words Derek had said to her a couple of days before – 'I would die for that girl.' She texted a quick reply of thanks and then put her phone in her pocket as she reached the vicarage. The downstairs curtains were open but upstairs were still shut. She thought it best to knock quietly.

Anna opened the door with a sleeping Sam on her shoulder.

'Hi,' she said softly. 'I thought we'd see you soon. Jessica is asleep. I persuaded her to take a herbal sleep remedy about four o'clock this morning. She's in a terrible state. Come through to the kitchen. Davy and Paul are in there. Do you want some coffee? Anything to eat?'

Bernie put her hand to her stomach. It was beginning to complain from all the rubbish food she'd been eating. 'Maybe an apple if you have one please. I think my stomach is starting a revolution against my eating habits.'

Anna grinned. 'I'm sure we can spare an apple.'

Bernie stepped into the kitchen and felt she was stepping back in time. Although the appliances were new, the cupboards were circa 1970s with frosted glass sliding doors. Very retro.

Davy and Paul Bentley were sat round a wooden table. Both men had mugs and Davy had two slices of toast on a plate. His dishevelled hair and the stubble on his face suggested he hadn't been up long. Bernie sat in the chair opposite.

'Hi, Davy. How are you this morning?'

When Davy raised his head, his eyes were bloodshot. He clearly hadn't slept.

'It's all a bit shit, isn't it? Sorry, vicar, didn't mean to swear,' Davy said.

Paul Bentley smiled. 'You can say whatever you want. We won't be offended in the least.'

Bernie sighed. 'You're right, Davy. It's completely and utterly shit. And I hate the fact I have to be here now and ask you and Jessica lots of questions. My priority is to find Molly. Otherwise I wouldn't intrude on you at this time.'

Davy sniffed and wiped his nose on the sleeve of his jumper. He lowered his eyes. 'I know.'

Bernie pulled out her notepad and pen. 'Let's start with you telling me what you know about Derek.'

Davy took a swig from his mug. 'Well, I first met Derek about six years ago. Me and Jess had been going out for a few months – we'd met at a party in Bristol. She was living with him at the time and I had to go and tell him I'd got his daughter pregnant. Oh God, I was terrified. Thought he was going to kill me. He probably would have done if I was smaller.' Davy half smiled at the memory. 'But I told him I'd look after Jess and that I wanted to marry her. We've been engaged ever since. And he was all right. Really supportive. I'd only just joined the army so Jess carried on living with him and had Molly. But it wasn't ideal. Her room was small. I tried to get accommodation at the barracks but couldn't for ages. Eventually we got a house and lived together for a bit before I had to go on tour. We should have got married last year but Jess got pregnant with Sam and she didn't want to have fat wedding photos. She struggled living at the camp and Derek knew that. Said he had a wedding present for us – the house in Otterfield.

It seemed ideal. I could still get to camp and Derek would stay when I was away. It needed work but he did all of that. Look, I don't know what you've got on Derek but he's been a really good granddad to Molly and Sam and really supportive of Jessica. She doesn't get on with her mum at all.'

'No, that's because she's a bitch.'

Bernie looked up and saw Jessica standing in the doorway. 'You're awake. I'm glad you got some sleep,' she said to the young woman. Her hair was as unkempt as Davy's and Bernie was quite sure Jessica hadn't washed all week – stale sweat and baby sick lingered around her.

Paul Bentley stood up. 'Here, Jessica, take my seat. Would you like some tea or coffee? Something to eat?'

Jessica shook her head.

'You need to have something,' said Anna, 'for this little one's sake at least.'

Sam stirred as he was passed into his mother's arms and he immediately started to root around.

'Do you mind?' asked Jessica.

'Not at all, go ahead and feed him. I just won't do the burping for you this time.' Bernie half grinned but the joke was lost on Jessica.

'So, Jess, tell me about your dad and why your mum's a bitch.'

Jessica made sure Sam was settled and latched on before she spoke. 'My mother's Spanish. I was born there. Dad went for a holiday, met my mum and decided to stay for a while. She got pregnant with me so Dad had to marry her very quickly. He wasn't given much choice really. They ran a bar in Marbella. It was good for quite a while but they weren't particularly suited.' A greasy strand of hair fell onto her face. She pushed it back and sighed. 'If they hadn't had me I'm sure they wouldn't have married. I was a real Daddy's girl which my mother hated. They lasted until I was sixteen then they separated and divorced. I was supposed to stay in Spain with my mum but she's really bossy and controlling. Dad said I could come for a holiday but Mum wouldn't let me. So when I was eighteen, I packed my bags, left Spain and came over here to Dad. And I haven't been back since.' Jessica wiped her eyes. 'I can't believe he'd leave me like this.'

Bernie wrote a few things down and then looked up at Jessica. 'Do you know what year your father went to Spain?'

'Nineteen ninety. Some time in the summer. I don't know when exactly.'

'Would your mother know?'

Jessica rolled her eyes. 'I guess so. But I'm not ringing her. Not after last night.'

'Can you tell me what you were talking about?'

Jessica paused. 'She… she was saying some really awful things about Dad, about his past.'

Bernie put her pen down. 'Jessica, do you remember what I told you last night about Derek?'

Jess started to cry, her body heaving as the sobs increased.

'Did your mother tell you the same thing?'

Jess raised her hand to her mouth but she couldn't stifle her tears. 'Oh God, oh God. He did it, didn't he? He did it.'

Bernie had the window down as she drove along the winding country lanes back to Devizes. The sun had made her car stuffy and she needed a slight chill on her face to keep her awake. She wondered if Jessica and Davy would ever be able to come through this. She thought of Sophie's parents who had never recovered, who couldn't even bear to stay alive for their son's sake. Would Sam endure the same fate as Steven Newell?

On the seat next to her was the photo of Steven and Sophie and the apple that she hadn't eaten at the vicarage. Jessica had been in too much of a state to answer any more questions about her father but Bernie now had a number for her mother. She had a feeling that the former Mrs Cole would only be too happy to dish the dirt on her ex-husband.

It looked as though Matt and Kerry were drowning under paperwork when Bernie walked into MCIT.

'Oh God. How much have you got through?' Bernie asked.

'Not nearly enough,' said Kerry. 'I know we should start at the beginning but we've skipped straight through to the transcripts of Derek Hayes' interviews. He was a slippery one. Stuck to the one statement that he'd been with Sophie's aunt, Lesley Cooper, and then taken his dog for a walk. Everything else was no comment. Was it Lesley you saw?'

Bernie pulled up a chair. 'Yes, and she's now willing to retract her alibi. She doesn't know what time he left her house. Obviously, when she told me she didn't know Derek was dead. She still hoped for justice. Closure is the best we can offer her now.' Bernie pulled out her notepad. 'I have a telephone number for Derek Hayes' ex-wife in Spain. She and Jessica were arguing on the phone last night when I got there. Apparently, Jessica's mother was saying some terrible things about Derek. We need to know what she knows. I don't know how good her English is, though, as Jessica was speaking Spanish to her.'

Kerry held out her hand. 'I speak Spanish. Number please.'

'Yeah, but how good is your Spanish? We might need something more advanced than GCSE.'

Kerry raised her eyebrows. 'I got an A in my A-level Spanish, thank you very much. And I worked in Spain as a travel rep for three years before joining the police. I think I'll manage. Number.'

Bernie found the relevant page in her notepad. '*Voilà!*'

'That's French.'

They both laughed as Kerry walked over to Bernie's desk.

'So, Matt, has the courier arrived yet for the tapes?'

Matt glanced at his watch. 'Yeah, came about forty minutes ago.'

'Damn.' Bernie huffed.

'Why? What's wrong?'

Bernie held up the photo of Steven and Sophie.

'That's Sophie Newell. There's a photo in the file but not that one,' said Matt.

'Yeah. You said your super-duper guys have a forensic artist.'

'Yes, they do.'

'I want an age progression on Steven.'

Matt pushed back his floppy hair. 'Oh God, ma'am, that could take a while.'

'I don't need all the different variations. What did our telephone witness say? A man in late thirties, early forties with light brown hair. Steven Newell was ten at the time which would make him around the right age.'

'It's a bit tenuous. Where is he?'

'Lesley Cooper doesn't know. He left after his parents killed themselves. They couldn't cope with Sophie's disappearance.'

'Shit. I didn't know that. God. That would give him motive.'

'And there's something else,' said Bernie. 'Steven found Sophie's teddy bear – under a bush. Lesley didn't know if it had been dropped or deliberately placed there. We'll need to check the records.'

Matt's eyes met Bernie's with a knowing look. 'Under a bush? Like the fleece and the buggy? OK. Give me the photo. I'll scan it and email it to them. I'll ask for their best shot. I'll check the case notes for the teddy bear. Then I'll start searching for Steven Newell.'

'Lesley thought he joined the Royal Navy when he was eighteen, so around 1998.'

'I'm on it.'

Bernie glanced at her watch. It was almost twelve fifteen. Nearly time for check-in.

Bernie sat down in front of DCS Wilson. He raised his eyes.

'So, where are we up to?'

'The Sophie Newell case seems to be our best lead so far. Sophie's aunt, Lesley Cooper, had been Derek's alibi but she's now retracted it. Sophie had an older brother, Steven. He was ten at the time. His parents never recovered from Sophie and killed themselves when he was eighteen. It's one hell of a motive for revenge.'

'Hmm, maybe. Do we have any idea where he is now?'

'Lesley said he joined the Royal Navy in 1998. She hasn't heard from him since.'

Wilson leaned forward in his chair. 'It's a possibility. Of course, there are alternatives, Bernie. Derek Hayes may not have worked alone and his partner may be back. Or it could still be completely random.'

Bernie shook her head. 'I think it's unlikely, sir. DS Anderson has found a suicide note saying Derek was doing this for Molly. Hopefully he'll find more evidence. I'm going over after this. And I'm waiting on Forensics for results this afternoon on the buggy and the hair we found. Kerry's trying to make contact with Derek's ex-wife as well. There were a few things she told Jessica that sound interesting. We're definitely moving forward.'

Wilson scratched his face. 'Good, but be cautious with the ex-wife. She may have an axe to grind and effectively it's hearsay.'

'Maybe. But as an ex-wife, I think she'll be more likely to spill some family secrets.'

CHAPTER TWENTY-FIVE

Bernie pulled up outside Jessica and Davy's house. A CSI van and Anderson's car were in the driveway. A few curtains twitched from the neighbours as she got out. She contemplated knocking on their doors to see if any of them would speak to her but knew they wouldn't.

The PC on the door nodded at her as she went into the house.

'DS Anderson?'

'Up here, ma'am.'

Bernie followed the voice up the stairs and into a small back bedroom. The decor was neutral – magnolia walls and beige carpet.

'Oh, this is small for a grown man.'

Anderson was down on his hands and knees, searching under the bed. One uniformed officer was rifling through clothes in a wardrobe. Anderson knelt back up.

'Ma'am.' He gave her a quick smile. Bernie found herself smiling back. Anderson was growing on her.

'Where are the other two officers?'

'One should be on the door and the other is helping the CSIs in the garage. We can't all fit in here anyway.'

'Yes, it's a bit of a squeeze. Surely not all his stuff's here? Is the rest in the garage?'

'Some, and in his flat in Bristol. He still had that. He'd been living here more since just before Sam was born. I'd like to go to the flat later if need be. I have all his keys.'

Bernie glanced round the small room. There was just room for a bed, a wardrobe and a small chest of drawers, in matching light oak veneer. 'Yes, of course. You said you'd found a suicide note.'

'Yes, it's downstairs on the table. We're gathering evidence there.'

Bernie went first down the stairs. Anderson was close behind and she was sure his fingers had brushed her back.

They went into the lounge and then through to the dining room. She saw on the table a few bags of evidence, including a mobile phone and a tablet.

'What about a laptop or computer?'

Anderson shook his head. 'Not for Derek but Jessica has one. Do you think we should take it?'

'Did you ever see him use it?'

'No, he only used his tablet.'

Bernie tapped her fingers on the table. 'Take it. You never know. Right, suicide note.'

Anderson pulled a bagged piece of paper towards him. 'It's here. It was found in the garage on a work bench. We have photos in situ.'

Bernie reached out and picked it up. She read aloud, '"I'm doing this for Molly".' It was all in capitals. She glanced up to the ceiling and looked for cracks before allowing her eyes to meet Anderson's.

'Bit short and sweet. Why didn't he just come to us? He knew something.'

Anderson sucked in his lips. 'I don't know, ma'am. Maybe I wasn't the right person for the job this week. Maybe Sergeant Turner would have been better for Derek.'

Bernie sighed. 'You can't blame yourself. None of us can. I'm beginning to understand now why the residents haven't been helping. He'd shamed the village. They thought it was retribution.'

Anderson's face flushed with anger. 'But it's not Molly's fault.'

'No, of course not. I'm just saying I get it now, not that it's right.'

A shout came from upstairs. 'Ma'am, sir.'

'Yes?' replied Anderson.

'You need to see this.'

They both ran up the stairs.

'What have you found?' asked Anderson.

The young officer held an envelope in one gloved hand and a letter in another. 'It was taped to the underside of one of the drawers,' he said.

'Can I see?' asked Bernie. Anderson passed her a pair of gloves. She put them on and then took the letter. She took a sharp intake of breath as she read the words.

'What does it say?' asked Anderson.

Bernie breathed out heavily and read the typed note. '"An eye for an eye, A tooth for a tooth, A child for a child, A life for a life." The law of retaliation. Well, a paraphrased version.'

'Old Testament, right?'

Bernie nodded. 'This is a ransom note from the abductor. It's got to be. And whoever it is, wanted Derek Hayes dead… Well, they got their wish. I wonder when he got this. Were you keeping an eye on their post, Anderson?'

'Yes, of course. But…'

'But what?'

'Sunday. There was a gap between me leaving and Alan Turner arriving. And I'd sent uniform home the night before. Sorry. I was wrong to do that. This must have been hand delivered. Which means someone was watching the house.'

Bernie was surprised by Anderson's apology but she didn't let it show.

The PC turned the envelope around. 'Looks like it was. Name and address is typed but there's no stamp.'

Bernie thought about the times recently when she'd felt she was being watched. Especially the flash of light from the other evening. 'That would make sense. Alan said Derek was in a bad way when he got here on Sunday. He must have just read this. Shame he didn't tell us.'

'There's something else in the envelope as well, ma'am,' said the PC.

Bernie passed the letter to Anderson and took the envelope. She gently pulled it apart. There was a golden curl, tied tight with a red ribbon. An image of a five-year-old in a school photo flashed in front of her eyes. She lifted it out to examine it more closely.

'Molly's?' asked Anderson.

'Possibly. But there's no root to get the DNA. It's the red ribbon I'm interested in. Lesley Cooper showed me an old school photo of Sophie and Steven together. She had red ribbons in her hair. Wait a minute.'

Bernie placed the lock in the palm of her gloved hand. She moved the ribbon to the side.

'Look at this. I thought it was a loose strand from the ribbon caught in the hair. But it's not. We'll need the lab to confirm it but this looks like blood to me. The question is, whose – Molly's or her abductor's?'

Bernie looked round the incident room. She'd called everyone in for the sixteen fifteen check-in. She'd added what they had learnt to a PowerPoint and was ready to share. As the room became quiet, Bernie clicked and the first screen came up on the interactive whiteboard. It was the picture of Steven and Sophie that Lesley Cooper had given her.

'This is Steven and Sophie Newell. Sophie went missing Thursday, 2 August 1990. Derek Hayes was the prime suspect but there was not enough evidence to charge him. He left the country shortly after. Coincidence? Well, let's look at the evidence. We know he went to Spain, reinvented himself as Derek Cole, married a Spanish woman and had a daughter, Jessica.'

Bernie moved onto the next screen, a photo of two letters. 'On the left is Derek's suicide note. As you can see, he wrote he was "doing this for Molly". On the right is what appears to be a ransom note. However, this note isn't demanding money. The abductor wanted something far more sinister – Derek's death. He clearly knew what it meant. The brown envelope was addressed to Derek and so it looked just like a bill. However, there was no stamp so it must have been hand delivered. We don't know when he received it but our best guess is Sunday morning. There was something else in the envelope as well.'

The lock of hair was displayed on the screen.

'Remember the photo I've just shown you of Sophie with red ribbons in her hair? I've checked with Sophie's aunt, Lesley Cooper, and Sophie always wore red ribbons. I think it was a message to Derek. We've sent it to Forensics for analysis. It'll be tricky to prove that it's Molly's but there appears to be a trace of blood on the hair and we're also hoping the ribbon may have some DNA on it.'

Bernie clicked again. A close-up of Steven Newell appeared. 'Steven was ten when his sister went missing. He helped with the search and found Sophie's teddy bear hidden under a bush. Matt had already suggested to me he thought Molly's fleece and the buggy being hidden under bushes was significant.'

One of the uniformed officers that had helped Anderson with the search raised his hand. 'Ma'am, can I ask a question please?'

Bernie wasn't keen on being interrupted but she let it go. 'Yes?'

'Do we know if the buggy was definitely used to take Molly from the park?'

Bernie nodded. 'I was going to come to that in a minute but yes, we do know. I heard from Forensics just before we started this meeting. The single strand of hair we found under the bush by the railway is definitely Molly's. DNA swabs and fingerprints from the buggy also show that Molly was in it.'

A murmur went round the room.

'On the surface this seems good news. But,' Bernie looked round at the officers, 'there is no other DNA or fingerprint evidence apart from Mick O'Connell's and we've already ruled him out. Which suggests the abductor wiped down the buggy before using it. Someone is looking at soil samples from the wheels which may help us place a suspect at the scene but doesn't really help us now. The two letters have also gone to be processed but I'm not holding out any hope of finding anything significant. This abductor is clever.'

Bernie pointed to the screen. 'OK, let's have a closer look at Steven Newell. His parents didn't cope with losing Sophie. They killed themselves when Steven was eighteen.'

There was a ripple of noise as people shuffled in their seats.

'I know. Pretty tough. He left and joined the Royal Navy and hasn't been heard of since. As the ransom note refers to "a child for a child, a life for a life", I think we have to consider Steven as a suspect. We had a call to Crimestoppers describing a man in his late thirties, early forties, who'd been seen hanging around Otterfield. And Eddie Parker mentioned they'd had a different delivery driver for the school meals recently so let's look into that in case it's the same guy. Age wise, the description fits with Steven. Items being hidden under bushes – fits with Steven. Red ribbon – fits with Steven. Local knowledge – fits with Steven. We need to find him ASAP. Matt's been working on that. Where are you up to, Matt?'

Matt stood up and glanced at his notes. 'So far, I've managed to find out when he joined up – September 1998. He served for twelve years, had an exemplary record and then left in 2010. Haven't found him since, still searching.'

Bernie bit her bottom lip. 'Right. Kerry, have you heard back from Derek's ex-wife yet?'

Kerry shook her head. 'No. I've left a message in my best Spanish' – she winked at Bernie – 'asking her to call me back. There's always the possibility she's on her way here. DS Anderson told me a phrase he'd heard Jessica saying over and over again last night on the phone to her mother. It translates as "No, you're not coming". So don't be surprised if she pops up here.'

Bernie rubbed her temple. Another headache was brewing. She needed water. 'Oh God, I think we could all do without that. Well, if she does appear – you're in charge of her, Kerry. And also, I'd like you to check out Lesley Cooper's alibi for last Friday.' Bernie paused. Her gut instinct told her Lesley wasn't involved in Molly's abduction. As Sophie's aunt, she knew the pain it would cause Jessica. But equally she'd had a few days to prepare herself. She'd been expecting Bernie. Maybe Lesley was more 'ready' than she needed to be.

Bernie heard Detective Chief Superintendent Wilson cough to her left. She glanced at him and recognised his knowing look. She nodded slightly at him.

'Of course,' she said, 'we also have to consider the possibility that Hayes had an accomplice back in 1990 and that's who's responsible now for Molly. Maybe something went wrong back then. So, DS Anderson, I want you to look into Derek's background. See if you can find anything at his flat in Bristol. Look through his past record and see what other names crop up. In the meantime, I have a post-mortem to go to. Considering what Derek was accused of we need to be one hundred per cent sure he killed himself. Otherwise, we're looking at murder.'

*

The chill and the smell hit her at the same time. Goosebumps appeared on her arms and she placed her hand over her nose and mouth. The antiseptic was barely masking a sweet, rotting stench. It reminded Bernie of when she'd left chicken out to defrost and then had to go away for a weekend. Her small one-bed flat had stunk for days after. She pulled her jacket on to minimise the cold but morgues could make her freeze in a ski jacket. It went beyond her skin and into her bones. She hated post-mortems more than anything. She'd fainted earlier in the year at one. Dr Nick White, the pathologist, had treated her with derision that time. He still did.

'Oh, DI Noel. I hadn't realised you were coming. You normally try to avoid this like the plague. I would have waited for you. Sorry about the smell. Had a bad one yesterday and it's still lingering today,' said Nick White. He had already started on his patient and there were flecks of blood on his scrubs.

Bernie stood back from the table and looked to the side, just keeping the body in her peripheral vision. 'Yeah, well, I'm heading this one up. What have you got so far, preferably in English?'

Nick White laughed. 'OK. Well, our victim died of a massive coronary. I can't be sure if it's in direct relation to the blow to the head.'

'What? Didn't Derek Cole die from carbon monoxide fumes?'

'Oh, sorry, wrong victim. I thought you were here for this guy.'

Bernie flicked her eyes towards the victim. It wasn't Derek but another man of a similar age. 'No. Who was he?'

'David Chaucer. The man hurt in the betting shop raid. Sorry, my fault. I assumed you'd taken the case since his death.'

Bernie shook her head. 'No. It's staying with Serious Organised Crime and Avon and Somerset. I'm here for Derek Cole.'

'I'll be doing him next. I did get a look at him when he came in though. At first glance I would say that Derek Hayes, or Cole, whatever we're going to call him, died from carbon monoxide poisoning from car fumes. His skin is still fairly lifelike – an indicator of carbon monoxide being present in the body. Toxicology will show the concentration of levels in blood so it's hard to give you a time of death at the moment. I'm sure your police officer at the scene can give you a better idea. I heard you had an officer there. He or she must know what time Derek went out to the garage.'

Bernie wanted to wince at the subtext to the pathologist's words – you had someone there, why wasn't this stopped? She took a shallow breath, enough to stop her from passing out but not too much to take in the smell. She still couldn't bring herself to look fully.

'I already know time of death. I was there myself. We did our best to save him.' She wasn't going to let him get away with his barbed remarks. 'Actually, I'm more interested in knowing if it's definitely suicide.'

Nick White continued to look at David Chaucer's innards. 'I heard a note was found, isn't that enough?'

'Oh, we all know it isn't always that simple. Considering what he was accused of I have to check all avenues.'

'I will examine Derek Cole carefully before I make any incisions. I'll even take X-rays if that will make you feel better. However, my job is to establish cause of death, not motive. That's your job. I'll be able to give you my initial findings later but I can't confirm anything until all the toxicological results are back in. And as you know, that can take a few weeks.' White now raised his eyebrows at Bernie. 'Is that good enough for you, *Detective Inspector?*'

'It is for now, *Doctor,*' Bernie smiled a false smile. 'Anyway, I must love you and leave you. I have a child to find.'

CHAPTER TWENTY-SIX

Bernie smelled Jane before she saw her. She was wearing a heavy, cloying fragrance, the sort that stuck in the back of your throat. Jane was draped over Anderson's desk in MCIT, her skirt hitched up a little to show off her black nylon-covered legs. Her hand was on Anderson's shoulder.

Anderson turned towards Bernie and mouthed, 'Save me.'

'So, Jane, to what do we owe the pleasure of your company?' asked Bernie.

Jane uncrossed her legs and recrossed them the other way. Static buzzed through the air.

'Careful, you'll give me an electric shock,' said Anderson.

Jane opened her mouth to say something but Bernie interrupted. 'Jane, what can we do for you?' She clenched her hands.

'Oh, yes.' Jane slowly turned her head away from Anderson. 'I was talking to the super about the ransom note. It seems to me if we make Derek Cole's death public then the abductor is more likely to let Molly go, don't you think?'

Bernie's fingernails dug into her palms as she clenched her hands tighter.

'There are a number of problems with doing that. Not only would we be causing terrible pain to Jessica, the press will assume Derek's guilt in relation to Molly's disappearance, despite him having a reliable alibi. The Newell case will be exposed and Lesley

Cooper will have to endure that all over again. And if Molly was just released immediately, then we may not catch the perpetrator.'

Jane slid off the desk to stand in front of Bernie. 'If *you* play this correctly then you should still be able to catch the abductor. I think the real question is, how long are you going to leave Molly to rot? Release the information and she could be free tonight, assuming she's still alive. It's all down to *you*, isn't it?'

Bernie felt her breathing quicken. The pressure to punch Jane square in the face was building up, threatening to erupt at any second. She was aware of Anderson standing up.

'Well,' he said, 'that's something for us to consider. And when a decision is made, one of us will get back to you. In the meantime, keep it quiet.' He placed his hand on Jane's back and guided her towards the door.

Bernie closed her eyes and tried to regain her composure. She hated Jane but she also knew there was a kernel of truth in her words. Anderson's hand touched her shoulder. He whispered into her ear, 'She's gone.'

She opened her eyes to see him standing close to her, then glanced around the room. 'Where are the other two?'

Anderson shrugged. 'Not sure. They may have gone to get a coffee. How was the post-mortem?'

'I walked in on the wrong one. Nick White hasn't even started on Derek's yet. Have you done your statement yet from last night?'

Anderson looked sheepish. 'Er, no. There hasn't really been time. I've been too busy with the search and now looking into Derek's past. I've still got to go over to Bristol as well to Derek's flat. Besides, I told you last night. The door was locked so I smashed the window to open it. Then I dragged Derek out.'

'It needs to be written up. It's important to get all the details down. You could leave Bristol until the morning. Have you found any associates for Derek Hayes?'

'Some, but I think you're right about Steven Newell. He's our best lead at the moment. I will look into these others too.' He hesitated. 'You know, I hate saying this but Jane may be right. The abductor is probably relying on the press for information. If we release—'

'I know,' Bernie interrupted. 'I know. I think we might do a plea for the person who rang Crimestoppers to come forward. Try and get a better description. We'll see if the forensic artist comes up with anything and it's possible the navy may have a more recent photo. If we could get the Crimestoppers' witness identifying Steven then that would help us enormously.'

'Lots of "ifs" there. We're running out of time, remember?'

Bernie stepped back, her hackles rising. 'I hadn't forgotten.'

'Hey, I'm not the enemy here.'

'Just go and find Kerry.'

Anderson backed away. 'OK. I'm going. And then I'll go to Bristol. I don't want to leave it until tomorrow. I guess I'll see you in the morning.'

Bernie looked up briefly and nodded. 'Yes, see you in the morning, unless you find a major lead.'

Bernie rubbed her eyes and stretched in her chair. It had been a long day and her adrenalin was spent. She looked across at Matt, bent over his computer. He was still trying to track down Steven Newell. Opposite him, Kerry was typing up Anderson's statement when the phone next to her rang.

'MCIT. Yes, she's here… Right, OK. I'll tell her.'

Bernie waited as Kerry put the phone down.

'Gary again.'

'What? I don't have time to deal with anything outside of the investigation at the moment.'

'He's called for you twice so it must be important.'

'And both times, the message he's left has said that it's nothing to do with the case. I don't even know who he is,' answered Bernie.

'Well, he's clearly not taking no for an answer. He's at the front desk.' Kerry hesitated. 'You don't think...' She nodded towards Bernie's desk drawer.

'What? Oh. That.'

'Have you spoken to the super yet?'

Bernie lowered her head. 'No. I haven't.'

Kerry came over to Bernie. 'This is serious. You must tell him. Tomorrow. In the meantime, you can't be sure this Gary isn't involved.'

'Involved in what?' Matt asked.

Bernie rolled her eyes at Kerry and mouthed 'thanks'.

'Bernie had a threatening card delivered to her grandparents' house on the day of the funeral.'

'Kerry!'

'What? You're not taking this seriously enough.' Kerry shook her head. 'Honestly, Bernie. Why haven't you told the super? And tell me the real reason.'

Bernie looked up. 'Because if I tell the super and enter it as evidence, it becomes real. And I can't handle that at the moment.'

'Do you want me to come with you, ma'am?' asked Matt.

'Where?'

'To see this guy.'

'Why?'

'Well, in case he's the person who sent the card. Or maybe he could actually be Steven Newell, trying to wheedle information out of us, or he might just get a thrill meeting you.'

Bernie walked over to Matt and placed a hand on his shoulder. 'Matt, I think you're overreacting. Only a stupid person would send a death threat and then walk into a major police station. But if it makes you feel better, you can come with me. Especially if I have to interview the guy. Come on.'

Headquarters was quiet as they walked down the stairs to the front desk. She used her security pass to let her through to the front office.

'You have a Gary to see me?' she asked the officer on the desk.

'Yes, he's just sitting down in the foyer at the moment but room one is free if you need to interview him.'

'Did he say why he wanted to see me?'

'No, not exactly. Said it was personal.'

She glanced through the window. A black man in his late forties was flicking through a newspaper. He suddenly looked up and their eyes met. He smiled and she saw him mouth her name.

Bernie stiffened. She turned to Matt. 'I have never seen that man before in my life. He's clearly not Steven Newell. But he might have sent the card. Stay with me.'

She was buzzed through to the foyer and Matt did as she asked – he was right behind her, perhaps a little too close.

She held out her hand. 'Gary? I'm DI Bernie Noel. I gather you want to talk to me.'

He stood up. He smiled again as he shook her hand. 'Yes, I do.'

'Well, I need to warn you I have very little free time at the moment. I'm in the middle of a big investigation—'

'Yes, I know,' he interrupted. 'I saw you on TV.'

'Told you,' Matt muttered behind her.

'Then you'll know,' Bernie continued, 'I can only spare you a few minutes.'

The man smiled again and gave a half laugh. He had a strange look on his face that Bernie couldn't work out. *Did you send the card?*

'You really don't know who I am, do you?'

Bernie sighed. She was in no mood to play games. 'No. I have no idea who you are. Especially as I only know your first name and not your surname.'

'To be honest, I thought if I told you my surname, you wouldn't talk to me.'

Bernie was confused. 'What do you mean?' Her heart was thumping. Was he connected to the London gang?

'It's Noel. Same as you.'

Bernie looked properly at the man before her. He was as tall as Matt, eyes as black as coal. And there was no mistaking that smile. She'd seen it in enough photos of herself.

'I…' She tried to speak but her voice failed her.

'I think we need to speak privately,' said Gary Noel.

'Yes, of course,' Bernie said, trying to reclaim her composure. 'This way please. Matt, could you get some tea? Is tea all right?'

'Tea would be great, thanks.'

'And maybe some biscuits or something? I haven't eaten any dinner,' she explained.

'We could go out for some food. I saw a pub on the way here.'

Bernie thought about it and then shook her head. She wanted to stay in headquarters where she was in control. 'No, I can't. Just in case something comes in. Please, after you.'

Room one had a few comfortable chairs and a coffee table. Bernie gestured to Gary Noel to sit down and then she sat.

'I'm sorry to turn up like this. I did leave some messages for you but when you didn't return my calls, I knew I had to come and see you. I'm leaving the country tomorrow for a while so thought I'd seize the opportunity. I saw you on the TV, my little girl, all grown up.'

'I was never your little girl.' Bernie bit her lip. This wasn't how she wanted to do this: she wanted to remain calm, in control, but she could feel years of resentment bubbling to the surface.

Gary nodded. 'I deserve that. I don't know what you've been told. I just want to present my side to you. What you decide after that is up to you. Is that OK?'

'How do I know you really are my father?'

'You don't but I'm willing to take a DNA test to prove it. And your mother has a scar on her right inner thigh from when she fell out of a tree when she was seven.'

Bernie's hands went clammy and her arms limp. She nodded.

'Firstly, I want you to know that I really loved your mother. She was my first love and I always think of her fondly. My parents owned a fried chicken and chip shop and she used to come in on a Friday night after youth club at her church. I fell head over heels for her. My friends thought I was mad for going after a white girl – blacks and whites didn't mix that much back then in Brixton – but I never saw her colour. For me it was all about her smile and her incredible blue eyes. She was just gorgeous.' Gary paused and wiped his eyes. 'Sorry, I'd forgotten how strongly I felt about Denise… I started meeting her after school and things moved very fast, faster than either of us could cope with really. We were naive. Denise fell pregnant fairly quickly. We'd only been together a few months.'

There was a knock at the door. Bernie stood up to answer it. Matt was there with a tray.

'Everything OK?' he asked quietly.

'Yes. You and Kerry can go home if you want to. I don't need you here. Thanks.'

Bernie put the tray down. 'Do you want sugar in your tea? I normally have one but they say sugar is good for shock so maybe I'll have two.'

'Bernie, please sit. I know this is hard to hear. I've been rehearsing it on the drive down.'

Bernie nodded and sat back down, sipping the hot, sweet tea.

'When I found out Denise was pregnant, I was shocked. But I wanted to stand by her. I loved her and she loved me. The problem was, we were both only fifteen. I think if we'd been sixteen then maybe it would have been easier but probably not. No matter how old we were, there still would have been your grandfather to deal with. And to say he was unhappy would be an understatement. He was bloody furious. He threatened me and although I was a slightly bolshie kid, he scared me.'

Gary picked up his tea and drank a few mouthfuls before continuing. 'I wrote letter after letter to Denise but I think he intercepted every one of them. I was going out of my head. Then there were riots in the area and your grandparents decided to move to Clapham. A friend wrote and told me you'd been born. I'm not surprised she called you Bernadette. That was the name of her favourite teacher at school.'

Bernie smiled at the memory of Sister Bernadette. 'Yes, she really supported Mum. She was there when I was born, along with my grandmother. I think Granny was a bit peeved her name, Susan, is only my middle name and not my first.'

Gary laughed. 'I can imagine that. My mum used to say that your grandmother could turn water into lemonade with one glare.'

'She does have a particularly sour look,' said Bernie. She decided not to mention her grandmother's sour temperament, especially when it came to her only grandchild.

'I did see you once though,' said Gary, 'when I went to the fair on Clapham Common. You were a toddler and Denise had taken you. The two of you were on the carousel and you were laughing. A big part of me wanted to run over and scoop you up and take you away.'

Bernie looked up at him sharply.

'Sorry, I know how that sounds with everything going on at the moment. But I didn't do it, obviously. I could see you and Denise were happy. And that was enough for me.'

'And now? You said you're leaving the country tomorrow. Where are you going?' Bernie asked.

'To Jamaica. I'm… I'm taking my parents' ashes home. They both died last year.'

'Oh.' Bernie had never really thought much about the other side of her family. Her little unit of four had been enough. 'I'm sorry. It's a shame I never got to meet them.'

'It is. They would have loved you. In fact, they offered to adopt you. It was probably that that spurred your grandfather into acceptance. He wasn't about to let his grandchild go. The one concession my parents' got was our surname. You would be given it in case you ever wanted to find us. But I guess you never did.'

Bernie lowered her eyes. 'It wasn't like that. I just didn't feel the need to. Pops was everything to me. He was my father figure. What about other family? Are you married? Children?'

Gary shook his head. 'I was an only child. I married briefly in my twenties but it didn't last long and we didn't have any children. You're my only family in the UK. I have relatives in Jamaica – aunts, uncles, cousins.'

'Why now?'

'I heard about your grandfather's death. And then I knew I could finally contact you. I sent a card…'

'You did what?'

'I sent a card.'

Bernie closed her eyes briefly. 'Did it have flowers on the front? And did you write it in capitals?'

'Yes. Sorry, my handwriting is awful.'

'You didn't sign it.'

'I didn't? No wonder you didn't know my name. I remember now. I wasn't sure how to sign it and then I saw Denise in an upstairs window and I panicked. I stuffed the card in the envelope and put it through the door.'

Bernie gripped the wooden arms of the chair.

'Oh God, Bernie. I'm so sorry. Did I scare you?'

She bit back tears. All the fear she'd pushed down was building back up. 'You have no idea. No bloody idea. You know nothing about my life.'

'But I want to. I really do.' He leaned forward. 'I should have fought harder for you and Denise.'

'You ought to tell my mum that.'

Gary reached inside his coat and pulled out an envelope. 'Actually, I have. I've written it all down. Would you give it to her please?'

Bernie hesitated and then shook her head. 'You know the address.'

Gary nodded. 'Yeah. You're right. I'll post it. And maybe see her when I get back from Jamaica.' He paused. 'I'm guessing you want to do a paternity test. I've got sample sticks with me. I'm sure you know how to take a DNA sample.'

Bernie looked at the man opposite her. She was still angry and upset with him over the card but she did want to know for certain if he was her father.

'Actually, it would be better for another officer to do that. To avoid any cross contamination from me. And I'll use one of our DNA kits. I'll ask the duty sergeant. And I'll get our lab to do the test. They deal with private DNA requests. If you wait here.'

Gary took her hand. 'Thanks. I'll pay for it obviously. Thank you for listening. And I'm really, really sorry about the card.'

Bernie waited in the foyer as Gary's DNA was taken. She was relieved the card had been from him. Kerry would laugh. Although now her location was known, it would only be a matter of time before the death threats started again. Last time she'd had Pops standing by her. Would Gary Noel be willing to do the same? Searching her feelings, she was surprised to find she hoped he would.

She smiled at me today. Not a scared or worried one but a genuine beam. She's beginning to trust me now. We played hide and seek. She's such a funny thing. She hid under the table every time. I let her win and she shrieked with delight each time she found me, her curls bouncing. I can't cut any more of them. Not since I sliced my finger doing it. They'll probably give her away when we finally leave here but it's a risk I'll have to take.

CHAPTER TWENTY-SEVEN

Thursday

Bernie woke with her alarm. It felt as though she'd only been asleep for five minutes but she knew she'd gone out like a light the moment her head had hit the pillow. She lay still for a few minutes, trying to think about Molly, but Gary Noel kept filling her head. She reached for her phone and found the selfie she'd taken of them both. He had thought it sweet she wanted a photo. She didn't let on she would be sending it to her mother to see if she recognised him. Part of her didn't want to let her emotions run away with her, and even though he'd initially scared her, excitement bubbled in her stomach. Kerry had been ready and waiting with chocolate when Bernie got back from talking with him. They had both laughed when Bernie said who'd sent the card, but it was more relief than a joke. The DNA tests would normally take about five days. She would speak to the lab and see if it could be speeded up a little. She felt bad about asking with all the pressure they were under but she had to know. She had waited thirty-two years to know her father.

She flicked back to the main screen of her phone and saw the text icon lit up. It was Anderson. *Nothing doing in Bristol. See you in the morning.*

Bernie was relieved she had missed the text. She had to suppress the conflicting feelings she had for Anderson. Something had shifted between them in the last day. With that and her father, too many things were diverting her energy away from the search for Molly. Bernie made a decision. Molly was her number one priority. The men who were starting to crowd her life could wait.

Wilson called Bernie into his office after the morning briefing.

'Bernie, I was talking with Jane earlier.'

Bernie resisted the urge to roll her eyes.

'She made an interesting point about releasing the news of Derek's death. It might just spur the abductor into letting Molly go. That's if the ransom note was from him.'

Bernie looked down at the floor, planning her words carefully before she answered.

'I do see her point. But if we're going to go public then we should at least have the courtesy to let Jessica and Lesley Cooper know first. And before we do that, I'd like to issue a plea for the phone caller to get back in touch, see if we can improve the description of the man they saw. That might lead to other calls.'

Wilson pursed his lips. 'You're playing a dangerous game, Bernie. I hope you know what you're doing.'

'Sir, we always tell people to not pay the ransom, to allow us to do a controlled drop with us there ready to arrest. We don't have that opportunity this time. Derek has paid the ransom with his life. I'm just not happy letting the abductor know he's won and, more than that, give him a chance to escape.'

She looked at Wilson, trying to stare him out. But the super wasn't backing down.

'Bernie, our priority is, and always was, Molly. Derek made the decision to not involve us and yes, we screwed up in not finding out about his past sooner but we must do everything in our power to find her. And if that means releasing the news of her grandfather's death, then we *must* do so. I suggest you see Jessica and Lesley this morning. You're right about notifying them first. I'll hold a press conference at two p.m. I expect you to be there.'

Bernie found Matt and Kerry in MCIT, working their way through the Newell case file, and Anderson checking out Derek's former associates.

'How's it going? Have you managed to check Lesley's alibi yet, Kerry?'

Kerry opened her notebook. 'Yes, I spoke to the manager of the charity shop. Lesley was there all day. But the manager did say she kept checking her phone in the afternoon, as if she was expecting news. It might not be anything.'

'Or it might be something. Well, I'm off to see Lesley now, and Jessica, if anyone needs me.'

Anderson glanced up. 'I might need you later, ma'am. There are a few interesting people who used to hang out with Derek. Some have done time.'

'OK. We'll chat when I get back.' She grabbed a Belgian bun from the bakery box and walked out the door.

She bumped into Sergeant Alan Turner on the stairs. 'Morning, Alan. Are you escaping from custody?'

He laughed. 'Sadly not. Unless you need me?'

Bernie stopped in her tracks, a sudden thought occurring to her. 'Maybe. When did you join the force again?'

Alan nodded knowingly. 'Ninety-nine. After Sophie Newell's disappearance, I'm afraid. I don't really know anything about the case. In fact, I don't think you'll find anyone here from that time now. And I know the detectives who were on the investigation are all dead bar one and he has dementia.'

'Which is why we need the locals to help us.' Bernie thumped the stair handrail in frustration.

'Once people know Derek's dead, some may come forward with information. I take it his death is under wraps for now?' Alan asked.

'Yes. Until the press conference later today.'

'Then I'll keep my ear to the ground.'

'Thanks, Alan. You're a star. By the way, there are some buns left in MCIT. Help yourself.'

Bernie chose to go to Lesley first. The lounge curtains were shut but she saw them twitch as she rang the bell. The door was on the chain when Lesley opened it.

'Lesley, it's DI Bernie Noel. Can I come in please? I need to talk to you about something.'

Lesley opened the door and Bernie barely managed to hold in her shock at her appearance. She was wearing a threadbare pink towelling dressing gown, her hair was in disarray and her face was red and puffy from crying. Was she really involved in Molly's disappearance? If she was then she was a good actress.

'I'm sorry about the bombshell I dropped on you yesterday about Derek's death. There was no easy way of telling you.'

Lesley smiled weakly. 'You were just doing your job.'

'Can we sit down?'

'Well, that sounds ominous. You always have to sit down for bad news, don't you? Come in.'

Bernie perched on the edge of the sofa, determined to not be sucked into it again. Lesley sat in her armchair, her hands gripping the armrests once more. She took a deep breath.

'OK, I'm ready for whatever you have to tell me.'

Bernie wondered where to begin. She decided to start with Derek. 'Yesterday, my officers searched Derek's house in Otterfield. They found a suicide note and also what appears to be a ransom note. The ransom wasn't asking for money. I can't tell you exactly what it said but it was indicating that the abductor wanted Derek dead. That was the ransom. Given Derek's probable involvement in Sophie's disappearance, we have no choice but to investigate the possibility that Steven is Molly's abductor.'

Lesley raised her hand to her mouth and let out a sound like a wounded puppy. 'Oh no, oh no.' She shook her head. 'I can't believe it.'

Bernie placed her hand on Lesley's arm. 'I know and it's only a possibility. But he's probably our strongest lead at the moment. He has motive and...' She paused. She guessed that Lesley would be discreet but it was her nephew after all. 'There are some similarities with Sophie's disappearance. I can't go into details. But I didn't come just to tell you this. There's going to be a press conference this afternoon and we're going to tell the press about Derek's death.'

'And Steven?' asked Lesley.

'Yes, we're going to talk about Steven. We'll ask him to come forward so if you know where—'

'I haven't seen or heard from him since 1998. Do you have any idea how painful that is?'

Bernie bit her lip. 'I'm sorry, Lesley, I'm so sorry. My priority is Molly and we're hoping that if the abductor, whoever it is, hears of Derek's death, then she'll be released.'

Lesley gave a slight nod. 'I do understand and I want Molly home with her mother more than anyone but...'

'But you want to know where Sophie is. You wanted Derek to answer that question.'

'Yes. I want Sophie to be with her parents in the churchyard. I want to know they're together.'

Bernie sighed. 'I'll do my best to find her after we've found Molly. In the meantime, if you hear from Steven...'

'I won't. He blames me, you see, for bringing Derek into our lives. For saying that he was with me when he wasn't.' Lesley looked down. 'It's quite tempting to follow Derek into that dark abyss… but don't worry, I won't. If there's any chance of finding Steven and Sophie then I'll stay alive.'

Bernie pulled her hand back from Lesley's arm. 'I'm sorry but I have to ask you this. We checked your alibi and we know you were in the shop. But you kept looking at your phone. Why?'

Lesley nodded. 'I was expecting a delivery. They were due to take it to the pub for me. I wanted to make sure it had arrived. I can show you my phone if you like?'

Bernie looked at Lesley. Her wretchedness was clear. 'Sorry, but yes, I will need to see it.'

Lesley rose from her chair, a little unsteady. 'Wait a minute, it's in the kitchen.'

Bernie glanced quickly around the room. There was no obvious sign that a child had been in there. Could she be upstairs? Bernie strained her ears but she could only hear the ticking of a clock.

Lesley came back and held out her phone. 'There. Feel free to look around. I've nothing to hide.'

Bernie took the phone and looked at the text messages. She could see one from a courier, confirming delivery of Lesley's parcel. It was timed at 17.22. Bernie checked Lesley's phone calls too. She recognised the people Lesley had called in the last week, and the ones she'd received. They were all from Marchant. Nothing out of the ordinary. Bernie turned her attention to Lesley's emails. Most were junk. Satisfied, Bernie handed back the phone.

'Thank you,' she said. 'I'm sorry I had to do that.'

'Don't be sorry. I understand. I know what it's like. Her mother must be going through hell. I hope she has someone to take care of her.'

'She does.' Bernie didn't dare mention that Jessica was only a few minutes' walk away at the vicarage. 'And you? Is there anyone who can come here, or better still, anywhere you can go? We won't mention your name when we release the news of Derek's death but the press may find out where you are.'

'Yes, Sue at the pub has said I can go there. She's a good friend of mine. It'll be ironic. The press camped on my doorstep, going into the pub for food and drink, and I'll be upstairs above them the whole time.'

'Well, I'm glad someone will be looking after you.' She squeezed Lesley's hand. 'I'll see myself out.'

Bernie hesitated before knocking on the vicarage front door. She was wondering how Jessica would take the news about the press conference. With the people of Otterfield already hating them, it would be hard to maintain public support with Derek's past revealed. She knocked lightly, in case Sam was asleep. There was no answer. She knocked again, louder this time. Still no answer. She pushed open the letter box to look through. The house appeared empty.

'Where the hell are they?' It was then she noticed Paul Bentley's car wasn't there. She reached for her phone to call Anna, just as it began to vibrate with an incoming call.

'Hello?'

'Bernie, it's Kerry. You need to get over to the Coles' house in Otterfield. The PC on duty has radioed in a disturbance and asked for back-up.'

Bernie sighed. 'Let me guess – Jessica Cole is there.'

'Yes, how did you know?'

'Because no one is in at the vicarage. OK, I'm on my way.'

As Bernie drew up outside Jessica's house, she saw her screaming at another woman, much older with long dark curly hair streaked with grey, who was screaming back. Even with the car window shut she could hear them. Bernie couldn't understand what they were saying and then she realised they were speaking Spanish. The older woman had to be Jessica's mother. Oh God. She needed back-up of her own for this. She quickly called Kerry back.

'Hi. I'm here and you were right about the mother coming over.'

'Oh God. Do you want me to come?'

'No, I'll bring her to headquarters and we can have a chat with her there. We need to get her away from Jessica. She's very upset.'

Bernie stepped out of the car and gave the door a good slam, hoping the noise would attract the two women's attention. It didn't but she saw Anna look up.

'Oh, thank God you're here, Bernie. I can't get them to stop.'

Bernie reached into her pocket and pulled out her warrant card. She walked straight up to the two arguing women and stood between them, shoving her ID into the older woman's face.

'Excuse me, I think we've all heard enough. I'm Detective Inspector Bernie Noel and I'm assuming you're Jessica's mother. Do you speak English?'

Bernie stared hard at the woman. Jessica's mother had once been beautiful but bitterness was now etched on her face – it wasn't laughter lines around her eyes.

The woman sucked her lips in and for a moment Bernie wondered if she was going to be spat at.

'I speak some.'

'And your name?'

'Bonita Cole.'

'You kept your married name?'

'Yes.' She nodded towards Jessica. 'For her.'

'Don't bloody bother on my account,' Jess said.

Bernie put her hand up. 'Now, ladies, let's just stay calm. Bonita, I would like to talk to you some more but we'll do that at the police station. We can't go into the house here and I think neutral ground would be better. But for the moment, I need to talk to Jessica and Davy alone. Perhaps you could wait in my car, Bonita.'

Bernie looked across to the PC standing by the front door to the Coles' house. 'Could you escort this lady to my car please?'

'Yes, ma'am.'

As Bonita was led away, Bernie pulled Jessica in closer and Davy joined them.

'I'm really sorry to do this but we have to go public with the news about your father's death. Due to things we found in your dad's bedroom, we have reason to believe that Molly's abduction is tied in with the disappearance of Sophie Newell and that your father was responsible for taking Sophie.'

'What things?' asked Davy.

'I can't tell you the exact wording but there appeared to be a ransom note sent to Derek and it wasn't asking for money. It was asking for his life.'

Jessica slumped down to the pavement. Davy stroked her hair.

'OK, Jess, it's going to be OK,' he said. He looked at Bernie. 'You want to tell people because you think the abductor will let Molly go if he knows Derek is dead.'

'Yes. We think it's a possibility. Davy, can you go and get Jess some water please? It's all right for you to go into the house.'

Bernie crouched down next to Jessica. 'There's something else I need to tell you. Your father didn't buy the house, Jess, he inherited it from his parents. This is where he grew up. All the people from Otterfield recognised him. They knew what he'd been accused of. That's why they blanked you.'

Jess looked confused for a moment. 'Oh, Dad. If only he'd said something. Why didn't they turn him in?'

Bernie shook her head. 'God knows. Maybe they're not the kind of people to grass. Maybe they thought if they were really horrible to you then you'd leave.'

Bernie heard Davy coming back with the water, his feet stomping on the pavement.

'I think after having some water you ought to go back to the vicarage with Anna. Hang on, where's Sam?' asked Bernie.

'He's with Paul. He was taking him for a walk,' said Davy.

'How did you know Bonita was here?'

'She called Jess on her mobile. Anna drove us over. I don't know where she's going to stay. There's no more room at the Bentleys'.'

'She's not staying,' muttered Jessica.

Bernie glanced across to her car. Bonita Cole was sitting on the back seat.

'Don't you worry about Señora Cole. I'll deal with her.'

CHAPTER TWENTY-EIGHT

'Where is she?' Kerry asked, getting up from her desk.

'In interview room three. The family room is being used,' said Bernie. 'I'm just going to get her a coffee.'

'Ha! You'd better make it strong. Spanish coffee is mostly espresso based.'

'Oh, great. Well, you make it then and bring a Belgian bun if there are any left. Something tells me we're going to have to sweeten her up.'

Bernie watched as Bonita Cole grimaced at the coffee placed before her.

'I'm sorry,' said Kerry. 'We only have instant but I've tried to make it as strong as possible.'

Bonita lifted the mug and sniffed before taking a small sip. 'It's OK.'

'Well, Bonita – may I call you that?' asked Bernie.

'Of course, it's my name.'

'Thanks. I'm glad you're a bit calmer now. Did Jessica tell you about Derek? That he's dead?'

Bonita nodded. Her eyes were downturned. The earlier anger in them had gone.

'Jessica told me you spoke to her about Derek, told her things about him she didn't believe. Can you tell us please what you said?'

Bonita took another sip of coffee and eyed up the Belgian bun.

'Please eat if you're hungry,' said Kerry.

'*Gracias*. I've not eaten.'

Bernie watched as Bonita tore into the bun, obviously much hungrier than she was willing to admit. She wondered if the pinched cheeks and lined face were a result of poverty rather than bitterness. Did Derek Cole leave her with nothing? She glanced at the woman's clothes and noticed a repair on her jacket. Her hands were raw and dry. Bernie began to revise her first impression of Jessica's mother. This was a woman at her lowest point.

'Bonita, when you're ready, please tell us about Derek and what you said to Jessica about him.'

Bonita wiped her mouth with her sleeve and nodded.

'Oh, *Dios mio*. I can't believe he is dead,' she said, speaking slowly and carefully. 'He was a bastard to me. It was a holiday romance, erm, a fling, but I got pregnant with Jessica. My father, very strong Catholic, he made us marry and he got Derek the bar. We didn't love each other, we didn't want to be together. But we had to stay married while my father was alive. The week after he died, Derek asked for a divorce. He was not a good husband. He slept with many, many women but not me. After Jessica, he never touched me again. I would have liked more children, but no.'

'What did you tell Jessica?'

Bonita drank more of her coffee before speaking. 'One night, a long time ago, I don't know when, Derek got very drunk and told me something. He told me about a little girl called Sophie. He said he took her away. Next morning, he said I dreamed it, not real, not true. But I didn't forget. And when Jessica rang about Molly, I knew.'

'Knew what?' asked Bernie.

'It must be Derek. I told Jessica and she started shouting. She always believes him, never me. Always. He left me with nothing. He sold the bar and took all the money. Then Jessica left to be with him. She loves her father more than me. I have nothing. I live with my mother.'

Bernie leaned forward towards Bonita. 'He definitely said he took Sophie?'

'*Sí.*'

'And did you ever look into it?'

'No. I was too scared to find out. What if he then hurt me or Jessica? So…' Bonita shrugged her shoulders. 'Do you think he took Molly? I've never seen her.' A single tear began to trickle down her cheek, followed quickly by more. 'I've never seen her.'

Bernie reached out and gently touched Bonita's hand. 'We're doing everything we can to find her. We've got another press conference in about an hour's time. We're going to mention Derek's death and some possible leads. Do you have somewhere to stay tonight?'

Bonita shook her head. 'No. I thought I would stay with Jessica but I can't. Maybe I just fly home.'

'No, I think you should stay. Kerry will find somewhere affordable for you. At some point Jessica is going to need you so you should stay. In the meantime, can we get you some more food?'

Bonita nodded. 'Yes please. *Gracias.*'

'Kerry, can you take care of Bonita please?'

'Sure, no problem. Come with me, Señora Cole, and we'll see what we can find.'

Kerry ushered Bonita out of the door but looked back at Bernie. She knew they were thinking the same thing. Sophie's name wasn't out in the public domain yet. Bonita was telling the truth. Derek had taken her.

*

Bernie looked through a small window in the door to the press conference. The room was packed. It wasn't just the local press this time. She recognised some of the reporters from the national newspapers, mostly the tabloids. She sighed. Last time had been bad enough but this time she knew she was about to be fed to the lions. Jane had invited the big guns.

'We need to stretch far and wide if we're going to find Steven Newell. We can't just leave it to the local rags,' Jane had said. 'Matt has found no trace of him since he left the navy so we have to go big. Honestly, Bernie, I don't know what you're worried about, this could make all the difference.'

Yeah, Bernie had thought, it's not your job on the line.

She felt the super's hand, lightly on her back.

'Are you ready, Bernie?'

'No, not really. I'm still not convinced we're doing the right thing.'

'We'll do it just as we rehearsed. I'll read out the statement and then take questions. I'll only direct something to you if I know you can handle it. There's no room for mistakes with this. Right, let's go.'

Bernie sidestepped to let the super go in first. 'No pressure,' she muttered.

Flash bulbs started to go off the minute she walked into the room. She was blinded for a few seconds and the clicks of the cameras drummed out a beat in her ears. The photographers focused on her, not Wilson. She was going to be the pin-up girl whether she liked it or not.

Wilson reached the desk and raised a hand. 'Ladies and gentlemen, if you could stop the photos for a moment please. We have an update for you, and an appeal.' He and Bernie took their seats.

Bernie watched as everyone in the room settled down. The super picked up his notes.

'Last Friday, at three forty-five p.m., Molly Reynolds was reported missing from Otterfield playground. We've followed up lots of leads, searched a five mile radius, used sniffer dogs and the police helicopter – we still haven't found her. Her family has been under terrible pressure and this pressure became unbearable two days ago on Tuesday evening. It is with enormous sadness that I announce the death of Derek Cole, Molly's grandfather.'

Bernie heard a collective intake of breath. At least Jane had managed to not let the story leak.

'Tests are ongoing,' Wilson continued, 'but at the moment it looks as though Derek's death was a suicide. This has been a terrible shock for his daughter, Jessica Cole, and her partner, Davy Reynolds. We would ask you to allow them to grieve in peace.

'We have two appeals we would like to make. We received a call through Crimestoppers from a woman, giving us a description of a man she had seen acting suspiciously. We would like her to get in contact with us again so we can improve the description. Secondly, the name Steven Newell has come to our attention. Steven used to live in the area until 1998. We know he was in the Royal Navy until 2010 but hasn't been heard of since. If Steven is watching this, or if anyone knows where he might be, then please get in touch. I'll now take questions.'

Hands darted into the air with the urgency of small children in a classroom. Wilson pointed to a local journalist first, despite Jane waving frantically and mouthing 'Tabloids' from the back of the room. Bernie allowed a flicker of a smile to form.

'Trudy Smith from the *Swindon Advertiser*. I was here at the first press conference on Saturday and it seems to me that nothing much has changed since then. What do you say to allegations that this case has been handled badly?'

Bernie winced. She hadn't expected such a tough question from a local journalist. *Maybe she's got one eye on the nationals, trying to impress them.*

'I would say we have run the case as well as we can. We have covered a huge search area. Evidence has been found and leads have been chased up. People have been eliminated from the inquiry. Next question.'

'Patricia Roberts, *Daily Mail*. It's very sad news about Molly's grandfather but I have to ask, was his suicide a statement of guilt? Did he take Molly?'

Wilson gave a sideways glance to Bernie. She cleared her throat. 'There is no suggestion that Derek abducted Molly. He was in a business meeting at the time she went missing.'

Wilson pointed to another eager hand.

'Sally Stewart, *The Sun*. What happened about the car you were asking about earlier this week? Did you find it?'

'Yes, we did,' said Bernie, 'thanks to a tip-off from a member of the public. We found the owner and have eliminated him from the investigation.'

Wilson gestured to another reporter, Clive Bishop, who had been around for years.

'Clive Bishop, *Salisbury Journal*. As you know, Detective Chief Superintendent Wilson, I've been in this job even longer than you.' There was some laughter in the room. 'I know the name Steven Newell.'

Bernie thought her heart had stopped beating.

'I hadn't heard of Derek Cole until this last week but I did know a Derek Hayes,' continued Bishop, 'and I certainly remember the name Sophie Newell. What is it you're not telling us?'

'Bloody press! Trust Clive Bishop to remember the case,' said Wilson as he wiped sweat from his forehead with a handkerchief.

'I think you handled it well,' said Bernie, although she was lying. Wilson had shut down the conference at that point with 'We're not at liberty to discuss that particular line of enquiry at the moment. No further questions,' and had immediately stood up and left the room, leaving Bernie to follow in his wake, the press muttering in the background. At least it won't be my name in the headlines later, she'd thought.

Wilson looked wary. 'Don't flatter me, Bernie. I screwed up on that one. Our policy of not revealing the Sophie Newell case backfired. I know you wanted to spare Lesley Cooper but I'm not sure that's going to be possible. All the papers are going to be looking into it now. I'm sorry. You were right, we shouldn't have released news about Derek and Steven at the same time.'

Bernie wished Jane were in the room to hear that but she had been left to placate the journalists and encourage them out of the building.

'Well, maybe, like the car, it will work to our advantage. Anyway, I'd better get back to it. I'm pretty certain Lesley isn't involved. She has an alibi and she knows what it's like to lose a child. I don't think she'd do that to Jessica. On the other hand, I think Derek's drunken confession to Bonita has a lot of truth in it. There's no way she would know the name Sophie without Derek telling her himself,' said Bernie.

Wilson made a humph noise. 'Fat load of help though. The man's dead. There won't be a trial.'

'No, but it does give closure to Lesley. After we've found Molly, I want to go through Derek's things to see if there are any clues as to where he left Sophie.'

Wilson wiped his forehead again. 'Yes. But Molly is priority. Let's just hope the abductor sees the news and lets her go. Otherwise, DCI Worth will be taking over the case in less than two days.'

Bernie took a deep breath. She was being doubted again and she'd had enough. She'd worked hard for her promotion and she wasn't about to give up on Molly now.

'Sir, I do understand that normally a more experienced officer would run this case but I've got to know Jessica and Davy these last few days and they trust me to find Molly. Despite the locals' hostility, we've discovered there's more than one missing girl here and we need to find them both. *I* need to find them both. Marchant and Otterfield are two communities that have been ripped apart and we owe it to them to get closure for Sophie and to find Molly. Now. And to take me off the case at this moment when we're so close to finding the truth would be counterproductive, not to mention a slap in the face for my team after all their hard work getting us to this point. DCI Worth would have to forge new links with the family. It would push the investigation backwards rather than forward. Please, sir, give me a chance to solve this case.' Bernie clenched her hands together.

Wilson stared at her. 'Have you finished?'

'Yes, sir. Sorry, sir.'

'Don't be sorry.' He nodded. 'The thing that struck me most about you when you arrived last December was your professionalism. But it was clear you didn't want to be here. You still wanted to be in London. This is the most passionate I've seen you in six months. I'll try to delay DCI Worth until after the weekend, although the chief constable will have to agree. Fortunately, you're in his good books because you were right about the betting shop raids matching up with sporting events – horse racing in this instance. But if he says no and DCI Worth does come in, it'll be on the understanding that you stay on alongside him. Is that good enough?'

Bernie beamed. 'Yes, sir. I won't let you down.'

'Good. Because between you and me, I can't stand the damn man.'

CHAPTER TWENTY-NINE

Kerry raised her head as Bernie walked into MCIT.

'So I heard the press conference went well?' she said. She gave a wink.

'Oh God. It was bloody awful. The press are going to be all over this now. We have to find Molly, and fast.'

'I know the pressure is on, Bernie, but we can't let the press dictate to us.'

'It's not just that. If we don't find Molly by Saturday morning then DCI—' Bernie stopped. She realised she hadn't told Kerry about the deadline.

'DCI who?' Kerry folded her arms. Matt shifted uncomfortably in his seat. Anderson didn't look up at all from his computer.

'Oh, wait a minute,' Kerry said, looking around. 'Do these two jokers know but not me? I'm your sergeant.'

Bernie sighed and briefly closed her eyes. 'Kerry, I'm sorry. I originally hadn't planned to tell any of you but it slipped out with Matt and Anderson. DCI Worth is possibly coming to take over on Saturday morning if we haven't found Molly by then. The super's going to try and delay him if he can but the chief constable has to agree first.'

Kerry put her head in her hands. 'Shit. DCI Worth? He's utter crap. How long have you known?'

Bernie moved from one foot to the other. 'Since Tuesday.'

'Two days ago?'

'I didn't want to put any extra pressure on the team.'

'But you told these two.'

'Only yesterday, and like I said, it slipped out.'

Anderson gave her a sideways glance. She had told him Tuesday night but she didn't want to admit to that.

Kerry stood up. 'I'm going to the loo, and you,' she pointed to Bernie, 'are not going to follow me.'

Bernie chewed her fingernails as Kerry stormed out of the room. She sat down in her chair with a thud.

'Is she always that touchy?' Anderson asked.

Bernie glared at him. 'She's unhappy about being left out of the loop. And I can't say I blame her.'

'Even so, throwing a hissy fit isn't going to help us. It's just coming up to three o'clock now on Thursday so if we go with the original deadline then we have until, say, nine o'clock on Saturday morning, then that gives us…'

'Forty-two hours if we don't sleep at all,' answered Matt.

'Thanks, Maths Boy. Then we'll take shifts sleeping and working,' said Anderson. 'Ma'am, go and get Kerry back. We don't have time to waste.'

Bernie noticed an authority in Anderson's voice. Her instinct was to rail against it but she stopped herself. You've done this before, she thought. You're not just an FLO. Who are you?

Bernie reluctantly got out of her seat and was halfway across the room when her desk phone rang.

'Matt, could you?' She gestured towards the phone.

'Of course.' He reached across and answered. 'MCIT. Oh hi… Right… Oh no. Oh that's awful… I'll let her know right away. We'll be in touch.'

Matt replaced the phone and looked up at Bernie. His face was pale.

'Molly?' she asked.

Matt shook his head. 'No. That was Terry West. Emma O'Connell died at lunchtime. Terry just heard from Mick O'Connell.'

Bernie put her hand to her face. 'This is really turning out to be a shitty day. Poor little girl, and to think we put so much pressure on her family these last few days. We need to arrange some flowers for them. Can you…'

'Yes,' said Matt. 'I'll sort it. Go and get Kerry. DS Anderson's right. We have to get on.'

Bernie knew which cubicle Kerry would be in. It was always the end one; she wouldn't use any other. Bernie asked her once why and Kerry just shrugged her shoulders. 'Habit, I suppose.'

'Kerry?'

Silence.

'I know you're in here and I know you didn't want me to come after you but we've had some news. Some bad news. Some really crappy, shitty news.'

Bernie heard the lock being released and Kerry came out.

'What? Molly?'

Bernie shook her head. 'No. Emma O'Connell died at lunchtime. She was only five.'

'I'm sorry I was huffy with you,' said Kerry, putting her arm around Bernie.

'I'm sorry too. I just didn't want to put more pressure on any of you. I really need you, Kerry.'

Kerry leaned her head against Bernie's arm. 'And you've got me. I'll stop being a silly cow.'

'Thank you.' Bernie walked over to the nearest cubicle and got some tissue paper to wipe her eyes. 'Right. Need to focus now on Molly. At least I don't have to worry about the condolence card any more.'

Kerry laughed. 'Yes. What a silly sod. How long have we got before old Worthless appears?'

'About forty-two hours. Anderson is suggesting we work and sleep in shifts through the nights.'

Kerry nodded. 'I agree. Your place would be best.'

'Mine?' The thought of Anderson back in her flat with the others there alarmed her.

'Well, yeah. It's not fair on Debs to have everyone round and both Matt and Anderson only have one room. So it has to be yours.'

'But I only have one bedroom.'

'That's not a problem. You and I will pair up and the guys can do the same. God, Bernie, I'm not suggesting you sleep with Anderson.'

The smell of Chinese food filled Bernie's small flat. There wasn't a huge variety of takeaways in Devizes and Bernie still missed the global kitchen of London. They sat around the coffee table, balancing plates on their laps, reading through paperwork.

Bernie had been worried when they'd all first arrived that Anderson would let on he'd been there Tuesday night – all night. She still wouldn't put it past him to stir up trouble like that. Thankfully, though, all he had said was, 'Nice place you got here' and then offered to make drinks. He had had the good sense to ask where things were, as well, even though he already knew.

'This is so bloody frustrating,' said Kerry. 'I feel as though we're going round in circles.'

'I know,' said Matt. 'It's driving me insane. We know Steven Newell has got to be found but there's no record of him anywhere.'

'Name change?' suggested Anderson.

'Like Derek?' said Matt. 'It's possible, I suppose. There must be records for that. But they won't be open now.' Matt put down his plate. 'I need the loo.'

'It's by the front door,' said Anderson.

Bernie froze. She didn't dare make eye contact with anyone.

'I noticed it on the way in,' Anderson continued.

Bernie slowly exhaled.

'You all right?' asked Kerry.

Bernie glanced up. 'Yeah, fine. Just feeling the pressure.'

The doorbell rang. Bernie looked up in surprise. 'Has anyone ordered more food?'

'Er, no. Not as such. I'll get it,' said Anderson.

As he left the room, Kerry whispered, 'What's he done?'

Bernie could hear voices in the little hallway and when Anderson returned, he wasn't alone. Someone was hovering behind him.

'Don't be angry with me. But it seemed to me we needed someone who had some knowledge about the Sophie Newell case.'

Anderson stepped to one side and a man appeared in the doorway. He was wearing a tweed jacket and had permanently ruffled grey hair.

'Clive Bishop?' Bernie looked at Anderson. 'You gave my address to a bloody journalist?'

'After I heard about the press conference, it made perfect sense to contact Clive. He covered the case all those years ago.'

Clive smiled awkwardly. He held up a plastic bag. 'I brought all my notes from that time. Don't throw any of them away – drives my missus mad. There's stuff here that you might not have. Look, I'm not going to lie to you. I'm always looking for a good story. But this one has been incomplete for too long. And I want to help you. There may be nothing in here that can do that but I want to at least try. Please?'

Matt came back from the bathroom. 'What's going on?'

Bernie shook her head. 'Well, Anderson has recruited a new member for our team. Meet Clive Bishop from the *Salisbury Journal*.'

Bernie watched as Matt looked from her to Bishop to Anderson.

'You've brought a journalist in?' Matt said. 'The super will do his nut if he hears about this. First you suggest we work all night and now you bring in a reporter. What are you playing at?'

A vein throbbed in Anderson's neck. 'Well, I'm trying to get the job done, instead of moaning because I can't find the main suspect.'

A shooting pain whipped across Bernie's head. She had to stop this before her two alpha males started a fight. They might be out of the office but she wasn't going to let them jeopardise the case.

'Right, OK. Enough. Matt, you need to back down. Despite appearances, DS Anderson is still your senior officer.' She looked at Anderson. 'But I'm *your* senior officer and I'm not happy you've gone behind my back. But Clive's here now. I suggest you make our guest a drink. What would you like, Clive? Tea, coffee?' She looked back at the older man.

'Cup of tea would be nice. Strong. No sugar. I've got my own sweeteners. Trying to break the habit.'

Bernie flicked her head towards the kitchen and Anderson sloped off.

'Let me introduce you to the team. Clive, this is DS Kerry Allen and DC Matt Taylor. And obviously, you know DS Anderson. I'm sorry about the welcome, or lack of. It could be worse, though, you could be Jane Clackett.'

'The Wicked Witch of the West?' asked Clive.

'Oh God, I shouldn't have said that. I'm too tired to think straight,' said Bernie. 'What's Jane done to upset you?'

Clive laughed. 'More like the other way round. She's really annoyed with me for asking that question earlier. Told me I won't be invited any more. Bloody cow.' He put his plastic bag down on the coffee table with the rest of the paperwork. 'So, anything I can do to help you find Molly, and hopefully Sophie, well, just ask.'

Bernie paused. It wasn't ethical to let a journalist help in this way but she'd already broken the rules by bringing the case notes home. And if it meant they found Molly then…

'OK. What have you got?'

Bishop reached out and tipped the contents of his bag onto the table. Various notebooks and newspaper clippings fell out.

'Sorry, I'm not very organised. Probably explains why I'm still a local hack when all my contemporaries have moved on to better things.'

'And there I was thinking you just love being a local reporter,' said Bernie.

Bishop gave a quick grin. 'I do love it really. Anyway, I was a young lad when Sophie Newell went missing, so it was easier to send me to talk to Derek Hayes' friends. Now, which one is it?'

Clive began rummaging through the notebooks, flicking them open until he found the right one. 'Here we go. Do you mind if I sit down? Back's playing up a bit.'

'No, of course. Please do,' said Bernie. 'And here's your tea.'

Clive plonked himself down next to Kerry. He took his time getting settled into a comfortable position before reaching into his pocket and pulled out his sweeteners, dropping two into his cup. He stirred it slowly.

Bernie's muscles tensed. She still wasn't used to the more leisurely speed of life here. It was taking all her energy to not shout at him to hurry up.

Clive lifted the mug to his mouth and blew across the surface of the tea, creating little ripples, before taking a small sip. 'Ah, that's a good cuppa. Right, well, as I said, I went and hung out a bit with Derek's friends.'

'Did they know you were a journalist?' asked Kerry.

'Hmm, no. I wasn't overly happy about being undercover. I'd only been on the job a couple of years at that point but I had worked myself up from being the tea boy to cadet reporter. Anyway, I managed to get an in through a friend of a friend of a friend. Ended up playing pool with some of them in a pub after Derek had done a runner. Oddly enough, they were quite open about it. I think they were trying to show how much they hated him for doing such a terrible thing.'

'So they thought he'd done it?' asked Bernie as she sat down next to Clive, eager to see what was in his notebook.

'Oh yes. Quite sure.' He put down his mug and opened his notebook. To Bernie, it seemed to be full of squiggles. 'Everything's in shorthand, my own special version. No one else can read it. Anyway, the thing that kept coming up, time and time again, was that Derek had money problems – big money problems. He was heavily in debt. He used to go to Bristol a lot. Said he was working but some of his friends thought his bookie was there. A couple of guys mentioned a woman in Bristol, thought he was probably two-timing his girlfriend. I take it you know about Lesley Cooper?'

Bernie nodded.

'But what's a gambling debt and another woman got to do with abducting Sophie Newell?' asked Matt.

'Well, the woman – probably nothing – but the gambling? A lot of his friends thought he had abducted Sophie and sold her to clear his debts. Especially if the person mentioned really was his bookie.'

'Who was that then?' Kerry asked.

'A very nasty piece of work called Tommy "Toolbox" Brown. Sounds ridiculous, I know, but he didn't use guns or knives. He had a toolbox and he'd choose which tool he was going to use to torture you. In some ways it's not surprising that Derek did what he did.'

Bernie felt sick. She thought about Eddie Parker and his ten grand debt and how worried he was. How much had Derek's debt been if he'd agreed to abduct a child?

'So his friends didn't think he'd killed her? They thought he'd sold her to this Tommy Brown who, I guess, would have sold her on to a paedophile ring?' Anderson asked.

Bernie looked across at him, glad he could ask what she couldn't.

Clive Bishop simply nodded. The anguish on his face said it all.

Bernie covered her face with her hands. An image of a smiling girl with blonde plaits and red ribbons swam into her mind. All along she had hoped it had been quick and painless for Sophie; that she hadn't suffered. She wiped one escaped tear away.

'Did you go to the police at the time?' Kerry asked.

'Yes. But Derek was already gone. And some blokes talking in a pub wasn't really evidence. They did check it out though. In fact there were lots of rumours about Tommy and human trafficking over the years. But back then, I hate to say it, Tommy had friends on the force. Nothing ever stuck.'

Anderson nodded. 'That would make sense. I found some statements in the original file from a few of Derek's friends and associates and his gambling was mentioned but I don't remember seeing that particular name.' He sat down next to Bernie, on the edge of the sofa, leaning into her. She found his close presence both reassuring and alarming at the same time.

'So what happened after that?' Bernie asked.

'Not a lot. There were no other suspects. The story was shelved. But it stayed with me and I wrote the article on Bill and Karen Newell's deaths. That was bloody awful.' He sniffed.

Pain was etched on Clive's face. Bernie put her hand on his arm and he patted it. He couldn't speak for a minute. There was a small buzz and Matt reached into his pocket for his phone. He gave her a little nod and walked into the kitchen.

Clive sniffed again. 'I can't begin to tell you how much pain there was around here after their deaths. That's what did it for Otterfield and Marchant. Any ties of friendship between the two villages were severed completely that day.' He reached for his tea and took a gulp. 'I spoke to Steven, briefly. I was quite well known by then. I was known for being fair. I just asked him what he would do and he said he would sell the farm and go. "Nothing to stay for," he said. So that's what he did. He had to split the farm up, though, sell the land and buildings separately. No one wanted a big farm.'

'Hang on, the Newells had a farm?' asked Bernie.

'Yes,' said Clive. 'It was called Newell Farm. It was between Marchant and Otterfield.'

Bernie's mind began to tick. 'Who bought the land?'

'Ron Willis did. Wanted to expand his farm for his boys but he didn't have enough money for the buildings as well.'

Bernie's heart beat faster. 'And the buildings?'

'They were sold to a woman who now does holiday lets.'

'Name?'

'I don't know her name but the place is now called Pear Tree Farm.'

'Oh God. Matt! Did you hear that?' said Bernie.

Matt came back from the kitchen. 'What? No, sorry. I was a bit more focused on this email. It's from the Royal Navy, with an attachment. I think this is going to help speed up the search for Steven Newell.'

He handed his phone to Bernie. She looked at the image of the man before her. Light brown hair, albeit a little thinner, still with a sombre look in his eyes and his lips tightly shut. She wondered if he had known any happiness in his life since Sophie had gone. She didn't blame him for wanting Derek dead but taking Molly was a step too far. She made a decision. It was time to flush Steven Newell out.

'Clive, I'm giving you a scoop. Put this photo on your website. You'll have ten minutes before any other paper. Matt, circulate this photo to all the police forces and Interpol. Airports and ports too.' Bernie glanced at her watch. It was close to eleven o'clock. 'Kerry, get on to Jane. We need to get this out on TV, and fast, and into the morning papers. Social media too. Anderson, contact the super and let him know what's happening. I'm going to ring Jessica and Lesley. They need to know before it's headline news. Let's get moving. This is the break we've been waiting for.'

CHAPTER THIRTY

Despite the late hour, MCIT was now a hive of activity. Steven Newell's photo was on all the major newspapers' websites and was guaranteed to go front page. Jane had got out of bed to mastermind the media coverage. Sitting at her desk in her office, without her make-up on, Jane actually looked human to Bernie.

'Glad to see you've taken my advice for a change,' said Jane. Bernie looked for a sneer but didn't see one.

'Yes, but it's having the photo that makes all the difference. Matt sorted that one out. There wasn't much point putting out a name without a picture. And Matt managed to catch the forensic artist just before he went to bed. He was more than willing to help and he's going to focus on different variations of how Steven Newell may look now – beards, longer hair, that sort of thing. So hopefully tomorrow, or' – Bernie glanced at her watch and saw it was past midnight – 'rather, today, we may have some extra images to put out there. Thank you for coming in. You can probably go home now and we'll see you in the morning.'

She turned to leave.

'Oh, Bernie?'

'Yes?' Bernie flicked her head back round.

'It's so much better when we work together, isn't it? The super will be pleased.'

Bernie stared at Jane, trying to work out what she meant. Her face was more readable without her heavy eye make-up and red lipstick and Bernie saw slight desperation. She'd heard the super had torn a strip off Jane after the press conference. In that brief moment, she felt some pity for Jane, although not a lot.

She paused before saying, 'It's all about working to our own strengths. Go home, Jane. There'll be a lot to do in the morning. If we need you before then I'll let you know.'

Bernie walked back to MCIT, fighting tiredness. Adrenalin was trying to kick in but wasn't quite working yet. She just hoped releasing Steven's photo would have the desired effect.

'Do you think he'll let Molly go now?' Jessica had asked her when she had rung earlier.

'If he's the one who's got her, then maybe.' Bernie couldn't bring herself to say to Jessica that Molly might already be dead.

Bernie had contacted Lesley next.

'If you catch him, can I see him please?' Lesley had asked.

'I can't make you any promises. He may not want to see you.'

'I know. But he's all I have.'

Bernie stood in the doorway of MCIT, watching her team work. They'd done everything she'd asked for and more. Although she knew there was a small possibility of someone ringing in with information in the middle of the night, she thought it unlikely.

'OK,' she said, as she walked towards them. 'We've done what we can for now. There's no point us all staying up. You might as well go home and I'll stay here.'

Matt looked up from his computer and smiled. 'With all due respect, ma'am, you've had a rough week. I can sleep anywhere, anytime, so if I do a night shift, I'll have no problems sleeping during the day.'

'Same here,' said Anderson. 'You and Kerry can go home and get a few hours before taking over from us at eight o'clock. It was what we were going to do anyway.'

Bernie looked across at Kerry, who looked worn out.

'I'm not going to argue,' said Kerry. 'I'm dead on my feet. Come on, Bernie, let's go before they change their minds.'

Bernie didn't like being overruled but she realised the main action would be in the morning. She sighed. 'OK. I know when I'm being told. See you at eight.'

She and Kerry both grabbed their coats and bags and headed out.

'I'm glad I've got you on your own,' said Kerry as they walked to the car park.

'Oh?'

'You asked about checking out my police grapevine for info on DS Anderson.'

Bernie felt embarrassed by the memory. 'Oh God, yes. I was probably a bit hasty. He's proved himself since then.'

'Yes, but,' Kerry hesitated, 'I think you should know anyway. Especially with how he's been today.'

'What do you mean?'

'Well, acting like he's in charge. He used to be a DI.'

'What?' They had reached her car and Bernie pressed the key fob to unlock it.

'In Scotland, he was a DI, had his own team and a good success rate. But he hit a fellow officer. Apparently, there were extenuating circumstances so he wasn't charged. Instead he was demoted and he came down here to escape it. So, sex on legs and a bad boy image. You'd better stay away, Bernie. I know your type.' Kerry waggled her finger and laughed. 'See you in the morning.'

'Yeah, bye.' Bernie got into her car. She sat in shock for a few seconds but then realised it all made sense. He was clearly used to giving orders, not taking them. And what extenuating circumstances? She was tempted to go back up and ask him but didn't want to have that conversation in front of Matt.

'Matt. Damn. I didn't tell him about Pear Tree Farm. I'll have to do it in the morning. And now I'm talking to myself. God, I've got to get some sleep.'

Bernie started the car. Reversing out of the parking space, she felt incredibly tired. The roads were empty and the drive home would only take five minutes without traffic. Her eyelids were drooping so she blinked to keep them open. She was almost home when her eyes shut. A bell ring woke her, and her eyes sprang open. She had narrowly missed a cyclist. She raised her hand to say sorry, not sure if the cyclist would see in the dark or not. Bernie indicated left to turn into her road but waited for the bike to go past before raising her hand once more to apologise. Bathed in the orange light from the lamp post on the corner of the road, Bernie saw the cyclist scowl.

'Oh, well, I deserved that.'

Bernie turned left and pulled into her allocated parking space. And then it hit her. The cyclist was the South African woman staying at Pear Tree Farm. What was she doing out so late?

We made the room into a cinema earlier. All the curtains were pulled shut and the lights were off. It was a Disney princess movie. I don't know which one, I wasn't really watching. But she didn't want to sit on the comfy sofa. She wanted to be under the table, lying on her tummy. I lay next to her and watched as she stuffed popcorn into her little mouth, her eyes fixed on the screen, barely blinking. I don't know why she likes being under the table so much. Maybe it makes her feel safe. But not me. I've been remembering so many things since this all started. Things I'd blocked out from years ago. A time when I hid under a table, curled up like a ball, listening to two people shouting, blaming each other for things going wrong. The voices in my head from the other night. They're clearer now. I've been lied to and manipulated. I'm no longer safe. More importantly, Molly isn't either. We have to move soon. I've started to make plans. The game of hide and seek is nearly over.

CHAPTER THIRTY-ONE

Friday

Bernie woke with a start. She desperately tried to hang on to the remnants of her dream. She was sure someone had called her name and there was something about Molly she couldn't quite remember. She could almost hear her grandfather saying to her, 'If it's important, it will come back. The Lord talks to us while we sleep.' She wondered if she would see Pops again in her dreams. She was worried about forgetting the sound of his voice, the deep and rich bass that would boom down the road if she was home late.

'Bernadette Susan Noel! What time do you call this?'

'Ssh, Pops, you'll wake everyone.'

'What do you mean? I'm not the one tap-tapping down the road in silly high-heeled shoes.'

Bernie shut her eyes tightly as she felt a wave of grief rushing towards her. She had done her best to keep her emotions at bay during the investigation but it was no good. She tried to catch the sob but her throat ached so much she had to let out the pain for the man who had raised her. Even though her real father had possibly come back into her life, no one could replace Pops.

She sat up as the tears continued. It felt as though the grief was coming up from her stomach and she thought she might be sick. She drew her knees up and sobbed into her bedding.

She wasn't sure how long she cried for. But eventually, the tears subsided and stopped. She grabbed a handful of tissues from a box beside her bed and blew her nose. She took a few deep breaths to try and calm herself and glanced at the clock. It was just before six thirty, when her alarm was due to go off.

Friday, she thought. Unless the super could persuade the chief constable to give her more time this was the last day to find Molly before DCI Worth took over the case on Saturday morning. She picked up her phone to check for messages but there were none. She sniffed. She felt completely drained and totally useless.

'Bernadette Susan Noel, are you feeling sorry for yourself?'

Pops was back in her head.

She felt her lip quiver slightly. 'Mmm.'

'Well, Bernadette, you know what you need to do. You need to give this day to the Lord and ask Him to go before you. So stop feeling sorry for yourself and go out there and do your job. Find. That. Girl!'

Bernie pushed open the front door of the police headquarters.

'Morning,' she said breezily to the officer on the front desk. She punched in the code to release the internal door and jogged up the stairs with renewed vigour. She wasn't really a religious person but she did have a new sense of determination after she had prayed. Or maybe it was the thought of Pops watching over her. Fragments of her dream were still playing around in her head. She still wasn't sure who had called her name but she was sure she recognised the voice. And she was certain Molly was still alive. She couldn't explain how she knew; it was just a gut feeling.

'Good morning,' she said as she walked into MCIT.

Matt and Anderson were bent over their desks, working. They both looked up with red-rimmed eyes.

'Right, quick handover and then off home. Come back when you've had enough sleep,' she said.

Matt shifted in his seat and yawned. 'Nothing much overnight. Hopefully, it will all kick off this morning.' He picked up a newspaper from a pile next to him. 'One of the uniform lads brought these in. Jane's done her job well. It's front page on all the nationals. It's headline news on the TV this morning and on the radio. Hashtag Find Molly is trending on Twitter with Steven's picture so if he has skipped the country, we've gone international. Interpol has it too. We've increased the number of officers for the phone lines this morning so we're hoping for a good public response.'

'Matt, that's brilliant. Well done. DS Anderson, what about you? What have you been up to?'

Bernie looked at him. His dark hair was tousled and he had stubble on his face. She was starting to see the attraction of him but managed to stop herself. She couldn't afford to go down that route.

'Ma'am,' he said, wearily. 'I've been going through the Sophie Newell case again, and the info that Clive Bishop gave us last night. I know you're sure we're looking for Steven Newell but I'm wondering if there could be a connection with Derek's past and his friends in Bristol. When I come back from Derek's flat, I'd like to look into that old gambling debt Clive mentioned. And whether or not Tommy Brown was his bookie.'

Bernie remembered what Kerry had told her about Anderson the night before. In some ways it was a sensible plan but was this him trying to exert authority again? She pulled a face as she spoke.

'It'll depend on the public response. We may have too many leads to chase up for you to be looking in another direction. Let's see how things are when you come back in.'

She waited for an angry response, noticing his mouth tighten. But he kept his anger in check.

'OK, ma'am. We'll see later.'

'Good. Come back in when you're ready but if I think I'm going to need you sooner, I'll call. Off you both go and get some sleep.'

Matt and Anderson staggered up.

'Make sure you drive home carefully,' Bernie said. 'Oh, that reminds me. Matt, you were in the kitchen last night when Clive Bishop was talking. Pear Tree Farm used to be Newell Farm, where Sophie lived. I saw Ellie Du Plessis last night when I was driving home. Oh God, I nearly hit her. So I won't be making jokes about your driving any more. Matt, are you OK? You look a bit confused.'

Matt shook his head. 'It's probably nothing but it was quite late to be out. You went home after midnight.'

Bernie shrugged her shoulders. 'I wondered about that too. Maybe she'd been for a night out. Anyway, I thought it was interesting.'

They all heard a bump and turned to see Kerry pushing open the door with her back. She carried a small brown box in her hands.

'Compliments of the bakery,' she said.

Bernie pointed at the box. 'That's not a big white box full of bakery goodies.'

'Er, no. Their oven packed up last night and they didn't want to let us down, so they've sent a box of Penguin biscuits. They've just got it fixed so they've promised sandwiches and sausage rolls for lunch instead. They hope that's OK.'

Bernie laughed. 'That's fine. It's very kind of them to think of us. Oh well, I had got used to having pastries for breakfast but I'm sure a couple of chocolate biscuits will be just as good. Perhaps you could go and hand some of them out to the officers who are waiting in the incident room. I saw a few in there already.'

Matt walked past Bernie. 'Wait for me, Kerry, I think I might need a couple of those to help get me home.'

Bernie smiled as Kerry and Matt left the room. She turned to see Anderson leaning against his desk, his arms crossed.

'Oh, I'm sorry, did you want one? I'll get Kerry back,' said Bernie.

He shook his head. 'No, I want to talk to you, while the others aren't here.'

Bernie swallowed. 'Good. I'd like to talk to you too. Please go first.'

'Why are you undermining my ideas?' Anderson asked. 'I genuinely think there's something in this Bristol link.'

Bernie took a step nearer. 'I could ask you the same, former Detective *Inspector* Anderson.' She slipped her hands into her black trouser pockets.

Anderson looked shocked and wiped his face with his hand. 'How long have you known? That was supposed to be kept quiet.'

Bernie kept her face stony as she replied. 'I only found out last night. I know you hit a fellow officer but I don't know why. I need to be sure I can trust you, if you're going to stay on my team. I'm more than happy for you to look at other lines of enquiry but you need to be prepared to follow my lead. Message understood?'

Anderson appeared to regain his composure. He pushed himself up from his desk and sauntered over to Bernie. 'If you must know, I hit the officer who was screwing my wife, well, almost ex-wife now. It's not something I'm particularly proud of.'

He brushed past her as he left the room. She felt herself shiver slightly but it wasn't with desire. She was unnerved. Bernie reached out to a desk to steady herself. Anderson hadn't said anything particularly scary to her but she couldn't shake the feeling of menace. She shook her head.

'Get a grip, woman,' she told herself.

'Bernie, are you OK?'

She turned to see Kerry at the door.

'What's happened? You were fine a moment ago, really upbeat.'

Bernie waved her hand dismissively. 'It's nothing. Just a little power struggle with DS Anderson. You're right, I was in a better mood. I had a good cry over Pops this morning. Think it released some tension.'

Kerry came over and put her hand on Bernie's arm. 'Good. I didn't want to say anything but I was a bit worried about you taking on this case so soon after his death. You do know there'll be more tears to come?'

'Oh yes. But I heard Pops's voice encouraging me to keep going. So, that's what we'll do. We're going to find her and I don't know why, but I'm convinced she's alive. Let's go and flush out Steven Newell.'

The media coverage had worked and a steady flow of calls was coming into the incident room. Kerry was making a list of credible sightings for uniform to follow up. Bernie tapped her on the shoulder.

'So, where are we up to?' she asked.

'Well, so far, Steven's been spotted in Swansea, London, Manchester and Fife. And those were all phone calls. According to Twitter, he's in Portugal, Istanbul, Sri Lanka and Australia.'

Bernie laughed. 'Right, so a busy boy then. Any of them actually worth checking out?'

'London and Manchester seem the best two options at the moment as we were given actual addresses. I've got onto the relevant local forces already. Just waiting to hear back. Oh by the way, front desk called up. There's a Paula Parker in reception for you,' said Kerry.

Bernie was surprised. 'Really?'

'Yep. Is she anything to do with the caretaker at Otterfield School?'

'Yes, his wife. Eddie was going to talk to her. See if she would help us. I'm amazed she's come here. I better see what she wants.'

*

Paula sat in reception, biting her nails. Nervous, are you? thought Bernie. So you should be. You all treated Jessica and Molly like dirt.

'Mrs Parker.' Bernie held out her hand. 'I'm DI Bernie Noel. We met briefly the other day.'

'Er, yes.'

Paula shook Bernie's hand. Her fingers were wet from the biting. Bernie resisted the urge to pull her hand away.

'Let's find somewhere to chat. After you.'

Bernie wiped her hand discreetly on her trousers.

They settled into the comfortable chairs in the family room. Bernie had briefly considered using a proper interview room but Paula had come of her own free will. Intimidating her now would not be helpful.

'What do you want to tell me, Paula? Is it OK to call you Paula?'

'Yes.' Paula's eyes darted up. She pushed her dark fringe away. 'Eddie spoke to me.' Her voice was similar to the shopkeeper in Otterfield. Slow, with the vowels stretched out.

Bernie nodded. 'And?'

Paula looked at her. 'Well, first things first. Eddie's told me about the gambling so you can leave him alone now. That other policeman wanted to know where he was Thursday evening. I told him Eddie was home with me.'

It took Bernie a second to realise an officer from the betting shop raids inquiry had obviously been in touch. 'OK. But what do you want to tell me?'

'It's a bit awkward, see. Apart from Eddie, no one else from the village knows I'm here.'

'Whatever you tell me will be in the strictest confidence.'

'Hmm. Things have a habit of getting out. Like Derek Hayes.'

'Do you think he took Sophie Newell?'

'Seems likely, doesn't it? Slipped away one night. Left a note for his parents. If he was innocent, why run? His poor mum and dad.' Paula shook her head. 'If he made contact with them, they never said. They were too ashamed. We all were. I mean, who wants someone like *that* living nearby?' She began to bite her nails again.

Bernie glanced at her watch. It was after eleven a.m. She really needed Paula to get a move on.

'So when Derek came back, how did the villagers respond?'

'Couldn't believe it. After his parents died, we thought the house would go on the market. A few people wanted to buy it. Took us a while to realise someone was there cos it was winter and he'd leave in the dark and come home in the dark. Didn't recognise him at first with the beard but there was something about his eyes. Like his father's.'

Bernie wondered if Paula would ever get to the point.

'Then this young woman turned up. Pregnant, with another kiddie in tow. I'm really sorry Molly's gone missing but there's something not right with her. Kicked my little Oscar at school. Anyway, we all thought she was his partner. Seemed wrong to us. A young woman with an old man. And then the girl. She reminds me of Sophie. I was the same year as Steven at school. Knew her quite well. Such a pretty little thing.' Paula looked up. 'We had to do something. So we called a meeting.'

'And what happened?' Bernie had been listening intently to Paula's voice. Was she their mystery phone caller? It was hard to tell. 'Please tell me no one from the village has done anything stupid.'

'Like what? Kidnap Molly? What you take us for? We might not be the friendliest but we're not monsters. Not like *him*!' Paula's voice rose up. Her cheeks flushed.

'Sorry. But the lack of help from the village has been so frustrating. What did you all decide at this meeting?'

Paula narrowed her eyes but continued. 'By the time we had it, we knew Jessica was his daughter not his partner. But we didn't want them in Otterfield. Thought about calling the police, letting them know he was back. Some of us thought they might want to reopen Sophie's case but none of us wanted the trouble we had when she disappeared. So, we thought it best to ignore them. Be unfriendly so they'd want to leave. And it was working. I heard Jessica muttering about "getting out as soon as possible".'

'But none of it was Jess's fault. And definitely not Molly's.'

Paula lowered her head. Her fringe covered one of her eyes. 'I know. We know. When Molly first went missing, we all just thought it was for attention. That Jessica had hidden her. But now…' Paula shook her head. 'Best thing that young woman can do is sell up and move away.'

'It won't be that easy. We don't know if Derek had a will.'

'Doesn't matter. It's Jessica's house.'

'What do you mean?'

'Grandparents left it to her. That's how we knew she was Derek's daughter. The neighbours witnessed the will. They knew her name.'

Bernie was confused. She was fairly certain Jess didn't know this. They'd have to look into it.

'Thank you, Paula. You've been very helpful. Just one last question – do you have any idea who might have taken Molly?' Bernie still couldn't tell if Paula was their mystery caller or not.

'No. None.'

'So you didn't call Crimestoppers with a description of a man then? A stranger who'd been spotted in the area? Eddie said it was a different delivery man bringing the school dinners lately.'

Paula looked puzzled. 'No. I haven't called. And it's a young lad bringing the food. Only strangers I've seen in Otterfield are you lot. Obviously we get a few tourists, especially at Pear Tree Farm. I'm the cleaner there.'

Bernie remembered Eddie had said Paula had two jobs and Naomi had mentioned her cleaner had taken the booking for the O'Connells. 'So you took the call from Mick O'Connell then? He booked one of the cottages.'

'Yes, I did. Oh, Naomi was so cross with me. I thought she'd want the money but apparently she'd been hoping for a break for a few days before the season really kicked in.' Paula shrugged. 'Oh well, you can't always get everything right.'

No, thought Bernie, aware of all her own mistakes, you can't. 'Thanks for coming in, Paula. If you think of anything else then please get in contact.'

She showed Paula out. If she wasn't the mystery caller, then who was?

CHAPTER THIRTY-TWO

Bernie sat at her desk, tapping her pen against a notepad. She was lost in thought, trying to pull together her dream. She'd been at a farm and kept catching sight of Molly. Or was it Sophie? The girls were quite similar. It wasn't her first dream about Molly but this one seemed more significant somehow. There was something about the voice who called her. Was it a woman or a man? Someone she knew? She shook her head. She knew her brain sifted information as she slept; she just needed to find the bits that had made it through the debris.

She looked at the notes she had started to write on her pad. The sightings in London and Manchester had been dead ends. A few Steven Newells had rung in to rule themselves out. Bernie was still hoping the woman who had given them the initial description would ring back. Otherwise, nothing.

Bernie glanced at her watch. It was just past midday. The super had asked for a briefing at one o'clock. She put down her pen and ran her fingers through her hair; it needed a proper wash, not the quick rinse she'd done after Sam had vomited, but that was the last thing on her mind. Especially since she'd left her new products in London, rushing to leave. She wished she could see Mrs Lloyd, the lovely old lady at her grandparents' church who used to do her hair when she was little. Her mother and grandmother had had no idea what to do with Bernie's burgeoning hair. She would sit for ages while Mrs Lloyd plaited her wild curls, telling her tales of the Caribbean. The stories hadn't really sunk in but Mrs Lloyd's kindness had. She was now in an old peoples' home, her arthritic fingers too gnarly to braid. By leaving so quickly, Bernie had missed the chance to see her. Once the case was over, she'd go back to London for a weekend. She needed to talk to her mother face-to-face about her father's appearance in her life anyway.

Bernie got up to make herself a coffee when she remembered something Paula Parker had said – might be worth checking out the will that left the house to Jessica.

She quickly searched for solicitors and found there were only four in the immediate area. She picked up the phone and started to call them, one by one. The first two hadn't dealt with the Hayes family but the third had.

'I'll just put you through to the solicitor that handled the will,' said the receptionist.

'Thank you.' Elevator music. 'Greensleeves'. She decided it could be worse.

'Natasha Rowley,' a sharp, efficient-sounding voice said.

'Oh, hello. I'm Detective Inspector Noel from Wiltshire Police. I'm hoping you can help me with a query.'

'Oh, right. Well, fire away. I'll help if I can.'

'I believe you handled the wills for Mr and Mrs Hayes in Otterfield. They both died last year.'

'Er, yes, I did.'

'Would it be possible to check who the house was left to? I need to know if it was their son, Derek Hayes, also known as Derek Cole, or their granddaughter, Jessica Cole.'

There was a short pause. 'This is to do with the missing girl, isn't it?'

'Yes. I'm just trying to find out if Jessica already owns the house. It would help her to know that.'

'One minute.'

Bernie could hear the swish of a filing cabinet being opened and then papers being rummaged through.

'Right, here we go.' Natasha's brisk voice was back. 'Really, I shouldn't be divulging this without a warrant… but if it helps Ms Cole, then I'm willing to reveal this. Initially, Mr and Mrs Hayes left everything to each other, as you would expect. But in the event of them both dying at the same time, or closely after each other, as did actually happen, there were instructions. Yes, the house was left to Jessica Cole. Derek was executor, along with myself. He was left a small amount of money and everything else, including the house, went to Jessica.' Natasha hesitated. 'And the jewellery went to her too.'

'The jewellery?' asked Bernie.

'Yes. Mrs Hayes had some very expensive pieces of jewellery – family heirlooms worth around thirty thousand pounds. We had to take them out of the safe at the bank. I suggested they should stay there but Derek insisted Jessica should have them.'

'So you gave them to her?'

'No, Derek took them, to give to… Oh God, Derek took them. You think she didn't get the jewellery?'

Bernie rubbed her forehead, she could feel another headache brewing. 'We didn't find anything when we searched the house and she's made no mention of any jewellery. A lot of work has been done on the house so maybe he sold them and used the money for that. Or maybe he didn't and he spent it elsewhere.' Bernie remembered Anderson's insistence about the gambling debt. Bookies often had long memories. Maybe she should let him look into it. 'Thank you very much, Natasha, that's been most helpful. I'm wondering if there's something else you can look into for me please.'

'Yes, sure.'

'It's probably before your time though. Could you see if Bill and Karen Newell were clients of yours? And Steven Newell as well?'

*

Bernie's finger hovered over the call sign on her phone. At best, Anderson would've only had about four hours' sleep. She wondered if her hesitancy was to do with being proved wrong but she knew that was just a smokescreen. In reality, she didn't want to have to speak to him again so soon after their last encounter. She was still uneasy. But Molly was more important. She pressed and waited for him to answer.

A sleepy voice answered, 'Hello?'

'Anderson, it's... Bernie. You don't have to come in straight away but I think it might be a good idea for you to look into that gambling debt after all. I've found out some information that might be relevant. I'll explain more when you get here.' She heard him take a deep sigh. 'I'm sorry I woke you. Were you fast asleep?'

'Mmm.'

'Right, well, just come in as soon as—'

'I'm sorry I was a sod earlier.'

'What?'

'You heard me. You caught me unawares. I wanted to be the one to tell you what had happened. I wanted you to hear it from me and not make up your mind before you knew all the facts. The look on your face earlier, I... I reacted the wrong way. I'm sorry.'

Bernie wasn't sure how she felt. There was relief at his apology but she still had misgivings. She shut her eyes and tried to steady her voice. She didn't want him to hear how vulnerable she felt. 'OK. We have to find Molly first. Everything else has to wait for now. Just come in.'

She ended the call and let out a long breath.

'So despite throwing everything we have at the media, we still have nothing concrete,' said Wilson.

'No.' Bernie lowered her eyes.

'Well, continue monitoring every lead that comes in, but you need to start preparing for a possible handover with DCI Worth for tomorrow morning. The chief constable hasn't come back to me yet. Make sure your logbook is up to date. Every piece of evidence, every interview, a map of the search area – everything.' Wilson rubbed his hands over his frog-like eyes. 'I know I'm sounding harsh but I want to show DCI Worth you did all you could.'

Bernie pushed aside her rising anger. 'There's still the missing jewellery I think Derek stole from Jessica. DS Anderson is looking into that now. He thinks there's a Bristol link here from Derek's past.'

Wilson nodded. 'The team can continue to work the case but *you* need to prepare the logbook. Understood?'

Bernie closed her eyes and nodded slowly. This wasn't how she'd hoped the day would turn out. She was just relieved Jane wasn't in the room to witness her humiliation. 'Yes, sir. I'll get on to it now.'

Bernie closed the door behind her and raced down to the toilets. She splashed water over her face and then dried it with a paper towel. She exhaled slowly, trying to keep her breath even; trying to slow down her racing heartbeat. She stared into the mirror and saw dark shadows under her eyes.

'Oh, Bernie.'

She winced at the voice that cut through her like a knife. It was Jane. She hadn't heard the door open.

'I've been looking for you everywhere. Are you OK? You look a little peaky. BBC *Points West* want to do an interview with you for this evening's show.'

Bernie sighed and allowed herself to glance at Jane. 'Wouldn't it be better if the super does it? I have paperwork to do.'

'Paperwork? You're supposed to be looking for a missing child.'

'I need to bring the logbook up to date. Double check everything before tomorrow.'

Bernie was aware of Jane looking at her.

'Oh, right… oh. They're taking you off?'

'Ssh, keep your voice down.' Bernie glanced down the line of cubicles, just in case anyone else was in there. 'Possibly. DCI Worth might be taking over in the morning.' Bernie waited for a snide comment, or a laugh or whatever it was Jane was about to do.

'Well, as I see it, you have two choices. You can either lie down and accept defeat, or you can get out there, do that interview and let the bastard abductor know you're onto him and coming for him. So what's it going to be? The BBC specifically asked for you.'

Bernie looked at Jane in surprise. She hadn't been expecting a pep talk. She suddenly felt suspicious.

'Why are you being so nice to me? I thought I wasn't good enough to talk to the media.'

'Well, you can't be any worse than yesterday's fiasco. And DCI Worth is a dirty old leech who can't keep his hands off my bum. I am *not* going to work with him on this case. So, I'm not really being nice, I'm thinking entirely of myself. And Molly. A week is too long.'

Bernie smiled. Maybe Jane wasn't a total vampire after all.

'What about the super?'

'I'll square it with him.' She looked Bernie up and down. 'Of course, you can't wear that. You'll have to go home and get changed. For God's sake, woman, you've got biscuit crumbs on your shirt. And you'll need to do something with your hair. And put some make-up on – you look like death warmed up. Come back to me in an hour and we'll go over what you're saying. Camera crew will be here at five p.m.'

Bernie laughed. This was the Jane she knew.

Bernie smoothed her hair down. She'd pulled it back into a tight bun and added a minimal amount of make-up. Jane had been right about her clothes. Without even realising it, she had put on her outfit from yesterday. Now in a new trouser suit and a clean shirt, she felt more professional and more confident about finding Molly. She'd been fairly diligent with keeping the logbook up to date anyway – it could wait; Molly couldn't.

Jane had gone through the questions with her. Her piece would be recorded and then edited with a film the presenter had made earlier.

They stood just outside headquarters; the weather was behaving itself for a change and Bernie felt a little warm in her suit jacket. The young female presenter was talking with the cameraman about the best position to stand in. Jane came and hovered over Bernie's shoulder.

'Happy with what we went through?'

Bernie nodded. 'Yes, I think so. Are you sure the super's all right with this?'

'Yes, he's fine. Of course, the chief constable may not be as happy so you've got to do your best and make this count. I'll just be inside.'

As Jane walked away, Bernie thought Jane was wasted in the press office. She didn't think it would be long before some political party spotted her ruthless potential and employed her to run an election campaign. She'd definitely win.

'Right, Detective Inspector Noel, we're ready for you now.'

Bernie smiled at the young woman. 'OK.'

'So I'll ask you some questions which you'll answer. We'll have a quick look at the footage to make sure it's all right. If there's anything you're unhappy about, we can record again. We'll start with me and then I'll turn to you and ask you your first question. At the end, when you do your appeal, you can either look at me or, if you feel comfortable, look directly into the camera. Right, let's start.'

The woman nodded to the cameraman before speaking. 'I'm outside Wiltshire Police headquarters with Detective Inspector

Noel who's been leading the investigation. Detective Inspector' – the presenter turned towards Bernie – 'it's now been a week since Molly Reynolds went missing from the playground in Otterfield. How confident are you about finding Molly at this stage?'

Bernie swallowed. 'We're still treating this as a missing persons' case, and as such, we're confident we'll be bringing Molly home soon.'

'Now, you've done a thorough search of the area but not much has been found.'

'No, but we have found some key items of evidence which have helped us piece together an idea of what may have happened to her. We believe she was taken away from the park in a buggy, along a path by the railway.'

'Overnight, you issued the name of a man you'd like to speak to in relation to Molly's disappearance. Can you tell us any more about that?'

'Yes. Through our enquiries, we've discovered a possible link with another missing person's case from 1990. A local girl called Sophie Newell disappeared from the farm she lived on; it's now Pear Tree Farm. We'd like to talk to her brother, Steven Newell. We don't know for certain if he's connected with Molly's abduction but we'd like to speak to him so we can rule him out.' Bernie turned her head a little and looked directly into the camera.

'Steven, please come forward, or if anyone knows where he is, please get in contact with us here at Wiltshire Police or on Crimestoppers. And to the person who has Molly: it's time to let her go now. We believe you've got what you wanted out of this. Her parents are distraught. Please, let her go.' Bernie glanced back at the presenter.

'Thank you very much, Detective Inspector Noel. If you can help in any way, then the telephone numbers you'll need are on screen right now as well as our website. This is Gemma Proctor, reporting for BBC *Points West*.'

Gemma smiled at Bernie. 'Wow. You're a pro. I think that was all OK. We'll just check back and see. Is there anything you're unsure about?'

Bernie shook her head. 'I think it was fine. Best to check with Jane.' Bernie beckoned to Jane to come out.

'How was it?'

'Good, I think, but I'd like you to check.'

Jane was silent as the film was played back.

'Ah, that bit there. Bernie, are you sure about mentioning Pear Tree Farm?'

'Well, it's only there to give some context. It might jog some memories for those who were living round here in 1990. Why should it be a problem?'

'Because if the owners start to lose bookings over it, they won't be happy. Let's hope it doesn't come back to bite you on the bum.'

CHAPTER THIRTY-THREE

Matt was waiting by Bernie's desk when she walked back into MCIT.

'Good to see you back in, Matt. Did you get some sleep?'

'Yeah, some. I actually got woken up by my mate from the digital forensics lab. He's emailed a few pictures of what Steven Newell might look like now. Having the more recent photo pretty much finished the job for them. They're still working on the other stuff.'

Bernie's brow furrowed. 'The other stuff? God, they're keen.'

'Yeah. The phone call giving the description of the man seen wandering around Otterfield.'

'Oh, that.' Bernie pulled out her chair and sat down at her desk. 'I'm not sure we're ever going to find out who that was. Is it worth carrying on with?'

'They've already started the work so we'll have to pay. Might as well let them finish. And this is a big case for them so it'll help with their profile.'

'OK. Let's see these updated pics then.'

'I emailed them to you.'

Bernie switched on her monitor and a few clicks later, had the pictures in front of her. 'Wow, these look good.'

There were three pictures; one showed an updated image straight from the original photo, another had Newell with less hair on his head and the last had him with a beard.

'There are still other variations they can do, like glasses or dyed hair but I think these are pretty good for getting on with,' Matt said.

Bernie nodded. 'Absolutely. Get these over to Jane and see if the BBC can add it in to their report tonight. And then get them released to all other media as well.'

'Social media too?'

'Hmm, yes, that would be good.'

Bernie was aware of Matt staring at her.

'What?' she asked.

'You just said Jane's name without any hint of a comment about her. In fact, you called her Jane and not "the vampire".'

Bernie gave a wry smile. 'We've come to an understanding. Now, hop to it.'

Matt laughed and started to leave the room. 'Oh, by the way, DS Anderson told me to tell you he's gone to see the solicitor. She called while you were doing the interview. I did suggest he wait for you but he said it came under his remit.'

Bernie rubbed her forehead and sighed. 'That's OK, Matt. I'm beginning to think DS Anderson is a law unto himself.'

Matt smiled. 'I don't think it, I know it. Right, I'm off to see your new BFF. Kerry's in the incident room if you need her.'

Bernie shook her head with a laugh. Jane, her new best friend forever? Not likely.

Bernie connected her laptop to the whiteboard in the incident room.

'Do we really have to do this?' she asked Kerry.

'Yes. We all want to see your moment of glory.'

'It's hardly glory and I did a very short piece the night Molly went missing.'

'Yes, but that was on the late-night programme. No one here saw it. We all want to see the detective inspector, don't we?' She turned to the other officers in the room.

'Yes.'

'OK then.' Bernie ran her fingers through her hair. She'd taken down the tight bun; it had made her head throb a little. She glanced around. The room was filling up. Even Wilson and Jane had come in.

Bernie had a sudden thought. 'Has anyone warned Jessica Cole and Lesley Cooper about this?'

'Already done,' said Jane. 'I called the vicarage and spoke to the vicar's wife and she was going to pass the message on. I spoke to Lesley in person. No need to thank me.'

'Well, thank you anyway.'

Kerry sidled up to Bernie. 'Oh my God. Are you two going to, like, move in together? I can just see you as roomies.'

Bernie grinned. 'Nothing as exciting as that. We're united in our dislike of DCI Worth, that's all. Right, this is about to start. I think we're on first.'

Everyone hushed down as the theme music came on and then the main presenter spoke.

'It's now been a week since five-year-old Molly Reynolds went missing from a playground in Otterfield, near Devizes. Gemma Proctor is reporting.'

The studio switched to outside footage with Gemma Proctor at the playground. Then she was at Molly's school with the head teacher, Tim Jenkins.

Bernie put her hands over her eyes as she came onto the screen and she watched through her fingers. The first time had been bad enough but this interview was longer. She pulled her hands away to see the three images of Steven Newell on the screen.

'This is how Steven Newell may look today,' said the female studio presenter. 'If anyone has any information they think may be relevant, then please contact Wiltshire Police or ring Crimestoppers on 0800 555 111.'

There was a round of applause and shouts of 'Well done, ma'am.'

Bernie raised her hands to silence the officers. 'OK, enough now. You know I hate doing this sort of thing. We had a burst of phone calls this morning after the newspapers ran Steven's name and photo. I'm hoping for the same this evening. There will of course be a shift change, so please make sure you're up to date and do a proper handover with the night staff.' Bernie looked across to Wilson. 'Is there anything you want to add, sir?'

Wilson coughed a little. 'Not really, other than do your job, *all* of you.' He looked pointedly at Bernie and she knew what that meant – the logbook.

A phone started to ring, and then another. Officers picked up the calls and began to write notes. Bernie wanted to stay but knew she had to leave Kerry in charge.

'I'll be in MCIT, writing up bloody notes if anything important comes in,' she said.

Kerry nodded. 'I saw that look. God, what's his problem?'

Matt came up to Bernie. 'What do you want me to do?'

'Firstly, order a lot of pizza. Secondly, double-check the visitors' list from the school. Go through it and see if there's anyone who might be Steven Newell.'

'I'm on it.'

Bernie could feel someone staring at her. She looked across and saw Anderson standing by the door. He beckoned her with his head and she followed him to MCIT.

'You did very well, ma'am. You have a face for TV.'

'Suppose that's better than being told I have a face for radio. Is this you trying to get back into my good books?' Her tone was crisp. 'Now, Matt said you went to the solicitor before I could brief you.'

Anderson gave a wry grin. 'I didn't want to disturb your interview. Besides, Natasha was very… obliging.'

I bet she bloody was, thought Bernie. Showered and shaved and smart in a fresh suit, Bernie could imagine Anderson charming the pants off Natasha – she hoped not literally.

'So, do you want to know what I found out, or not?'

Bernie's mind snapped back. 'Yes.'

'You were right about the Newells having their will with the same solicitors'. In their will, there was a codicil that set apart ten thousand pounds for any information leading to the arrest and conviction of whoever took Sophie. It's been sitting in a savings account ever since.'

'Since 1998? That's going to be a lot more than ten grand now.'

'Yep. And earlier this year, someone rang the solicitors to ask if the reward was still available.'

Bernie looked at Anderson, sharply. 'Name?'

'*She* didn't give one. Which begs a couple of questions. Why hasn't this person come forward if she has information? And how did she know about the reward in the first place?'

'Because she's local and close to the Newell family?' Bernie suggested. She thought for a moment. 'I'm wondering now if Lesley told me the truth when she said she didn't know Derek was back.' She shook her head. 'No, that doesn't fit. She wouldn't have to check about the reward money, she'd already know. But it's got to be someone who's been around a long time. At least from 1998. Maybe even from when Sophie disappeared.'

Bernie stared at the logbook in front of her. She didn't know what else to add. She knew by reputation that DCI Worth was a very picky detective. It was normally his officers who did all the legwork while he meticulously recorded information in his office. He had a high turnover on his team. He claimed they moved onwards and upwards thanks to his training, but Bernie had heard enough rumours to know they were escaping their DCI.

She could hear phones ringing in the incident room. Kerry hadn't disturbed her so she knew nothing significant had come in yet. Matt was working his way through the school visitors' list. So far, everyone he had rung had had an alibi. Anderson was looking into the information the solicitor had given. A thought occurred to Bernie.

'Anderson?'

'Yes, ma'am.'

'Our mystery woman who asked about the reward money.'

'Yep.'

'Is it possible that she has given us info?' asked Bernie.

Anderson looked up. 'What do you mean?'

Bernie pointed her pen at him. 'Could she be our mystery phone caller?'

Anderson sat back in his chair and folded his arms. 'Possibly. But why hasn't she called back to give better info and claim the reward?'

'Matt?' asked Bernie.

'Yes?'

'When will your forensic guys have any info on the telephone call?'

'Erm, let me just check.' Matt went into his email. 'They're hoping to have something for us by tomorrow. They said there were a few more checks to do. But even if they clean it up, do you honestly think someone from the solicitors' office will recognise the person? And she didn't leave her name there either.'

Bernie started to chew the bottom of her pen. 'I'm clutching at straws, aren't I?' She glanced at the clock; it was just after seven thirty p.m. She threw her pen down. 'Sod the bloody logbook. I'm going to see Kerry.'

She was about to walk into the incident room when Kerry came out and they nearly collided with each other.

'Bernie, I was just coming to get you. We've now had three lots of information, all corroborating each other.'

'Saying what?'

'That Steven Newell is in Australia.'

'What?' Bernie couldn't quite believe it. 'Wasn't there something on Twitter about that this morning?'

Kerry looked down. 'Er, yes. There was that this morning and then we've had two phone calls this evening. Both of them served with Steven in the navy and both men said they thought he'd gone to Australia.'

Bernie leaned against the wall. 'Doesn't mean he didn't come back here and take Molly. Did either of them give an address?'

'No. But one of them thought another old colleague might know. He's going to ring back later.'

Bernie sucked in her cheeks before blowing them out. 'But they're both certain it's the Steven Newell we're looking for?'

Kerry nodded. 'Oh yes. One of them knew about Sophie. Steven had confided in him. He was in charge of Steven when he was a new recruit. It's definitely him.'

'OK. You stay in the incident room. I'll get Matt to look into this.'

Bernie walked quickly back to MCIT.

'Matt, stop work on the school list for now. We've had reports Steven Newell is in Australia. We're waiting for an address but can you look into it? Start with the High Commission here. They should be able to point you in the right direction.'

Anderson turned towards her. 'Looks like Clive Bishop was right. Derek's bookie was Tommy Brown and he was a mean old bastard.'

'Was?' asked Bernie.

'Yes, died in 2009.'

'So, how is that relevant now?'

'That's what I'm working on. Looks like the business carried on. I'd like to go to Bristol tomorrow to find out who runs it now. Find out about Derek's debts and see if he paid them.'

Bernie paused. She was so certain that Molly's disappearance was tied up with the Newell family it was hard to entertain any other possibilities. She nodded slowly. Anderson would do whatever he damned well pleased anyway. 'OK.'

'Bernie?'

She turned to see Kerry in the doorway. 'You need to come now and speak to this lady on the phone. She's going apeshit.'

Bernie ran down to the incident room. She could see a uniformed officer trying to placate someone on the other end of the line.

'Madam, please, just try to calm down. Detective Inspector Noel is here now.'

Bernie mouthed, 'Who is it?'

The officer turned her notepad to Bernie and she read the name. Bernie made an O shape with her lips. She took the phone.

'Detective Inspector Noel. What can I do for you, Mrs Phillips?'

'You can bloody well pay me for the three cancellations I've had tonight after you mentioned my farm on the TV! And my phone has been ringing non-stop with journalists. Even caught one on my property.'

'Mrs Phillips, Naomi, I'm so sorry for mentioning the farm. I only did so in the hope it might jog someone's memory about Sophie Newell.'

'Well, that was before my time and it's me who's paying the consequence of your slip-up. I didn't know she'd lived here when I bought it. And to think how helpful I've been to you – letting you know about my dodgy customers and all that.'

'Yes, Naomi, you've been very helpful. Of course, the O'Connells are in the clear. They had nothing to do with Molly—'

'But there's something not right with them. Are you sure their little girl is ill or did they just tell you that to put you off the scent?'

Bernie took a deep breath and raised her eyes upwards. 'Naomi, I hate to tell you this but Emma O'Connell died yesterday.'

There was a pause at the end of the line. And then a whispered, 'What?'

'Very sadly, Emma died yesterday. She had meningitis. I thought DC Taylor had told you how ill she was.'

'Well, yes, but I didn't think she'd die. Oh God, this is awful.'

Bernie could hear Naomi's breathing quicken. 'Naomi, are you OK?'

'Oh, that poor girl. That poor family. And I made it worse for them these last few days. If I had known…'

'Naomi, you can't blame yourself. You thought it was Molly and in that sense, you did the right thing. My colleagues over at Thames Valley were discreet in how they handled the situation and I know they're helping the O'Connells now. We've sent them flowers, not that it helps much.'

Bernie waited for a response. 'Naomi, are you sure you're all right? I'm so sorry to have to tell you like this and I am very sorry about the cancellations. Do you want me to send someone down to the farm to get rid of the journalists?'

'No, don't worry about that. I can deal with them. I'm just so sorry about the little girl. I lost a cousin to meningitis many years ago now. Oh God.'

'I know. It's awful. I know you didn't have direct contact with Emma but you did clean up her vomit. So you might want to check in with your GP to make sure you're not infected. Don't want anyone else to be ill. And with her death, this makes us even more determined to find Molly.'

'Yes, of course, her poor mother has suffered enough, with losing her father as well. Her suffering needs to end, doesn't it?'

'Yes,' said Bernie. 'We're hopeful for a breakthrough.'

'Yes, well, I'm sorry I shouted at you. I'll get off the phone now. There must be others trying to get through. Goodbye.'

'Bye, Naomi.'

Bernie handed the phone back to the officer.

'Thank you, ma'am. I didn't know what to say to her.'

'Don't worry. But any more weirdos, get DS Allen to handle them.' Bernie nodded in Kerry's direction and smiled.

'Oi! I heard that,' said Kerry. 'Everything OK?'

'It is now, I think. Not the best way to tell her about little Emma. Stopped her in her tracks though.'

There was something about Naomi Phillips that Bernie couldn't quite put her finger on. Generous on the one hand but then scathing on the other. Maybe it was mood swings. Maybe it was just her age. Or maybe there was more to Naomi than met the eye.

I've seen the papers. A photo and name for everyone to see. It's time. I tell her to not make a sound. I tell her we're going on a journey, a magical mystery tour. She squeaks and I put my finger to her soft lips.

'Hush,' I say, 'not a sound, remember?'

She nods, her blue eyes solemn. I lift her up and she cuddles into my neck. I smell her washed hair. I carry her to the door and then out, into the night.

We're leaving. And we're never coming back.

CHAPTER THIRTY-FOUR

At just after ten p.m., Bernie shut the logbook with a thud.

'Right. That's as damn close to perfection as possible. If DCI Worth makes any quibble with it then I won't be responsible for my actions.'

She stretched back in her chair until she caught sight of Anderson looking at her, and quickly shrank back. 'How are you two doing?' she asked him and Matt.

'Still waiting for the Australian High Commission to get back to me,' said Matt. 'They did say it might take a while. I've finished looking at the list of visitors from the school. All the men check out so nothing suspicious there.'

Bernie yawned. 'Oh, sorry. Lack of sleep is getting to me now. Anderson, anything more on this bookie?'

'Yes and no. He had some very nasty associates so if Derek did owe money, I wouldn't put it past them to kidnap a child for ransom.'

'Except there wasn't a financial ransom,' said Bernie. 'It was a lot darker than that and more than just a pound of flesh.' She sighed. 'Have you checked with police in Bristol?'

'Yeah. The officer who dealt with Tommy Brown the most is back on duty first thing tomorrow. What time is DCI Worth due?'

Bernie sighed. Despite the super's best efforts, the chief constable was adamant that DCI Worth would be arriving in the morning. 'I think it's nine a.m. He likes his beauty sleep.'

'OK, I can be in Bristol for seven. Catch this guy as he comes in. You know, if Steven Newell really is in Australia, then this is the next best lead.'

Bernie looked at Anderson and nodded slowly. 'I know.'

There was a sudden shout of 'Bernie', and then the sound of running out in the corridor. Bernie ran to the door as Kerry got there.

'What?'

Kerry paused to catch her breath. 'A phone call. Came through on nine nine nine. It's short but recorded. Come and listen.'

Bernie looked over her shoulder and beckoned Matt and Anderson. 'Come on.'

Bernie made sure there was silence in the room as the call was played back. The voice was muffled but the words were clear enough.

'She's back in the same place.' Click.

Bernie looked at Kerry. 'Telephone number?'

'Yes, it flashed up. Not a mobile so it's being checked now.'

'Ma'am?'

Bernie looked to see a male uniform officer waving at her.

'Confirmation just through. It was a phone box in—'

'Otterfield,' finished Bernie. 'Of course it bloody was.' She closed her eyes for a moment to compose herself. Was this a hoax? A cruel trick played by someone in Otterfield? Or could it really be Molly? She almost didn't dare to hope.

'Ma'am?'

Bernie opened her eyes to see Kerry there, waiting for orders, along with everyone else. Time for action.

'Matt, send that to your tech guys and ask them to compare it with the lady who gave the description,' Bernie said. 'Kerry, I need you to stay here – this could be a false alarm. Anderson, go to the vicarage in Marchant but wait outside. Don't go in until I confirm it. I want two cars and a silent approach. Make sure we have bolt cutters so we can get into the park. Do we still have an officer outside Jessica's house?'

'No,' said Anderson. 'We padlocked it instead. Are you sure you don't want me to come with you?'

Bernie shook her head. 'No. If Molly is there and alive, then I want you to break the good news. But if she's... dead... then wait for me.'

Bernie put her hand to her mouth. The initial exhilaration that Molly was possibly back had been replaced by a chill. Was she going to find a girl, alive, or a dead body?

CHAPTER THIRTY-FIVE

With lights flashing, the car Bernie was in zipped down the winding lanes towards Otterfield. The hedges rose up on each side, creating a dark tunnel. She'd had the good sense to get another officer to drive. The car behind contained four officers, ready to fan out and search for Molly in the park. But Bernie was fairly certain she knew where Molly would be – in the playground. An ambulance was en route as well.

Bernie's heart was hammering away. She'd left Kerry to contact the super. She started to bite her nails. She was grateful for one thing. If Molly was there, it would be them who found her. Not a dog walker or a bunch of teenagers having a booze-up in the park. No one had been near it for a week. No one had dared.

'Ma'am? How do you want to do this?' asked her driver, a male uniformed officer.

Bernie pulled her hand away from her mouth. 'The gate should be locked so we'll use the bolt cutters to get in if we have to. Obviously we'll need torches. I suggest we head to the playground first. Put shoe covers on before we enter. I think she's there. If not, we work in twos, covering the park. I bloody hope this isn't a wind-up. I haven't got time for that.'

'If the main gate's locked, how did they get in?'

'Same as us. Bolt cutters. The abductor must have some. A chain was cut when she was taken.'

The driver slowed the car as they entered Otterfield.

Bernie spoke into her radio. 'Blue lights off. Don't want to draw attention.'

Curtains were drawn in all the houses. Light leaked out from some but most were dark. Good, thought Bernie, no audience.

A couple of minutes later, they drew up outside the park. Bernie was tempted to jump out of the car and just run but she held back. She waited for one of the officers to fetch the bolt cutters to cut the chain on the main gates. But they weren't needed.

'You were right, ma'am. Already cut.' He pushed the gate open. Bernie winced at the high-pitched squeak.

'We'll need to bag the chain. Just in case. But let's look for Molly first,' said Bernie.

'After you, ma'am.'

Bernie stepped forward. She took a deep breath and then switched her torch on.

'Everyone got their shoe covers?'

'Yes,' came the chorus of replies.

'OK.' She repeated her orders. She felt sick with anticipation. What were they going to find? She had promised Jessica she would get Molly back but she'd never promised her she would be alive.

They followed the path round to the playground with Bernie leading. Bushes and shrubs loomed in the shadows. Moonlight-silhouetted trees swayed gently in the breeze, the leaves whispering secrets. Myriad stars sparkled overhead. In one sense it was a beautiful night but... Bernie shuddered. The sense of being watched was back. Was the abductor here, now, observing them? Or maybe it was just adrenalin causing the prickling sensation on the back of her neck. The park was silent except for the rustling of the shoe covers as they walked. Their combined torches lit the way and it wasn't long before they could see the railings around the playground and the little gate.

The padlock on the gate was also cut. If this was a hoax it was an elaborate one.

Although the playground didn't have much equipment, it was still quite large, with a few bushes dotted around it. Bernie swung her beam slowly across the area, trying to track each part. She hovered over the swings and slide but couldn't spot anything.

'Shall we go in, ma'am?'

Bernie looked at the officer who had spoken to her. His face was eerily pale in the torch light. She turned to them all. None of them really wanted to go in. None of them wanted to find a dead child.

'Right,' she said quietly. 'Let's just do our job.' Bile rose up from her stomach. She swallowed it back down. As the senior officer, she had to lead.

She stepped into the playground and began swinging the torch around again, slower this time. The other officers did the same and discs of light danced across the ground as though in a nightclub. She was fairly certain the swings and slide were clear but checked anyway. She searched carefully under the slide, looking for any clue that Molly had been there. The others were behind her but were holding back a little. She cursed herself for not bringing one of the duty sergeants with her. She even missed Anderson. But she didn't want him to see her like this – hesitant and anxious.

Bernie moved past the empty swings. She bumped one and the chain squealed in protest. She tensed. She reached out and steadied it. She headed towards the rear of the playground. Her beam picked out the edge of the roundabout – a red and blue striped base with yellow handles. Then she saw something else. She started to run out of instinct. She couldn't help herself.

'Molly.'

The inert bundle she had spotted wasn't moving, wasn't responding in any way.

'Molly!'

Bernie stopped as she reached the roundabout and lowered her torch. A child was lying on it, perfectly still, curled up as though asleep, blonde curls trailing down over her face.

'Molly?'

Still no response. Bernie reached into her pocket and pulled out some gloves. Her own breathing was ragged as she struggled to get them on while holding the torch.

'Let me take that for you, ma'am,' said a voice from behind.

Her driver was holding out his hand for her torch. The other four officers stood behind. Bernie thought it was partly out of dread but also not wanting to contaminate the area.

Bernie looked at the child, hoping to God this wasn't going to be a murder scene – a white tent over the body with CSIs and Nick White analysing Molly's death. Jessica's face when she broke the news. She shut her eyes and whispered a prayer. 'God, please.'

She reached out but wasn't quite close enough. She shuffled forward and tried again. This time her fingers brushed Molly's cheek. Was it warm? It was so hard to tell with the gloves on. She gently moved her fingers down, searching round her neck for a pulse. She couldn't find one. She raised her fingers and held them under Molly's nose. Was there something?

'Bloody gloves.' She peeled one off and placed two fingers under Molly's nostrils. A faint breath tickled Bernie's skin. 'Thank God,' she whispered.

Rain started to fall down gently. It was so light Bernie could only see it when she looked at the yellow glow of the lamp post. The hospital car park had a few cars in it – one of them a police car. Bernie had come in the ambulance. She had held Molly's hand the whole journey. Jessica and Davy were already at the hospital with Anderson when they arrived. Bernie stayed with Molly while the doctors did an initial examination before allowing her parents in. Jessica had gone straight to Molly's side but Davy had scooped Bernie into his arms and given her the biggest bear hug she'd ever had. No one said anything – words weren't needed. Bernie had looked at the reunited family and for a moment her heart had lurched. For a week, Molly had been hers – her responsibility – and now, she had to give her back.

The rain was fine, drenching. The kind that looks harmless but completely soaks you to the skin. She stood, allowing it to wash her and mingle with her own tears.

'What are you standing in the rain for? You're getting soaked, ma'am.'

Bernie didn't turn to face Anderson. If he wanted to talk to her, he could join her in the rain. She felt his arm brush against her. She looked at him.

'Hey,' he said, raising his hand to wipe her tears from her cheek. 'Why are you crying? You should be happy. You found her.'

Bernie struggled against her sobs to get her words out. 'She wasn't moving. I thought… I thought she was…'

'Dead?' he said. 'That must have been scary.' Anderson turned her round to face him. 'That's why I didn't want you to go without me. I've found a dead child before. It's bloody awful. Reaching out your hand to check? Well, that takes courage. And you did it. And she's alive.'

He pulled Bernie in for a hug as her sobs continued. 'You found her. You kept your promise to Jessica.' He rested his head on hers.

Bernie relaxed into him. A big part of her wanted to stay there but it wasn't wise. She reluctantly pulled away.

'Bernie, I think we need to talk.'

'No. Not until the case is over.'

'It is. You found her.'

'But we don't have the abductor.'

Anderson touched her arm.

'Let DCI Worth handle it.'

'I'm not letting him take over now. Not when we're so close.'

'Bernie, we've worked our backsides off for the last week. You got the main result – you got Molly back.'

Bernie stepped away from him and shook her head. 'No. I'm going home to sleep. And in the morning, we are going to nail the bastard who did this. Molly is drugged up to her eyeballs, and yes, we've got her back. But we don't know for certain she's going to be OK. We don't know what she's been through. So, we're not going to stop now. And you're going to Bristol in the morning to find out about this Tommy Brown. And I'm going to go to Otterfield, because there's a whole bloody load of female suspects there.'

'Fine. If that's how you want it.'

'It is.' Bernie turned and started to walk away.

'At least let me drive you home.'

'No. I'll get uniform to take me.'

'Bernie, this is ridiculous.'

She carried on walking and heard the sound of something being kicked, probably a rubbish bin, and then the sound of 'Fuck'. She didn't look back.

The engine started as she approached the police car. She opened the passenger door and got in. She glanced sideways at the driver as she did her seat belt up.

'You didn't see a thing,' she said.

'See what, ma'am?'

It's dark. My head throbs. My body aches. My eyes are too heavy to open. The smell of pennies fills my nostrils. I struggle to move. I try to reach out with my right hand but feel only empty space. She's gone. This wasn't the plan. It's out of my control now. Molly's 'too hot to handle'. 'Too dangerous to keep her'. But is she safe?

CHAPTER THIRTY-SIX

Saturday

'God. I think the bakery has sent the entire shop this morning,' Kerry said. 'You can tell the news about Molly has spread.'

Bernie smiled. There was a huge selection – Danish pastries, Belgian buns, eclairs, cookies, muffins and their famous giant ring doughnuts. She pulled out a raspberry Danish to have with her statutory morning coffee. The incident room was full of beaming police officers. The tension of the last few days had lifted. Molly was alive and Bernie had heard from Jessica that she had woken up this morning and asked for juice.

Bernie was about to start the morning briefing when there was a cough. The super came into the room, followed, unexpectedly, by the Chief Constable of Wiltshire. Everyone went quiet.

'Good morning. Before you start the briefing, Bernie, I have something to say. Well done to everyone who has been involved in this investigation,' said Wilson. 'We got Molly Reynolds back and that's an excellent result. The chief constable would like to say a few words.'

Bernie's palms were clammy as the highest officer in Wiltshire stepped forward. No mention had been made yet of DCI Worth.

'To all the officers involved in this case – I give you my personal thanks. It's not been easy and the press have been a bit tricky at times. Thank you, Jane, for handling them so well.'

Bernie spotted Jane in the doorway, blushing, adding some much needed colour to her cheeks.

'You've all played your part, whether you were on the search or handing out leaflets or manning the phones.'

Oh God, thought Bernie, he's buttering us up before pulling us all off the case, or maybe just me.

'Being part of a team is incredibly important. But a team only works well with a strong leader. Detective Chief Superintendent Wilson…'

What? Bernie couldn't believe what she was about to hear. He's sat behind a desk for pretty much all of it.

'…I'm sure you will agree with me, that this team has been very ably led by Detective Inspector Bernadette Noel.'

Bernie's eyes shot up to meet the chief constable's gaze. He smiled at her.

'You showed bravery last night, going into the playground. You didn't know what you were going to find. You have led from the front from the beginning. However…'

Bernie's heart sank. This was the moment she'd been dreading, the moment when DCI Worth would be introduced.

'…your work is not over yet. Molly is back but her abductor is still at large. By all means, have a good breakfast this morning. But then, go out there and catch the perpetrator. And when you do, the first round of drinks is on Detective Chief Superintendent Wilson. That's all.'

Laughter rippled round the room. Bernie stood there stunned. The chief constable came over to her.

'Not the speech you were expecting?' he asked.

'No, sir, I thought you were going to introduce DCI Worth.' She looked at the man before her, smart in his uniform, the reputation of Wiltshire Police resting on his shoulders. Only his eyes gave away the strain of responsibility. She had never met the chief constable personally before.

'What's the saying? "A rolling stone gathers no moss"? It would be stupid to stop you now, while you have momentum and passion.' He held out his hand to Bernie. 'Good luck, Detective Inspector. I'm sure you'll have news for me soon.'

She took his hand and matched his firm grip.

'I'm sure we will, sir.'

Bernie smiled as he left the room. Then she turned to her colleagues. 'Right, you heard the chief constable. Eat up your breakfast and then get cracking. We've got an abductor to catch.'

'Matt, where are we up to with Steven Newell?'

'I got an email this morning from the Australian High Commission. There's a Steven Newell who's British and lives in Darwin. Whether he's our Steven Newell remains to be seen. The local police are trying to make contact with him so hopefully we'll get some more news today.'

Bernie smiled at Matt. Although he'd had some sleep, he still looked a bit wrecked. He hadn't shaved and there was baby fluff growing on his chin. She was grateful Anderson hadn't yet called in. She'd tossed and turned over their conversation to begin with when she'd gone to bed, but thankfully exhaustion had taken over and it was the best night's sleep she'd had in over a week.

She'd left Kerry running the incident room. Phone calls were trickling in still, although some were just congratulating them on finding Molly.

Jane came into MCIT with a huge pile of newspapers and plonked them down on Bernie's desk. She held up the first paper.

'"Molly's home!"' she said. 'They're all like that. Lots of praise for you, Bernie. I had to mention the tip-off. Didn't want it to look as though she'd been in the park the whole week and we just hadn't found her.'

Bernie smiled. Jane had said 'we' and not 'you'. Maybe she wasn't so bad after all.

'Thank you. The chief constable was right. You've done a good job, handling the press,' said Bernie.

Matt looked surprised at Bernie's response. 'Oh my God. Can we all join this love-in?'

'Of course,' said Jane, with a wink. 'More than happy for a threesome with you, Matty boy.'

Matt turned bright red and buried his head in his work.

Jane and Bernie giggled together. 'I'll catch you later, Bernie. You know where I am if you need me.'

Bernie waited for Jane to leave before she spoke to her DC.

'Oh Matt, you did ask for that.'

'Hmmph.'

The phone started to ring on her desk.

'Saved by the bell,' said Bernie.

Matt avoided Bernie's eyes as she answered the phone.

'MCIT. DI Noel speaking.'

'Er, is DI, sorry, DS Anderson there please?' The voice was female with a soft Scottish accent. Alarm bells started to ring in Bernie's head.

'I'm afraid he's not in the office at the moment. Can I take a message?'

'Erm, I probably don't need to leave a message. I just need to know where to send some of his stuff. I'm Louise Anderson, his ex-wife, well, almost. Shall I just send it to headquarters? It's only one box.'

Bernie felt awkward. 'Oh, right. Yes, here is probably best. It can be left at reception.'

'OK... Can I ask you something else?'

'Yes,' said Bernie.

'Are you Dougie's boss?'

Bernie could feel a trickle of cold sweat on the back of her neck. 'Sort of, yes.'

'This is going to sound like a really stupid question but, are there many female officers on your team?'

The trickle was working its way down her back. 'Why?'

'It's... maybe I'm wrong for saying this but... I couldn't face myself if another woman goes through what I went through...'

Bernie's shirt felt damp.

'You see,' Louise Anderson continued, 'he comes across so charming and he's very good-looking. He's not violent, he's never hit me but... he's controlling, manipulative. I've had three years of hell. I don't want another woman to go through that. Am I wrong to tell you?'

Bernie closed her eyes and took a deep breath. The safety of Anderson's arms the previous night seemed a long way away. 'No, you're not wrong. I'll keep an eye out.'

'Good. Thank you. It's a weight off my mind knowing that someone else knows. Bye.'

Bernie replaced the handset. It felt as though Louise Anderson had just plunged a knife into her heart.

CHAPTER THIRTY-SEVEN

Anderson's name flashed on Bernie's phone. *Bloody perfect timing.* She'd let it go to voicemail for now. She knew it would probably enrage him but she didn't care. After her brief conversation with Louise Anderson, she really didn't want to talk to him just yet.

The email icon flashed up on Bernie's PC. *Who's trying to get through to me now?* She clicked and found two messages. The first was from Therese at the lab saying they were still analysing the lock of hair. The structure was similar to Molly's but the blood definitely wasn't hers. The other was from Nick White, the pathologist.

'About bloody time too!' Bernie said.

'What?' Matt asked.

'The preliminary post-mortem findings for Derek Hayes. We won't get the full report until toxicology comes back.'

Matt moved his chair next to Bernie's. 'Open it up then.'

Dear DI Noel,

Apologies for the delay in sending my first thoughts. A full and thorough examination of Derek Cole/Hayes took place, including X-rays. I have a new technician who labelled the X-rays with initials rather than full name. As a result, I thought there had been a mix-up with the other body you saw, David Chaucer, the victim from the betting shop raid. I ordered new X-rays yesterday and was amazed by the results. Both men had similar head wounds – a closed fracture to the back of the head. The fractures are recent, not historic. It's possible the same kind of weapon was used for both men – a blunt instrument of sorts. I will need to do some more tests but at the moment it is possible that Derek Cole was incapacitated by a blow to the head prior to his death. I will let you deduce from that what you will.

I'll be in touch when I know more.

Yours,
Nick White

Matt stared at the screen, rereading the email. 'Is he saying what I think he's saying?'

'Yes,' Bernie said. 'And if this is the case, then Derek didn't commit suicide. He was murdered. And there may be a connection with this other victim. The one who was injured in the betting shop raid.' She shook her head in confusion.

'But what about the suicide note?' asked Matt. 'Did someone else write it?'

'Looks like it. We need to get that letter checked against a sample of Derek's handwriting. And Anderson told me that the car door was locked. He had to smash the window. Derek couldn't have locked it if he was knocked out. There must have been a second set of keys. We'll need to check with Jessica.'

'Check what with Jessica?'

Bernie looked up to see Kerry. 'Post-mortem report. Derek was hit on the head and probably unconscious when put in the car. So how was his door locked if the keys were in the ignition?'

'Spare set?'

'That's what we need to check. Matt, can you ring the vicarage and speak to Jessica and find out please?'

Kerry sat down next to Bernie and read Nick White's email. 'So, not suicide then. Murder.'

'Exactly.'

The phone on Bernie's desk rang. She answered, her mind still distracted by Nick White's revelation.

'MCIT. DI Noel speaking.'

There was a slight pause. Oh God, thought Bernie, this is all I need – a call centre has got through to me somehow.

'Is that Wiltshire police?'

'Yes, sir, it is. I'm Detective Inspector Noel. How can I help you?'

She put her hand over the phone. 'I think somebody has put this call through to me instead of the incident room.'

'Sorry,' mouthed Kerry.

'Oh good. I wasn't sure if I'd dialled the number correctly.'

Bernie frowned. What kind of nutter was this man?

'Well, you have. Can you tell me your name please?'

Another pause.

'Oh yes, of course. I'm Steven Newell. I'm ringing from Australia. I gather you've been trying to get hold of me. Is it about Sophie? Have you finally found her?'

Bernie grabbed Kerry's arm and mouthed 'Steven Newell' and she switched the phone over to speaker.

'Yes, well, no. We haven't found Sophie. I wanted to ask you about something else that might relate to Sophie's disappearance.'

A slight delay. 'OK. I apologise if you can't hear me very well. I'm ringing on a satellite phone. I'm on a boat in the Pacific at the moment. I'm a marine biologist.'

Bernie and Kerry looked at each other. 'How long have you been on the boat for, Mr Newell?' asked Bernie.

Pause. 'Coming up to two weeks now. We're on our way back and the station radioed me to say you wanted to talk to me. They gave me this number.'

'Can anyone verify that?'

Pause. 'Yeah. Five other crew members.'

Bernie shut her eyes briefly. 'Your local police will need to take statements from you all but I'm very glad you called me, Mr Newell. A young girl went missing last week but we found her last night. Her grandfather was Derek Hayes.'

There was silence. 'Mr Newell? Are you still there?'

'Yes, I'm here. It's just... hearing that name again. You wondered if I was involved.'

'Yes.'

Pause. 'Well, I'm not. Didn't even know that man was back. Have you arrested him for Sophie?'

'No. I'm afraid...' Now it was Bernie who paused. In light of what she had just read, it looked as though Derek's death was murder rather than suicide. She continued, 'I'm afraid Derek Hayes died earlier this week.'

Pause. 'What? Shit. He's the only one who knows where Sophie is. I want to be able to bury her with Mum and Dad.'

'I know, Mr Newell, I understand your frustration.'

Pause. 'I take it you've spoken with my aunt. Did she tell you what she did? How she gave him an alibi?'

'Yes, she did. And she's very sorry about that.'

Bernie could just hear a faint echo of her own voice.

'Too bloody late for that now. But you said the little girl is back. Is she all right? Doesn't she know who took her?'

'She's not ready for questioning just yet and it will be a specialist team of officers who do that. Can you think of anyone else who would want to harm Derek Hayes and his family?'

Pause. 'I'm not sure. I was only ten when Sophie went missing. He may have had money problems. He was always either skint or loaded. I think I remember my dad making a comment one day – something about how Derek must have had a win because he suddenly had a wodge of cash. So maybe there was something with that.'

'Thank you, Mr Newell. You've been a great help. I'm planning on looking into Sophie's case so I may need to speak to you again at some point. When you get ashore, you'll find the local police will have an email address for me. Please send me a message with your contact details. Thank you for your time.'

Pause. 'Yes, OK, I'll do that. I appreciate you taking another look at the case. Thanks. Bye.'

'Oh, just one other thing.'

Pause. 'Yes?'

'Your parents left a reward in their will for anyone who may have information leading to the arrest and conviction of a suspect. Do you have anything to do with that?'

Pause. 'No. The solicitor deals with it. Nothing to do with me at all. I'm starting to get crackling on the line my end. I'm going to have to go but I'll be back in two days if you need to contact me. Bye.'

'Goodbye, Mr Newell.'

Bernie switched the phone off. 'Shit. I really thought it was him.'

Kerry reached out and touched Bernie's arm. 'He was a good candidate. But now we can eliminate him, we have to start again. Besides, the caller last night was female. And I'm totally thrown by Derek's post-mortem report.'

'Yeah. Both men had similar head wounds. That really doesn't make sense. Unless Anderson…' said Bernie. She remembered his missed call. She looked at her phone. She wasn't sure she wanted to listen to his voicemail with Kerry there.

'Unless Anderson what?' Kerry glanced at Bernie's phone. 'Has he called? He has, hasn't he? He might have found something. Go on. It might be important. And stick it on speaker. I've missed his dulcet Scottish tones,' Kerry laughed.

Bernie picked up the phone. 'I'll listen to it first, just in case he's slagging me off for not answering.'

'All the more reason for me to hear. I'll be a witness.'

'Kerry, no. It's my phone…'

'Don't be so stupid,' and Kerry snatched the phone from Bernie and pressed play.

Anderson's voice sounded tinny in the large room. 'Bernie…'

Kerry raised her eyebrows. 'We've progressed to "Bernie" then.'

'…look, I don't know if you're not answering because you're busy or because I was a dick last night…'

'What did he do?' asked Kerry.

Bernie just bowed her head.

'…but, I'm sorry. You've asked me to wait until we finish the case and I will. Just give me a call now because I'm starting to make some headway in Bristol. Please.'

Kerry switched the phone off. 'Well, I can see why you didn't want me to hear that.'

'Kerry… I…' Bernie shook her head. If she couldn't explain it to herself then how could she explain it to Kerry?

'What the hell happened last night?'

Bernie raised her head a little but couldn't bring herself to look at Kerry. She kept her voice low. 'Nothing happened but we had a… moment.'

'What, like a "kissing" kind of moment? God, Bernie. I mean, it's not the done thing but you wouldn't be the first police officer to have a relationship with a colleague.'

Bernie sighed. 'No, it was just a hug. But his wife rang earlier. Well, almost ex-wife. She wasn't exactly complimentary about him. I think there's more to him than meets the eye.'

'Well, we all know that. And exes aren't exactly reliable. You must know that too.'

Bernie gave a half smile. 'Oh yes. All too well. But there's something… I just can't put my finger on it. I mean, he's intense but… I don't know.' She shook her head.

'Ma'am?' said Matt.

Bernie looked across at him.

'You were right. Two sets of keys. He kept a spare set in a drawer in the garage. Do you want me to go and check it out?'

'Send uniform. I need you here.'

'I can sort that,' Kerry said. She stepped away from Bernie but said in a quiet voice, 'And you've got a phone call to make.'

Bernie nodded and grabbed her phone.

'Anderson, it's Bernie. What have you got for me?'

'Derek Hayes had a massive gambling debt when he left the country in 1990,' Bernie told Matt and Kerry. 'According to the copper Anderson spoke to, Hayes was a marked man.'

'So, Derek probably only came back because he thought he was safe. From Tommy Brown, anyway. He knew he'd died and thought the debt had gone as well,' Matt said.

'Except, it probably hadn't,' said Kerry. 'That would explain why Derek took the jewellery that should have gone to Jessica. Did this bookie have family or a business partner?'

'It appears that way. That's what Anderson is looking into next. He's liaising with Avon and Somerset Police in connection with the betting shop raids. Two dead men with similar head wounds can't be ignored. But if Molly's abductor is from Bristol, why use the phone box in Otterfield?' asked Bernie.

'To throw us off the scent? Make us think it was a local?' suggested Matt. 'Talking of which, just going back a moment, Derek thought he was safe from Tommy Brown but what about the people in Otterfield? It was a massive risk coming back.'

Bernie tapped a pen on her desk. 'Unless… he knew somehow that he, and in particular, Jess, would be blanked. And he was banking on that hostility to make her want to leave. Derek would have put the house on the market and pocketed the money to pay his debt.'

'It's possible,' Kerry said.

'Hmm,' said Bernie. 'It still feels as though we're missing something, and it's probably right under our noses. Can you try your tech guys, Matt? See if they've come up with anything yet.'

Matt reached for his desk phone and dialled a number.

'Kerry, you'd better go back to the incident room and check on the calls.'

Bernie glanced at her watch. It was close to eleven o'clock. 'I'm going to call the hospital, find out how Molly is. I still don't think they'll let us interview her yet. But if we don't make any progress here, then we may have to.'

Bernie picked up her phone and was about to dial the hospital number when she saw Matt waving at her.

'What?' she asked.

'That's brilliant, thank you. Yes, I can see the email in my inbox now. Thanks. Bye.'

Matt put the phone down.

'They've sent a provisional report. They worked through the night on this. There's still more to do but this is what they've discovered so far.'

Bernie came round to his desk and pulled up a chair. Matt clicked on the email to open it. There were a couple of attachments but they read the email first.

'Wow. So they're ninety per cent certain that the woman who gave the description and the woman who gave the tip-off about Molly being back in the park are the same,' said Matt. 'That's good news.'

'Yes but without a name, it's not much use,' said Bernie. 'Unless we talk to every woman in Otterfield until we find the voice that matches.'

'Oh, ma'am, I'm not sure that will work. Right, what are these attachments?'

Matt clicked on the first one. It was a detailed report on the phone calls. He opened the next one. Bernie noticed he seemed to freeze.

'What's the matter, Matt?'

Bernie looked at the monitor.

'Shit. Oh shit, oh shit, oh shit!' she said, looking at the image on the screen.

Matt started rifling through some paperwork until he found what he was looking for.

'Here.' He pushed it towards Bernie. 'It's the visitors' list from school. I only checked the men. I thought we were looking for Steven Newell. I remember seeing her name but didn't think anything of it. Look, she went in February and March and… again, here in April. And always to the reception class. She was there doing art classes.'

Bernie buried her face in her hands and took a deep breath before speaking.

'Did we ask these guys to do this?'

Matt looked at the image on his computer screen. 'I just asked for age enhancement. Obviously they did Steven first. It says here at the bottom that this is a rough calculation and they have more work to do but…'

'They don't need to do any more. It's bloody obvious who it is. Right, we've got to get over there now, and fast. She may have already left. I want you to put an alert out for her with all forces and ports and airports. Let the super know too. And get onto Keith at the Dog Section. We might be needing them again. I'll

Joy Kluver

get Kerry and some uniforms and get over there now. I just hope we're not too late.'

Bernie grabbed her bag and ran towards the door. Her mobile began to ring. She glanced at the screen before answering.

'Therese.'

'Hi, Bernie. I've got a DNA hit. Sorry it's taken a while. We were looking at suspects when we should have been looking at—'

'Victims,' said Bernie. 'We know. Email it across. Thanks so much, Therese. Sorry but I have to go.'

Bernie had almost reached the car park with Kerry following behind when her mobile rang again. This time she answered without looking.

'Yes?'

'I've got something.'

'What, Anderson? I'm on my way out.'

'You need to go to Pear—'

'Pear Tree Farm. Yes, I know, she's been under our bloody noses all this time.'

My head still hurts. I'm drifting in and out. Strange dreams. Or are they memories? An argument. A man and a woman. And I'm a little girl. Hiding under a table. Crying because I don't have my teddy.

'You're not selling her to the highest bidder,' says the man. 'She goes to a family or the deal's off.'

'You're not in a position to bargain with us,' replies the woman.

'Oh yes I am. I know she's not the first child you've sold. I know about the others. She goes to loving parents or else I'll take you all down.'

Now I'm really crying. The man who took me also tried to save me. I trusted the wrong person. This was never about what I wanted. This was always about her. She lied. And she took Molly from me.

CHAPTER THIRTY-EIGHT

Bernie pounded on the cottage door. There was no answer.

'Police! Open up!'

Bernie listened carefully but couldn't hear anything. She gave a nod to the officer behind her who had the battering ram ready.

'No! Wait.'

They turned to see Naomi Phillips hurrying across the court-yard towards them.

'Don't break the door down. I've got keys.'

Naomi's hands trembled as she turned the key in the lock. 'Whatever is the matter?' she asked.

Kerry and four other officers pushed past them and ran into the house.

'Where's Ellie?' asked Bernie.

'Ellie? What do you want with her?'

'Yes, Ellie Du Plessis, or as she used to be known, Sophie Newell.'

Naomi looked shocked. 'What? You mean the girl who was taken from here? She's Ellie?'

'We don't know for certain but we believe so. And we also think she abducted Molly Reynolds and kept her here.'

'What? Oh my God. I swear to you I had no idea.' Naomi raised her hand to her mouth. 'It would explain why she's been taking extra food this week. But… are you sure? I cleaned in there yesterday and there was no sign of a child.'

'Really?'

'Well, I don't think so.'

Kerry came to the door and shook her head. 'It's clear and by the looks of things, she's done a bunk already.'

'Damn. OK, get Forensics over here anyway.' Bernie turned back to Naomi. 'Is there anywhere you can think of that she might have gone?'

Naomi was beginning to cry. 'Oh, I don't know. She's a… painter. She's been doing a study on the White Horse over the last few months so she's stayed here on and off. She's sometimes slept there and painted pictures in the moonlight. There's a little wood near it – the Leipzig Plantation. She may have pitched a tent. I can't believe she came back here, to the same place.'

'I think that was all part of the plan, Naomi.'

'Bernie?' asked Kerry.

'Yes?'

'Do you think she's gone to her aunt's?'

Bernie smiled. 'Now, that's a possibility. Leave one officer here to secure the scene. You take one with you to Lesley's and I'll take the other two with me to the White Horse.'

'Is there anything I can do to help? I feel so awful about this, Detective Inspector,' said Naomi Phillips.

'Well, I'm sure the Forensics team will appreciate a cuppa at some point. And please call me Bernie.'

Naomi nodded and sniffed a little. 'I think I can manage that.'

Bernie signalled to a couple of uniformed officers and ran to one of the cars.

'Oh, Bernie?'

She turned to look at Naomi.

'I hope you find her.'

*

'I take it you know how to get there,' Bernie said to the young male officer driving the car.

He grimaced. 'I can get you to the top of the hill but not into the plantation. Have you been up there?'

'No.'

'Well, it's just as well you're not wearing heels, ma'am. You've got some walking to do.'

'Great.'

Bernie thought for a moment. 'So how did she get up there with Molly? She must have cycled. God, why didn't I think about that before? That's how she got Molly away last Friday after she crossed the train tracks. She must have had her bike where we found the buggy, with a child seat or a trailer. It's a very short ride from there to Pear Tree Farm.'

'Well, she could definitely cycle up here, especially at night, although it does get quite steep.'

'That's probably where she'd been on Thursday night when I saw her. Shit.'

The officer glanced at Bernie. 'She's obviously had it all planned out. The woods are to the left of the road; the White Horse is on the right. There are a few clearings where she might have pitched a tent. I camped there once when practising for my Duke of Edinburgh award. It belongs to the council but you can get permission to camp there.'

Bernie smiled. 'So you know the woods well then, PC...?'

'PC Rogers, ma'am. I used to. It's been a while. I suppose you could ask for the Dog Section to come and help if need be.'

'Of course. I was going to send them to the farm.' She quickly texted Matt to divert the dog team to Roundway Hill.

Bernie's phone buzzed an incoming call.

'Kerry?'

'She's not with Lesley. Poor woman was so shocked when I told her we thought Sophie was alive – assuming it is her.'

'She's not on her own, is she?'

'No, she's at the pub. She's being looked after. And I checked. She's been here for the last couple of days. She certainly didn't leave here last night. So she's not been helping Sophie.'

'OK. Come over to the White Horse at Roundway Hill. Need to look for a tent in the woods.'

'We searched there last week. There was nothing at the time to indicate anyone was camping there.'

'Ellie might not be there,' said Bernie. 'It was only a suggestion from Naomi Phillips. She could've had Molly at the cottage the whole time and just moved her yesterday.'

'I've asked Matt to sort out Forensics at the cottage so we'll know soon enough if Molly was there.'

'And I've asked Matt for the dogs to come here. Poor guy. I left him with lots to do.'

'Any word from Anderson?'

'I'm not sure. Let me just check my texts.'

Bernie scrolled through her messages. She put the mobile onto speakerphone.

'Yes, there is one. It must have come through while I was talking to Naomi Phillips. It says, "Just arrest on suspicion of abduction for now. You don't know the half of it." He clearly does though. We'll switch to radio once we get there. Don't know how good reception will be. See you soon.'

Bernie tucked her phone back into her pocket.

'Nearly there, ma'am.'

'As the one with the best local knowledge, you can lead the way.'

PC Rogers blushed a little. 'I hope I don't let you down.'

'I'm sure you won't.'

*

The road was a steady incline but not too steep. The sun was trying to break through the cloud, making the car stuffy. Bernie wound down her window. She saw the White Horse to her right, further up Roundway Hill.

'Wow. It's bigger than I'd realised,' she said.

'Yes, it was cut in 1999, to mark the millennium,' said PC Rogers. 'It's the newest of all the white horses in Wiltshire but there used to be one here in Victorian times.'

'Well, I can see why she's been painting it… if she's been painting it. Maybe all of that was false. No, wait, Megan Williams said Molly had done a chalk drawing of a white horse. Of course! I bet that's what Ellie had been doing with them in the art classes. Anyway, when we get to the woods, take me to the likeliest places first. If we can't find anything then we'll use the dogs.'

Bernie turned to the female officer behind her. 'I want you to wait at the entrance for DS Allen. Radio through when she arrives.'

'Yes, ma'am.'

The sun almost disappeared as soon as Bernie and Rogers stepped into the wood. The tree canopy allowed only a few slivers of sunlight through. The air was cooler and smelt damp. Bernie waited for her eyes to adjust to the gloom. There was a pathway that PC Rogers started to follow.

'She's more likely to be off the track but probably best to stick to it for now,' said Rogers.

'So you didn't search here last week?'

'No, I was on leaflet duty. I've only been an officer for just over a year. I'm still a rookie really.'

Bernie nodded. She could remember being a new recruit and being given all the shitty jobs to do. 'Sorry about that. Sounds as though we could have done with you up here.'

Rogers smiled at Bernie. She noticed dimples in his cheeks. 'I'm sure DS Allen did a thorough search. I'm pretty certain it was mentioned on the news we'd searched here.'

'Ah. So if Ellie Du Plessis has been keeping an eye on media reports, and I'm sure she would've, she would have known this area had been done. So it was safe to move Molly. Although if she is here, it seems odd she hasn't left town completely.'

'Oh, I don't know, ma'am. If Ellie is actually Sophie, then maybe she's reliving the trauma of being kidnapped. Or perhaps she's revisiting places where she felt safe as a child. Plus, if she's been in South Africa for most of her life, she's not going to know the UK particularly well. Where do you run to if you don't know where to go?'

Bernie nodded. 'You stick close to home. That's why she chose Pear Tree Farm to stay at in the first place. It was her old home.'

They were further into the woods now. Bernie could hear a few birds chirping. She saw squirrels running up the trees, chasing each other's tails. Twigs were snapping under their feet.

'Not exactly a silent approach,' she said. 'Are all these trees the same? I'm rubbish at this kind of stuff.'

'Yes, they're mostly beech trees.'

'So I'm not going mad thinking they all looked the same. Honestly, I know my way round most of London but I can't fathom this wood out at all.'

Suddenly Rogers stopped and raised his arm.

'What?' Bernie whispered.

'Did you hear that?'

'What?'

'It sounded like moaning.'

Bernie raised her eyebrows. 'Oh God. Are we about to rumble a couple in mid throes?'

Rogers shook his head and smiled. 'No, ma'am. Not that kind of moaning… there it is again. I think it's from that direction.'

He pointed to his left, off the main track. 'I'll go first, ma'am. I'll try to keep back the branches and brambles for you.'

They walked as quickly as they could, the brambles snatching at their clothes. Bernie could hear the noise now as well. Rogers was right; it wasn't *that* kind of moaning. It sounded like someone hurt. They pushed on past branches until they could see a very small clearing in front of them. A small, dark green tent was pitched and the sound was coming from inside.

'Hello?' called Bernie. 'Ellie, is that you?'

More moaning. They were right by the tent now. Bernie gave Rogers the nod. He unzipped and pulled back the canvas. It was dark inside. What little light there was wasn't penetrating through.

'Have you got a torch, Rogers?'

'Yes, ma'am. A small one.'

He pulled it out and switched it on. A small but fairly bright beam illuminated the tent. Bernie could see a woman, who winced with the light.

'Ellie?'

Bernie climbed in. Ellie moaned again. Bernie was relieved to know she was alive, for now at least. She could see blood on the woman's head.

'She's been hit, I think. But she's alive.' Bernie put her fingers on Ellie's neck. 'Pulse is erratic. Radio for the air ambulance. We can't afford to lose her. We need to get her to hospital fast.' She took hold of Ellie's hand. It was sticky with blood.

'Yes, ma'am. Right away.'

Rogers stepped away, taking the torch with him. The tent was dark. Bernie thought about getting out her phone but then remembered the blood on her hand.

'It's OK. We're going to get you to hospital. We know what happened with Molly. We know you're really Sophie Newell. But who did this to you? Do you know?'

Ellie moaned again but it sounded as though there were words as well. Bernie moved in nearer, her ear close to Ellie's mouth.

'Say that again.'

'Is she safe?' came the whisper.

'Molly? Yes, she's safe. She's back with her parents.'

'Don't trust…'

'Don't trust who?'

There was the start of a name but then Ellie's head lolled to the side.

'Ellie, stay with me.'

Ellie murmured but her words were unrecognisable. Bernie sat back up. Thoughts started to trigger in her brain. The woman on the phone, the voice in her dream; she had heard that voice before. The voice that knew it was time for Molly to go back; the voice who had told her where to find Ellie.

Rogers put his head through the tent flap.

'Sorry, ma'am. I took the torch away. DS Allen has just arrived along with the Dog Section. Do you want me to go and get her?'

'No. I need you to stay here. She's in a bad way. She's slipping in and out of consciousness. Keep talking to her. I have to go somewhere. I'm going to need your car keys.'

Bernie headed back to the track, wiping her hand on her trousers. She pulled out her phone. It had one bar of reception. She hoped it was enough. She found the contact she was looking for and pressed 'call'.

'Anderson? Where are you?'

'Heading towards the A342. Still about fifteen, twenty minutes away at least.'

'That was quick.'

'I've put my bloody siren on. You don't want to know what speed I was doing on the M4. Let's just say I've probably triggered a lot of cameras.'

Bernie could only just hear him. 'Look, reception is bad. I'm at Roundway Hill, in the woods by the White Horse. We've found Sophie Newell.'

'What? Dead or alive? And why the hell are you there? You're supposed to be at Pear Tree Farm.'

'We were but Sophie, or rather Ellie, wasn't in her cottage. And she is alive but only just. She's been attacked.'

'Bernie, I've got no idea what you're talking about. You've got this all wrong.'

'No, Anderson, only half wrong. There was more than one abductor. I've got one and you know about the other.' Bernie pictured the toolbox she nearly fell over when she first visited Pear Tree Farm. 'I'm guessing Tommy Brown had a daughter, right?'

CHAPTER THIRTY-NINE

Bernie called Matt as she ran down the hill towards the police cars.

'Matt, I haven't got time to explain. Just meet me at the farmhouse.'

'But ma'am—'

'We have Ellie or Sophie or whoever she is. It's not her we're after now.' She ended the call.

Bernie spotted Kerry talking to Keith and Dan, the dogs sat by their sides.

'Kerry, can you wait for the air ambulance please? We found her but she's in a bad way. Keith and Dan, if you're able, help PC Rogers with her. She's... oh God, I don't know how to describe whereabouts she is.'

'Is she bleeding?' Keith asked.

'Yes.'

'Then Bonnie will find her. Don't worry.'

'Where are you going, ma'am?' asked Kerry as Bernie unlocked the police car.

'Back to the farm. I've been so stupid.' She opened the door and threw her phone down on the passenger seat before driving back down the small road as quickly as she could.

As she attempted to drive through Devizes' stationary traffic with blues and twos on, she desperately tried to work out how she'd missed it. Naomi Phillips had seemed so nice. She was the kind of woman you would expect to be chairwoman of the local WI, not the daughter of a bookie who kidnapped children to get people to pay their debts. And now she was following in her father's footsteps. With the similarities between Derek's head injury and the man at the betting shop, it looked like she was probably behind the betting shop raids too. Bernie was sure the two women had worked together on Molly's abduction. Both had grievances against Derek Hayes, but how had they met? Was it just coincidence? Or had Ellie knocked on the front door of her old home expecting her parents to be there? Bernie shook her head. She hoped Anderson had some answers because she as sure as hell didn't.

Devizes was soon behind her. From here, at the speed she was doing, she could make it in about seven minutes. But she knew that wasn't safe and she might miss the hidden left-hand turn into the farm. She slowed, wondering if Matt was there already. Did I tell him, she thought, did I tell him that it's Naomi we need to arrest? She glanced at her phone. There wasn't time to stop to ring. Radio? She knew Matt was a bit hopeless with his radio. Wait, there's an officer already there, securing the scene.

She pulled the radio out of its cradle.

'Control. This is DI Noel.'

There was a crackle.

'DI Noel this is Control, go ahead. Over.'

'Yes, Control, I need to contact the uniformed officer left at Pear Tree Farm but I can't remember who it is.'

'One moment, DI Noel.'

Bernie's heart raced with the speed of the car.

'DI Noel, this is Control. Transferring you over now. Go ahead, PC Mills.'

'This is PC Mills. What can I do for you, ma'am? Over.'

Bernie felt a wave of relief.

'Can you keep an eye out for DC Taylor please? Pull him to one side and tell him we need to arrest Naomi Phillips but he's to wait for me.'

'That could be difficult, ma'am. He's already in the main house with her. She invited him in for a cup of tea.'

'Shit. Go in but be careful. She's a suspect in Molly Reynolds' abduction. I'll be there ASAP.'

Bernie floored her accelerator and her speed jumped up to sixty mph. She felt slightly out of control on the bends. She was grateful not many people were out this Saturday lunchtime and the roads were clear. The radio crackled.

'Control, this is PC Mills. Officer down, I repeat, officer—'

And then nothing. Bernie grabbed the radio with her left hand.

'Come in, PC Mills, come in! Control, I've lost PC Mills. Over.'

'Control to DI Noel. Copy that. I'll try to raise him.'

Bernie could hear Control trying to get PC Mills on the radio to respond. *What have I done?*

'Control to DI Noel.'

'Go ahead.'

'I can confirm that PC Mills has activated his SOS button. So possibly two officers down. Will send all available back-up immediately and two ambulances to Pear Tree Farm. What's your ETA?'

'Control, I'm almost there.'

Suddenly Bernie saw the sign advertising Pear Tree Farm. She hit the brakes and skidded into the turning. She drove into the deserted courtyard. Naomi's car was still there. Adrenalin was pumping into Bernie's bloodstream as she jumped out of the car. She'd always been a fight girl. Got herself into too many scrapes as a child. One of the nuns at secondary school had told her she'd be a good police officer. A strong sense of justice and little fear would work in her favour. But she felt fear now. *What had happened to Matt and to the other officer? Did Naomi have a gun?* She certainly had plenty of knives in her country kitchen – Bernie had seen them. Even used the bread knife herself. Would they have blunt force trauma wounds like Derek, Ellie or the man killed in the betting shop? Or were there other tools Naomi liked to use from her father's toolbox? Bolt cutters, for example. Bernie couldn't believe just how brazen Naomi had been.

Bernie rummaged in the boot of the police car for a stab vest. There wasn't one but there was a can of pepper spray and a baton plus she had her cuffs. It was better than nothing but the thought of not having a stab vest made the scar on her abdomen itch. She closed her eyes briefly to steady herself. She knew she should wait for back-up. She knew. But the adrenalin was pumping harder and the fight instinct was kicking in, stronger than ever. No one messes with my officers, she thought. *No one.*

The front door swung open as she gently pushed it with the tip of the extended baton. She willed herself to be calm. If it was possible to negotiate with Naomi, then she would. But if not, she was ready. She walked slowly up the hallway, checking the stairs as she went past, looking behind her as well. She remembered the kitchen was at the very back. She thought that was where Matt and the other officer were most likely to be.

She was right. She saw the PC first, face down on the floor by the table, his radio beeping the SOS call. Matt was slumped over the table top, blood oozing from a head wound. She checked them both for a pulse. Both were still alive. Not wanting to speak, she pulled out her phone, putting it on silent first, and sent a text to the super detailing the assistance required. She quietly opened a couple of drawers and found a clean tea towel. She pressed it on Matt's wound. He stirred slightly.

She whispered, 'Ssh, Matt. It's Bernie.' She lifted his arm and placed his hand on the tea towel. 'Try and keep some pressure on it if you can.'

'Trying to leave,' Matt mumbled.

'Naomi? I guess so. And you two were in the way,' she whispered.

She wanted to stay with her officers but she was a sitting duck. A quick glance around the kitchen showed it was clear. Bernie walked quietly back into the hallway. The house was silent. She strained her ears listening for any signs of movement. She stood at the bottom of the stairs. Was Naomi up there, packing a bag? Or was she in one of the downstairs rooms? Bernie had just placed her foot on the first stair when she heard a noise from outside.

The courtyard was empty. Bernie thought she must have imagined it but then she heard the noise again – some kind of ripping sound. The door to Ellie's cottage was open. Bernie moved swiftly.

The cottage was tiny. A small lounge led through to an even smaller kitchen. The whitewashed walls had a few paintings hanging up, all of them of the Devizes White Horse. Bernie peered closer and saw Ellie's signature. Rather than the ubiquitous paintings found in holiday cottages, these were good.

Bernie moved to the stairs. She was now wondering if she'd imagined the ripping sound but Naomi had to be somewhere. She cautiously stepped onto the bottom stair before creeping up, aware that any creaks would herald her appearance. Two closed doors were at the top – one to the right and one straight ahead. Bernie pushed open the right-hand door, banking on it being the bathroom. Seeing she was correct and the room empty, she stepped forward to open the other door.

Light seeped in through a break in the curtains. A double bed was behind the door, the duvet rumpled up. There were built-in cupboards on the far wall. One of the doors was ajar. Bernie hooked her baton in the gap and pulled the door open. A hanging rail was empty but the back of the cupboard was plastered with newspaper articles about Sophie and Molly, with photos of Derek and Jessica, and… photos of her – at the playground, at Jessica's house, even outside headquarters. Some of the paper had been ripped down. She picked one up. It was a photocopy of an article written by Clive Bishop all about the Newells' suicides. Someone, she imagined Sophie, had underlined passages with a yellow highlighter all about her disappearance and the reward offered for information that would lead to an arrest. A yellow circle framed a family photograph taken in happier times with a smiling Sophie held by her father. Bernie couldn't even imagine the pain the young woman must have felt to discover her parents were dead.

Footsteps from outside caught Bernie's attention. She turned to leave but her foot caught on something and she crashed to the floor. She hit her head, stunning herself for a few seconds. As she came round she was aware of movement next to her and turned over just in time to see Naomi Phillips standing over her with a raised hammer in her hand. As she swung it towards Bernie's head, Bernie raised her arm with the baton. The hammer caught the baton in her right hand, jarring it, and she lost her grip. It clattered to the ground next to her. She tried to use the spray but Naomi was too quick with the hammer and smashed Bernie's left wrist. Pain radiated up her whole arm. The can was on the floor too. Naomi raised the hammer again. Bernie rolled and grabbed the can. Flinging her injured left arm across her eyes she sprayed the pepper spray into Naomi's face.

Almost immediately, Naomi dropped her weapon and put her hands to her eyes, coughing and screaming. Bernie staggered up. She knew she didn't have long to cuff her but with only one hand working properly, it wasn't going to be easy.

'On the floor, now!'

Naomi didn't obey, though, and stumbled out of the bedroom towards the bathroom, Bernie following, groping her belt for her cuffs. Naomi found the sink, blindly reaching out to turn on the tap. 'You bitch!' she screamed back at Bernie.

'Oh no, you don't. Naomi Phillips, I'm arresting you on suspicion of abducting Molly Reynolds and assaulting three police officers and Ellie Du Plessis. And for the murders of Derek Hayes and David Chaucer. You do not have to say anything, but it may harm your defence if you do not mention, when questioned, something which you later rely on in court. Anything you do say can be given in evidence.'

Bernie tried to wrench one of Naomi's hands down from her face, but with only one hand working, she couldn't get the cuff on. Naomi's other arm came back, elbow pointed, ready to hit Bernie, when another hand grabbed it.

'I don't think so, Mrs Phillips,' said Anderson, as he cuffed one hand and then the next. Bernie stepped back, holding her left wrist.

'You OK?' asked Anderson.

'Yeah, although I think my wrist might be broken. It's Matt and the other officer in the main house I'm worried about. She hit them on the head with the hammer. They were both alive when I left them though.' Bernie tucked her left hand inside her shirt to keep it supported.

The sound of sirens outside invaded the little cottage, followed by doors slamming and shouts of 'Ma'am!'

'In here,' she called back. She looked at Anderson, holding Naomi Phillips, her eyes and nose streaming. 'We found Sophie or Ellie. Unfortunately for you, Naomi, she's still alive. I suppose you thought you'd sneak away while I went searching for her. Murder, abduction, GBH on four people, three of them police officers – you'll be going away for a long time.'

Anderson smirked. 'And that's before we even take into account the betting shop raids and fixing sports matches for years.'

'Oh dear, Naomi,' Bernie said. 'You didn't do a very good job of looking after Daddy's empire, did you? Anything you want to say?'

Naomi made a coughing noise and then spat phlegm out at Bernie.

'I think that's a no, DS Anderson.'

'I think you might be right, DI Noel.'

Anderson pulled Naomi down the stairs and handed her over to two uniformed officers. Bernie followed behind.

The paramedics were already in the kitchen, dealing with Matt and the other officer. Bernie was cursing herself for not warning Matt.

'Are they going to be OK?' she asked.

The paramedic looked up. 'Can't say for sure. They'll need X-rays. Both of them have strong pulses and are breathing well. Head wounds always bleed lots. Hopefully it looks worse than it actually is. But we'll let the doctors decide.'

'Come on, let's go outside and let the paramedics do their job,' said Anderson. 'Someone needs to look at your hand as well.'

Bernie allowed herself to be led outside by Anderson. Her hand was throbbing and her wrist was starting to swell.

'You need to go to hospital. I can take you.'

'No… I'll go in the ambulance with Matt.'

Anderson sighed and shook his head. 'God, Bernie, why didn't you wait for back-up? She could have killed you. I heard it all on the radio.'

Bernie looked back to the house and saw Matt being brought out. 'Matt was down. I sent another officer into danger. I should have told him to wait for me.'

'Bernie, this isn't just about your professional duty. I care about you. Let me take you to hospital. You don't have to be brave all the time. We can talk on the way there.'

Bernie remembered her earlier conversation with Louise Anderson. She wasn't sure if she could trust Anderson any more. 'No. You need to stay here. Look for evidence. In particular, check out the bedroom cupboards in the cottage. Look for anything that places Molly here. In fact, the dogs are at Roundway Hill. Get them over to see if they can find her scent. And get the hammer to Forensics ASAP. The clock will be ticking as soon as Naomi's booked in, and you said Bristol police want to talk to her as well.

I need you to run things here for me. Kerry's busy with Sophie and someone needs to go with Matt. I'll see you later.'

Bernie walked across to the ambulance as Matt was loaded inside.

'Can I come with you?' she asked the paramedic.

'Of course. And I'll have a look at that wrist of yours on the way to the hospital.'

Bernie found it hard to look at Matt, with the oxygen mask over his face and a compress to his head. She felt herself sway but wasn't sure if it was the movement of the ambulance or a memory trying to surface – her on a stretcher, warm blood pumping out of her side as the rest of her went cold. Her boss's voice telling her they'd arrested all the gang members and that, thanks to her, they had all the evidence they needed. The teenage girl on the ground, still in her netball kit, who would never get up. And then the death threats after the trial and her move from the Met to Wiltshire Police for her own safety. At least the sympathy card was from her father and not from them. But it was only a matter of time. She thought the counselling had worked. Maybe it hadn't.

The temporary cast was heavy on Bernie's arm. She'd been given an appointment to come back later in the week for a proper cast to be fitted.

'And now, you need to go home and rest. No more work for today,' said the A&E doctor.

Bernie gave a wry smile. 'There's just one more thing I need to do first.'

They appeared to be the perfect family. Davy had Sam in his arms and Jessica was reading to Molly.

'Knock, knock,' said Bernie. 'Can I come in?'

Jessica's eyes widened as she took in Bernie's arm in plaster.

'What's happened to you?' she asked.

'Oh, nothing really. Just a fractured wrist – all in a day's duty. I just came to let you know we've got them.'

Bernie smiled at Molly. Colour had returned to her cheeks and her golden curls sparkled in the sunlight that filtered through the Venetian blind. 'Hi, Molly. It's so nice to meet you properly at last. My name's Bernie and I've been looking for you all week.'

Molly gave Bernie a quick glance. 'Like hide and seek?'

Bernie laughed. 'Yes, Molly, a bit like hide and seek. You're very good at hiding.'

Molly smiled and her eyes lit up. 'That's what the lady said to me. She liked playing hide and seek too. First we hid in the cottage and then we hid in a tent.'

'What did the lady look like?'

'She was very tall and had hair the same colour as mine. And she talked funny. But she was nice, not like the other one.'

'The other one?'

'Yeah. She was old and grumpy. At first she was nice. She gave me lots of cake to eat but I always felt sleepy afterwards. And then she wasn't nice. She hurt the other lady and I was crying. She shouted at me to eat some cake so I did. And then, when I woke up, I was here with Mummy and Daddy.' She looked across at Davy and beamed. 'I love my daddy. And Sammy. And Mummy. And Granddad. Where is Granddad?'

Bernie saw Jessica's eyes fill up at the mention of Derek. She reached out and took Jessica's hand.

'You know,' said Bernie, 'Bonita hasn't gone back to Spain yet. She's still here.'

Jessica sniffed.

'I can give you the address of where she's staying if you like. Up to you. No pressure.'

Bernie saw Jessica give a slight nod.

'I'd like that, thank you.'

CHAPTER FORTY

Monday

Bernie looked through the window in the door. MCIT was quiet for a Monday morning. Kerry was tapping away on her keyboard, writing up her reports. Anderson was on the phone. Bernie wondered if he was talking to the Serious Organised Crime team in Bristol. Once they'd heard Naomi Phillips was in custody, they'd swooped in.

Bernie had slept most of Sunday. The super had ordered her to stay off work until Monday. Ellie Du Plessis, or Sophie Newell, was still in hospital and not ready for formal questioning, but she'd told Kerry about her part in it all. How she'd been taken by Derek Hayes to help clear his massive gambling debt. She'd been abducted to order, originally destined for a paedophile ring.

'But,' Kerry told Bernie on the phone, 'Derek persuaded Naomi to find a family for her and she was sold to a South African couple instead. Which was less money.'

'So Derek was still in debt.'

'Yes. Fortunately, Ellie had a good life but when her adopted parents died she set out to find what had happened to her real family. I really felt for her when she came back here and found out about her parents' suicides. Revenge is powerful, no doubt about it.'

'So how did she end up at Pear Tree Farm?'

'She looked up the details when she got here just before Christmas last year, hoping for a big family reunion. She'd remembered her name. Told me she used to write it down and then burn it so her adopted parents wouldn't see. When she got to the farm, she recognised Naomi. She'd been the one who'd taken her out of the country, disguised as a boy. Naomi had cut her hair short. She remembered being quite traumatised by that. I guess at the time everyone was looking for a man with a girl, not a woman with a boy. Ellie went apeshit when she saw Naomi in her old house and not her parents. She was devastated when Naomi told her about her parents' suicide. Naomi took advantage of Ellie's grief, told her she was remembering it wrong and managed to convince her it was all Derek's fault. That he was going to sell her to a paedophile ring and that she, Naomi, was an innocent party in all of this. She claimed she bought the farm so that Steven would have some money. Personally, I think she was waiting for Derek.'

'Long wait. How did they know he was back?'

'Oddly enough, that was Paula Parker. She gossiped to Naomi that the "black sheep" of the village was back. She didn't have to say any more than that. Naomi knew what she meant. She went to see and recognised him straight away. He still had a debt to pay. She's definitely her father's daughter in that respect. So she and Ellie hatched a plan. He was supposed to sell the house to give them the money, but couldn't because it was in Jessica's name.'

'So he stole the jewellery.'

'Yes, but it still wasn't enough. Ellie wanted revenge. She still believed Naomi's account that Derek had intended to hand her over to paedophiles. She wanted Derek to die like her parents had. Ellie got to know Molly through the art classes at school and then she planned the abduction with Naomi's help. Although Paula nearly scuppered that by taking the O'Connells' booking. The other cottage was meant to be empty. But when Naomi heard we were looking for their car she decided to use it to her advantage.

She knew we'd want to search the farm at some point and she decided to redirect us to them. Of course, the biggest problem was that, through the abduction, Ellie started to remember what really happened to her and that it was Derek who had tried to save her. She feared Naomi would sell Molly to the highest bidder. So she decided to leave and take Molly with her.'

'But Naomi spoke to me,' said Bernie. 'Of course. She said Jessica had suffered enough. She put Molly back. She did the right thing. At least, that's what it looks like. More likely no one would take Molly. Too much press coverage. Journalists starting to hang around the farm. Plus she had the pressure of the last betting raid going wrong. She'll try and put all the blame on Ellie at interview, except we have her voice on tape, giving us false information. She's the one who really organised this.'

'Yeah, but even if we can't get her on the abduction for now, we can get her on GBH and, potentially, Derek's murder. Forensics are working on the hammer as we speak. There are a number of DNA samples on it so they're having to separate them out. But Matt's a definite.'

'How is he and the other officer?'

'Both are fine. Matt's desperate to get out of hospital and get on with the job. Thankfully Naomi didn't hit them as hard as Derek and David Chaucer. Anyway, you need to rest. I'll see you in the morning but don't push it. If you need longer, we can cope.'

Now, Bernie pushed open the door to MCIT.

'Morning,' she said.

Kerry and Anderson turned and smiled.

'Good to see you, ma'am. I was kind of hoping you'd stay off for a few more days so I could hold the fort for a little longer,' said Kerry.

Bernie laughed. 'You can't get rid of me that easily. But I probably won't stay too long today. And we'll celebrate when Matt's out of hospital. Remember, the chief constable promised the super would get the first round in.'

Kerry's phone began to ring. 'DS Allen speaking… That's great… Does she want a lawyer?… OK, it's her choice. I'll leave straight away.'

Kerry got up. 'That was the hospital. Ellie is well enough for formal questioning and wants to give a statement. She asked specifically for me. Do you want to come too, ma'am?'

Bernie was about to say yes when Anderson caught her eye. She needed to talk to him about his ex-wife and with Kerry out of the office, now would be a perfect opportunity. 'I think you can handle this one by yourself. I might put her off.'

'OK. She's asked to see Lesley as well.'

Bernie smiled. 'Has she? Oh good. Maybe hang around for that, just to make sure nothing kicks off.'

'I'd better be there when Steven arrives in a couple of days' time then. He was overjoyed when I spoke to him. But he might not be so happy to see his aunt.'

'No. But that family could do with some healing. Call me later and let me know how it all goes.'

Anderson put the phone down as Kerry left.

'Any news?' Bernie asked.

'Naomi's been charged with a great long list of stuff and remanded. She's considered a flight risk. We'll get a chance to question her tomorrow. See if we can get her for the murder of Derek Hayes as well as abduction.'

'I'd like you and Kerry to do that.'

'Don't you want in on it?'

'No, I'll watch if I feel up to it. You've earned the right to interview her. It was your lead, after all. And Kerry will have Ellie's statement to go by. I'm sure the two of you will do a good job. Anderson…'

'Please, call me Dougie, it's what my friends and family call me.'

Bernie swallowed. 'So, we're friends, are we?'

'I don't know what the fuck we are. I called you yesterday, lots of times.'

Bernie had seen seven missed calls on her phone this morning.

'I was sleeping. My phone was on silent. Dougie…'

The door to MCIT swung open. It was Jane.

'Oh, Bernie, you're back. So glad you're all right. I don't know if you saw the papers yesterday but you were headline news. Again. Who knows, maybe officer of the year? Anyway, I need to *drag* DS Anderson away to the super's office for an update. We need to put a statement out.'

Anderson rolled his eyes. He clearly didn't want to be dragged by Jane anywhere.

'This might take a while,' he said. 'Let's meet for lunch, say twelve thirty at the bakery?'

Bernie nodded. 'OK. I'll just catch up on a few things here.'

It was almost time to leave for lunch when there was a ping on Bernie's phone. An email had arrived. It was from Therese at the lab. Were the results back on the hammer already? But why send them to her private email? She read it quickly and then again, more slowly, taking in exactly what it said. She closed her eyes briefly, trying to take in the enormity of the words. There was another ping. She smiled when she saw the sender.

Dear Bernie,

I'm sure you've had the email from the lab too. Thank you for agreeing to take the DNA test. I know my turning up like that was difficult for you. You were in the middle of a big case and I didn't help. I saw on the news you found Molly. I am so very proud of you, my daughter. I can't tell you how much it means to me to write those words – my daughter.

I hope we can build a relationship but I'll understand if you don't want to. I've thought about you every day since you were born. And I really mean that. I began saving money for you when I first got a job and have continued to do so. There's about seventy-five thousand pounds, enough for a deposit on a house, or you may want to go travelling. Whatever you want to do, it's yours. I'll be in touch soon.

Best wishes, Gary.

Bernie sat down, aghast at the amount her father was offering her. Could she really accept it? 'Of course you can,' she heard Pops say. 'It cost me more than that to raise you.' She smiled. Her first thought was for her mother. Had Gary's letter to her arrived in the post yet? How would she feel having to share Bernie? Would she resent Gary coming back into their lives? Or would she be happy?

Bernie glanced at her watch. She needed to leave. Her father's email had helped her to make a decision.

Bernie stood outside the large glass window. She could see him sitting there, his dark head down, reading something. She willed him to raise his head and as he did so, he smiled broadly. She pushed the door open.

'I thought you were never going to come,' he said.

'What made you think I'd come in the first place?' asked Bernie.

'Knew the first time I saw you.'

'Isn't that a bit presumptuous of you?' She smiled.

He smiled back. 'So, what do you want to do? Do you want to stay here and chat first? Or…?'

'Or what?'

He laughed. 'Or we could just go straight there now? I guess I'm driving.' He nodded towards her arm.

She laughed. 'Yes, you'll need to drive, Alex. Going straight there would be good.'

'OK. I'll just grab the keys. And…' He pulled a folder out of a drawer. 'A little light reading for the journey, if you can manage it.'

Bernie put the folder on the table and opened it. She pulled out a few pages stapled together. The front page had a picture of a cottage – her cottage in Marchant. It was time to make Wiltshire her home.

'Perfect.'

EPILOGUE

I'm playing with my dolls and teddy bears in the garden when I see him. He looks sad. I can see the dog lead but Sandy's not with him. I start to run towards him and call his name. He spots me and opens his arms wide. He picks me up and tosses me in the air.

'Why are you sad, Uncle Derek?'

'Oh, Sophie, I've lost Sandy. I can't find him anywhere.'

I love Sandy. He's golden all over and has the softest fur. I like to bury my face in him.

'Don't worry, Uncle Derek. I can help you find him.'

'Are you sure?'

He looks like he's going to cry. He must love Sandy very much.

'Of course.'

He puts me down. I pick up mine and Sandy's favourite teddy bear. He likes to play hide and seek with it. I'll put it under a bush for him to find. I take Uncle Derek's hand and together we walk away.

A LETTER FROM JOY

Dear reader,

I want to say a huge thank you for choosing to read *Last Seen*. If you did enjoy it, and want to keep up to date with all my latest releases, just sign up at the following link. Your email address will never be shared and you can unsubscribe at any time.

www.bookouture.com/joy-kluver

I hope you loved *Last Seen* and if you did I would be very grateful if you could write a review. I'd love to hear what you think, and it makes such a difference helping new readers to discover one of my books for the first time.

I love hearing from my readers – you can get in touch on my Facebook page, through Twitter, Goodreads or my website.

Thanks,
Joy

joykluverauthor

@JoyKluver

kluver.co.uk

ACKNOWLEDGEMENTS

Although writing is quite a solitary occupation, there are a lot of people working behind the scenes or cheering on from the sidelines. So I'd like to start with my editor, Therese Keating, and all the rest of the incredible team at Bookouture. It's so wonderful to find an editor who loves my characters as much as me. To my agent, Anne Williams – thank you for answering my questions before I've even asked them! It's great to know I'm in such safe hands.

To Sara Starbuck, thank you for your early wonderful edit. It really did make all the difference.

Thank you to Karen Bate and Rebecca Bradley for their police expertise and also to Kerri Cooke for an early proofread. I've had to use some artistic licence with the story so any police inaccuracies are my own.

I ventured into the crime genre world about five years ago and I couldn't have found a more welcoming community. It would be impossible to name everyone but there are some I have to highlight. Firstly, to my BBFs (Best Book Friends), Vicki Goldman and Alex Khan – thank you for sharing the lows and now the highs! To Rod Reynolds, the first author to ask to read my MS: I'm not sure if you'll ever know how much that meant to me. To Susi Holliday, Jane Isaac and Sam Carrington, thanks for all the advice. To the First Monday Crime crew – William Ryan, Katherine Armstrong, Sophie Goodfellow and Liz Barnsley – thank you for your support.

Alongside the wonderful crime authors are the fabulous crime bloggers. Again, impossible to thank them all but I want to mention Jen, Mandie, Jacob and Karen. Thank you for your friendship and putting up with me at literary festivals!

I've been writing for twenty years and there's a particular group of people who have listened to my stories, week in and week out. A huge thank you to Elizabeth Kay, my tutor at the Malden Centre Writing Class. Without your guidance I wouldn't have started to write novels. The class has changed a lot over the years with people coming and going but there are some stalwarts who have endured hearing my stories – John, Viviane, Jean, Mike, Sue, Aleks, Marilyn, Caroline and Clare. Special thanks to Sue and Aleks who took it in turns to be the voice of Bernie.

To Cathy and Terry – thank you for our school-run literary chats. The school runs may have ended but your encouragement carries on.

Thank you to Jean Noel for allowing me to use her surname.

Thank you to Tracey Shepherd for helping to make Bernie more authentic. You may think you didn't do much but you said one thing that changed everything.

To my amazing church family, thank you for your prayers and encouragement.

To Sarah McAlister, my partner-in-crime at the Friends of West Barnes Library. Thank you for taking a risk with me and hopefully we'll have our events back in the library soon.

Thanks to Claudine, Su, Rachel, Becky and Kathryn for your steadfast friendship over the years.

And finally, to my family, in particular my husband Phil, and our three children, James, Beth and Hayden. Thank you for your editorial guidance (!), for putting up with rubbish dinners but mostly, for not laughing at my dreams.

Printed in Great Britain
by Amazon

17938339R00200